# RAINA'S WITNESS

## The Tragedy of Human Trafficking

By

Barbara J. Bolton

Printed in the United States of America

ISBN: 0989791394
ISBN-13: 9780989791397

*I dedicate this book to an old friend, my loyal cat, Randi*

*For eighteen years you were by my side my friend, the last four and a half of which we spent writing this novel. The winters by the fireplace will be lonely without you my little orange, furry tiger, but someday in a beautiful place beyond this physical world, I believe our spirits will meet again. Melani and I miss you.*

# CHAPTER ONE

## 1983

## Hell Bound and Tied

Raina's ribs are cracked and broken, stabbing at her side and sharp pain wracks her body with every breath she takes. Chunks of her scalp are flayed and gouged and her hair is matted with blood. She is naked and shivering, curled up against the cold cement steps, her body shrouded by the coastal fog of November. She lifts herself onto her elbows, then pushes up with her hands to try to stand, but her knees start wobbling and she collapses. Woozy, stupefied, her heart racing, she instinctively recalls the night of the date rape almost five years ago. As bad as that memory is the events of the last few hours are even worse.

Up until college she had spent little time away from the southwest reservation where she was born and raised and leaving for college on a full blown scholarship should have been like walking into a beautiful dream for her and her family. But instead, fate's fickle *modus* ensued and Raina's dream turned into a living hell.

She can hear the muffled banter of the rowdy young men in the fraternity house kitchen who had tossed her out on the stoop like garbage, their drunken voices vulgar and cruel. Raina thinks about her mother and her child, how beside herself her mother would be if she knew what has happened and she wishes she was back home on the reservation with her family right now. Exhausted, she curls up again and within seconds she is fading in and out, dreaming about the smells of home and her mother's warm embrace.

Time always flew on the weekends when she went home to her family. After putting her baby boy to bed, she would go out on the porch to immerse her senses in the wonder of her peoples' land, standing tranquil under the dazzling stars of the desert sky and breathing the night's sweet bouquet. Her mother often came out behind her, wrapping a cozy shawl around her shoulders. They would talk for hours.

She is awakened from her reverie by guttural voices. Before she can identify where the voices are coming from a thick blanket is thrown over her, covering her face. Raina realizes she can't move her arms. She is half conscious, but she cries out, "Help! Someone! Help!" In seconds her torso is rolled up in the heavy mantle and she is lifted off the cement. She struggles but the serrated edge of her broken rib scrapes her lung and takes her breath away. Her mind whirls, trying to comprehend what is happening to her. She can't see, but she hears voices and feels a rope binding her. The men wrap her so tightly she can hardly breathe. Then a man throws her over his shoulder and she bounces down the steps with him, gasping in pain.

Raina hears a callous voice and a lock click, "Throw the bitch in." The voice is hard and cold, but not one of the frat boys.

She lands in the trunk with a thud, the impact knocking the wind out of her.

Then another man's voice, "She better not piss in my trunk."

She hears the trunk door slam down above her and she stiffens, lying petrified from fright and held motionless by the rope.

A muffled laugh and then a second voice taunts, "Dogs don't piss when they're in transit."

Tears fill Raina's eyes as she struggles to breathe. She hears and feels the jolt of two car doors banging shut and the engine start. The car rolls forward and she is so frightened and oxygen-starved she falls into a dreamlike state.

She relives what happened a few hours ago in the kitchen of the fraternity house. Why had she thought it was a good idea to go along with a classmate to a fraternity party? Why had she trusted him? And why, when she wanted out, had she agreed to chug beer as a penance for wanting to leave.

It all happened so fast. Eight drunken young men, loud and obnoxious, faces geering as she chugged her beer, "Drink, chug-alug! Drink, chug-alug!" They had blocked the door and told her they wouldn't let her go until she chugged two cans of beer back to back. She was desperate to get out of there so she drank. She choked down the last beer and started for the door, but was swarmed by what seemed an army of hands grabbing and clawing at her clothing.

They ripped off her clothes, then shoved her into a sizeable dog kennel and locked her in. She withered in the center of the cage, arms folded, trying to cover herself. She was embarrassed and disgraced, but still her pride, her innate sense of dignity, gave her courage. She felt her blood rising to her face and heat prickled her ears. She was seething with rage, but she could do nothing. Caged like an animal, powerless, stripped of her humanity and fearing for her life, Raina watched the frat boys as they smoked, drank, snorted and staggered around, goading each other into doing absurd and vile actions.

She had curled herself up, trying to disappear, hoping they would stop the torment. After enduring their verbal abuse for what seemed an eternity she asked for her clothes and demanded to be let out of her cage so that she could go to the bathroom. They had just stood there laughing and told her to, "Sit up and beg."

Tears stung her eyes and she covered her mouth with her hand, trying to keep from sobbing out loud.

"You're not getting out until you sit up and beg."

Raina flinched at the sound of the voice. She was terrified, but she wouldn't swallow her pride and beg. Instead, she asked them once more for her clothes and for her freedom. She promised she wouldn't tell a soul, but the more dignity she displayed the more arrogance they demonstrated. It didn't take long for her to grasp that speaking invoked their anger, so she knelt in her prison, tucked her knees close to her chest to cover what she could of her body and closed her eyes. She used her mind to transport herself away, trying to dismiss the swelling of her bladder, while obnoxious music pounded her brain. As a macabre accompaniment to the blaring music, a pornographic movie played without sound on a TV in a dark corner. The light from the screen flickered through a smoky haze so thick it burned her nostrils. She turned away from the screen when it pictured a blindfolded girl being brutalized.

Suddenly, an onslaught of stinging jets of beer from close range pelted her face, taking her breath away. All she could do was move a few inches away from the edge and even more toward the center of the cage as the raucous crew shook their beer and sprayed her.

She knelt in front of them, morose, her shoulders slumped and her graceful hands covered her eyes as drenched strands of jet black hair dripped white foam onto her thighs. Suffering, wet, naked and shivering, she now felt a desperate need to use the bathroom. Her bladder was sending her brain urgent messages of pain. She pressed her knees together hard, trying to hold back and asked them one last time to set her free.

One of the fraternity brothers began to chant, "PEE, BITCH, PEE!" and at once was joined by a chorus of thunderous voices growing louder with every rendition, "PEE, BITCH, PEE!"

She had covered her ears, "PEE, BITCH, PEE!" She squeezed her eyes shut, "PEE, BITCH, PEE." She had curled her toes and clenched her fists, "PEE, BITCH, PEE." She held it as long as she could, "PEE, BITCH, PEE," but then she felt a warm stream of relief flow out of her, impossible to stop. She exhaled and cried as the flow turned into a warm puddle pooling around her knees.

For a long moment there was a pause and silence filled the room. Then the voices roared as beer bottles pounded the top of the cage and one of the men howled, "Bad Bitch! Bad Dog!" as he wrenched the door open.

At last, she thought, they're done, they'll free me now.

But instead, they grabbed her by the hair and dragged her out. They howled obscenities in her ear as they smashed her face into the puddle of urine so hard that her nose broke and blood mixed with the urine splattered into her eyes. She closed her lids tightly as they grabbed handfuls of her hair and banged her head against the floor. At last they let go and she collapsed.

One of them kicked her and swore as he screamed, "Get her the fuck out of here."

Then they all rushed her, kicking her and rolling her toward the door, fracturing her ribs. Raina tumbled onto the steps, her cheek sliding across the gritty cement. Then a thickening liquid crept into her mouth and with her throat engorged, she heaved, oozing warm vomit across the cold cement. At last she fainted.

The sudden braking of the car rolls Raina to the back of the trunk and the thump stirs her consciousness. She awakens to someone lifting her out of the trunk and again heaving her onto his shoulder. She winces in pain with every step as she bounces up and down; Her splintered ribs stab at her side and her breath catches in her throat. She is once again close to being unconscious. Who are these people? Did the fraternity brothers turn her over to another gang? The man carries her into a house and drops her on a mattress on the floor.

Raina hears a quiet whisper at first and then a clear order, "Untie it and let me look at it."

The men pull at the rope and Raina twirls around like skewered meat until she rolls free. Cool air rushes at her. It's fresh and glorious and she gasps for a huge breath, but the broken rib piercing her lung forces her into short, quick pants instead.

Raina looks up at the man standing in front of her. He is a hard looking, humorless man with his hand to his chin stroking his beard. He's dressed in an extravagantly expensive black suit. Even in her pain and desperation she can't help but notice the bright shiny ring on his finger, bright silver and stamped with a black moon and star. She senses that the others fear him. They call him Daboia, a name which she was later told was a Hindi-Urdu word meaning, *that which lies hidden*. He came to the United States in 1980 from Pakistan, then disappeared into the shadows. He studies Raina from head to toe with grim, sooty eyes. Then he inspects her every orifice, cruelly using his hands to check for cocaine use, tooth decay and rectal damage, much as if she were a prized animal he was purchasing at auction. She is insignificant to him. He has the power to kill her or let her live. He deliberates for a moment, then makes an offer. The men begin to barter with him.

Raina feels as though she is outside her body. She has never been so humiliated. She cannot believe what is happening to her, she is actually being sold! Those fraternity brothers had turned her over to human traffickers. Her mind reels, this cannot be possible. This can't be happening in her country, a free country.

Daboia makes a final offer for two hundred dollars.

Her captors squabble and argue back, "It's got teeth and it's not used up."

Daboia counters, "I said I want them young and this one is not a cherry."

The two men grumble, but give in. They are each handed a hundred dollar bill and they leave the house.

Before he leaves, Daboia claps his hands twice and a girl bustles into the room. Raina can tell the girl is young but she looks much older than her years. Her eyes are dark and austere, her body is scrawny, yet she has ample breasts and one of her cheeks bears a scar from a burn. She is wearing a black micro-mini skirt, fish net stockings and a tight leather halter with bright crimson ties that gather loosely in the front. Her breasts slop out at the top. Her tall black boots are cracked and weathered.

She looks Raina up and down and in a sultry voice says, "Follow me."

It was the first time that anyone had directed words at Raina since she'd been thrown into the trunk of the car wrapped in a blanket and she strains to clear her parched throat to deliver an answer.

"Where am I? Who are you?"

"I'm Zoa. Shush now, or theys gonna punish us."

"Who's they? . . . Punish us for what?"

Zoa puts her finger to her lips, "Shh. I'm gonna say it jist once, so listin up or yer gonna die. Do what yer told and don't complain. Ya ain't free no more, Daboia just bought ya."

"This is the United States of America. You can't buy people in this country, it's against the law."

Zoa leans closer, "Ya be a foo' girl, if ya don't believe me. This is how it works on this side of the tracks. You been trapped and sold like an animal, but ya got street value, jist like dope. Men of all kinds will pay ta have sex wit ya, or watch ya having it. They is loads of money in porn and sex; that be reality, girl, so git real. Daboia owns ya now and he'll do what he wants wit ya. America can't protect ya. How can it? It don't even know where's you at, girl? Daboia can have ya killed and ain't nobody gonna know it. If yer lucky, you be sent to a strip club where ya gonna dance and turn tricks in the back room."

But Raina is not willing to give in despite Zoa's grave warning. Holding her side, Raina slowly stands up to leave, "I won't do this," she whispers, "they can't force me. I'm not a stripper or a prostitute and I don't want to be." Not more than five hours ago she'd been on the campus of one of the best known colleges in California, enjoying an academic scholarship. There would be people looking for her. "My mother and father will file a police report off the reservation."

"Foo', you think Daboia don't know dat? Believe me, they knows what they doing, few of us ever get freed or escape." Zoa grabs Raina by the arm, "Ya think I'm here 'cause I wanna be?" Raina winces in pain and tries to pull away. Zoa's expression turns to stone, "Listin up, foo', I left my parents' house when I was thirteen 'cause they was strung out an fightin' all the time. So one night I snuck out and one of Daboia's men found me on the street. He talked nice, told me I was pretty, that I looked like a model. He said I could make a good livin' modelin'. Said he'd get me started in the business. He brought me home to his dig and things was nice at first. He told me he loved me. But it wasn't long before he started taking pictures of me naked and showing them ta the men who come 'round buying his smack. They offered him money ta have sex wit me and he forced me in ta doin' it. Then he started filming me while they raped me. He say it was time I earned my own way, but he kep' all the money.

One night I got into it heavy wit' him and I tried ta leave, but he grabbed holda my hair and beat me so bad

I just 'bout bled to death. After dat I wished I woulda, 'cause he sent me ta a strawberry farm somewhere and put me ta work. I 'member the cars lined up in a parking lot by the dozens and the men standing in line for their turn like they was standing in line at Taco Bell. They each got three minutes. I had ta do twenty men an hour. Later, he sent me ta a strip club where I danced. I never got ta keep a penny, they took it all from me. It was better than the strawberry farm though, and girl, ya didn't dare talk."

Raina's jaw hung open in horror, but her look was firm, "I'm not going to be dragged into this hell. I'm going to get away from these monsters and tell everyone what they're doing. This is slavery disguised as prostitution."

Zoa presses her finger to Raina's lips, "I had ta learn the hard way, like I 'spect yer gonna. But I'm warnin' ya, foo'; you better submit 'cause these is brutal men. If ya helpful and no trouble ta them, ya get extra food, or a bitch treat; that's when they take ya to get your nails done or a hair-cut."

Raina hobbles to her feet and her eyes lock onto Zoa, "You have to help me. I can't live like this. Help me find some clothes."

"Ya gonna have ta do this. Ya might not be willin' at first, but ya gonna do it. I'm warning you." She sticks her finger in Raina's face, "Ya do what ya told ta do. If not, ya gonna suffer."

"No!" Raina chokes out a groan.

"Oh yeah, ya smile at the men, make them believe that ya enjoying every second no matter what they do ta ya, most of all when theys filming. If ya don't, they gonna hurt you in ways ya can't believe."

Raina covers her face with her hands, "How can they get away with this?"

"They blackmail, they torture and threaten yer kin folk. They list things they gonna do ta ya like nobody's business. Girl, they'll beat ya 'til ya do what they say."

Tears pool in Raina's eyes, "There must be families out there missing daughters who the police are looking for."

"Yeah, sure they is, but Daboia moves us 'round so much we don't even know where we at, how ya expect anyone else is gonna find us?"

"There's no way that they can –" Raina starts to say, but Zoa interrupts and covers Raina's mouth. Zoa looks toward the door and stiffens, she listens hard, then after a few breathless seconds she whispers, "A while back, a Mexican girl on her way ta a hair-cut got free and ran. I heard tell she made it to a store before Daboia's men caught up wit her, but no one knows what happened after dat. There was hope for a while, but after not hearing nothin' for months." Zoa's eyes moisten and she surveys Raina's face, "They is no hope girl. She be dead."

For a moment Raina's stare holds tight and she swallows hard. In the next instant, they hear footsteps in the house. Zoa's expression changes from woe to dread. She motions for Raina to follow her. Raina limps behind, holding her side, thinking the woman is leading her to a way out. Instead, they enter a bathroom with no mirrors. The sink and tub are rust-stained and scummy. The window is boarded and nailed shut. Zoa turns the bath water on and tells Raina to get in.

Raina hesitates, but the water runs steamy and clean into the tub, and she is drawn to its soothing warmth. Guarded, mindful of the pain in every move she makes, she climbs in the tub. She figures that after her bath she'll be given some clothes, and that's when she'll try to escape on her own.

Zoa helps her wash her hair and Raina is grateful because she can't lift her arms above her ribs. The water is warm and comforting and she smells the soft clean scent of soap. She flinches when Zoa rinses the dried blood from her cheek and swollen nose. Her face is swollen, an angry purple bruise has spread across both eyes and she feels tiny nerve endings pulsating and stinging beneath her scalp. She is tired, all she wants to do is fall asleep, and wake up in her own warm, soft bed.

When Zoa finishes helping Raina bathe, she takes an old worn towel and dries her while whispering, "Ya gonna be spending the night at this house, then they gonna take ya away in the mornin'."

Trembling, Raina whispers back, "Where are some clothes for me and who's taking me where?"

It seems as if Zoa wants to say more, but she keeps silent. Instead she motions again for Raina to follow her.

Raina's voice is a faint whisper, "Will they take you, too?"

Zoa doesn't answer, walking ahead in silence. They return to the room where Raina had first been thrown onto a mattress. She looks around. The mattress is the only furnishing in the room. No blankets, no sheets, no pillows. There is one dim and dingy light bulb hanging lopsided from the ceiling, its pull string dangling in stark blankness. The window is covered with an old yellowed shade that is nailed around its entire perimeter. The entrance to a closet is bereft its door, nothing but hinges hang loosely from the frame. The air in the room that once seemed cool and glorious in reality is stagnant and smells of decay.

Zoa whispers as she turns to leave the room, "Now 'member, be quiet and obey, or ya gonna wish ya was dead." As she leaves she locks the deadbolt on the other side of the door.

Raina stands naked in the middle of the room, abandoned and shivering. Suddenly feeling self-conscious she covers herself with her arms, then, like a scared rabbit entering a fox's den, she freezes, fearing that if she moves it will draw the predator's attention.

She stares down at the worn, stained mattress, deciding she needs to collect her thoughts and come up with a plan of escape. Raina crouches down, and while trying not to make a sound she creeps toward the mattress. She sits down on the cleanest corner trying to pull her thoughts together. She has to figure out how to get away.

Soon, she curls herself into the fetal position and closes her eyes while clutching the small worn towel to her chest, her one possession. She holds the damp and tattered towel as if it is her baby. Dear God, how she misses her baby boy. She stirs at the memory of him, his birthday is next week and soon she is reminiscing about his *first* birthday.

Her mother, Anna Rose, who was always called Rosa for short, had baked him a white cake with chocolate frosting. Raina can almost smell the sweet scent of fresh, crushed vanilla beans wafting through the kitchen. She smiles tenderly, thinking back, watching her baby boy, Ira Samuel, in his highchair with his hands submerged in his first cake. She named her son Ira, after her mother's father, a tribal medicine man and Samuel after her own father. Rosa and Samuel babysit for the boy while she is at school during the week. The four of them are very close.

Raina and Grandpa Sam had taken Ira to his first Padres baseball game when he turned three and he loved it, so for his fourth birthday they bought him a brand new baseball mitt. Raina can't wait to see the look on her son's face when he opens his present and she really can't wait to play catch with him. Ira is a smart boy, advanced for his age and Raina is very proud of him.

She dreams of happier times, drifting back to the time last Saturday, less than a week ago, when they had been sitting at the kitchen table playing a game of Peon. Out of the blue Ira began to sing a song he'd learned in preschool. They looked at each other in amazement as he named all fifty states in the song. When he was finished, he sat there in his booster chair with his sweet face beaming from ear to ear.

Without warning the dead bolt slams to one side and the door to the room bursts open. Raina is startled from her reverie and wracked with pain in her side from the sudden movement. Daboia is standing in the doorway with three other men. She cowers on the corner of the mattress as she reads the look in their eyes.

They cross the room and Raina throws her arms out in defense while wincing in pain, "Oh, no. No! Please, I have a baby! I have a son." She tries to make them see her as human, "No, let go!" She kicks her legs, trying vainly to keep the men away. Daboia narrows his eyes, "You will obey bitch!" He yells. In a frenzy, she swings her fists and begins cursing, using a mixture of English, Spanish and her native Kumeyaay.

Raina is crying as they shove her down on the mattress. Despite the pain in her side, she pounds and claws, screaming and scratching, trying to get them off her. They shove a gag into her mouth. One of them sets up a video camera and the other three hold her arms and legs down. She tries to twist free, but they are too strong and they pull her up, forcing her on her hands and knees. Daboia watches intently, then he takes his turn first. The more she struggles the rougher he gets. Each one of them takes his turn at sodomizing her while the camera is filming. The pain is searing and the penetration tears at her. She screams out in muffled agony, gagging and gasping for air. After each man finishes, he uses her towel to wipe himself.

Tears stream from Raina's bruised and swollen eyes, gushing down her cheeks. Her nose begins to bleed again as the last man grabs her hair, pulling her head so far back that her eyes roll to the back of their sockets. She sees the ceiling, then his face and then he rams her so hard that her nose smashes against the wall. When he is done, he stands cleaning himself with her towel while she gags and sobs. Once finished with the towel he throws it at her, hitting the back of her head.

Daboia gives Raina a warning before the men file out of the room, "If you do not obey, I will know for sure that you enjoyed this and I will find all kinds of ways to please you." Raina only faintly heard his warning as she began to black out from the excruciating pain.

When Raina wakes up, she is on top of the blood-soaked mattress, her feet and wrists are tied and she is staring up at the squares of the dirty ceiling tile defiled by nicotine and covered with stains the nature of which Raina can only surmise. She is dizzy and it feels like her cheeks are stretched with a coat hanger and stuffed with cotton. Her face is redish purple and bloated, her eyes are scratchy and raw. She squeezes her lids shut and rolls her eyes back and forth, trying to regain moisture in them. Her anus is throbbing in agony. Her entire bottom is so swollen that it feels like a grapefruit has grown between her legs.

Zoa is in the room. When she sees Raina blinking her eyes she whispers to her. "What they done is a warning of what will happen if ya try ta escape or disobey. 'Member this night. Obey they every command. If ya don't, they gonna make it worse."

Raina could not believe that anything could be worse than what she had just been through. All she can think about is a way to escape these demons. Then Zoa pulls a syringe out of a bag and ties a tourniquet above Raina's elbow. She lays the needle on top of her skin and pushes it into her vein. Within seconds all the pain that Raina feels doesn't matter. She welcomes the warm, floating feeling of comfort as it flows through her body. She has just been given her first of a series of drug doses especially designed to force her into addiction.

Later that day, while Raina is still incapacitated by the drugs, a team of four men transport her to a middle-class neighborhood. There she will begin her education as a sex slave.

She and the other new girls are ordered to greet all men with a smile. If they dare disobey they are beaten. They are told to speak in low, seductive tones. They are forced to use sleazy, degrading phrases about themselves and such language is the only type of dialog that they are allowed to use. The traffickers intend that their victim's own voices and personalities be erased from their memories.

Raina refuses to degrade herself, and after being slapped around over and over again is finally told that she is no longer permitted to talk. They tell her clients that she is a dumb bitch who can't read, write, or speak. Raina doesn't care, she has nothing to say to them and as long as she doesn't talk, they don't beat her up.

The girls are forced to watch pornographic videos daily. They're expected to imitate the women in the films. Some of the men pay a premium to watch a video of a violent sex act and then choose one of the girls to act out the part of the girl in the video. The men are allowed ten timed minutes with a girl. If they want more time they have to pay more. None of the girls are paid.

Raina now lives her days in modern-day slave quarters in the middle of a city. As far as Raina can tell from quick peeks out the door when someone enters or leaves, she is still in California, though she can't be positive. She is not allowed to leave the house. Her meals are fixed and brought to her in a room where the curtains are never opened. None of the girls even dares to approach a window. If Raina needs to use the bathroom she asks for someone to take her. When it is time for her menstrual cycle, there's no rest. During those times she is forced into oral or anal sex.

Raina is a slave in an underworld of hopelessness, and misery. Through no fault of her own she now lives in a place where the one purpose she has on earth is to provide sex. She is bound to a life of sexual servitude and nobody knows where she is. When people hear rumors about the strawberry farms and ask why the white flags are hung on the reeds along the side of the highway, they are told it's where the migrants bring their whores. It's as if the women and children are willing participants. And people turn away in disgust.

After Raina has been enslaved for a month they move her again, depriving her of what even death row inmates are given; a space to call their own. She has nothing. She is no longer even considered as valuable as a dog. Pimps supply her and the other women with drugs and alcohol to subdue them and increase their dependency. All the victims, women and children, are kept as isolated as possible. There is no other condition in human life which is so low, so desperate and so terrifying as is the horror of an existence as a sex slave. When Daboia is present all are made to get down on their knees in reverence to him and smiles are the golden rule. The victims must always smile and act as if they love what they are doing so they don't spoil the clients' pleasure.

They have turned Raina into a robot, but she still has life behind her eyes. There is not one moment of the day that she does not think about her baby boy, her parents and her freedom. It has been many weeks now since her abduction and she wonders if Ira still asks for her and questions why she doesn't come home to him. Her eyes tear up and her chin starts to quiver when she pictures him crying for her, but she has to choke back her feelings because of the brutal punishment inflicted upon her for showing any emotion other than lust.

But it has become too hard for Raina to hold her feelings inside and they manifest themselves in other ways.

Quite often she has to ask to be taken to the bathroom so that she can vomit between servicing clients. Her neck and shoulders ache and she bites her fingernails until they bleed. She is forced to earn a quota of six hundred dollars per day. The pricing is set and written on a board that travels along with her. It is meant to be a constant reminder of what she now is.

Vaginal or anal sex with condom $20/10 minutes.
Without a condom $30/10 minutes.
Oral sex $10 per five minutes.
Disclaimer:
"Without a condom is at your own risk."

There is no concern for any of the girls' health because they are not considered human. They are reusable, disposable chattel. Since the women and girls are usually from poorer neighborhoods or male dominated cultures their disappearances are often ignored. It is assumed they have become willing prostitutes, or have been married off by their families.

Most of the girls Raina meets are very young, many times between the ages of fourteen and seventeen, with some as young as ten or eleven, but one day Raina is present when a new girl is brought in who can't be more than six years old. She is tiny and her skin is a flawless milk chocolate brown. She has the most beautiful brown eyes that Raina has ever seen. Her face is angelic. She is pure innocence and they are withholding her from the lines of men in the fields until after she is deflowered by the highest bidder. The man who won the bid is tall and muscular and wearing a suit. He won the bid to pillage her innocence for the sum of two thousand dollars.

Raina is so sickened by the man that before she can think about the consequences, she is scrambling across the room to aid the child. She stands like a shield, fixing herself firm between the client and the tiny girl. She speaks out loud for the first time in weeks, begging the client to take an experienced girl like herself instead. The man looks down at her with wild eyes. He grabs her shoulders and shoves her to the floor. In an instant, two of Daboia's men seize Raina, yanking her to her feet and insisting that she apologize. She refuses, so they apologize for her. They explain that Raina is an exceptionally horny bitch and she is jealous because she is eager to have a good looking, muscular man like him for herself. The man nods in jovial acceptance, pleased with the explanation.

Then one of the house women motions for him to follow her and she takes the child's hand and begins to lead them into another room. The child turns back to Raina, her eyes reflecting both uncertainty and fright and tears pour down her cheeks. She reaches out to Raina, *"Por favor! Por favor! Senora!"* Raina extends her arms toward her, but she is stopped by Daboia's men.

She pleads, hot tears stinging her eyes, "Please! Please! I beg you, please let me go for her! I'll do anything for you. Please just let me go for her," but Raina can only watch as the child is forced through the door. Raina tries to free herself, but Daboia's men hold her back. "I'm so sorry, baby! I'm so sorry!" Her words echo hollowly as she watches the door close.

For a moment there is silence, then enraged, Raina turns around, her eyes so cold that Daboia's men stand immobile, held by her frosty glare. Inside, her blood is boiling. She clenches her teeth trying to hold her emotions in check, but they spew from her like molten lava.

For a moment she becomes like they are, soulless and violent.

Raina displays a blind fury that the men have never seen before. She begins swinging at Daboia's thugs with a force and strength that she never knew she had. She claws one of them in the face with her nails, raking four bloody gouges into his cheek. She picks up a lamp and breaks it on top of the other thug's head. She struggles and wrestles with them, her fists pounding into their necks and ears, delivering strike after strike. She digs her nails into their hands and when they grab her hair she kicks, aiming at the groin area. They slam her to the ground, but she gets up and hurls a coffee table across the room sending both men stumbling backward. She jumps on one of them and he shields his face with his hand. She crunches down on his arm with her jaw, crushing and tearing his flesh to the bone with her teeth. But then, she feels a blow to the back of her head followed by a burning and roaring in her ears and she goes limp and falls to the floor.

When Raina awakens, her entire body is stinging and her muscles are throbbing. Two men are standing guard over her, each of them holding a thick rubber hose. One of them bears four long scabs across his cheek, scabs which will result in scars. Raina has no way to know this, but those scars will stay with him. For the rest of his short life he will be called, "Rakeface." The other thug has a thick gauze bandage binding his arm courtesy of Raina. When Rakeface sees that she is awake, he makes a mock strike at her with his black rubber hose, his eyes wild and burning with rage, "I'm gonna kill you slow, bitch."

Raina shrinks, pulling her knees tight into her chest and covering her head with her bruised arms. She peeks up at them, tells them that she will obey and begs them not to hit her again. Raina is tied up and transported to a new camp.

Her new captors give her an initiation of their own. She is forced to clean up all of the rooms in the house including cleaning up the human excrement in the bathrooms. She will also be expected to meet her client quota along with her clean-up duty. Her clients are workers from the fields and she can smell strawberries mixed with alcohol and tobacco on every one of the dozens of men who file through the house.

She has been moving from room to room all day long and she has counted at least thirty girls at this house. The men at this farm are timed as they rape their victims, spending no longer than five minutes with a girl. Each girl is forced to service twelve men each hour. If a girl is extra pretty, the word spreads and she becomes a high demand commodity. The men are allowed just three minutes with those particular girls because they will have to service twenty men each hour. She will do this every day for the rest of her life until she is full of disease and so spiritually empty that she can earn no money. She is then left to die.

Raina thinks back to the first night of her captivity. She thinks about the woman she'd met named Zoa, wondering if she is still alive. Zoa's low sultry voice drifts through her mind. "*Very few people are freed or escape with their lives,*" she had said. But even after all this time Raina still plans on escaping.

Several months later, Raina happens on a chance to escape while she is scrubbing filth from a bathroom floor. She hears Daboia's voice for the first time since the night of her kidnapping, it seems to come from just down the hall.

Her ears pick up bits of conversation. Raina thinks this must be a significant meeting place, maybe even a headquarters. From what she can hear, Daboia and the men seem to be having a business meeting, a criminal think tank so to speak. All the bosses of the houses, camps, and farms must keep track of the profits that are made off the girls' backs. Slavery is the oldest business on the planet and it is run like any organized business, except that the workers get no wages and the owners pay no taxes. Daboia pockets the lion's share of the millions of dollars earned by the girls. The others split what is left of the profit made by the individual areas that they manage. The women and children who live in these houses, farms or camps last from two to seven years. They end up either beaten to death, or die alone in a dark, filthy room, ravaged by AIDS or other diseases.

Raina begins cleaning the room next to the men and she can plainly hear Daboia telling his followers, "Brazil is becoming a major player in the sex industry. The lack of opportunity for female workers, the reduction in jobs on farms because of the decline of the farming industry and the general infrastructure of the country has resulted in the sex trade down there booming and the boom should continue right on through the eighties," he tells them. "Some of the most powerful men in the world are calling it a paradise for the commercial sex trade. They think it will grow well into the nineties. They're selling females down there before they reach puberty, clean, without disease and before menses, so they have no sanitary needs and require minimal food. The demand is becoming great for nine year olds and younger. I hear they are offering travel packages because of the growing appetite for child pornography. Actors, athletes, politicians, and businessmen are all heading down to Brazil. They are paying premium prices for sex and many of the peasant farmers down there are selling their females for next to nothing. The buyers are making a killing off the profits."

Raina hears another member of this brotherhood speak up, but she doesn't recognize his voice, "We should be doing the same; we need a greater demand for the young here in this country."

Daboia answers, "Yes and that's what this meeting is about. The fastest way to weaken the countries of the West and their infidel religions is to weaken them from within and I believe we can speed the process through the spread of pornography. Porn is like heroin; it's progressive and addictive. What I'm proposing is that we start slow. We start by filming the "Mufa'khatha," the placing of the penis between the thighs of a toddler. Get American pornography users acclimated to the idea. Make viewing of such sexual acts commonplace by flooding pornographic web sites and book stores with sexual acts of that nature and then progress from there. Tell them that children are both cooperative and responsive and actually enjoy the experience. Like the Western Psychiatrist, Dr. Frued said, 'Sex is born into us and comes naturally to children.' We'll make users of porn feel good about themselves and their pornography habit. We can create a demand for child masochism and legitimize it with the theories of Western doctors such as Freud."

Another man's voice, a hollow voice, also unfamiliar to Raina says, "Child pornography isn't rampant enough. How do we make it more popular?"

"Remember, not long ago pornography itself was very unpopular in this country," Daboia answers, "At one time it was usually hidden and men caught buying pornography were shamed and extensively prosecuted by law enforcement. Now, the entire Western world is desensitized to it and prosecutors cannot keep up with the violators. Pornography is on TV, on the radio, in magazines and in advertisements. It's everywhere in one form or another in the West. The most desirable adult entertainment capital of the world is here in this country, Vegas, where the streets are crowded with examples of pornography. I predict the same will happen with child pornography. It will stay hush-hush and people will continue to close their eyes to it because it's too messy for them to deal with. Men don't tell on each other and what happens behind closed doors, stays behind closed doors. Last week, I was introduced to someone who may be interested in getting the process going for us; he's got heavy connections in Vegas. Pornography will spread like a plague. We'll make sure of that. I'm sure that child pornography will soon be acceptable and men will pay exorbitant prices to have sex with children. The more the Federal Government and Immigration and Naturalization Service try to bust it up, the more people will take a chance. The users of pornography will risk the danger involved because of the adrenaline rush such use will create and it logically follows that we can then charge more for providing the service. All we have to do is create the addiction—the demand will follow."

A dramatic pause, then another voice asks, "How can we be sure it'll work?"

"Listen to what I am saying to you! At first pornography was just about nudity and sex. Then it progressed into deviant sex, violent rape, bestiality, and finally snuff films, the actual killing of the enslaved sexual partner. Remember the golden shower? At first there were a smattering of customers, but once users became accustomed to seeing victims forced to smile as someone defecated or urinated on their bodies, films and magazines illustrating that horrifying practice started flying off the shelves. Westerners even have their wives go to local pornography shops to pick films or magazines. This proves how intellectually and spiritually deficient Western women are. They will sit and watch as other women are forced to do unspeakable acts and then pleasure their man after. Then, of course, the men want to buy more." He throws his hands up in the air, "The process feeds itself, it's addictive and it's growing. The same will happen with child pornography."

A wave of excitement sweeps through the room. Daboia waits for the excitement to calm down, he continues, "Pornography is the most lucrative product around, because it creates demand for the slaves we buy and the product sells itself over and over again. Believe me, it will be a lot less trouble using children. We'll raise them on pornography. Pornography will be their life. We'll be making more money in twenty years than most major businesses and all sports venues combined. By providing a service like this, our brotherhood will command the world."

Raina hears excitement in the men's voices and her face flushes as she realizes Daboia is serious. She is enraged. How can this be happening? How can they be so callous and be so disconnected from the suffering of women and children?

Then a skeptical voice shouts out in the other room, "You're saying that the more porn a person watches, the more it influences their appetite for sex? If so, won't it drive up the price of the slaves we have to buy? What if it gets too expensive to supply the demand?"

Other voices break out in agreement. Daboia hushes them and answers in a confident voice with an iron tone, "When we are close to having that type of demand, we'll start breeding farms."

A hush settles in the room. Raina gasps.

"We'll breed women for the sole purpose of selling their offspring into porn for male pleasure. After all, it is written that, 'females are created as toys, born for a man's pleasure.'"

One voice filled with rising excitement asked, "Why don't we just start a breeding farm now? We could cut out the cost of abortions and we could eliminate the cost of buying women and children off the street. Our profits would soar."

The others begin murmuring in agreement, another man laughingly says, "In this country, we'll probably be able to lobby the government, to get 'em ta pay the medical expenses of the births with the welfare system."

The room fills with sarcastic laughter.

Raina is aghast; a farm to generate sex slaves. Her stomach is swirling, her face is hot and crimson. All she can think about is getting out of here. She has to tell the authorities what's going on. She has to try to stop this lunacy. People are never going to believe this. She can't believe it herself, but, then again, at first society did not take Hitler seriously either. She feels as though she is in a vacuum, living in a parallel world. She can't stand this life any longer; she'd rather die than to be part of this absolute misery. To be forced to have sex again and again with men who stink of sweat, dirt and booze. Men who are allowed to be brutal if they so choose. Men who are short, tall, fat, thin, and bald. Men with no teeth, no hair, no scruples. Men of every race, creed, color and religion, married or unmarried. Men who come to buy women and girls for less than the price of a T-shirt and then treat them as if they are dumpsters for dying sperm. Even animals do not do this to each other.

Raina knows how fast the daily sexual and physical abuse can thwart the ability to feel pleasure, even simple pleasure, like seeing the blue of the sky, feeling a warm spring breeze, or hearing a bird chirp in the early morning. How you simply become detached from everything, your one earthly purpose to supply filthy and stinking sex.

Raina's deepest hope and immediate purpose is to get far away from these demons before they notice her missing. She has been on clean-up duty now for months and her captors consider her a low flight risk. She has a tiny window of opportunity right now, because most of the men are attending this meeting. Even though she will be on foot this is as good a time as any.

Raina drops her soapy rag in the pail and turns to leave. She gets down on her knees and pushes the bucket along the floor with one hand while dragging her trash bag with the other. She doesn't want to arouse any commotion at this point, so she crawls on her hands and knees down the hallway, her head bowed, as quietly as possible. The men stop talking for a moment as she passes. She lowers her chin to her chest and keeps quietly crawling along the hall. After a few moments the men resume their talking.

When Raina reaches the kitchen she stands up and steadies herself. She waits a moment, regaining her balance and letting an attack of lightheadedness pass. Then, in quiet increments, she opens the refrigerator door, covering its sound with the voices of the men. She'll be punished if she is caught stealing food and she will lose her chance to run. She bends down at the refrigerator and as noiselessly as possible, peels the packaging off the back of a luncheon meat container. The men stop talking. She freezes. She stays motionless, holding her breath. She waits, fixed in a bent position for someone to say something. She releases her breath in relief when the voices resume. Raina pulls some lunch meat from the package, stuffs a handful into her mouth and the rest into her skirt. She moves to the sink and turns on the tap just enough so that she can cup some water into her hands. She needs the fluid so she has to risk it. After she drinks enough water and she feels herself gaining strength, she tiptoes to the back door and surveys the area.

It is hilly and rough, but she sees no one. There is a grove of trees about eighty yards up a slope that is straight ahead. If she can make it to the trees she may have a chance. All she has to do is make it to the edge. A couple days before, as she risked a glance out of a window she saw a faint glimmer beyond those trees; a glimmer which could have been a headlight. There might be a highway back there where she could flag someone down for help. If that is the case, she'll be free.

Raina is ready to leave. She takes a deep, but soundless breath and then another. She clenches her teeth together, stares straight ahead at the trees and hits the door running. She is surprised at how fast her legs are able to move and she pushes them hard.

The men sense movement from within the house, then the thud of her hand hitting the door. For three stunned seconds they are so startled they are unable to move. Raina is thus able to gain some added precious steps. Her mind is wild with fear as she runs.

Then all hell breaks loose and the men are scrambling for their weapons. It seems to her that they emerge from everywhere, yelling and chasing after her. They're carrying guns, and whips; one even carries a meat hook. Raina knows they won't shoot her, because the sounds of the shots will raise suspicion and they'll want to punish her and watch her suffer before she dies. She runs as fast as she can without looking back, determined to reach the trees. The men are shouting threats, but they no longer scare her. Blocking all else out, she is singlemindedly focused on the trees in front of her, her eyes fixed on the spot of that glimmering light of hope. Her legs feel strong, her attitude is changed and she feels in control for the first time in months. She is running up the hill, getting closer and she pushes harder. The heels of her bare feet slam against the parched sedge. The dried craggy soil cuts and burns her soles, but Raina doesn't let up. She feels nothing but the hope that her mad dash for freedom succeeds.

The men begin to gain on her, their voices getting louder. Adrenaline surges through her. She pushes herself to the brink. She is running faster than she ever has in her life and it seems she is going to make it. The trees are just forty yards away. She is halfway there. She is going to make it. She knows she will. She'll be free to see her baby boy again. What joy she has waiting for her if she succeeds. She is almost there now, a few more steps and she'll be free to tell the world of the horror she has lived. She is gasping for breath, her heart is racing. A branch snaps beneath her foot, she is almost at the edge of the trees and she surges ahead with excitement. She picks up the branch that she stepped on and brandishing it like a weapon, heads into the safety of the trees.

A whistling sound, then a crack and there is a sharp stinging on her foot. The whip catches her ankle just enough to make her stumble. She lands painfully in the tree roots and the men are on her. They gather above her, their arms hanging over her like deformed branches of the trees. She peers up at them, bright rays of sunlight separate the dark human forms above her and she squints as the light stabs her eyes. She knows what's coming next, her eyes blink and she covers her head with her arms. Even though she wants to die, her body reacts spontaneously, protectively, trying to cling to life.

She screams obscenities at them, hoping to get them to finish their grisly business quickly. She does not want to survive this attack only to be tortured again and again. She has lost her one chance to escape and she wants to die. She swears a solemn vow that she will find a way back from the dead to tell the world about them and what they are planning.

She is on her back, they pull her arms and legs apart and pound the butts of their guns into her ribs. Whips slice through the flesh on her face and eyelids, but it is the meat hook that does the most damage. One of the men gouges her legs and arms, then picks her up and tosses her around with the hook. Finally, she lands on her stomach and he tears the hook into her back slicing through her rib cage and puncturing her lung.

She screams in agony and calls out her son's name. Blood gurgles in her throat. She whispers, "Ira! Baby, Mommy loves you." Blood bubbles and oozes from her mouth and nose while they keep pounding at her.

There is no mercy. Raina does not expect any. The men are worse than rabid beasts and they don't stop even as Raina stops fighting, lying inert and gasping for breath. She expels one last breath, crying out. "Ira, Samuel, Notah - my son, I love you." and she dies.

Raina lies lifeless in a dark swath of dirt and blood, bouncing listlessly with each blow from the butt of the men's guns.

At last, Daboia, who is standing close by watching shouts at them. "It's over! Get that trouble making bitch out of my sight." Two men scramble down the hill to grab a tarp from the back of a pickup truck and throw it over her.

After 5:00 p.m., when the farm shuts down for the day, Daboia brings the other girls out to look at Raina's body. He stands in a wide, callous stance, his lips curled in a sneer as he throws the tarp back. Raina's eyes are open, her body is bluish-white and she is still clutching the tree branch in her hand, its leaves are torn, and it's soaked with blood.

"This is what happens to bitches when they try to escape."

There's no reaction from the girls, they're not surprised by his brutality. Daboia tells the men to clean up the mess and to feed the carcass to the animals. Two of Daboia's men, Wasif and Rakeface, take a filthy blanket, roll up Raina's body and toss her into the trunk of an Oldsmobile Delta 88 Sedan. They cover the spot where Raina's blood is spilled with shovelfuls of fresh dirt.

Later that night they drive Raina's body to a remote location in the desert close to the Mexican border. Wasif stops and puts the car in park. "This is good enough. Let's throw her out here, nobody's gonna find the bitch's body way out here." They pull Raina's body out of the trunk of the car and dump her in the sand.

"Yeah, but maybe we should bury it, or pour some gas on it and burn it," Rakeface says. He pulls the collar of his jacket up around his neck, and looks out into the night as an uneasiness runs down his spine. He then turns to Wasif motioning him to hurry up, and they drag her a couple feet from the car. Wasif un-sheaths his knife and cuts the blood-soaked blanket open, exposing her body to the elements and the animals.

A swirl of sand whirls around them, and Rakeface can't shake the edginess and chill in his body. "Leave it and let's get out of here. Something ain't right about that bitch, even though she is dead. Let the coyotes pick her apart. Nothing's bad enough for this whore. My wife's still pissed about the scars the bitch left on my face."

Daboia's men get in the car and start down the road, "Yeah," Wasif says, "That bitch gave me a nasty infection when she bit my arm. I had to tell the doc a dog bit me." They both sneer, "Yeah, that's the truth," Rakeface answered, "a dog in heat, the stupid bitch."

They turn onto a desert back road and head north for San Diego's back country. In the beam of headlight's ahead, they can see nothing but sand and scrub brush. After kicking up dust for a few miles they notice lightning flashing and the wind picking up. Even though they are going slow the car begins to careen.

Rakeface checks the mirrors while Wasif glances out from window to window.

"Looks like we're in the middle of a dust storm," Wasif says.

Suddenly they are hit by a dust devil, a monstrosity, spewing its sand particles at fifty miles an hour and sucking their car right toward its center.

Rakeface turns the wheel and tries to swerve out of its path, but the dust-devil changes course at the same time. The car smashes into the twirling spiral of dirt and sand pelts the car like buckshot from a shotgun.

Rakeface leans forward and looks up through the windshield, "What the hell? It's worse than a tornado. You ever seen anything like this?"

"Shit, no."

"Me, neither. I thought they don't happen at night."

"My guess is they do. Step on it."

Lightning is flashing and the wind is roaring, growling and whistling through the windows. Rakeface speeds the car up and the devil moves with them, making the visibility zero. They circle round, backtracking without knowing it, ending up back where they came from deep in the desert with the dust devil hovering above. Dust is blowing in through the vents and it clouds the inside of the car.

Rakeface can't see where he's driving and his nostrils are plugged with sand. They both fumble for the vents, slamming them shut, but the storm is so violent that sand blows in from the floor boards, the trunk and the bottom of the doors, filtering in through every crevice.

Wasif covers his mouth, "Stop! Maybe we should just stop and wait this out, we can't see anyway."

"What the—! Whoa!"

The giant dust devil picks the car up, catching it by the hood and whirls it around. Twirling and turning like a carnival ride, the dust devil spins the car. The men use their shirts to cover their faces. The air is filled with ozone generated by multiple lightning strikes and its strong almost chlorine like odor starts to burn their nostrils. Their eyes begin stinging, their stomachs churn and both men feel like vomiting. As the car drops to the ground and stops spinning, a huge tunnel of sand collapses around them.

For a minute all is quiet. The worst seems to be over. But then steam begins to seep in through the vents from under the hood. The burning stench of sizzling rubber invades the passenger compartment as gasoline fumes combust and ignite near the engine. The smell is putrid and the corrosive vapors singe their noses. They take off their shirts and try to plug the vents.

Rakeface reaches for the door, "I can't take this anymore! I'm getting out of here!" He pulls the handle and pushes on the door but it won't open.

The dust devil had dropped its load of sand, burying the car up to its windows. Rakeface pushes with all his strength but he can't budge the door. He bangs it with his shoulder again and again, but it doesn't move. He tries the windows, but they won't open.

"Were trapped, we're fuckin' trapped. Find something to bust out the window with," Rakeface screams.

They scramble, looking on the floor, under seats and in between them. Wasif grabs a .45 pistol from the glove box and starts bashing at the window with the gun, but the window doesn't break. He decides to try shooting out the window instead, but he's shaking and he can't hold the gun still. One bullet ricochets off the metal frame of the door and cuts off the tip of Rakeface's nose and another bullet ricochets off the metal brace of the roof and grazes Wasif's groin on its way back down through the seat and the floor board. Tears sting their eyes and they both howl in pain. One bullet hits the window and the rest blast holes in the roof, but the window, although spider-webbed with a hole and cracks, holds together, and dust and dirt sifts down through the holes in the roof like sand passing through an hour glass.

Rakeface grabs his nose. "My nose! Son of a bitch! Oh, shit! Watch it, the engine's on fire!"

Wasif grabs his crotch. "My *zibbe! Ooh my zibbe*'s hit! Turn the key off, dumb ass."

"Me, a dumb ass! You're the one that can't shoot a gun straight, you fuckin' idiot!"

Wasif looks at Rakeface, whose nose is squirting blood, then he looks down at his crotch and it's bleeding, too, "Damn! It hurts! My balls hurt! How we gonna get out of this?"

Rakeface turns the key and shuts off the engine. He crawls into the back seat and lays on his back, putting his boots on the door window, "I'm gonna kick out the window, that's how." He starts to kick at the window but can't get enough leverage to break it. Annoyed, he shoots Wasif a glare, "Git back here and help me, fuck head. I need you to sit behind me so I'm closer when I kick it."

Groaning and holding his *zibbe,* Wasif climbs into the backseat and squeezes next to the door. Rakeface leans his back on him and begins to kick. Every time he kicks at the window, it thumps Wasif's crotch, "Stop, stop, stop it!" Wasif reaches round the front of Rakeface and grabs his nose squeezing it.

"Ouch! You stupid fuck!" Rakeface gives up on the window and climbs back into the front seat, "You kick for a while, dickhead!"

An explosion from beneath the hood rattles the car and peels open a hole in the hood, a surge of oxygen is sucked under the hood and the vent covers blow off. All the lights go haywire, blinking and flashing, except for the dome light. The dome light stays on. In less than half a second, the driver's side air bag detonates and slams into Rakeface, smashing him against the seat. "Fuck! Git this thing off of me. Git it off! Cut it, git the fuckin' knife and cut it."

At once, a series of "pops" buffet the air like firecrackers and hundreds of puffs of smoke erupt, filling the car. Bombardier Beetles invade the cab, blowing in through the vents, unleashing their caustic flatulence into the air. The stench is awful and their bites scourge and burn.

"Oh, shit, git 'em out of here!" Wasif swings, thrashing his arms in every direction.

Rakeface is pinned, his nose squashed, broken, swollen and bleeding. "Git the knife and pop this thing!"

Wasif, holding his crotch with one hand, climbs over the seat. He gropes under the passenger's seat with his other hand. He finds a knife and stabs the airbag. It explodes, launching both men off their seats, ramming their heads into the roof of the car and knocking them unconscious. They settle in a slump, leaning shoulder to shoulder.

A few moments later, the pair are roused as caustic and evil smelling fumes envelope them. They come fully awake to find the car is filling with sand from the holes in the roof. The men are already buried to their necks, arms pinned to their sides, while the little exposed flesh they have left is crawling with beetles. The insects bite and chew like flesh-eating piranhas, while at the same time the sand keeps pouring in.

Wasif confronts Rakeface, his eyes stinging and tearing, "We're gonna be buried alive! We're gonna die like this!"

Rakeface spits and sputters, throwing his head from side to side. He struggles to move his arms. "She did this. That fuckin Indian voodoo bitch did this! She cast a fuckin spell. The bitch put a hex on us. I knew there was something spooky about that whore."

The sand keeps pouring in. It reaches their bottom lips, they both try to blow and spit it away, but it sails into each other's eyes and the beetles keep gnawing at their flesh. The sand advances above their mouths. They look at each other fearful, unable to speak. Their lashes heavy with sand, eyes filled with dirt, they battle to blink it away. Within moments the sand has reached their nostrils. They stretch their necks, desperate to breathe. The sand stops pouring in just before it covers their eyes and for the next few minutes they watch each other suffocate, unable to scream for help.

Sucked into the desert by the dust devil, the two men are buried alive inside their car on the ridge of a mass grave. They die on an ancient Indian burial ground, the same spot where a short time ago, they dumped the ravaged body of Raina Notah, an innocent woman, a mother, a daughter.

# CHAPTER TWO

## Bad Medicine

"Rosa. Rosa." Sam shakes his wife's shoulder in a gentle manner, "Wake up," he whispers, "The baby cries. Rosa."

Yielding to her deep slumber, Sam swings his legs off the side of the bed. His bare feet hit the cool floor and he fumbles for his slippers. He shuffles down the hall and flips the light switch in the baby's room. He finds Ira on the floor, clutching his baseball mitt. He bends down and scoops the boy up.

"Oh, no, what's this? Why is grandpa's boy crying?" He cradles the boy in his arms and rocks him back and forth, "What's wrong, partner?"

Ira sniffles and rubs his eyes, "Mommy was pwaying wiff me, now she's gone."

Grandpa Sam sighs and with a despairing moan lays his grandson down on the bed. "Mommy isn't home, buddy. I wish she were."

"Ah huh, Papa, she has a stick wiff her, it's a wed one, she wants to pway wiff me, but I don't know where to go."

Holding back his tears, Sam swallows hard as a lump rises in his throat and he pulls the covers to Ira's chin and tucks him in.

"A red one, huh? I think you had a dream, son, but your mommy will be home someday soon and we'll play ball on Saturdays like we used to do." Sam turns away to hide his angst while he tucks the blankets around the boy's feet. "Now you go back to sleep so you can grow up to be big and strong."

Ira, clearly frustrated, lets out a huge breath and folds his arms across his chest. "I telled her you wouldn't baweave me, but she said she is waiting in the desert and I don't know where to go. Will you take me, Papa?"

Sam studies his grandson in silence for a moment and wonders why he suddenly seems so grown up. Then at last, he nods. "We'll take a ride tomorrow, buddy, after preschool, but for now you go back to sleep."

"Okay, Papa, tomorrow I bring my ball and mitt. Good night, Papa."

After kissing the boy on his forehead, Sam turns out the light and leaves. He walks down the hall to his bedroom and stops in the doorway for a moment to watch his wife sleeping.

She is no longer the women he married. The medication they've prescribed for her is strong and she now seldom interacts with people. Since Raina's disappearance, his wife seems to have disappeared too. Before this happened she would have never chosen pharmaceutical drugs over her herbal medicines. She is blocking everything out. She even forgot to bake Ira a cake for his fourth birthday and that wasn't at all like her. Sam had to quickly run to the store to get a cake, covering her forgetfulness.

He has been covering for her more and more in recent weeks.

Sam collapses onto his bed and his head hits the pillow. His wife doesn't stir. He tosses and turns as he has done every night since Raina's disappearance, worrying about her while his wife is sedated into a coma-like state. It feels as though there's a heavy jagged rock in his chest where his heart used to be and if he's lucky he'll fall asleep before morning. Sam lies motionless and drained, staring straight up at the ceiling. Thoughts of his daughter fill his mind deep into the night and sleep, slow to arrive, turns up just before sunrise.

"Grandpa! Grandpa!" Ira jumps off the mini-school bus that takes him to and from preschool. He runs, shouting grandpa all the way across the yard. Out of breath, he reaches the porch and grandpa scoops him up in his arms at the top of the stairs.

"Hi, partner. How was school today?"

"Guess what, Papa, we cutted with scissors today. I made a heart for you and Gramosa. See, here it is. I made one for Mommy, too. I made Mommy's really big, it's in my pack. I'm gonna give it to her when we see her today. Can we go now, Papa?"

"It's very nice, thank you. Let's give Gramosa the heart and see if she wants to ride with us today."

"Okay, Papa."

Sam takes Ira into the house. When they walk into the kitchen Grandma Rosa is standing at the stove, staring out the window in a trance-like state. She turns and offers the pair a soft smile while stirring a pan of soup. She has been going through the motions since her daughter disappeared, trying to use sheer will to regain a sense of normalcy back in her life. Grandpa hands Ira to her and takes three bowls out of the cupboard. They sit down and Ira hands Grandma Rosa the heart, his expression beeming with pride. Sam, pleased at Rosa's appearance comments, "Rosa, I'm glad to see you're dressed."

She sets the heart on the table and folds her hands taking a moment to summon the courage to tell her husband that she has asked their close family friend and village priest, Father Lelonis Kendall, to take custody of Ira. Father Lelo, as he is called, is also a Colonel in the U.S Marine Corps.

"I have an appointment with Father Lelo." She tries to hold back tears, "He's coming by today; we're going to discuss Ira's future."

Ira looks up from his soup, "Is he coming wiff us to pway with Mommy today?"

Sam also looks up, "What are you talking about, Rosa?" His wife's manner is confusing him.

Rosa looks at him through tired and worn eyes, "Not now, Sam, not in front of the boy."

"Gramosa, me and Papa are going for a ride to pway wiff Mommy today. Want to come wiff us?"

The look on Rosa's face turns to shock. She turns to her grandson, then back to her husband. "What have you told him, Sam?"

"Nothing. He had a dream about Raina last night, so we're going to take a ride in the desert today. I promised him we would, that's all."

"No, Papa not a dream, she was here wiff her bat, 'member? She is waiting for us in the desert."

Rosa stares at the boy and for a long moment there is silence.

Sam chokes up and tears fill his eyes, "Son, why don't you go and change your clothes. Put your play clothes on and find your mitt, okay?"

"Okay, Papa."

Ira runs out of the kitchen and Rosa turns to her husband. "I've been having visions for weeks, Sam. I can't shake them." She pauses, tears spill from her eyes, "They're bad, they drain me. I'm still trying to make sense of them. In my visions –"

Sam interrupts. "Wait, Rosa, what is this about Father Lelo? What do you mean about Ira's future? I'm his grandfather. I have a right to be included in this conversation. Besides, there's nothing to discuss, our grandson stays with us." Sam swallows hard, then continues. "If Raina is never found alive, he stays with us."

Grandma Rosa bows her head and begins to wail. Emotions slog through her like a tsunami on an ocean beach. Unstoppable, it propels the debris of overwhelming grief and she begins crying out to Sam in her native tongue and with a mournful lament. "Listen to me, listen to what I'm saying!"

Ira runs down the hall, frightened by the blood-curdling cry. He drops his ball and steps on it. He flies through the air and lands on his back, knocking the wind out of his lungs.

Sam runs to his side. "It's all right, buddy, breathe, breathe, keep trying, keep trying."

After a few moments, the boy arches his back and draws in a huge breath, then coughs as he expels it.

Rosa is still in the kitchen, vocalizing in her native tongue, words that do not make any sense to Sam and words that frighten Ira. She wails as if she is at a funeral and she rocks back and forth. Sam picks Ira up and sets him on a kitchen chair. He walks to Rosa where she is doubled over sobbing and helps her to their bedroom. He picks up the bottle of tranquilizers from the nightstand and stares at it. "She must have gotten a new bottle, he mumbles." He hands her one of the capsules. She puts it in her mouth, tempted, but doesn't swallow it. He tucks a light blanket around her and waits for her breathing to calm down.

"Rosa, I'm going to take Ira for a ride like I promised him and when I come back we'll have a talk about your vision. Just rest here now. If Father Lelo gets here before I do, tell him I'll be back soon." Rosa looks at him with such grief stricken eyes, that Sam wonders if the visions she is having are going to kill her; he prays they don't, "Close your eyes and rest now, Rosa, I'll be back in an hour or so."

Sam leaves the room and Rosa turns on her side, taking the capsule from her mouth, she reaches for the bottle on the nightstand and puts it back in. She curls her knees to her chest. Her body is shaking and she prays hard, asking the Great Spirit to make these visions nothing but bad dreams. But she continues to see the future in her heart and she trembles in mourning.

Sam walks back into the kitchen.

"Papa, is Gramosa okay?"

"Grandma Rosa is okay, she just needs some rest. How 'bout you? You okay? Any bumps on your head?" Sam checks the back of Ira's head, "Nope, I don't feel anything. That's good."

"I'm just like Gramosa, right, Papa? I'm okay."

Grandpa Sam looks into his grandson's eyes. "Yes, son, I believe that you are just like your Grandma Rosa." Then to himself. "Much more than I ever realized, until now."

"What, Papa?"

"Nothin, partner. Let's go."

They climb into Grandpa's white pickup truck. Ira notices the ATV in the truck bed and pulls on Grandpa Sam's arm, "Can I sit on your lap and steer, Papa?"

"Later, when we get out into the desert. For now, put your seatbelt on."

They head out of the village and off the beaten path. Sam doesn't have a clue where they're going, but if it makes the boy feel better he will take him for a ride to the end of the earth and back again. It feels good to be out of the house and who knows, maybe his grandson did have a vision and maybe Raina was trying to get home through the desert. At least that thought gives him something to hold onto, something that makes him feel as though he's doing what he can to find Raina.

After driving for fifteen minutes, Sam spots a linear path of huge looping tracks that trails alongside the road then turns toward the desert. At first he drives past, but something stirs in him and he hits the brakes hard. He throws the truck in reverse and backs up to have a closer look. He puts the truck in park.

Ira, looks up at his Grandpa. "My turn to steer? I get on your lap now, Papa?"

"No, not yet. Grandpa wants to look at something."

"Can I see, too?"

Sam started to say no, but then he looks down at his grandson, his expression so innocent and hopeful. He is the reason we're here after all, he thinks.

"Okay, come on."

Sam puts the truck in park and opens his door, he pulls the boy out and sets him on the ground. They stand in silence as they study a huge path of sunken ground made with swirling hoops, which leads into the desert.

"What is it, Papa?"

"The tracks of a dust devil. I've never seen one so wide. If I weren't standing here looking at it I'd say it was impossible."

"No, Papa, you're not cwazy. I see it, too."

Sam casts a double take at his grandson, he smiles, "I didn't say I was crazy son, I said it seems impossible."

"Oh, yeah, sawry, Papa." Ira looks down at his feet, then pops back up, changing the subject, "Can we go, Papa? Maybe Mommy fawode it and she is stuck."

Grandpa Sam stares out into the distance, then murmurs, "We'll have to take the ATV." He turns and looks down at Ira, "We'll follow it for a ways, but it's going to get awful dusty, dry and dirty."

"I know, Papa. It's okay."

"Okay, you get our gear out of the cab and I'll start unloading the ATV."

Ira runs to the door and climbs up into the extended cab. He grabs the helmets one at a time, hiking them into the front seat. Then he digs in grandpa's duffle bag, looking for their gloves and face masks. By the time Ira gathers the gear, his grandfather has already opened the tailgate, propped up the ramps, fastened the ramps on the tailgate and has mounted the ATV.

"Stay back," he yells, as he fires the ATV up.

Ira stops in his tracks and nods. He watches his grandpa back it down the ramps. Once down safely, Sam motions to Ira to bring the gear. The young boy toddles to his grandfather, carrying both the helmets stuffed with gloves and masks just like grandpa had taught him.

"I 'membered to save myself a trip," he said with a cheeky smile.

Grandpa throws his head back and laughs, "You're a smart boy. How about the water? Did you bring the water?"

"Oops, I go back and git it."

His grandfather smiles, "No, buddy, Papa will get it. I have to get the keys and lock up anyway." Sam walks back to the cab, grabs what he needs, pushes the lock and slams the door shut. As he walks back to the ATV, Ira climbs up on the seat and scoots to the back. Sam unbuckles his belt and pulls it off. As usual when he takes his grandson for a ride, he makes a makeshift seatbelt and attaches Ira and himself to it. They leave the road they were on and head out into the desert, riding alongside the huge, looping tracks.

Sam drives slowly, while both he and Ira observe the desert winter scenery. The backdrop of the snowcapped mountains is breathtaking and Sam is savoring the reprieve; the temporary escape from his emotions. It's a much needed distraction from the stress and worry he has endured for months. The boy seems to be doing okay, but Sam still worries about the emotional toll Raina's disappearance is having on him. Sam, a spiritual man, a man of remarkable calm is, himself, feeling the strain. Of late, he suffers from heartburn and has dizzy spells. He thinks its anxiety, stress and improper nutrition that's taking its toll. He keeps promising himself that he'll start eating better for his grandson's sake, but he's having trouble keeping the promise since he just doesn't have an appetite.

Ira has become so relaxed that his cheek is resting against his grandpa's back and he's fallen asleep. Sam, slows down and checks the homemade seat belt to make sure it's secure. His grandson's state of repose has begun to seep into him and he can feel some of the pressure easing. Why didn't he think of this sooner? The desert is exhilarating, containing a healing power of its own.

They cruise through the sand encased in their protective bubble, appreciating the scenery as they pass. The cactus flowers, soft and beautiful, protected by their harsh thorns. The tumbleweeds dried and scorched, loping along the rippled sand. They pass by the rare and scattered red wisps of the desert palms, and see prairie dogs peeking out of their earthy homes. To Sam the desert is full of an implicit spirit of peace, and he is connected. Soon a peaceful feeling overtakes him and he takes a deep breath, relishing the moment, knowing it will be over all too soon.

Sam's peaceful state is interrupted sooner than he thought. Ahead he sees a glimmering sheet of metal, foreign to the desert, on top of a pile of sand. As he edges closer, Ira stirs and Sam is stricken by a seemingly mystical presence. He stops the ATV and shuts it down. The tracks of the dust devil stop just ahead at a sand dune and the rays of the sun illuminate the top of the dune like a shrine.

Ira's eyes grow wide, "Papa, what's that?"

"Stay here, son, Grandpa is going to find out." Sam unfastens his homemade seatbelt, throws his leg over the ATV and gets off. He approaches the sand dune with caution, but when he's within ten yards a commanding wind roils up around his feet, knocks him to his knees and in a matter of seconds a pile of sand buries him almost to his waist. Frightened, he turns toward his grandson, but it appears the boy is oblivious to what has happened and Sam feels as if a spirit has entered his body, a dominant influence fills his mind.

*"Go back. Take the boy home. You have found her."*

Sam stares in disbelief. He cannot move a muscle. Again his own thoughts are overcome by what seems to be a spiritual entity.

*"Protect the child's eyes lest he be blinded to the goodness in his soul. Protect the child's eyes. Do not proceed. Take him home."*

Sam tries to move, but he can't. Then he hears Ira calling to him.

"Papa, Papa! I scared! Papa!"

Sam's mind is released, while at the same time another tempest of wind swirls away the sand. He is freed and he jumps to his feet, making a mad dash to Ira. He knows the presence in the desert is a spirit and he does not want to take Ira anywhere near the mysterious dune of sand. He doesn't know exactly what is happening, but he knows it has something to do with Raina. He hustles to buckle Ira to himself and the ATV, then zooms back toward his pickup. As he drives his heart is pounding so hard it sends tiny waves of darkness through his brain and he feels as though he may pass out before he can get back to the truck. *He has to hold on, stay calm, get Ira back home. He must tell Rosa what happened.*

After they arrive home, Sam plucks Ira from the truck and dashes to the back porch. A gust of wind blows a piece of paper across the steps and Sam flinches when the swirling squall sends it airborne, rustling the paper past his face and whirling it through the yard.

He holds the boy tight and notices that Ira is very quiet. Sam knows the boy must have questions, Sam is just afraid he won't have the answers. He takes the steps of the porch two at a time, calling for Rosa when he reaches the door. He sets the boy down and grabs the phone to dial the tribal police. He calls for Rosa again, but she doesn't answer. The phone rings at the station and the sheriff picks up.

"Chief Dewey speaking."

"Dewey it's me, Sam."

"Sam? What's up, you sound winded."

"I took a ride in the desert today with my grandson and I came across something that I think you should check out."

"What's going on?"

"I think it might have something to do with –" Sam hesitates, looks down at his grandson, then turns his head and lowers his voice, "Raina, my daughter."

"Tell me what's going on. Why do you think it has to do with Raina?"

Sam turns his back to the boy and whispers, "Dewey, the boy is right here, I don't want to talk in front of him. I think something bad has happened. Can you come pick me up so I can take you out there? You'll need your four by four, or a dune buggy. It's in the middle of nowhere."

"Aw, yeah, sure, Sam, Ben and I'll be right there."

Sam hangs up the phone and hurries to his bedroom where he had left Rosa napping. "Rosa, I think we may have found something. Rosa? Are you here, Rosa? Rosa, where are you?" Sam checks the house; there's no sign of his wife anywhere.

Ira comes into the room.

"Papa, what this say?"

Sam takes a note from the boy's hand.

"Where did you find this?"

"On the fwoor by the door, papa."

Sam reads the note.

*I'm sorry I missed you,*

*I must exile myself by taking part in a cleansing ritual. It is with regret that I will not be of any help to my grandson in this crisis at such a young age. Still, it is best I leave. For today I have witnessed visions so horrifying it has left me hollow, and in anguish. I no longer trust myself to raise a child alone, or even live among people. Please watch over my grandson, I trust you without fail.*

*Sincerely,*
*Rosa*

"Damned medication."

Ira looks up at his grandpa, "What, Papa? Bad medcin?"

Sam picks the boy up and holds him in his arms. "Yes, son, bad medicine. You'll have to come with us back into the desert. Do you wanna go for another ride? This time we'll go with Chief Dewey and Deputy Ben."

"Okay, Papa, but what 'bout Gramosa?"

"We'll look for her when we get back; I think she went to visit great grandma."

"Okay, Papa."

They step out onto the porch just as the two officers are pulling up in their dune buggy. Once again Sam and his grandson set out, this time with the sheriff and his deputy, driving slowly down the old, tribal road that's not much more than a footpath. The locals call it Sacred

Ridge Road, named for a mass Indian Burial Ground that lies somewhere along it. Only the local tribal members know exactly where it is. The location of the mass burial site is kept secret to protect it from souvenir seekers.

At last the dune buggy and ATV arrive at the pile of sand. The steel roof still shimmers in the light and Dewey asks Sam to stay with the boy so he and Ben can get a closer look. As they approach, the men are astonished at what they see; a car buried to its windows on the outside and almost filled to the top with sand on the inside.

Sheriff Dewey takes off his hat and wipes his brow, "Well I'll be a son of –" he pauses, amazed at the sight.

His deputy peers into the window and his jaw drops in disbelief. "There's people in there! How the hell did that happen? I'm gonna go around and have a look at the other side." Ben walks around to the front of the car, noting damage to the hood. He stops dead in his tracks when he gets to the other side. Less than two feet from the driver's door a woman's body is face down in the sand, a tree branch gripped tightly in her fingers.

"Chief, com'ere quick!"

"Why?" Chief Dewey bustles around the vehicle, he stops dead, a horrified expression grips his face.

Before they can stop him, Sam, carrying Ira in his arms, also runs around to the other side of the vehicle. Chief Dewey puts his hand out. "No, Sam! Stop! Wait!"

But it's too late. Sam falls to his knees, clutching Ira close. He begins to sob. The little boy stares at his mother's ravished body, her flesh torn, metallic green blowflies infesting the wounds. There were obvious signs that predators have added to the carnage, eating the flesh and dragging bone fragments off in the desert. Sam passes out and topples onto the boy.

While trapped beneath his grandfather's body, Ira begins to see everything moving in slow motion. He feels no pain as the two officers pull him out from beneath his grandfather. The sheriff reaches to his side to unsnap the strap of his two-way radio. He lifts it to his mouth and begins speaking in a tense voice, while looking around, trying to explain their whereabouts.

Ben rips Sam's shirt open and starts pumping on his chest. He puts his ear to Sam's mouth, then nose. He begins to pump harder.

The squad car's bubbles flash red, late into the evening hours as the police and detectives investigate the scene. Sam is taken away and Ira is taken to the squad car where he seems to be swallowed up in the vastness of the back seat. A forlorn figure, he sits petrified, his hands folded in his lap, while visions he does not understand overcome him. He is trembling, worrying about his grandfather and he's never felt so lonely in his life. He sits helpless, cold, sniffling, waiting for someone to take him home to Gramosa. Then out of nowhere, he senses rather than sees, a soft mist looming above his head and he feels a gentle breeze drifting through the vehicle. The mist surrounds him like a warm blanket and he feels gentle hands caressing his cheeks. His chin settles to his chest and he falls asleep.

# CHAPTER THREE

## The Prodigy Refugee

"How did this happen, Cheryl?" Chief Dewey holds the receiver in one hand, while scratching his head with the other. "How does a scholarship daughter disappear and then show up a murdered prostitute, leaving in her wake a father who's dead from a heart attack, a mother who's vanished into thin air and a four-year-old son who's now an orphan. How does something like this happen? We're gonna have to comply, that's all there is to it. We're gonna have to send the boy down there. It's against my better judgment but there's nothing else we can do. It's final." He hangs up the phone and looks up from his desk.

The deputy, Ben, is leaning in the doorway with his arms crossed. He steps into Dewey's office.

"What did Cheryl say? Is there any paperwork filed anywhere?"

"Nope, nothing. She can't find anything and it stands to reason. It all happened so fast with Raina. Before we found her body, her parents were certain she was coming home; they hadn't given up hope. Everyone assumed that if she didn't come back the boy would live with the grandparents." Chief Dewey picks up the phone to call Social Services.

"I hate to do this but I'm gonna have to let them release him to the family members across the border, distant as they are, they are the closest living relatives."

Ben runs his hands through his hair, "But he don't even know 'em. Why can't he just stay with the Cocopahs? He's been with them for two weeks now and he seems to be adjusting pretty well. Isn't there anything we can do?"

Chief Dewey opens a file folder on his desk.

"Nope. Zip. The relatives down yonder were notified about the situation and have agreed to take the boy." He shuts the folder. "They can't afford to feed the kids they got, but my hands are tied. I've petitioned family court to keep him in this country, but the hearing is set for two months out. Best I can do is go down there on occasion to check on him 'til his hearing comes up."

Ben plops down in a chair and sighs, "That's a long time for a young child. He's going to be scared outa his wits. This whole thing is awful."

Frustrated, Dewey picks up the folder from his desk and crosses the room to his filing cabinet. He draws in a huge breath and opens the drawer.

"What kind of a mother becomes a prostitute and puts herself in a position to get herself killed? It's the shame of the matter that killed her pa and drove her ma away, not to mention what she has done to her son." He stuffs the file in, "There aren't any words to describe a woman like that. It's downright despicable, that's what it is." He slams the metal drawer shut.

Ben shifts in his chair. "It just don't seem like her to do something like that, you know?"

"What do you mean not like her? She's been a black sheep since she was fourteen when she hooked herself up with that Salazara kid, got herself pregnant and cried rape. Haven't seen hide nor hair of that poor kid since. What was his name again? Domingo? Yeah, Domingo Salazara, that's it. She disgraced her parents and the whole village for that matter. Some scholarship student."

Ben shrugs his shoulders.

The phone rings and Chief Dewey answers it in a rigid tone. "Chief of Police Dewey. "Ah ha, okay, meet me by the door with him. Oh and bring the Polaroid, would ya?" He hangs up and grabs his hat off the rack. "Well, here I go, cleaning up the mess left to me by a two-bit prostitute. I'm stuck with the fun job of picking up a four-year-old boy and delivering him to strange relatives in a foreign country. That's just what I wanted to do today, head across the border, risking my neck and the boy's neck in Mexico." Then he mumbles under his breath as he puts on his hat. "Most likely end up gettin' home late and missin' supper, too. Oh, well, I'll do what I gotta do. Gotta have that paycheck. Hold the fort down 'til I get back, will ya, Ben?"

Ben nods and puts his face in his hands. He feels terrible for Ira. The kid's been through so much at such a young age. He went from a secure home with his grandparents to nothing in zero flat. What a mess this is. He prays the relatives are decent and that they keep the boy safe until the Chief can bring him back for the court hearing.

Dewey drives down a prickly desert road for what seems like an eternity. The vastness of sand and rock is endless and the single topographical change is the difference in the height of the canyons. After a long ride in silence he and Ira come upon a narrow trail. He looks down at the directions Cheryl wrote on a slip of paper for him. The ink is smudged from the coffee he spilled on it, but he guesses this must be the place because there's the sign, a dingy white T-shirt hanging on a fence post next to a one-armed saguaro cactus.

He turns the wheel and steers down the narrow bumpy path that leads to a meager rancheria. The boy has not spoken a word the entire trip and Chief Dewey pities him. He stops the Jeep and puts it in park. He leans forward with his arms on top of the steering wheel, peering out above the dash. Perturbed, he examines the surroundings. There's nothing here but a rundown shack with a rusty horseshoe above the door and some old, makeshift sheds. It looks desolate, he thinks, but he tries to sound upbeat to the boy.

"Well, son, this is it. This is where you'll be staying for a couple months. Get your bag out of the back and I'll take you to meet your cousins." He shuts the Jeep off and gets out. Ira doesn't move.

"Son, this is where you're gonna stay for a while. Now come on out and get your bag from the back seat." Ira stares straight ahead as if he's deaf. Dewey walks around to the passenger side of the Jeep and opens the door. He looks down at Ira and coaxes him out. Ira's eyes are red and puffy and he stares up at Chief Dewey, but he doesn't say a word. Dewey reaches into the back and takes out the Padres duffle bag that the boy's mother bought him last Christmas and hands it to him. Ira doesn't take it.

"Now, son, don't misbehave, you're disrespecting the people that are offering to feed ya. I'm sure you're gonna be treated just fine here. Besides, it's just for a few weeks until I can get you into court and back to the U.S."

A young man and an old woman with a cane emerge from the door of the lopsided shack. They stand staring for a moment. A gust of wind kicks up, twirling some dust through the yard, scattering a flock of chickens. The pair approach the Jeep.

Dewey steps forward and extends his hand out as they approach, but neither one takes it.

*"Hablo un poco español pero mejor es mi Ingles o Kumeyaay. Usted habla Ingles, o Kumeyaay?"*

The two eye him for a long moment and at last the man answers.

"All three. I'm Anthony Cureo. This is Hallia Salazara, my mother-in-law. She speaks English, too and she owns the place. Her grandmother's tribe was from the Jamal Reservation in California, but her birth was never recorded and since the divide, our side of the family has been denied legal immigration. Is this the boy?"

Dewey takes his hat off. "I'm Chief of Police, Dewey Brown. Yep, this is him. His name is Ira. Say hello to the people, Ira."

Ira hangs his shoulders so low he looks like he's nearly bent in half. He has no desire to speak.

Anthony steps forward, eyeing Ira up and down. "He's tiny."

Dewey smiles. "Well, of course he is, he's four. What'd' ju expect, a linebacker? I sent word he's smart, not big."

The old woman bends down and takes Ira's chin in her hand, lifting it up. Ira pulls away and the woman remains bent over, staring at him. "He's got bad manners." She straightens and looks at Dewey, whispering. "Some tell he was raised by a whore."

The Chief pats Ira on his head. "He won't be any trouble. Wasn't his fault what his mother turned out to be, he's a good boy."

Bending down again, the old woman grabs Ira's Padres bag and starts digging in it. She shuffles through a few clothes, a Padres thermos and a Padres rain poncho. "These his things? He ain't got much, does he?"

Dewey steps closer and examines the contents himself. "Most everything was burned in a funeral pyre according to the old Kumeyaay custom, except for a few odds and ends and some papers laying around, this is it. We have them stored with the mother's evidence box down at the station, nothing of any value."

The woman nods and takes Ira's hand to lead him to the house. Ira turns and looks at Chief Dewey with tears streaming down his cheek.

Chief Dewey's shoulders slump and his heart aches. "I'll be back to visit, son." He looks at Hallia, then back at Ira. "I'll be back every week."

Ira yanks his hand away from the old woman and turns around. "I come wiff you now?"

"No, son, you'll stay here for a while."

Ira shakes his head and shouts. "I come wiff you now!" The expression in his eyes pierce the sheriff's heart as Anthony grabs the child and picks him up, carrying him across the yard to the hovel which is his new home.

The old woman waves her cane at Dewey. "He okay." Then she follows Anthony into the shack.

Chief Dewey walks to the back of his Jeep, a lump in his throat. He takes one of the spare gas cans and a funnel out and fills his tank. When he's done, he uses his handkerchief to wipe his brow and then looking at the shack one last time, downcast, he gets in his Jeep and drives toward the border. Tears well up in his eyes frequently on the way home and he can't shake the heaviness in his chest. He feels sorrow for the boy who has just been abandoned once again and wishes Ira was still sitting beside him.

Anthony sets Ira down on the dirt floor in the middle of the four-room shack. Hallia tosses his bag on an old armchair in the corner of the room with its stuffing busting through a tear in the cushion. She points at the chair. "That's where you'll sleep. We eat a breakfast, lunch and supper, no snacks. Everyone earns their food around here. You'll carry wood to earn yours tonight."

Five other children ranging in ages from two to twelve stand in front of the shack. They, and a pregnant woman begin to file into the shack, along with a rail-thin dog wagging his tail. They all stare at Ira.

The five-year-old takes a step closer to him. "Me, Tanny, dis is Rocko." She points to the dog. "How long you be here?"

The old woman pulls Tanny back and motions for the children to leave.

"You young'uns git back to your chores now. You all gonna meet him at supper." The old woman shoos the kids out the door, then she turns to Ira and points to Anthony, "Anthony is your uncle. He's gonna show you where the outhouse and woodshed is."

Ira and Anthony walk in silence to the makeshift lean-to where wood is stored and Anthony points out the outhouse that's twenty feet away. Halfway between, stands a rusty old pickup topper surrounded by mesh wire that serves as a chicken coop. Alongside the coop is a storage shack that's made of corrugated scrap metal and is slanted to one side. Next to the storage shack is a washhouse made of dry-rotted wood planks nailed up with tar paper, where each person washes his or her own clothes in a metal tub, then hangs them out to dry on a row of old bald tires leaning against the outside wall.

The homestead is without electricity and all the water is carried from a well. This Indian rancheria in rural Mexico somewhat mimics the lifestyle of the United States' Southwest Indian tribes, except in Mexico, the Kumeyaay tribe's poverty level is much worse.

Ira was accustomed to at least having a bathroom with running water and electricity. His Grandpa Sam and others from the reservation worked as firemen during the wildfire season and because they had long helped the State of California with fire control, the state brought electricity to their reservation. From now on Ira's life will be a life of hardship and rationing, at least until Chief Dewey comes to take him home.

The rationing starts right away as Anthony steps into the wood shed and begins to toss the next day's ration of wood out onto the ground. He tells Ira that because he will be sleeping in the chair in the kitchen where the woodstove is, he will be in charge of keeping the fire going. This is shocking to Ira, neither his Gramosa or his Papa would ever let him go anywhere near a woodstove and now at four years old he is going to be in charge of one.

Ira lifts his arms out to his sides and shrugs. "I dunno how."

Anthony looks at the child, and feels a twinge of empathy. "I'm gonna teach ya. I'll teach ya everything there is to know about surviving out here."

Anthony then takes three pieces of wood and stacks them in Ira's inadequate arms. He points to the shack of a house and sends him back with the wood. Ira can see over the top of the pile by a hair. His chin is tilted up and resting on the top piece of wood. His body arches backward under the weight of the heavy load. He drops the wood outside the door and returns to Anthony to make nine more trips. When he's done his legs and arms are so weak they're shaking; he sits down on the ground, exhausted. He rests there until his heart stops racing, then, left alone by Anthony, he spends the rest of the afternoon exploring his new surroundings.

He notices that the women sit outside the shack weaving baskets and the men go out mending and maintaining the miles of dirt roads that lead to other homesteads and rancherias. Ira is so lonesome for his family that throughout the day tears well up in his eyes. Rocko the dog begins to follow him everywhere, wagging his tail. Ira has never had a dog so he doesn't quite know what to make of it and at first he is leery, even shooing the dog away at times.

One afternoon as Ira is resting from hauling wood, he is again overcome by sorrow. He misses his grandparents terribly and he wipes his nose with his sleeve as sobs pour out of him. His loneliness is unbearable and nobody at the rancheria seems to care. None of them say much to him except Grandma Hallia on occasion and sometimes

Anthony when he comes home from working on roads. His sobbing doesn't go unheard today, though.

While his head is bowed, resting on his knees, warmth brushes up against his back. He looks up to see Rocko sitting next to him. He presses his nose into Ira's neck, then licks his face and nuzzles his shoulder. Ira is so taken in by the dog's perception of his pain and need of affection that he grabs Rocko and hugs him tight and from that day on they are inseparable.

At night while Ira is curled up in his armchair by the woodstove, Rocko sleeps right below him and sometimes when Ira wakes up in the middle of night crying, Rocko will stand in front of him with his chin on his lap. Ira has become so attached to Rocko that he has started feeding Rocko a portion of his own food at every meal. Although it seems as if Rocko is beginning to gain some weight, no one disapproves, instead they tell him it is his food, he can do what he wants with it, although they can't offer him a larger ration.

Time passes and Ira adapts to his chores and his position in the family. Chief Dewey has come to visit a couple of times, but tells Ira that Immigration is holding up the paperwork process. Ira is too young to understand what "Immigration" is and he has begun to settle into his new home. Rocko has made things easier, so it doesn't matter to him whether Chief Dewey shows up any more or not.

After a few months, his loneliness starts to lessen and there are longer times between Chief Dewey's visits. Ira turns five and doesn't even realize it. Nobody at the rancheria knows when his birthday is and neither does Ira, but he is growing and getting taller and he wonders why he doesn't have to go to school. He remembers Gramosa saying that he would have to go to school every day once he got bigger. Ira guesses that since school made his mother turn bad and Papa and Gramosa disappear, he won't go to school anymore. He guesses he gets to have Rocko, instead.

Ira and Rocko are as one; the dog does not ever leave his side. One night while Ira is dreaming, Rocko shows up in the dream carrying a stick in his mouth and he hears a soft voice reciting the English alphabet. Ira starts to repeat it in his sleep. From then on Rocko shows up almost every night in Ira's dreams with the same stick. He sits down with it in his mouth and a voice seems to start to teach Ira something new. Sometimes he dreams about adding numbers or spelling words, but his favorite dream is a dream about desert plants. He learns at night in his dreams and it's almost as if he were going to school. Hallia, Anthony and the rest of the clan are amazed at how smart the boy is becoming.

The weeks turn into months and then years. Chief Dewey no longer comes to visit and Ira has resigned himself to life in the rural foothills in Mexico. He no longer even thinks about leaving the rancheria to go to school, but continues to grow more knowledgeable every day.

One night, Raina comes to Ira in his dreams, this time she is not disguised as Rocko with a stick in his mouth, but she is holding the stick in her hand. It looks like the stick has been painted red, just like the night in his bedroom at Grandpa Sam's house. She begins talking to him, telling him that soon Rocko will go away. Ira wakes up in an anger induced sweat. He yells at her to go away, his arms flailing and swinging out at nothing as he clamors for her to leave him alone!

Hallia hobbles across the room with an oil lamp in one hand and her cane in the other. She sets the lamp and cane on the table, grabs Ira's hands and looks at his palms then turns them, checking the tops. "What's wrong, did you burn yourself boy?"

Ira shakes his head no, then he describes his dream and tells her what his mother said.

Hallia lets go of Ira's hands. "Ya just had a bad dream is all. We'll not let that bad woman take the dog away from you." Then she looks him up and down. "Yer gettin too growed up fer that chair. That's why yer having bad dreams." Her eyes turn a bit softer. "I think that sheriff's done given up on you a long time ago, so I think it's about time for you to have your own bed. I'm gonna send Anthony to find a bed for you tomorrow. Now git back to sleep, we'll see 'bout it when it's mornin'." She pulls his blanket up to cover him, takes her cane and the lamp and hobbles back to her bed. As Ira curls himself up into the chair he thinks about how he didn't even notice that he doesn't fit the chair anymore and he thinks about Hallia and what she just said. She said out loud what everyone has been thinking: The Sheriff has forgotten about him.

After eating breakfast, Anthony and his oldest son head out on horseback to Tecate, the nearest border village to try to barter for a used mattress. Ira does his part by taking on his cousin's chores for the day. As he makes his rounds, he notices that Rocko is not following him. Whistling, he calls for Rocko, but Rocko doesn't come. Ira claps his hands together. "Here, Rocko, here, boy! Come on, Rocko." Ira sees the dog across the yard and continues to call for him. Rocko sits and stays still, so Ira walks to him. As he gets closer he sees that Rocko has a stick in his mouth and it's red, like the one in the dream about his mother. Ira starts to run to Rocko thinking that he might be hurt, but stops frozen in his tracks, standing in deafening silence, unable to believe his eyes.

*A diaphanous white gown ripples in a soft breeze and standing in place of the dog is his mother. Her long dark hair floats on air, her facial expression grim, but tender. As she opens her mouth to speak, a lambent swirl of silver mist outlines her form and tiny flecks of gold appear to atomize through her, then colorful streams of light arch from her lips and the sounds from her mouth are indescribably beautiful.*

*Ira, my son. I am here, I've always been here. Rocko is going away.*

Ira covers his ears and yells. "No! No! *You* go away, I want you to go away, not him. Leave him alone, he's mine, I don't want you, I want him, leave him alone!"

*Ira, you must trust me now.*

From across the yard Hallia's basket topples to the ground when she stands up from her chair. She watches as Ira stands in the middle of the yard, waving his arms and shouting. She sees nothing around him, but he's yelling and swinging at the air in front of him. Hallia grabs her cane and hobbles as fast as she can across the yard to him. She reaches his side and takes hold of one of his arms.

"It's all right, boy, it's okay."

Ira swings at Hallia, hitting her again and again, then he gives her a shove. She stumbles backward. Ira yells at her. "You're a bad woman. Go away and stay away from Rocko." He keeps slapping her as she tries to protect herself with her cane, then he grabs the cane and twists it, thrusting her to the ground.

The others stand watching, flabbergasted and petrified. They can't believe their eyes. The boy must have lost his mind, it appears that he's going to kill Grandma Hallia.

After a few seconds, adrenaline spurns them into gear and they run across the yard, shouting at Ira. When they reach him they team up, capturing his arms and tackling him to the ground. It takes Anthony's wife and their four children to pull him off the elderly crippled woman. All of them stand silent, huffing and puffing in disbelief. Hallia lays on the ground with her arms covering her head. Ira stands rooted with a blank stare, his only movement the thumping in his chest. The group watches him circumspect as they help Hallia to her feet.

Rocko comes out from the house running straight for Ira, Ira has a look of confusion on his face as the dog nuzzles his nose into Ira's hand, then Ira's legs buckle and he collapses to the ground. Anthony's wife and the other children hold Hallia steady as they dust her off and help her walk to the house, leaving Ira sitting in the middle of the yard alone.

Ira is dumbfounded, he doesn't understand what has happened, he is troubled by the illusion and he cannot begin to explain it to anyone else.

Ira has been sitting for almost three hours since the incident. No one has emerged from the house. The sun has sunk to the horizon and Ira still remains in the same place with Rocko at his side. Anthony and his son ride up together on the back of one horse with an old twin mattress strapped to the back of the other horse. They stop to ask Ira why he is sitting in the yard by himself. Still numb, Ira points to the house and the two look at the capsized chairs and toppled baskets lying on the ground in front and they know something is wrong.

Jumping down off the horse, they dash across the yard to the shack.

Ira can hear the clamor inside, from outside across the yard, as Hallia and the others describe what happened. When Anthony emerges from the shack he has Ira's rabbit fur blanket and a rope in his arms. He storms to the horse, unties the mattress and drags it inside the woodshed. He comes back out and crosses the yard to Ira. "They say you lost your mind, boy, that you're possessed. They don't trust you in the house anymore. You'll sleep in the shed from now on until we figure out what to do. You must be close to ten years old now, boy, not four. You left bruises on an old woman. What's wrong with you?"

Ira says nothing. Instead, he stands up and mopes his way to the shed. He looks back to see if Rocko is following him but Anthony has put the rope around Rocko's neck and is leading him to the house.

"The dog stays with us in the house," Anthony yells back at Ira. Then he takes Rocko inside and closes the door.

Ira collapses on the mattress. It's dark and stuffy in the shed. He's lonely. He has been lonely since he arrived at the rancheria, but without Rocko it's much worse. He doesn't miss any of them, he's never felt like he belonged anyway. Rocko is the sole being on earth that makes him feel good.

It's a full moon and he stares up at the pinholes of light shining through the tin roof. He's wide awake late into the night thinking about his mother and wondering why she wants to hurt him. He waits for Rocko to come to him in his dreams, needing the comfort of his friend, but Rocko doesn't come and Ira doesn't sleep.

As the sun rises, faint light creeps through the cracks of the makeshift shed. Ira hears footsteps approaching and soon Anthony's wary face peeks through the door. He sets a plate holding three tortillas down on the ground. "You awake?"

Ira rolls onto his side, turning his back on Anthony.

"You can ignore me if ya want, but I'm the one friend you got here. Everyone else is as superstitious as a gypsy and they all believe you've been struck by *mal de ojo*. I stood up for ya and told 'em that given you're just nine and what you've been through, you should have another chance. You can stay for now, but another tantrum like yesterday and you're gonna have to go." Anthony starts to leave, but then turns around. "We gave a mess of eggs for that mattress you're on, so you'll go without your morning egg until you've paid it back. You got work to do, boy, so get up like everyone else and git to it."

After Anthony leaves, Ira sits up, wolfs down two of the tortillas and stuffs one in his pocket for Rocko.

He stands up and stretches his arms to the roof while yawning, then looks down at the mattress. He can't remember ever sleeping on a mattress before this. He's hoping that tonight he'll be able to fall asleep. He doesn't care if he has to stay in the shed, but he wishes Rocko could be with him.

Again he thinks about his dreams of Rocko and his mother. He wonders if Hallia is right and the dreams will stop now that he has a mattress. He likes it when Rocko is in his dreams, but he doesn't like it when his mother is.

She is bad. She left him and took everyone with her just so he would be all alone and sad. Everyone says she is a bad woman and this is all because of her.

Ira leaves the shed for the outhouse, then gets busy with his chores. He starts hauling wood, then totes the water for the wash. After he's done hauling, he chops and stacks wood while the other children gather acorns. Acorns are the main food source for winter, but this is a bad year and they're scarce. The children work harder and harder at finding them, but are finding fewer and fewer. This worries everyone because it's getting close to the end of the season.

When noon hits and Ira sits down to rest a minute he realizes that he still has Rocko's tortilla in his pocket. He hasn't seen the dog all morning. Ira turns to where the women are sitting in a circle weaving their baskets and decides to approach Hallia. They all stop and look up at him with suspicion, all except Hallia who refuses to even look at him. "I'm sorry about my dream and about hitting you. I thought my mother was there and I wanted her to go away."

Hallia was avoiding his eyes at first, but after a moment she looks up at him. She has a swollen cut above one eye and a bruise on her cheek. She stares at him for a long time. It makes everyone uncomfortable and they wait for her answer. Hallia knows that he has been plagued by bad dreams since he arrived. She believes it's not his fault and after a few minutes she nods acceptance of his apology. He smiles, thanks her, then asks her if she has seen Rocko. Hallia nods toward the door. "The dog is getting old, he sleeps in the house." Ira starts for the house, but Hallia calls out after him. "Have you finished your chores?"

"Yeah."

"If you promise not to think about your mother anymore, you can carry your mattress into the house."

"Thank you, Gramma Hallia. Can I go see Rocko now?"

Hallia waves a finger at him. "For a bit. The men are down the road mending a fence that needs fixin' and you can help."

Ira nods. "Okay." He turns and runs as fast as he can to the house. He barrels through the door and Rocko lifts his nose. Ira grabs him around the neck and hugs him tight. "What's wrong, Rocko *paco*? What's wrong with you? Are you tired?" He lifts the dog's snout and puts his forehead against Rocko's. "Ha, Rocko, what's wrong with my Rocko *paco*?"

Rocko wags his tail and licks Ira's chin.

After Ira pets Rocko for a while he stands up and digs in his pocket. "Rocko, you're just tired, so you rest now. I'll come back later. Here's your tortilla."

Ira pats Rocko on the head then leaves the house to retrieve the mattress from the shed. Once he has it in the house he lays it on the floor close to the stove and lifts the thin dog up on it. "I'll share with you, Rocko *paco*. I share everything with you." He hugs the dog one last time and leaves to help the others with the fence.

At sunset the women are cooking supper, they've made Sha-wii from acorns and cooked some rabbit meat. They're finishing up frying the last of the handmade tortillas and they've called the others in to have their evening meal. As they enter, they see a stack of tortillas rolled with grilled rabbit piled high on a platter. There's also a bowl of beans, some agave, wild plums, desert apricots and of course acorn pudding. Ira's hungry and eats his portion as fast as a lizard eats a locust. He's glad that no one brings up the incident about him and Hallia yesterday and he is thankful for the food.

There is a lot of chatter in the room at supper time as usual, but some of the conversation is not pleasant. Anthony's wife talks about the acorns being scarce and how the crops weren't very good this year, as she helps her youngest with his food.

Anthony looks at her with concern and nods. "The drought has been hard on the animals, too, the hunting will be poor. It's going to be a scarce winter for everyone."

Ira wonders if they wish he wasn't here to share their food, but nobody says anything.

The days are getting shorter and colder temperatures are creeping into the night air. Rocko seems to be slowing down from the chilly weather which worries Ira, but even though the dog is aging, he still wags his tail when he plays fetch with Ira and stays close by his side. His appetite is still pretty good and he can still smell the tortillas Ira stuffs one in his pocket for him.

Weeks go by and winter is in full force. Rations are getting meager and for the past two weeks the hunting has produced no meat. The only animals around are the coyotes yelping far off in the distance. The Salazara family is surviving on what's left of the acorns, buckwheat flowers and seeds from storage, their protein-rich mesquite beans are all gone. They need meat to supplement their diet so they butcher a chicken every other day, but that's leaving them with fewer eggs to eat at breakfast and none to take to market.

At the first light of every morning, Anthony and the boys go out to hunt on empty stomachs, vowing that they will even kill a coyote to eat if one crosses their path. Another few days go by and still no meat so they must kill another chicken. They know, however, that killing their chickens is a temporary solution. The chickens will soon be gone; they will not have enough food to sustain them, and no eggs to bring to market. Every evening they all crawl under their blankets with hollow stomachs and late into the night the sounds of children crying because of their hunger echo through the walls of the tiny rancheria.

As time passes they get more and more desperate and late one night the adults gather in one corner of the house, whispering among themselves. Ira can't hear what they're saying, but they occasionally glance his way and he guesses they must be talking about sending him away. He understands why they'd make him leave, but he doesn't want to go tonight. So he lies very still, pretending he's asleep, hoping they'll wait until morning.

When they're finished talking, Ira is relieved that they all head for their beds. He's thankful they're going to wait, because at least he can enjoy his mattress for one more night. He's way beyond hungry and tired, but soon he falls into a deep sleep.

He begins to dream about Rocko and he notices that this time in his dream Rocko doesn't have a stick. He just floats above Ira for a moment and then he's gone.

The shack is cold when the sun opens Ira's eyes. He must have fallen so deep asleep that he let the stove go out. He wobbles to his feet, opens the stove and stirs the ashes. They're still glowing so he shoves some wood in and soon the fire starts crackling. He stuffs in more wood and the stove begins to heat. He shivers while crouching back on his mattress and curls up beneath his rabbit fur blanket waiting for the rest of the clan to waken.

Anthony is the first to rise. He touches Ira's shoulder. "Get up, boy. You and I are going to fetch some yucca stalks. The women folk are out of wood for the burn pit and they need to make some pottery to sell."

Ira rubs his eyes and sits up. He looks around the room for Rocko but someone must have let him out already. Ira puts his pants on and buttons his flannel shirt. It's not yet light out and he almost has to feel his way to the outhouse. When he's finished he whistles for Rocko, but he doesn't come, so Ira calls his name. Anthony walks out of the house.

"C'mon, Ira, let's get going, never mind 'bout that dog, the sooner we get this done the sooner we can have breakfast."

They take a long walk into the desert in search of yucca stalks and as Ira's walking he's thinking about how hungry he is. He was already hungry for breakfast before he fell asleep last night, but he's downright starving this morning. He doesn't complain, though, because he knows Anthony is just as hungry. He can't wait to get back to the ranch just to have his plain tortillas.

Ira feels faint as he fills an agave net with yucca stalks. He's weak and even though it's chilly out, he wipes the sweat from his brow. He needs food and all he can think about is getting back home and eating his breakfast. He steadies himself and swallows some spit to ease the burning pain in his gut. He works hard and finishes filling the net as fast as his body will let him. When they've rounded up enough yucca, they can't help but stop and admire a huge pink sun that is now fully above the horizon. Then they drag the net of yucca stalks, stalks that seem to weigh a ton, back to the rancheria.

As they near the shack, the smell of breakfast wafts through the air. Ira inhales through his nose and his stomach starts to run a riot with hunger pains. Hallia must have butchered another chicken because he can smell meat along with an assortment of savory spices sizzling on the stove. His mouth starts to water and his brain is energized. He hasn't had meat in two weeks and he can't wait to spoon some onto his tortilla and gobble it down.

They leave their nets filled with stalks outside and enter the kitchen. The others are already lined up at the stove, holding out their plates. Hallia is spooning meat onto the tortillas and Ira is last in line. His stomach is in knots, grinding and growling. He can feel the glands beneath his ears engorge and his mouth begins to water. He can't wait until his turn; there is plenty of meat for two good-sized tortillas each. Hallia must have butchered two chickens.

After everyone else has been served Ira steps up to Hallia. She looks at Ira, her eyes tired and sad. She plops a scoop of steaming meat onto each of his tortillas, then she sets the spoon down and leaves the room.

The group is scattered about the room because the table can't accommodate them all at the same time. Ira turns and hurries to his mattress to sit down, he takes his first bite. "Mmmm." He can't chew and swallow fast enough. It's hot, delicious, heavenly; he chomps off another bite, then another. Before he knows it, he's finished with his first tortilla and starts on his second. All are enjoying their breakfast and the sound of people chewing fills the room. Ira finishes his second tortilla, saving a hefty chunk for Rocko. He gets up and walks to the door calling out for the dog as he steps outside, but Rocko doesn't come.

He claps his hands and yells again. "Rocko, *paco*, where are you?" He ventures through the yard checking behind all the sheds, but can't find the dog. He walks back to the house, deciding that Rocko must have gone hunting.

Everyone looks at him when he walks back into the house.

"Did anyone see Rocko this morning?" No one answers. He turns to Grandma Hallia. "Have you seen Rocko?"

Hallia doesn't answer, instead she looks at Anthony. "You didn't tell him while you were gittin wood?"

Ira looks at Anthony. "What? Tell me what?"

Anthony looks down at the ground, then back to Hallia, without saying a word. He switches his gaze back to Ira and for a long moment he stares into Ira's eyes in silence. "Rocko is gone, Ira."

"What do you mean he's gone, gone where?"

*An unexpected breeze blows past Ira's face, like the warm breath of a loved one and he flinches. For a moment he is mesmerized by it and he stiffens. It's as if he's standing in a thick crowd of people not able to move an inch. An overwhelming sensation of love and assurance overtakes him and he takes a deep breath, not wanting this moment to end. Then he hears a soft voice. I am with you son. Ira stands still, he couldn't move even if he wanted to and he doesn't want to, he has never felt such peace in all his life.*

He is pulled back to reality by Anthony's four year old. "Rocko *paco* is a taco." She blurts out as if singing a nursery rhyme.

Anthony's wife covers the child's mouth with her hand.

As Ira snaps out of his trance he flashes his dark eyes at Anthony. "What were you supposed to tell me Anthony?" Ira stares, waiting for an answer.

"Ira, Rocko died last night."

"Oh, he died, did he?"

Ira walks to the door and opens it. Turning back around he looks at all the faces in the room, then he leaves the shack without a word. With quick long strides he crosses the yard until he reaches the chicken coop, yanks the latch off and throws open the flimsy mesh door. He grabs the pickup topper, and flips it over. He counts the chickens. Then he counts again. Ira drops his chin to his chest and closes his eyes, the peace that he felt a few moments ago is gone. He feels lightheaded, his throat is thick, his stomach swirls. He drops down to his hands and knees, his back arches and he throws up again and again until he is gagging and there's nothing left inside of him.

When he's finished he stands up, wipes his sleeve across his mouth, takes a deep breath and tramps to the woodshed. He rummages inside until he finds a shovel, he walks back to the chicken coop and shovels his vomit and pieces of his friend Rocko in to the truck topper. Ira turns to the house where Anthony and some of the others are standing in the door, watching him. He marches across the yard, holding the spade of the shovel out in front of him, his dark eyes boring into them. As he gets closer, the children scatter and he stops in front of Anthony.

"Did you forget I know how to count? No chickens are missing."

Ira pushes Anthony out of the way with the shovel, walks into the house, looks at the kitchen stove where the pot of meat is and his throat constricts. Anthony rushes to protect the meat. Ira picks up some matches and plods across the yard back to the chicken coop, grabbing a net of yucca and dragging it with him. He takes the wood and dumps a pile of it on top of his vomit.

He strikes a match and sets the wood on fire. He puts the rest of the matches in his pocket. He shoos the chickens until he has chased every last one of them out of the coop. He keeps throwing wood on the fire until it's all gone and the flames are crackling and shooting up twice as high as the shed next to it.

Ira watches the smoke rise for a few minutes and offers up his prayer to the Great Spirit, just like they did for his grandpa and mother six years ago. He walks back to the house, takes a knife from the kitchen table, grabs his rabbit fur blanket off his mattress and stuffs them both into his Padres duffle bag. Ira takes one last look around. Hallia stands in the corner of the room, their eyes meet for a moment, he turns and walks out the door.

Ira must leave this life. He knows these are not his ways, not his people and not his dreams. The inner peace that he felt earlier made him realize that he has no connection to these people and he must search for something else. Something that feels right.

As the fire blazes and a stream of gray smoke rises to the sky, the boy of ten with a full heart of courage, but only half of a shadow wanders into the desert seeking his destiny. As he walks with his bag slung on his shoulder, he feels nothing, not hatred, not spite, not even hunger. He sets his face like flint and he never looks back.

# CHAPTER FOUR

## The Padre's Search

Father Lelo stirs up a cloud of dust as his truck skids to a halt in the gravel parking lot of the tribal police station. He throws it in park, slams the truck door and rushes to the entrance. Chief Dewey is standing on the steps waiting for him. Father nods as he walks past him and turns down the hall, stepping into Dewey's office. They close the door.

Father Lelo addresses the situation, unreserved. "What do you mean they don't know what happened to him? When I called you yesterday you said he was in Mexico with relatives. He's ten years old. How could they just let him go off by himself? He's ten for Pete's sakes." Father Lelo takes his hat off and slaps the dust from it. "I was supposed to have a meeting with Rosa the day I got orders from the Marines. I went to their house to meet with her, but nobody was home. So I left a note telling Rosa that the Marines Corps was deploying me to Honduras with the Bishop's blessing and that I was ordered to be packed and ready to leave base at 0500 hours. I wrote in the note for Rosa to stop by in the evening before 8:00 p.m. if she still needed to talk to me. She didn't show up that night. Nor did I hear anything from them all the while I was in Honduras."

Chief Dewey stands with his arms crossed, giving him his full attention.

Father Lelo lets out a huge sigh, "After my tour in Honduras was finished I thought I was on my way home, but I was handed orders to report to a Navy ship anchored in the Persian Gulf. After that, once again I thought I was coming home, but then I learned through a message from the Red Cross that my mother had been taken critically ill. My commander granted me an emergency leave so I bummed a flight from Bahrain to Malaga, Spain and stayed with her until she passed. I just got back to the States. I didn't get word that they found Raina, or that Samuel had died, or, for that matter, that Rosa left."

Chief Dewey moves across the room to the closet and takes a medium-sized box down from the shelf. He hands it to Father Lelo in silence.

Father Lelo lifts it up and peeks inside. The box contains all the evidence collected at the scene where Raina's body had been found. He sets it down on the corner of the desk and begins to examine its contents.

First he pulls out what's left of Raina's clothing: a shredded, bloody shirt and short skirt with some torn fishnet stockings; then a dead tree branch measuring a foot long stained with dried blood. Near the bottom of the box Father Lelo pulled out a Colt .45 revolver with an empty chamber, two wedding bands and a crumpled California license plate. Beneath those items is a vehicle registration card that doesn't quite match the plate numbers, a bunch of unopened letters postmarked Honduras, a funny-shaped brown package that's post marked Bahrain and two hand-scribbled notes.

One of the notes had been found in Sam's shirt pocket the day he died. The note was addressed to nobody, but signed by Rosa. The other note was the one Father Lelo wrote to Rosa that she had never received. It was trapped in the bushes near the porch, fluttering in the breeze. It was found after Sam had already died and Rosa had exiled herself. Father Lelo pored through the words recalling the day he wrote it.

*Dear Rosa,*

*I have been called out on deployment to Honduras as trouble brews with the Nicaraguans. My orders are to ship out at 0500 tomorrow morning. I will be at the rectory this evening packing, but will leave for base by 8:00 pm tonight. Please feel free to come by. I sense that the matter in which you wish to speak is of an urgent nature.*

*Sincerely,*
*Father Lelo*

Then Father Lelo picks up the note that Rosa had written. The one little Ira handed to his grandfather the day they rode out to the desert and found the gruesome remains of his mother. It was the note that was meant for Father Lelo, but the note that he had never received. Now standing holding both notes side by side, he reads Rosa's note for the first time.

*I'm sorry I missed you,*

*I must exile myself by taking part in a cleansing ritual. It is with regret that I will not be of any help to my grandson in this crisis at such a young age. Still, it is best I leave. For today I have witnessed visions so horrifying it has left me hollow, and in anguish. I no longer trust myself to raise a child alone, or even live among people. Please watch over my grandson, I trust you without fail.*

*Sincerely,*
*Rosa*

Father Lelo's heart sinks. He swallows hard, looks up at Dewey and drops his hand in disbelief, the note Rosa wrote falls to his side. He lifts his hand back up and skims the note again. He can't believe it, he is completely perplexed. "This note was for me, this note was meant for me. Why didn't someone let me know? They wanted me to take care of the boy."

Sheriff Dewey touches Father Lelo's shoulder. "It wasn't addressed to anyone specific, so we didn't know who it was for. You were already gone so we never even thought it could be meant for you. It was so vague, and nobody considered for even a moment that she would ask you to look after her grandson. We didn't find your note to Rosa until weeks later; nobody put two and two together. We all felt bad for the boy. We all loved him despite what his mother was. I didn't want to send him to relatives in a strange country but our hands were tied; there was nothing else we could do. I had to take him to Mexico."

Father Lelo picks up his hat and puts it on. "I would've been given guardianship; I would have had him placed with my brother and his wife until I got home." He pulls a white handkerchief from his pocket and wipes his nose. "I feel awful. I loved that boy like a son. I have to find him. I don't even want to imagine what that child has gone through."

Father Lelo puts the evidence back in the box, except the funny-shaped brown package. He stares at it for a moment, then looks at Chief Dewey. "May I take this? I sent this to the boy from Bahrain a while back."

Chief Dewey nods. "The post office didn't know what to do with it, so I took it and stuck it in the evidence box." Father Lelo stuffs the package into his jacket pocket.

"I'm going to get to the bottom of this," He picks up the box and hands it back to Chief Dewey.

"Where are you going?"

"I'm going to find Ira. I owe it to him and his mother."

Dewey steps forward. "I understand finding the boy, but the mother was nothing but a two-bit prostitute who got him into this mess in the first place. Look what it did to her parents?"

Father Lelo stops in his tracks and turns around. His gaze meets Chief Dewey's with conviction. "Judge not, Chief." For a moment their eyes are locked on each other. Father Lelo softens his tone. "We humans are limited in our perceptions; we don't see the world as God does, so be careful you are not putting the wrong spin on things. Always remember, Chief. 'Judge not, lest ye be judged.'" After an intense pause, he turns and leaves the station.

Father Lelo's thoughts are of Ira and Raina as he walks to his car. He had spent many hours counseling Raina while she was pregnant with Ira. He'd gotten to know her very well. Most of the people in the village had turned on her. They all whispered behind her back, gossiping about how she had been with so many boys she didn't even know who the father was. It was cruel and it hurt Raina deeply, *she'd* known who the father was. She was innocent. She had never willingly been with a man.

Raina was a young girl then, with special dignity and grace. She was kind, warm-hearted and very intelligent. She and her parents came to his Mass every Sunday and he spent most of his free time with them. You could say they adopted Father Lelo into their family. He was heart-broken that her son had been sent to live with the family of the boy who had raped her.

Rosa, the tribe's medicine woman, a sensitive mystic, as well as a visionary and a vital part of this Kumeyaay Indian community, spent time teaching Father Lelo the healing power of natural plants and herbs from the earth. Samuel spent time teaching Father Lelo about ancient Native American Religion. Father Lelo is a very prosperous man, rich in holiness, acknowledging God in everything that is good. He is determined now, first to find Raina's son and then to find her mother, Rosa.

Father Lelo steps up into his truck. He pulls the funny-shaped package out of his pocket, opens the glove box and sets it inside. He drives down the main street of the village to the far end where the church and rectory still stand. He has not been here since 1983. It has been six years and little is changed. The Diocese had not replaced him so the old rectory, nothing more than an addition to a now abandoned church, remains empty. It's where he'll be staying.

He pulls up alongside the church. He puts the truck into park while a flood of memories fill his mind; baptisms, weddings, funerals. He bows his head for a moment, remembering Raina and Samuel. He regrets that he wasn't here for his dear friends' funerals and murmurs a prayer.

Father Lelo turns the key off, gets out of the truck and goes into the house. It's dusty, in need of a cleaning. He picks up an old lantern and shakes it; it's empty. He lifts the cover off the woodstove; he'll need wood. It's getting close to noon so he decides to make the trek to Camp

Corners' convenience store to pick up supplies and gas up the truck, then get this place cleaned up and hit the rack early for a good night's sleep. He'll head out at first light to search for Ira and bring him home.

For the past ten days Ira has been spending most of his time walking, or thumbing rides on bumpy dusty roads in the beds of old pickup trucks. He's inherently attuned to the desert and not at all afraid. His grandparents and Anthony taught him all about the life and customs of his ancient desert ancestors. He's learned everything he needs to know about living in the desert.

When Ira comes upon a remote rancheria here and there, he stops to ask for work in exchange for food. He'll then haul, chop and stack wood for a meager breakfast, or he helps to mend a fence for an evening meal. The things he learned about ranch work from Anthony have come in handy, things such as, how to toenail boards together, how to patch a fence and how to hunt small game with a war club, throwing stick, or setting a snare. He has learned which plants are edible and what they are used for. He learned how to gather nuts, beans and acorns that are all loaded with protein.

Sometimes he can stay at a rancheria for one night like he did last night, but times are tough for everyone and none of his hosts can afford to let him stay any longer. They do allow him to fill his thermos with water before he leaves, though. He hasn't had to spend any nights without shelter yet, but it looks like he'll have to tonight. It's March, which is a good thing for him, for there is neither extreme heat, nor extreme cold and his rabbit-fur blanket will be enough to protect him from the crisp night air.

Ira sets out before light and walks all morning, tiring before noon. He doesn't come across a single living thing, not even a lizard or a mouse. His luck is about to change, though, because just ahead on the south side of a rocky *bajada,* he stops to stare at a rare retreat, a clump of old saguaro cactuses hiding beneath a slope of a rise. The huge old giants are casting their shadows on a formation of enormous white rocks. An orchard of Mesquite trees along with pink flowering ironwood and fat, twisted elephant trees have grown up from between the boulders. A cloak of burgundy prickly pear, succulent, orange-flowered barrel cactus and yellow poppies make a colorful congregation surrounding the stoic granite altar.

His senses come alive as he approaches this rare desert garden. He flares his nostrils and takes a deep breath, his lungs swell and his nose fills with lush, blossomy fragrances. He hears birds chirping in harmony and he sees the barrel cactuses all leaning to one side in unison, like a colorful choir frozen in motion, they're all pointing south. He knows the barrel cacti are the desert's compass. They reassure him like old friends that he's moving southwest, just like he planned.

As he enters this special oasis he thinks about what Anthony had said. He'd talked about a town called Vineyard that's south and far to the west, next to a thing he called the ocean. He said the town is a place where they grow purple fruit bigger than your head. The people of Vineyard are rich and offer other people jobs to help pick their purple fruit. It's because of Anthony's story that Ira is heading that direction. He doesn't know where Vineyard is, or what kind of people live in the town. Nor has he ever seen an ocean, but Anthony said it is so much water that you can't walk through it. Ira can't even imagine a puddle that size, but if it's still there, he'll walk around it. He needs to find work and a permanent place to live.

Right now, though, Ira's found a temporary haven. He's tired from walking all morning and in need of a break. He stops and surveys the oasis for a place to sit. He selects a huge boulder with a smooth side, plunks himself down and props his back against it. Then he digs in his Padres bag for his thermos and gulps the last of his water.

He leans back on the rock, closes his eyes and tilts his face to the sky. Sunbeams brighten the blank canvas of his lids. Warm energy flows into him and he begins to dream.

One by one, tattered black silhouettes glide across the sand, creeping ever closer to where Ira sleeps until the nimble, dark shadows slide across his face and awaken him. He looks up at the sky to see a carnival of vultures riding the air currents; a merry-go-round gliding up and down, delivering a low, enchanting tune. Ira's sleepy eyes are soothed by a twirling mobile of black floating wings drifting beneath a cerulean sky.

Suddenly, with an alarming shrill piercing the air, a rare bald eagle makes her appearance. Her telescopic vision focuses on a brown hare camouflaged by a community of desert scrub. The eagle plummets to the earth with her wings tucked to her sides, then turning up, she sweeps the sand with her tail feathers and clamps her talons into the hare. She sets her hooks deep into the rabbit's back then spreads open her giant wings, flapping and toiling, hauling her prey to the heavens. A paltry black bird darts here and there, making a nuisance of itself. It pecks in vain at the dangling quarry. There's a minor squabble, a slight tumble and the eagle flies away with her prize.

Ira watches as a feather floats down, rocking side to side, then twirling round and finally settles on a rock in the distance. He stands up and walks to the feather. It's a tail feather from the eagle. Ira knows that the eagle is sacred to his people and knows what this moment would mean to them.

The eagle flies higher than any other bird and is closest to the creator. So, like the creator, it has a different perspective of this earth and its inhabitants. Eagles are given the honor of flying messages between the physical world of humans and the spiritual world, so they are big medicine, a sign of nobility. Their feathers are powerful and filled with prosperity.

Ira stands looking at the feather in front of him; this is a rare occasion and he wonders if it's a message from the Great Spirit. He wonders if he's worthy of the honor of picking it up, or should he just leave it where it lies. He's so young and doubts that he's deserving of it, but then why did it land in front of him? He wishes someone with wisdom was around who could help him with his problem.

As he stares at the feather, unconscious of his actions, he slips his hands into his pockets. Then recognizing this gesture as a sign not to touch it, he turns to walk away. Then he stops again and his mood lightens. Maybe the Great Spirit meant for him to take it to someone who is worthy. Then once again he changes his mind and he stares at the feather, realizing that he doesn't know anyone he can give it to. He's alone in the world and so he turns and walks away.

He pulls his hands out of his pockets, walks back to where he left his Padres bag and picks it up. He considers the time of day; just a half day of sunlight left, he should get started preparing for a night without shelter. He'll think about the feather some more when he's done with his work and his mind is settled.

Ira crosses the desert garden with his Padres bag riding across his shoulder. He stops and surveys the area. There's a creek bed created by the runoff waters from the winter rains. It's scattered with animal tracks, a good sign. He walks alongside the dried bed until he finds a good sharp corner where the water would have run the deepest. He mentally maps out a spot of ground where there's no chance of any shade. He uses a flat rock and digs until the sand becomes moist. He digs two holes side by side. Once he's done, he places the cup in one hole and the thermos in the other. Then he gathers some plants with leaves and lines the holes with them. He pulls out his rain poncho, unfolds it and ponders for a moment at its size. The poncho is meant for a toddler. He has never had to use it. He places it on top of the holes, sealing its perimeter with sand and larger rocks to make it air tight. He then finds two smaller rocks and places them above each container on top of the poncho. This will make the plastic dip to a point above the containers, guiding the condensed water on the underside of the poncho to roll down and drip into them. The sun is hot and Ira knows that this make-do solar still will produce the water he needs to drink.

Ira then gathers stalks of dried and blown-down yuccas and stacks them close to a craggy opening in the rock formation. It's a crevasse with just enough room for him to slide into and it'll make a good shelter.

The next thing he needs is a weapon to catch a meal with. He searches for a rock that fits into the size of his palm and a decent-sized dead branch that he can use to pound on. He takes out his knife and cuts some yucca leaves. He lays the long, spiny blades on the dead branch and pounds them with the rock until the plant's casing is loosened. Then he takes his knife and scrapes the green sheathing away until its stringy fibers are exposed. He works them loose by holding the plant's long leaves between his palms and rubbing them back and forth. Once they're loose enough, he pulls the fibers apart. After he has a nice bundle of fibers, he sits back, relaxes in the shade and begins to braid some good thick cords.

Finished braiding cords, he takes a hike to where the eagle caught her meal. He fully expects to catch a meal here, too. The tracks in the sand leading to the brush and thorny bushes means this is a community hare house and the trail leading to it is very active. This is a good place to set his snare.

He takes the clasp off the zipper from his Padres bag and ties it to the end of one of his braided cords. He pulls the other end of the cord through the round opening, making a free-moving noose. He secures the opposite end of the cord to a choice branch toward the top of a bush, leaving it dangle. He then works at making a simple trigger by carving the end of a stick to a sharp point and pounding it into the ground next to the noose. Then he takes another piece of cord and ties one end of it to the stake in the ground, bows the branch down above it and ties the other end to the loop that is attached to the branch. He arranges the noose with briars and twigs so that it's opened and dangling a couple inches off the ground. When a rabbit runs through the snare, it will trigger the branch to snap up. The noose will catch him by the neck, toss him into the air and force him to dangle.

As the animal struggles the noose will tighten and the rabbit will suffocate.

Next he forms a funnel along the ground with branches, rocks and other debris that will guide the animal down the trail straight into his snare. It is not his intention to watch an animal suffer or have to use a club to finish it off, so he is careful to make the best snare he can, to ensure a quick death. This is not a sport to young Ira. He takes the life of the rabbit for the fats and proteins it will provide him. In return, Ira gives the rabbit back its life in a different form. He will consume it, transforming it into energy and the rabbit will live on in him.

Ira makes his way back to where he'll be camping for the night. He looks up at the sun and wipes his brow, it's hot. He pulls one of the braided cords out of his pocket and ties it around his forehead for a sweat band.

Things go from one extreme to the other in the desert and he thinks as long as it hasn't been getting too cold at night he won't make a fire. Animal activity is most prevalent in the dark and animals shy away from fire. However, a fire would keep dangerous predators away. He decides he'll get the wood ready.

Ira spends the rest of the afternoon gathering wood and preparing a one-match fire just in case the time comes that he has to light one pronto. He gathers tiny pieces of twigs and piles them in a light airy mound in front of the cave opening. Then he builds a teepee around the twigs with a layer of larger twigs, leaving an opening for his hands to slide into so he can strike a match, protecting it from any breeze. He continues to add larger sticks and branches, always leaving an opening in the same place until the teepee is thigh-high. Then he piles the largest pieces alongside, for when the flames are ample enough to handle them.

After Ira has done everything he can to ready himself for the night he sits down, stretches his legs out and puts his hands behind his head. The sun is reclining and so is he.

The sights and sounds of the desert come to life, as the air cools and the shadows grow tall. The moon begins another dress rehearsal, making its naked appearance huge and round at the horizon, and the sun makes its punctual exit, clothing her majesty the moon in a hue of purple as it leaves for the evening. The magnificent exchange of these two heavenly bodies brings the desert audience to an ovation. The birds chirp as they fly back and forth in the saguaros. A team of chattering squirrels scamper up and down a mesquite tree. Dozens of hummingbirds take advantage of the blossoms, drinking and pollinating as much as they can while the fragrant blossoms last. Ira watches them, amazed as they fly backward, sideways and upside down to get the sweet nectar of their choice. A pack of Harris Hawks in the trees a few yards away are busy building and protecting nests. Dwarf owls take part, peeping at him from the holes in the saguaros.

Everyone has a partner or kin, everyone except Ira. He looks down at his Padres bag. He remembers the day that Rocko stuck his nose in it, sniffing for the tortilla he had saved for him. As he tried to pull his nose from the bag, it got stuck. Ira smiles as he pictures Rocko standing in front of him, his head tilted to one side, the bag covering it and his tail wagging with joy. He takes a deep breath as tears drop from the corners of his eyes. He was just four when he went to live at the Rancheria and he has never been anywhere else. He misses Rocko.

Ira sniffles as he watches two hawks fly to the top of the tallest saguaro, their plumage a festival of black, chestnut, chocolate and bright white colors. Ira forgets his sorrows as he watches one of the attractive birds land on the back of the other. There they sit, like a totem pole. What are they doing, he wonders. All at once, the bird on top takes flight and lands near a bush. Before long he's crawling beneath it, flushing out a cottontail from the other side. The other hawk dives from the cactus, toppling the prey, but the rabbit regains its balance and zigzags across the sand with the hawk flying close behind. Then another hawk appears, then two more. They fly at the rabbit from every direction, cornering it so that it has no place to run. Ira has never seen anything like this; birds that help each other hunt then share the meal.

As Ira watches, he realizes that this is the second rabbit dinner he has watched being caught today and it means there's a good chance he'll catch one in his snare, too. He's also smart enough to know that where the prey is plentiful so are the predators.

A light warm breeze rustles the branches and coyotes begin to yelp as the gigantic moon rises. Ira digs in his bag for his matches and knife and sets them close at hand. He then picks up a long stick and shoves it into the cave, stirring it around. He listens for any reaction, whether it be rattling, hissing or growling; he hears nothing, so he crawls in feet first.

He has built the pile of firewood within reach in case the coyotes decide to intrude and it's assembled ready to light fast and intensify in a jiffy. Ira yanks his blanket from his bag, pulls it into the cave and snuggles in for the night. If everything goes well he'll have water, rabbit and cactus pears for breakfast. He's exhausted; he closes his eyes, pondering the day's events for what seems like an eternity.

Sleep finally grips him, his body becomes heavy and his muscles surrender their strength. He enters the realm of unconsciousness, somewhere between real and surreal.

*Ira drifts on the night air to the spot where he set the snare. He's suspended in nothingness, waiting for comprehension. Finally, he becomes aware. The snare is empty and off in the distance he sees an eagle feather blowing across the sand. It moves slowly at first, but then picking up speed it tumbles straight to the snare. The feather hits the cord hard enough to trigger the branch. It snaps up, catching the feather with it. The feather then dangles above the trail like a caution flag, a warning to all rabbits within miles that this is death row, the last mile, the end of the road. Ira tries to run to the feather; he has to get rid of it or the rabbits won't come. He steps in one of the holes that he dug and smashes the thermos cup. In slow motion, he trips and falls, overturning the thermos in the other hole. The water spills from both containers and Ira watches helpless as it disappears into the sand. He grabs his ankle; it begins to swell and turn purple. He tries to stand but he can't. How will he survive in the desert now? His stomach is growling, he's thirsty, the sun is an inferno and he can't walk.*

Ira wakes in a sweat. He looks around, trying to gain his senses. Then he lets out a deep sigh of relief. It was just a dream, but one that he can learn from, for sure.

He musters up some courage and crawls out of the cave. He pulls the blanket out and twirls it around his shoulders like a matador. Then he climbs to the tallest part of the rock and stands above his domain, surveying it for predators. He must take matters into his own hands and heed the warning of his dream. He looks to his left, then his right, then he turns all the way around.

Behind him is the black silhouette of a great horned owl perched at the end of a snarled branch. The owl twists her neck around and looks at Ira with huge yellow eyes. She hoots twice as if trying to communicate with him, then she lets out a deep eerie "whoo, whooo," that gives Ira goose bumps. She watches him for a moment - then flies away.

Ira looks around again and doesn't see anything else. Good, he thinks. It's safe to go get the feather. The moon is bright enough for him to see his way. He picks up his knife and walks to the dried creek bed. He watches where he steps so he doesn't trip in one of the holes. Squinting, he tries to locate the feather. He searches for the white tip that would stand out against the brown sand.

After a few moments he spots it and, bending down, he reaches for it in the same instant that a sizzling hiss spurts from the ground, then that familiar rattling sound. Ira stiffens, he freezes in mid-motion. The snake is so well camouflaged, he can barely see it, but he knows its head is just inches from his hand. His heart begins racing, its pounding filling his throat and ears. He doesn't dare move. There's nothing more perilous in the desert than to be bitten by a poisonous creature. He is days away from any form of help. He knows that if the snake sinks his fangs in him, he'll suffer a slow, agonizing death.

Even though he is alone in the world he's not ready to die. So without another thought he jerks the hand that holds the knife and slices the blade through the snake, severing its head from its body. Then he immediately jumps out of the way. He stands and watches as the snake's rattle slows, stops shaking and drops to the sand.

Ira knows that snakes, in most instances, give up and crawl off, but he didn't want it scaring away his rabbits. Besides that, he can eat the snake and use its thick skin. Ira picks up the feather and leaves the head of the snake where it lies, but drags the body back to his cave. When the sun comes up he'll skin it, roast its meat and make a sheath for his knife from its hide.

Father Lelo opens his eyes and yawns. The rusty old box spring squeaks as he peels back the covers, rolls to his side and reaches for his watch. It's early and still dark. He pulls on his sweat pants and tiptoes across the cold floor to the wood stove. He opens it and looks inside. The coals are throwing out some heat and he rubs his hands above them. He slides the coffee pot to the burner, then shuffles to the porch for more wood. When he opens the door he sees a sedate glow that has variegated the horizon. He takes a deep breath, filling his lungs with the crisp morning air. He stacks some wood into his arms and stands in the doorway for a moment. He loses himself in the sight of the first light of day and gives thanks for the morning.

Father Lelo shuts the door with his foot, drops the wood next to the stove and then stuffs some pieces inside. After a few minutes the fire is crackling and he ambles back to the bedroom for his morning meditation. When he has finished, he ends his prayers with a request for Ira's safety and a hope that he has a successful journey in finding him.

After he dresses, he stuffs his rosary beads into his pocket and goes to the kitchen. The coffee pot is percolating and the smell of fresh coffee wafts through the air. He begins to pack some survival essentials into a backpack for emergency purposes. Then he loads his military gear into his ruck sack. He knows that it's likely he'll be spending a few nights in the desert tracking Ira down after he has stopped at the Salazara ranch.

After loading the truck with supplies he pours himself a steaming cup of brew. He stands in the doorway of the tiny rectory sipping, while feasting his eyes on a thin crescent of golden pink that's emerging from the desert horizon. He wouldn't miss this for anything. A desert sunrise is the best show on earth and he stands watching until the life-nurturing crescent turns to a half circle.

Father Lelo climbs into his truck and drives through the village to the other side of the reservation, where he turns onto the highway and travels west. He follows a map that Chief Dewey drew up for him the day before.

He drives all morning on a principal but desolate highway, the road rough and bumpy. Some of the ruts from the wash out of the winter rains are as deep as brooks and the entire trip to the rancheria has been like driving an obstacle course.

The priest is worn out and thirsty. He's glad when he finally sees a structure off in the distance. As he approaches closer to the rancheria where he knows Ira spent the last six years, he feels a strong sense of presence. He stops the truck in the dusty yard and puts it in park.

*A gust of wind swirls the dirt off the ground, a dog appears. It sits down in the middle of the yard and a woman in a long flowing gown stands next to it. She is holding a red-tipped stick pointing out to her right.*

Father Lelo blinks and the mirage is gone. I better drink some water, he thinks, I must be hallucinating. He gets out of the truck, stretches and takes a good long swig from his canteen.

As he is drinking he notices an old woman emerge from the house, followed by a young couple and a trail of children. They stop halfway to the truck, their expressions showing their thoughts. They're looking at an alien. Father Lelo chuckles; he supposes it's not every day they see a man with a priest's collar wearing military fatigues way out here. He puts the cap back on his canteen and extends his hand.

"*Hola. Habla usted Ingles*?"

Their looks change to surprise as he speaks to them in Spanish.

Anthony nods, "Yes."

"Okay, good. I'm Father Lelo and I'm looking for the boy who was brought to you six years ago." Father knows the answer to his next question, but he asks anyway. "Is he still here?"

"No."

Father Lelo waits for embellishment, but none is offered so he steps forward. "Where is he?"

Anthony's expression turns suspicious. "Are you accusing us of something? Do you think we sold him? We didn't sell him."

This time it's Father Lelo's expression that changes. "I didn't imply that you had. I simply asked where he is."

Anthony stands with his arms crossed, his stature lik a stone monument. "The boy set our chicken coop on fire one morning, then walked off. I think there's something wrong with his mind. His mother was a, a." Anthony stops and turns and looks at the children. He waves his hand motioning for them to go inside and start their chores.

Father Lelo stops him from finishing his comment. "The boy was like a son to me. His grandmother, who is a tribal medicine woman, wants me to raise him and I want him with me."

"Then why did the sheriff bring him to us?"

"I'm a Marine as well as a priest. There was a mix up and I was sent away on duty without knowing her wishes."

Anthony is apprehensive about Father Lelo's answer. "Seems kinda dumb to give custody to a Marine Corps priest on active duty."

Father Lelo looks Anthony square in the eyes. "Forgive my frankness, but it seems even dumber to give custody to you. After all, he is missing now. Just tell me which way the boy went and I'll be on my way."

"I don't know, I didn't watch him."

"You don't know. We're talking about a ten-year-old child. How could you just let him walk away? Did you even call the police?"

Anthony shrugs his shoulders. "We all figured he'd get picked up by someone and brought back here safe."

Father Lelo throws up his arms in frustration. "Just who the hell would you be expecting way out here? Madonna? This isn't exactly Ventura running through your yard."

Anthony straightens his stance. He pulls his shoulders back and puffs his chest, "We had been expecting Domingo, my brother-in-law." Anthony shifts after he says this, as if he wished he hadn't.

Father Lelo arches his eyebrows in surprise. "Oh, yeah, that sounds reasonable, except Chief Dewey told me he's in prison on drug charges, so the word 'safe' doesn't exactly fit here, does it? When was he here?"

"Last week. Said his wife Anita was pregnant again. They came for some baby clothes."

"When was he here before that?"

"About eight months ago."

"Did he see the boy?"

"Yeah, he knew we took him in. He also knew we weren't going to let him have him."

"Does he know that the boy is out wandering alone now?"

Anthony clears his throat and shifts his weight. "Our youngest blurted out that he set the chicken coop on fire and about the dog before we could stop him. So, yeah, he knows the boy left."

"A dog? What about a dog?"

"We had an old dog that he got attached to and the boy took it hard when we – I mean when it, died."

Father Lelo lets out a sigh. He looks down at the ground, deep in thought then he looks up with troubled eyes. "I don't even know what he looks like anymore. He wasn't quite four when I saw him last. His birthday was last month. So he is ten now. I'm sure he's changed a lot."

Anthony relaxes a bit and recognizes the worry in Father Lelo's eyes. "He's taller than most kids his age, with a lean build. He's got a thin straight nose. He is a handsome Indian kid."

Father Lelo's eyes soften and he nods. "I don't suppose that you went out of your way to do any searching for him yourself?"

A surge of guilt washes across Anthony's face, but he says nothing.

Father Lelo stares for a moment, wondering how anyone can be so apathetic when it comes to a child. Then he thinks about the harsh reality of poverty. How it takes its toll and how every ounce of energy you have is spent just surviving, leaving not a drop for an extra crisis. He walks to the truck without further rebuke.

Anthony steps forward and stops him before he gets in. "For what it's worth, he took a knife from the kitchen, some matches and that duffle bag he came with. I taught him how to hunt and find water."

They stare at each other in silence for a minute. Father Lelo lets out groan then turns and gets into his truck. He starts it up, nods at Anthony and drives off down the road in the direction he came from. He figures he'll go to the nearest town and start asking people if they've seen the boy. He knows he has his work cut out for him, long hours and hot days are ahead.

A week passes with Father Lelo stopping to question everyone he sees. Today, he notices a tiny hovel just east of the dirt road he's on. He turns the truck onto the dry gravel path leading up to it. He stops in front of the shack in a cloud of dust. A woman with a worn and weathered face peeks out of the door. She speaks to him in Spanish, telling him she has seen nobody except her husband and children for months. She offers Father Lelo some water, but he declines. He carried plenty and knows how hard it is to come by out here. He holds up his canteen and smiles. She smiles back toothless, waving goodbye as he backs the truck up and turns it around.

As Father Lelo drives along, he thinks about Anthony and the rancheria where Ira grew up. It was humble to say the most, but at least Ira had a dog. He must have been quite attached to that dog to have thrown such a fit when it died.

In a sudden epiphany, Father Lelo slams on the brakes. He remembers his vision of the dog and the woman when he pulled up to the shack. It's just a hunch and maybe not even that, but the woman was holding that stick straight out to her side. Was she pointing it in a specific direction on purpose? *This is crazy,* he thinks, but he shifts the truck into reverse, backs up and turns down a road heading southwest. *Why not?* He shrugs, he's got nothing else to go by and it's as good a direction as any to continue looking.

# CHAPTER FIVE

## The Big Cluster

After many days of traveling through the desert, Ira has found a rocky path that seems to be leading to someplace other than hills and canyons. There are tracks on the hard sand that look pretty recent and he's hopeful there's a town nearby. It's been five weeks total since he left Hallia's place, hitching rides between rancherias. It's been three long weeks since he left the lush oasis where he spent his first night alone in the desert. He only came across one main highway and there were no cars around when he crossed it. He continues on via the way of the prickly pear cactus and manages to produce enough food from both cactus and snares along with water to stay alive.

He has suffered and survived the long hot days and cold dangerous nights. He learned how to avoid poisonous reptiles and scorpions and also learned that it's necessary to rig booby-traps to ward off nighttime predators like cougars and coyotes. The past two weeks have been a very trying time for him, and even though he is only ten years old, he feels proud at what he has accomplished. It's been a true test of his endurance, but he wonders if any kind of achievement matters when nobody knows you're alive. He also wonders how much longer he can stay alive, since his clothes no longer fit because of his lack of proper nutrition.

Ira's time alone in the desert has been hard and strenuous and the one thing that kept him from failing was the fact that he did not realize that it was possible to fail. It never once occurred to him that he might not make it to Vineyard and that's what keeps him moving forward; that and his will to reach the giant water. With a swirling wisp of a breeze, Ira is suddenly caught up in a vision.

*He's tired and staggering, he stumbles upon a monstrous puddle of water that goes on for as far as his eyes can see. He begins to laugh and everything is beautiful, children are laughing and playing. Everywhere he looks he sees the faces of happy people. Then a cascade of spray splashes out from the water and a misty figure appears. She's holding a stick in one hand and a clay bowl in the other. The bowl is filled with water and she holds it straight out in front of her as she glides toward him. She reaches the sand where he stands and he steps forward to drink from it. She waves the red-tipped stick above it and the water changes to blood. Tipping the bowl to the side she spills the contents onto the ground and as the red liquid hits the sand her dress absorbs it, soaking it up until her white flowing gown has turned crimson.*

He gasps as he snaps out of the vision, feeling empty and heavy. This time he is sadder than he's ever been. Why does she keep doing this to him? There are no answers, but the one thing he knows for sure is that the woman in the vision is his mother and that he hates her. She has taken everything he has ever loved away from him and now even his dreams are terrifying because of her.

He waves his hand as if to make her memory disappear and for the next two days pushes on. He begins to notice some changes in the scenery. There are cacti here that are even taller than the saguaros. The air seems to have a different quality; it smells unusual to Ira and it seems to him the air even feels funny. The land is becoming plusher and for the past half hour Ira has been hearing a faint tingling or clanking type of sound far off in the distance. The sound starts and stops in random intervals, sometimes it clanks just once, other times for a few seconds. He has never heard anything like it before.

The path widens as Ira walks. Then for the first time in his life he hears a soft bleating sound. Ira stops in his tracks and listens. He is amazed by the animals that appear through the thicket. The only animals that Ira can ever remember seeing are the ones on Hallia's ranch and she did not have any animals of this kind. They are smaller than horses and they have pointy horns that have grown straight up from their crowns. Ira stands for a long moment just staring, then his gaze shifts to another first. A man who is bearded down to his chest is walking toward Ira, holding a long stick that is curved at the end.

Ira is stunned at this scene. He stands watching as the shepherd taps his stick on the ground in a soft rhythm, guiding the herd that's nibbling on the undergrowth. Most of the animals are white, but there are a few brown ones mixed in and one that is as black as a raven. The black one has a leather collar with a bell attached. The herd is content and quiet, there is more shaking of tails than bleating and of course the occasional tingling of the bell.

When the old man is close enough he speaks to Ira in Spanish. Ira knows just enough Spanish to get by, something he forgot to take into consideration when he left the rancheria. His grandparents and mother spoke to him in Kumeyaay and English, and Anthony always spoke to him in English.

The wise old bearded man looks at Ira with a friendly smile. "*Hola, estas perdido*?" Ira drops his jaw and stares at him with a blank look. Nobody has spoken to him in five weeks and because he's not fluent in Spanish he misinterprets the word "lost" for "happy" and after a few seconds he answers no.

Ruby Dix smiles and nods, for the most part because now he knows that what he thought might be true, is true. The young boy did not understand him and doesn't know where he is. It doesn't take much to figure this out. The boy is not Mexican, rather looks like an American Indian. He has never seen the child in these parts before and he has a look of bewilderment on his face. Now Ruby is very curious as to why a young child who is not fluent in Spanish is wandering all alone in Mexico, an obviouslydangerous thing to do. He checks to see if the boy understands any Spanish.

"*Hablas ingles?*"

Ira looks down in embarrassment because he did not consider the language barrier that he was walking into and nods.

The old man is relieved that Ira nodded. He must understand some Spanish, so he introduces himself. "*Mi nombre es Rubert, Richardo. Me llamo Ruby Dix. Habla usted espanol?*" Ira shrugs his shoulders, answering with a few Spanish words. "*Un poquito. Habla usted ingles?*"

Ruby takes his two pointer fingers and places them an inch apart then he holds them up in front of Ira's face. "Little big," he says in English.

"Little big," Ira, repeats and can't help but chuckle at Ruby; it's the first time he has laughed in many months. He holds up his fingers, imitating Ruby. "Little *bit*. You mean, little *bit*," he says, emphasizing the "t."

Ruby smiles and repeats, "Little bit-taa." He tussles Ira's hair and laughs. "*Esto debe ser divertido*." Then he gestures to Ira with his hands, indicating food and sleep.

The gestures for food and sleep Ira understands well, it's all that's been on his mind for weeks. Ira smiles wide and introduces himself, "*Me llamo Ira*." He accepts the invitation by nodding.

Ruby smiles and repeats Ira's name, then he puts his hand on his back and points his shepherd's pole west.

Ira almost immediately feels as if he has known Ruby Dix forever. For the first time since his grandpa died, aside from Rocko, of course, he feels like he has a friend. He's a tad worried about the language barrier, though, but he figures he can teach Ruby more English and Ruby can teach him more Spanish. Ira feels safe as they walk side by side, another feeling he has not felt in a long time. His steps are light, his breathing is easy and he is thankful to the Great Spirit for sending Ruby Dix his way. *Maybe*, he thinks, Ruby is the one who is meant to have the eagle feather, but he decides he won't try to communicate that just yet.

Ruby and Ira walk with the herd to a secluded community that's close to the coastline, a community called Suelo Banya. As they walk they communicate the best they can. Ira points to the animals with a perplexed expression. Ruby tells him they are goats, "*cabras*," then he points to the black one and tells Ira its name is Poncho, "*el lide*r," the leader. He also teaches him how to say house, supper, dog, wife and daughter, in Spanish.

Ruby is surprised how quick Ira learns. Ira is surprised that Ruby has a wife and daughter, he just seems too old, perhaps it is the long beard.

They turn and pass through a stone archway onto an archaic cobblestone street. They walk downhill, passing a few *casas* on either side. None of the *casas* have any glass in the windows or doors, just openings in the walls and their floors are dirt. There is a group of children hitting a crinkled-up ball of tinfoil with sticks and two dogs that are barking and chasing alongside of them. Some older children have their arms full of wood and are heading toward something that he's never seen before.

Ira stops dead in his tracks; the scene overwhelms him. Beyond a stone fence at the end of the cobblestone street, he sees thunderous spools of green and blue-colored water pushing forward, washing up on white sand, then sloshing back into a heavy swell, only to turn, swell aloft and rush back again. Ira is amazed that it continues on and on; that it seems to have no end. Never in his wildest dreams could he ever have imagined this much water.

Ruby watches Ira's reaction with pleasure, he can tell Ira has never seen an ocean before. "*Se llama oceano.*" Ruby is anxious to learn about Ira, but he's patient and lets Ira absorb the ocean's majesty in silence.

After a while, Ira realizes that although there is big water here, there are no clusters of fruit as big as your head and as he looks around, his expression changes from splendor to worry.

Ruby notices the change and tries to gesture to Ira by opening his arms wide, "*Paso Algo?*"

It takes a long time before Ira speaks as he tries to figure out how to ask Ruby about the town that he is looking for. He decides it will be easier to ask about the fruit, so he makes a gesture with his two fingers like he did when they first met and says the word little. Then he pulls his fingers wide apart and says. "Big."

Ruby imitates him, nodding. "Big, *si grande*, big."

Then Ira gestures by pointing in his mouth.

Ruby smiles and nods in what he thinks is understanding. *"Tengo mucha hambre tambien."* He pats his stomach, makes a few eating gestures with his hands and gestures for Ira to follow him.

Ira's shoulders slump as he realizes communicating about the town and fruit that he's looking for is going to take time and effort, but on the bright side he senses food in his future. So he drops the subject for now and follows Ruby.

They walk down the hill to a casa that is close to the ocean and Ira is once again awestruck by the sloshing sound of the waves as they roll onto the sand, and also the skirl of the seagulls that soar nearby.

He helps Ruby corral the *cabras* into their pen, Poncho's the last one in. Then he follows Ruby to the house. As they walk through the doorway, Ruby's wife turns around, surprised to see a scrawny boy with a braided cord of agave tied around his waist drawn tight, holding his pants up. He stands looking rather oafish in the doorway with a matching headband holding his long black hair in place along with an eagle's feather. She turns to Ruby, her expression now inquisitive and he wastes no time introducing Ira to her.

*"El nombre de el nino es Ira. Esta perdido."*

She looks back to Ira, no longer curious but shocked. *"Esta perdido? El es tan jovan!"* She indicates with her hand that Ira is small.

Again, Ira mistakes *perdido* for happy, not lost and he smiles as wide as he can and nods. "*Si, muy perdido en tu casa*," which translates as lost in her house.

The woman scrunches her eyebrows and gives Ruby a funny look. He steps closer to her and tells her that the boy doesn't speak a lot of Spanish. She puts her hands on her hips and laughing says jokingly. "*Esta bromeando, de verdad*." Then she turns around to stir some beans that are simmering on the stove.

Ira's stomach is in knots and is growling at the smell of the food. It smells so good that he's having a hard time stopping himself from running to the stove, scooping it up by the handfuls and shoving it into his mouth. He takes a deep breath through his nose and looks at Ruby, his mouth thick with saliva and his body weak and jittery.

"It smells very good." Then he rubs his tummy.

Ruby understands and translates in Spanish to his wife. She turns around to acknowledge his compliment and introduces herself. "*Hola, Ira, mi nombre es Lolita la esposa de Ruberto. De ondde eres*?" Ruby translates it for Ira, best he can.

Ira stands silent for a moment. He doesn't know how to answer this question. He doesn't have the foggiest how to explain where he came from. So he just tells her that he came from the desert. "*El desierto*."

Lolita tilts back and laughs, sets her spoon down and throws her arms out to her sides. "*El desierto. Eres un fantasma*?"

Before Ira can explain that he is not a ghost a young girl walks in from outside. She's Ruby and Lolita's daughter and Ira figures she must be about nine years old. Ira has never seen a girl so pretty and he gets a funny feeling in his stomach. He swallows hard and his cheeks feel hot.

Lolita watches as the two youngsters eyes meet, she moves to her daughter's side. She tells the surprised girl that Ira is lost and will be eating supper with them.

Ruby walks to his daughter's side also, and puts his arm around her shoulder, then looks at Ira. *"El nombre de nuestra hija es Pela."*

Both Pela and Ira look down, they focus their eyes on their feet. It feels awkward for both of them. Ruby tells Pela that Ira doesn't speak much Spanish and that after they eat will she take him to play with the other kids at *la playa*. Pela nods, but doesn't look at Ira.

During supper the conversation is light as they teach Ira some Spanish words and watch as he shovels food into his mouth at an alarming rate. Lolita scoops more onto his plate each time he cleans it and Ruby pours him more *agua*, wondering how long it has been since the young boy has had water and a good meal.

After Ira has had enough, Pela takes his hand and leads him out the door to the ocean beach, but Ira turns around and runs back into the *casa*. He begins to rub his stomach and he shouts out to Ruby and Lolita. *"Muchas gracias, por la cena."*

Lolita is impressed that he said the Spanish words properly. She smiles and says, *"No hay de qué,"* as she waves them off.

Pela and Ira walk down to the beach where the other children are building a fire, they're struggling to communicate, but then a dog comes running towards them.

Pela points to the dog, *"El nombre de el perros es Oso. El es mi perro."*

Ira bends down and tries to call the dog to him. "Hi, Oso. Come here, Oso." The dog just stands and stares. Ira is sure he can get the dog to come so he calls him again.

This time he slaps his thighs while calling his name. "Here, Oso. Come here, boy." Again the dog doesn't come. Instead it sits down with ears bent forward, and a look of confusion. Ira looks at Pela, embarrassed. He holds his hands out to his sides, shrugging his shoulders. "*Oso no habla Ingles*?"

Pela doubles over, laughing.

Ira smiles.

She looks up at him. "No, "*No, que el perro no habla ingles*." For the first time the two understand each other and it is a moment that feels very good. Ira is glad that he could make Pela laugh and he stands grinning and enjoying the moment while she giggles, holding her stomach. Then she calls out to the dog in Spanish to come to her. "*Ven aqui, Oso*." She claps her hands together.

They stand there on the beach together, petting Oso while his tongue dangles from the side of his mouth and his tail wags.

Oso takes to Ira right away and Ira realizes that learning to speak Spanish is even more important than he thought. The way things are now he can't even communicate with the dog if he doesn't learn the language and he really likes Pela and Oso.

The three of them walk closer to the water where others have built a fire and the children are playing stick ball. Pela and Ira find some sticks and join the game. Ira never knew that life could be so much fun. Even though he cannot understand most of their words, he does understand the universal pastime of playing stick ball, although the ball game he remembers playing is one where you hit the ball while it's flying through the air, not rolling on the ground. Perhaps he can teach them to play his version sometime down the road. For now, he laughs with the children when they laugh, even though he doesn't understand why and Pela does her best to help him with communicating. For the first time that Ira can remember, the world seems like a nice place.

Ira grows into his new life as well as growing into his clothes and his Spanish gets better. He still makes many mistakes, which Pela seems to enjoy because when he says something incorrectly she laughs at him. This sometimes irritates Ira but he doesn't let it show. He loves his new people. Pela has become Ira's best friend and along with Oso, who is always following closely at their heels they do everything together.

Ira has been with Ruby's family for a year and a half now and the time has passed quickly. Life is so different here compared to the Salazara Rancheria. Sure, there are chores to be done, but nothing like at Hallia's place and here there is always enough food. Ruby takes them to the fishing village every so often to sell a *cabra* and buy supplies. Even though it's a tiny village, Ira has never seen so many people selling so many things in one place. Like Ruby, others are selling goats and the smells and the sounds are very strange to him.

There are people in this seaside village from places he has never heard of, selling things he's never seen and who look very different, but he is beginning to understand more each time he comes. There are Americanos who come to the village to buy fishing supplies or to eat at the *cantina* where you pay people to bring you cooked food. There are people wearing conical hats made of straw, that Pela calls, "Orientals," selling oysters and fish.

There is *mucho pescado fresco* served in this village and Ruby tells Ira that this is a port village where most people earn their money by going out onto boats or *barcos* to catch fish to eat and sell.

Today is Ira's fourth trip to the village, and as Ruby leads them through the community he teaches Ira how to barter and exchange *dinero*. There is much to learn and he's getting worldlier by the day.

After a while Ruby tells the kids that they may explore the many colorful stands of merchandise, but as before, he's stern in his instructions to both of them, to stay away from the *callejones* because there is always danger in alleys. Before he finished speaking Pela, Ira and Oso are already on their way down the street. The two walk side-by-side, chattering up a storm, while Oso's tail wags from side to side.

Suddenly, Oso's nose lifts straight into the air and he takes off barking, darting down the street, leaping over vegetable crates and barreling through a display of bright ponchos, before turning down an alley. Ira and Pela waste no time and engage in hot pursuit, chasing him as fast as their legs can go. They don't even hear Ruby and Lolita calling to them to come back.

As they turn the corner to the alley they stop, both of them bending and holding their stomachs to catch their breath. As they look down toward the end of the alley they see a hut made of wood in front of a miniature trailer house sitting on blocks. It has a small three foot by three foot pen in front of the hut that is filled with a dozen wiggling puppies. The chubby puppies are climbing everywhere trying to reach their mother, who's tied to a post a few yards away, and there stands Oso, nose to nose with her, both of their tails wagging. Pela puts one hand to her mouth and points with the other. *"Oh, mira que lindos cachorros."*

Ira would agree that they are cute, but in his entire life he can't remember ever seeing a baby dog. He's mesmerized by the sight. He grabs Pela's hand. *"Vamos déjà ver."*

Pela pulls her hand away. *"No. Papa dijo que no callejones."*

Ira tugs Pela's arm wanting to stay just for a minute. *"Vamos solo un minuto."*

*"No, no debemos."*

Ira is persistent and he pleads with Pela. *"Si. Por favor."*

Pela stands her ground; she folds her arms and clamors. *"No!"*

Ira huffs. He's annoyed at her and he puts his face close to hers. *"Esta Bien, quedate, voy a ver a los bebes."* Ira is fixed on seeing the puppies, and doesn't care if she wants to or not. He turns and ventures toward the puppies' pen. As he approaches he sees a man talking to a thin woman next to the tiny house trailer. The woman walks to the puppies and picks one up by the scruff of its neck and carries it back to the wood hut. She hikes the puppy up, dangles it with one hand in front of the man's face, speaking in a language Ira has never heard.

The puppy whimpers and a yellow stream sprinkles onto the man's shoes. He hops away on one foot, yelling at the woman, and Ira chuckles to himself. He thinks the man must be buying a puppy for some lucky kid, maybe for his son. He thinks how much he would love to have a dog of his own someday. Maybe when he gets his first job he will save enough *dinero* and buy a puppy for himself.

Ira looks back at Pela and waves, trying to coax her into coming closer, but she won't budge. She just stands with her arms crossed and yells out to him. Come on, let's tell mama about the babies, "*Vamos a decirle a mama acerca de los bebes.*" Then in an instant the look on her face turns to panic.

Ira turns around to see what she's looking at. He watches in horror as the woman lays the puppy down on a block with one hand and raises a machete with the other. With one skilled whack she lobs off the whimpering puppy's head. She then picks the puppy up by the back legs, tosses the head to the side and holds its body above a bowl to let the blood drain out of its neck into it. She grabs a brown sack, wraps the puppy up in it, and hands the package to the man. In exchange the man hands her a few coins.

Ira is horrified. He can't believe his eyes, then he flashes back to the vision he had long ago of the woman at the ocean with the bowl and the blood. After a few minutes he turns to look at Pela but she's not there. He searches the alley, twirling in every direction. She's nowhere to be found. She must have gotten scared and run back to her mother. Good, he thinks, she'll be safe, but he is still panicked and afraid for Oso so he calls to the dog with an inflexible tone.

"*Ven, Oso, Ven.*" The dog doesn't move. Ira is torn between going to get the dog and the danger that might be lurking down the alley. He calls again, clapping his hands and slapping his thighs in a dictatorial manner, but Oso stays with the female dog. Ira turns back again to look for Pela, hoping she has brought Lolita and Ruby back with her, but she's not there. He continues to call for Oso to come.

At that moment, the woman with the machete looks toward Ira. She yells something at him and begins waving the machete in the air. Ira is frightened, he wishes he had listened to Pela. The woman begins to run toward him waving the machete. Ira can't wait any longer. He thought they would kill Oso, so without another thought he runs at a dead sprint to collect the dog. The woman is hysterical and yelling, now pointing the machete straight at him as she runs. Ira is scared but he knows if he doesn't get to Oso she will kill him, so he keeps running. The woman is getting closer to him, she has a crazed look in her eyes and she's screaming something that he can't understand. She says it again and again while waving that shiny blade. As they get closer to one another, Ira thinks he may have to knock her down to save Oso, and himself. He hates to do that to such an old woman, thinking back to what he did to Hallia, but what else can he do? So as he runs he makes a plan to tackle her ankles and roll away from the machete as fast as he can.

Just then, the man with the butchered puppy drops the package and begins running at him, too. Now it's two against one; how did he get in this mess? He won't stop now, though, he has to save Oso. He knows once the man reaches him he'll get a beating or worse. The man starts to yell and points at Ira. Should he turn and run away, try to find Ruby, Lolita, but if he does that they will kill Oso before he gets back. "No!" he shouts, "I will fight for Oso. You leave him alone! Do you hear me, leave him alone!"

The man passes the woman in a dead run and reaches Ira first. Ira closes his fist ready to swing, but the man doesn't clobber Ira like he expects, instead he keeps running past him toward an old shabby building. The man is hollering and shaking his fist with the petite old woman running close behind him.

Ira is surprised that they pass him up, but he sees it as his chance to grab Oso and get away. So he runs to the dog and takes hold of his collar; as he pulls at Oso he realizes this is his chance to set all the dogs free. He lets go of Oso and seizes the rope around the mother dog's neck, and works at untying the knot while watching as the two run into the vacant building. Then he hurries to the puppy pen and knocks one of the walls down. The puppies scatter, waddling to their mother and she whimpers while licking them one by one. Oso stands, wagging his tail, as Ira tries to shoo the dogs and coax them to run.

He grabs Oso's collar again and starts dragging him down the alley, hoping the man and woman stay inside the building until he gets past. He wonders if one of them lives in that old rickety structure and why they ran there so fast. It must be because they don't want anyone to know what they do to puppies. Ira feels a twinge of guilt about turning the woman's dogs loose but he felt worse for the dogs.

Just as he thinks that he'll make it past the building without incident, Oso's nose once again lifts into the air. The dog yanks himself free and runs to the old building, barking. "*Maldito*!" Ira mutters, he can't believe he just let Oso get away. He calls for the dog to come but the dog stops, turns around, and starts barking at him in a drastic manner as if he were trying to tell him something.

Ira recognizes that Oso's mood has changed, the dog is stressed and tormented. Ira walks toward the dog, trying to grab hold of him, but every time he gets close to Oso, the dog turns and runs away, then he sits down and barks in dismay.

Ira doesn't want to go into the building where the old woman and man went but Oso seems to want to go there. He calls out to the dog to come again, but this time Oso runs into the building. Ira stands and watches, helpless to stop him, as Oso disappears. He is torn between going in after the dog and running to find Ruby. He decides to go in after Oso.

As Ira approaches the door of the old building he can see inside. There is shouting and a scuffle is going on, and there are more people than just the old woman and man in there. Ira stands on his tippy toes in the doorway, leaning from side to side, trying to see what's going on and trying to spot Oso. There are five people in all, three men, the old woman, and someone lying on the ground but he only catches a glimpse of the person's feet for a split second.

It's utter chaos inside the building with arms swinging, machetes and knives flying and the dog barking wildly. A crowd is beginning to form outside the door behind Ira. In a fast and furious fashion two of the men inside scurry to a broken window and climb out. Another man scales the window and chases after them. Ira sees the old woman fall to her knees alongside the person on the ground. For a moment Ira wonders why Pela is lying there with her pale blue dress all messed up, when she's supposed to be with her mother and father.

Then reality hits him and everything changes to slow motion. He runs toward her and it feels as though he has lead in his shoes, almost as if she's a thousand miles away. He makes it to her side after what seems like an eternity and kneels down next to her. He straightens her dress and lifts her body close to his. She's been stabbed multiple times and her face has been slashed. He holds her, rocking back and forth, telling her everything is going to be okay, her warm but faint breath on his cheek. Then he notices her dress is sticky, soaked in blood and turning crimson red like his vision. Ira begins to yell out her name but she doesn't stir. He gently shakes her, crying, and repeating her name; she doesn't answer. Then he watches as Pela's chest rises one last time and she ceases to breathe.

Ira holds her and weeps bitter tears that sting his eyes and burn his cheeks. He can't believe Pela is dead; it doesn't seem real. He has never felt such anguish and despair in his entire life.

Ira kneels, holding Pela close, willing with all his might for her to awaken. Then a hand touches his shoulder from behind. It is Ruby, he pries Ira away from her. Ira looks up at Ruby, whose eyes are red and glazed. Lolita stands behind Ruby, two people from the crowd holding her up. Both parents are beside themselves with grief and as they kneel down at Pela's side, tears stream from their eyes.

Ira feels as though his heart is being carved out of his chest as he watches Ruby and Lolita slump over their baby girl's body, they weep, moan, and lament without cessation or restraint.

The crowd stands and stares in silence with pity, thankful that it isn't their child lying dead.

Oso is by Pela's side, too. He stands alongside Pela with his tail tucked between his legs, nudging her with his nose. He licks at her face, trying to wake her up, then sits down and whimpers, looking lost and helpless.

Ira's chin drops to his chest and he covers his eyes with both hands; after spending every waking minute for the last year and a half with Pela, he realizes she is gone forever.

Forty minutes pass before a police car turns into the alley. Not because nobody cared enough to call, but because there were no telephones nearby. It takes almost an hour before an ambulance arrives. The attendants cover Pela up, put her on a stretcher, and slide her into the ambulance. The officer takes down some names and information and that is the last time Ira ever sees his best friend.

Three days later, early in the afternoon, Ira walks along, leading a slow procession with Lolita and Ruby to a tiny cemetery on the hill behind Ruby's rancheria. There's about seventy-five people walking behind; in essence, the entire village of Sulo Banya. The women, dressed in gray, carry arms full of colorful flowers that they pick on their way to the grave. The smell of flowers clogs Ira's already stuffed-up nose. A small band of musicians play music, making his temples throb even harder. When they reach the gravesite, a man lowers Pela's small wooden casket into the ground with a rope. One by one the people throw heavy spades full of dirt and flowers into the grave until the last shovelful is thrown on top of her. Ira stands numb, drained of life, his head and shoulders slumped with such grief that it appears he wants to crawl into the grave with her. Ruby and Lolita are so weak they fall to their knees, sobbing in each other's arms and they remain at the grave well past sunset.

Ira continues to live with Ruby and Lolita for the next six months but all three are distant to one another. There is a lack of acceptance about Pela's death. Lolita still sets a place for her at the table. They wake up at night, crying at times and Ruby seems to get irritated with Ira about next to nothing these days, something that he's never done before. Late one night when Ira believes both Lolita and Ruby are asleep, he packs his Padres bag with the few belongings that he has and without a sound, he slips out the door.

Ruby stares at the ceiling, listening as Ira's footsteps fade, then he rolls to his side, takes a deep breath and sighs.

Ira starts walking north along the coast.

# CHAPTER SIX

## Tijuana Brass

"Absolutely not! I will not give up. That boy is still alive and I'm going to find him," Father Lelo throws his hat on the chair in Chief Dewey's office. "Is there anything else you can think of that might help lead me to him?"

Chief Dewey shuffles through his desk drawers one by one. "I can understand your dismay, but the boy has been gone from the Salazara ranch for two years now. You've been out searching for him every free moment you have and you haven't turned up one lead, not one." He pulls out a photograph and holds it up. "With all due respect, Father, I don't think this snapshot of the boy when he was four is going to help, I almost threw it out a couple times, but here you go." He hands an old Polaroid to Father Lelo. "My secretary Cheryl snapped it just before I took the boy to his relatives in Mexico. He's got to be what, about twelve by now?"

Father takes the picture and stares at the tiny boy holding his duffle bag in one hand and Chief Dewey's hand in the other. He brushes the specks of dust from it, and in deep thought trails his finger along the boy's image recalling happier times, while he sticks the photo in his shirt pocket "He'll be twelve tomorrow. He's my responsibility. He was left in my custody and I'm going to keep searching."

Chief Dewey mumbles. "I have my doubts,"

Father Lelo interrupts, squaring his shoulders and lifting his chin. "Doubts about what, Dewey?"

"Well, it's just that, you know, he's illegitimate. His mother was a whore." Father Lelo scowls at Dewey. Dewey continues. "Well, what I mean is, it's an unstable, rough country down there, that's all. With all the drug cartels and smuggling going on, I just think that"

Father Lelo interrupts again. "What, Dewey, what is it that you think? You think he's a drug dealer? Or a smuggler? Or maybe he's a twelve-year-old pimp by now."

Chief Dewey huffs, then shuffles through some papers on his desk.

Father Lelo points his finger at him. "You don't have proof of any of this nonsense. I don't subscribe to the gossip theories about Raina and I'm certain her boy is a good boy. He's a child for mercy's sake, you should never have sent him out of this country in the first place. I'm going to keep looking for him and I expect to find him alive." Father Lelo picks up his hat and puts it on, "Good day, Chief," he turns for the door, "Thanks for the picture." He walks down the hall with quick long strides.

Dewey catches up, follows him out to the steps, "Father, I didn't mean any disrespect." Father Lelo keeps walking, Dewey continues, "I should mention," he pauses. This stops Father Lelo in his tracks, he turns around waiting for Dewey to continue, "I drove down to Mexico to check on the boy a few times and there is something that comes to mind, not sure its of any consequence though."

"What is it?"

"The last time that I went down there, Anthony Cureo was talking to his mother Hallia about the new vineyards cropping up along the coast; he said there was work for people there and at a good wage. The kid, I mean, Ira, was a tad older then and seemed to be listening pretty close. It's just a stab in the dark, a long shot at best, but maybe it's somewhere to start."

Father Lelo tips his hat and gives Dewey a nod. "I'll check it out."

"Good luck, Father, and if there's anything else I can do, just let me know."

Father Lelo, still upset with Chief Dewey's handling of the whole affair, slams the door of his truck, starts it up, and rolls away. As he drives he thinks about the whole situation and remembers the odd shaped brown package, the gift from Bahrain that he mailed to Ira many years ago. He pulls it out of the glove compartment. He stops the truck at the gas station at the end of the village and while the tank is filling up, he unwraps the parcel. He stares at the carving, recapturing the moment he bought the gift.

He had found the zebra carved from teakwood while he was stationed in the Kingdom of Bahrain on the streets of Saar, at their yearly heritage festival. He watched the woman place the finishing touches on the carving and he thought it would fascinate a three-year-old to see a horse with black-and-white stripes. But above that reason, he found it fascinating that a woman with a swollen red bruise around her eye, no doubt a gift of her husband's affection, living in a country where zebras were not indigenous, had carved it and painted it, while most people were weaving souvenir baskets or floor mats made of palm fronds and firing pottery in ancient kilns. He admired that a woman with no means and so few rights was broadminded and courageous enough to think outside of her country, if only in her mind. He bought the carving for the most part because it inspired him to ponder in depth on the subject of human rights and to think of a world void of oppression, a world where everyone was allowed to become the person God meant them to be.

There were so many things he wanted to teach Ira back then, things he still wants to teach him. He would like to build confidence in him, give him some worldly experience and give him a good education so that he might rise above poverty like his mother was trying to do.

He thinks about Raina and how much potential she had, about her compassion, ingenuity, and understanding of medicine, both modern and ancient, about the solutions and cures that might have been if she had not been killed before she could graduate from medical school and pursue her career.

Father Lelo's thoughts drift back to the vision he had at the Salazara ranch, the woman holding the stick with a red tip and pointing it west. The vision was flimsy at best, a vision frocked in a rolling white mist, yet even without a face he was sure the figure in the mist was Raina.

What if it weren't just a mirage, what if there was something more to it? Father Lelo pulls out his map of Baja California, and inadvertently sets the carved zebra figurine down on top of the word Tijuana. For a long moment he stares at the zebra as though he's entranced, his palms become clammy, and he senses a slight feeling of encouragement, maybe this is where I should start he thinks, but then dismisses the impulse. Tijuana is not exactly known for its vineyards. He puts his finger on Tecate instead, and traces the map south along Highway 3, then on to Highway 1, to the checkpoint at Guerrero Negro. He decides he will scout every vineyard and settlement along the coast from Tecate to Guerrero and back up to the U.S. border until he finds the boy. He knows that given his limited time to search it'll take months, but it was a good way to start.

Ira is fortunate to hitch a ride after leaving Ruby's in the wee hours of the morning by flagging down an old truck. The owner is on his way to Tijuana. He hops in the pickup's bed which is overflowing with squash, zucchini, corn, and beans. He rides along in silence, the wind blowing his hair. He doesn't have a plan. He just knows that he had to leave Ruby's place, the memory of Pela's face and the guilt he felt for Pela's death were tearing him apart. Though Ruby and Lolita never cast an accusing eye at him, his relationship with them had become strained.

Pela's death has changed him. He no longer feels that surviving in this world is a guarantee, rather he now feels burdened all the time, like there's a heavy net of agave stalks on his back that he just can't get rid of. He's hoping that moving on and away from the memories of Pela will help to alleviate some of that weight.

As they near the city the man driving the truck hollers out the back to Ira, "*Tijuana es una ciudad grande, ten cuidado.*" He knows it's dangerous for him to be in a large city alone, but Ira believes a large city is just what he needs to dull the pain of his battered mind. A good-paying job with lots of physical labor should do the trick. Maybe one day he will have enough money to buy his way into the United States of America, a place where Anthony told him that, "Life is like a beautiful dream." Nobody has ever bothered to tell Ira that he is already a U.S. citizen. Nobody has ever bothered to tell him anything about who he is or where he comes from, except that his mother was a whore and was found dead alongside a couple of dead thugs. He doesn't even know that the next day is his twelfth birthday.

The driver turns the corner and Ira rides into Tijuana with his nose in the air like a Labrador Retriever. Standing on top of a sack of squash, swaying with every movement of the truck, he takes in the sights. He has never seen the likes of such a city, the smells, sights, sounds and the high and multi-colored *edificios* have Ira's head whirling. The truck rolls to a stop at the curb next to one of the high buildings and Ira hops off the bed, grabs his duffle bag, and waves, yelling out to the driver, "*Gracias, adios*."

The driver sticks his arm out the window and yells back as he pulls away. "*Ten cuidado*." Ira does not need the caution to be careful, he has learned the hard way.

The city is noisy and congested, filled with exhaust fumes, pedestrians, cabs, carts and people. He walks past the wooden stands overflowing with shirts, statues, flags, flowers, ponchos and guitars. It appears that anything you want, you can buy in this city. To him it's almost overwhelming. Ira looks down near his feet. A painting of a naked couple intertwined on black velvet is displayed on the sidewalk. He doesn't know why, but his face feels warm and flush and he hastily moves past the painting.

As Ira strolls along, taking in the scenery, something stops him dead in his tracks. Standing in front of him hitched to a carnival cart is a petite donkey painted with black-and-white stripes. Ira feels his mind pull away, for a moment he's entranced as he stares at the black and white striped animal. Memories of early childhood stream through his mind, illuminating his past and then an impulse pulls his eyes down to his now clammy hands.

*A random collage like a black-and-white cinema picture travels across his palm. His grandfather, grandmother, and his mother carrying his duffle bag transpire then meld together forming the likeness of a zebra. As he stands, staring at the zebra in his palm, an image of a tall man clothed in black appears next to it, then in a mystic way the man splits into two; appearing as both an apparition, and a physical being. The apparition stares at Ira, while his corporal eyes stare at the zebra.* Ira is caught up in a revelation he does not understand.

*A dense white mist drifts through the street; it swirls and forms a cloud around the hitched donkey. The once vivid black-and-white stripes on the donkey are obscured. All Ira can see is a vague silhouette growing larger and taller. Then the cloud thins and standing in front of him is a regal stallion of pure white. A thick outline of red paint encircles one of its eyes. A woman with long, jet black hair, clothed in brilliant turquoise sits on its back. In her right hand she carries a spear that's dripping with blood from the tip. The mist swirls above the maiden's head, turning her hair to the palest of amber. Drops of blood from the spear land on the stallion's back, a cloud of steam roils up from the splatter. The maiden breaks apart, emerging into two figures, out from her chest flows a shirtless man who mounts in front of her. His skin, a creamy brown reveals the shimmer of a pallid scar resting on his shoulder in the unmistakable shape of an eagle's feather. The scar materializes: The feather becomes a quiver, arrows sprout forth from the top of it. The horse rears up and digs its hooves into a stormy sky. A thunder bolt flashes in the stallion's eyes; his nostrils flare as he whinnies and snorts. He stamps the ground, then charges forward. Then heavy mist spirals around and carries the vision away.*

The sound of brass instruments spilling into the streets stirs Ira's consciousness. He closes his eyes, trying to recapture the vision. But when he opens them he's left staring at a black-and-white painted donkey. He is unable to forget this vision. It had no beginning, or ending, only a picture of what seemed a true event in between and for the first time since his visions started, it was not about his mother. Or, he doesn't think it is about his mother. He reaches down, unzips his duffle bag, and stares at the eagle feather he found in the desert.

After a few moments the remnants of the sensation fade and once again his consciousness is in the real world. He puts the feather back into his duffel bag and begins to move on down the street. After walking a few blocks he stops again, this time to watch as a couple dressed in the fanciest clothes he's ever seen, say, *"Que hago,"* and exchange rings in front of a padre and a multitude of guests. Then the people begin to cheer, and the band begins to play, while the enticing aromas of chorizo sausage, beans, and tortillas, drifting through the streets make his empty stomach growl.

Ira continues down the sidewalk, then turns the corner and unintentionally enters into a red-light district.

The street sleeps in the bright mid-morning sun. None of the neon signs are flashing and what pallid life there is, is from owners throwing buckets of bleach water onto the sidewalk in front of their night clubs. Although Ira is very intelligent there are things he has never been taught and in his mind, he's found a nice quiet avenue.

A man wearing a colorful poncho and sombrero standing across the street notices the young boy standing alone. The stranger senses vulnerability and decides to cross the street to talk to Ira.

*"Hola, hijo, estas perdido?"*

Ira stops walking and looks up, the sun is in his eyes so he blinks, then squints. He tries to focus, but all he sees is the shadow of the sombrero, and a wide set of teeth grinning at him.

*"Usted necesita un amigo? Ese soy yo."*

Ira doesn't answer, he moves to walk past the man, but the man speaks up again, this time in English.

"What's wrong, you don't speak Spanish?"

Ira stops and relaxes a bit; he turns around. "I speak both English and Kumeyaay, and pretty good Spanish too. And no, I am not lost and I do not need a friend."

Now the stranger's expression changes and he believes that this is a boy who might be missed by someone. "You visiting here with your kin, son?"

Ira avoids the stranger's eyes, he looks at the ground.

This is one of the signs the stranger needs to tell him just how vulnerable Ira is. Ira's body language shows no assertion and the stranger believes he must be in the city alone. He introduces himself. "My name is Diego. I was given the name because my father was from San Diego. You know of the city called San Diego, right?"

Ira draws a blank, he's never heard of it, then he answers. "No, but I know about the city called Vineyard where clusters of fruit grow the size of your head."

Diego laughs and lifts the brim of his sombrero, he finds the boy amusing. He begins to ask Ira friendly questions concerning his wellbeing. Ira is in need of such companionship, he's deprived of someone who cares, so he pours out his life like water from a rain spout. As they walk, Ira tells Diego why he speaks English and begins to tell of his childhood at Grandma Hallia's place, not mentioning his mother, of course, not at first. But then as Diego's friendly and calming voice continues, Ira begins to confide in him. He tells him about the one thing he was ever taught about his mother. That she was a whore who left him with his grandparents when he was three and got herself killed by drug dealers. He told him that he never knew his father but that his grandpa died of a heart attack after they found his mother dead and his Gramosa just up and disappeared, that's when he was sent to Grandma Hallia's.

Ira carries on about how poor they were and how lonely and hungry he was all the time. He tells Diego how the family killed his friend, Rocko, a dog that he grew to love. How they tricked him into eating the dog to keep from starving. And how he left that rancheria that day for good. Then he told Diego about walking alone through the desert and how he survived with almost no food or drink and about how exhausted he became and finished by telling Diego how he was almost bitten by a rattlesnake.

Diego listens without interruption, Ira continues by telling him the sad story about the woman selling puppies and how his best friend Pela's death was his fault. Even after six months, he cannot hold his tears back when he thinks about her.

Diego achieves what he set out to do, he has motivated Ira to open up and confide about his life.

"It helps for one to know just how destitute they are, because then they can start to heal." Diego tells Ira. Then with solace in his eyes, Diego tells him he deserves a good meal and a safe warm bed to sleep in. He touches Ira's shoulder with a gentle hand. "I insist that you stay with me for the night. Then if you decide to stay longer, I will give you a job cleaning in my club, you don't have to go to Vineyard."

When Diego touches his back, Ira stiffens. He closes his eyes and for a moment time stands still. *A cloud of mist forms, he sees his mother's face. A searing pain pierces his shoulder. Her voice echoes his name then vanishes, disappearing into a cloud.* As Ira snaps out of it, he blinks away his tears to find Diego's face an inch from his nose while shaking Ira's shoulder.

"What's wrong boy, you see a ghost?" He pats Ira's head and straightens himself. "Didn't mean to make you cry, boy. C'mon, I'll show you where you'll be staying."

Ira is sick of the pain that his mother causes and he is glad the vision disappeared. When Diego shakes his shoulder again he accepts Diego's offer in hopes that it will free him from her torments for good. He rubs the back of his shoulder and follows Diego to a car. He slides into the back seat and the driver takes them to Diego's house. Ira's intention is to stay with Diego for a short while, just long enough to earn some money. Then he'll set out to find Vineyard.

As they approach the house, Ira can't believe his eyes. He sees the biggest, most beautiful house he has ever seen. It's surrounded by a tall stone fence teeming with thick foliage. Two men stand guard beneath an old arched gateway made of stone. Diego gives them a command with a wave of his hand and they push open the heavy, wrought-iron gate. Lofty stone archways line a brick path and giant potted plants lead to a colorful, mosaic-tiled bar with a waterfall behind, and tall wrought-iron chairs in front of. It's a beautiful receiving area for guests. Diego leads Ira inside and in Ira's eyes the inside of the house is exquisite. It is surrounded by a lush potted herb garden, refreshing fountains, and it's the first house that Ira has ever seen with giant glass windows, enormous heavy doors of wood, and floors that are not dirt, but covered with rich Spanish tile.

Diego secures an alarm system on the wall then orders a woman servant to bring lunch along with some *limonada.* He leads Ira to a colorful floral garden with a white marble table next to a trickling fountain and invites him to sit on one of its curved marble benches. Diego disappears and the woman emerges from the kitchen and sets a plate and glass in front of Ira. Two men stand watching as he devours a golden brown empanada, stuffed with chicken and vegetables, served with fresh salsa and guacamole, he washes it down with the lemonade. For the first time since Pela's death, Ira feels like it's all going to be okay. Then Diego comes back with a bottle of wine and two goblets.

"Have you ever tasted red wine? This is the best that France has to offer." He pulls the cork and takes a whiff from the top of the bottle. He pours some into each of the goblets and swirls the crimson liquid around.

The servant comes back to clear Ira's plate and Diego gives her an order in Spanish, *"Traenos pastel."* He sets the glasses down and waves her off.

"Got to let it breathe for a minute or two, son, then you're in for a real treat. I can teach you everything there is to know about wine."

Ira has never seen wine in fancy goblets, he stares at the beautiful etched crystal. "I've never seen that drink. What is it?"

"Nectar of the gods, son, nectar of the gods."

Ira vaguely remembers that God has something to do with heaven, though how he knows that he can't explain "Are we in heaven?"

Diego laughs at Ira and gives him a wink, "Yes, my heaven. It all belongs to me." He lifts his goblet and motions for Ira to do the same, then takes a sip.

Ira swallows the wine and immediately bursts into an uncontrollable cough. The drink is not what he expected, nothing like anything he has ever had to drink before.

Diego pats him on the back. "Drink up, you'll get used to it and you'll like it, I promise. Just give it a minute or two and it'll warm you from the inside out."

The servant returns with two elegant silver plates sprinkled with powdered sugar and garnished with a mint leaf. In the center is a personal sized pineapple cake, topped with coconut rum frosting, sprinkled with bits of toasted coconut, then crowned with fresh whipped cream and a cherry. Ira has never seen anything like this dessert before. He starts to feel his entire body relax, every muscle feels light yet also heavy. He devours his cake and drinks more wine. Soon Ira becomes intoxicated from the wine and sugar. He becomes very sleepy and Diego has the maid take him up to a bedroom. Ira soon feels right at home.

A few weeks pass. Diego makes it easy for Ira to adapt to his lifestyle and now he has everything he needs. He doesn't have to be hungry all day or struggle for food. When he's not with Diego at the shooting range for target practice, he spends his days exploring the house and grounds, with servants waiting on him, bringing him food and drink to his heart's content. He even has his own private bathroom with a toilet that flushes. It's a stark contrast to the outhouse at Hallia's place. Ira closes his eyes, thinking about how his life has changed. He never even thinks about leaving for Vineyard anymore and every night he drifts off to sleep worry free, safe, and content, although he has noticed a recent and negative change in Diego's attitude.

Early in the wee hours one Saturday morning, Diego slips into Ira's room carrying a bag. In the moonlight cascading from the window, he watches Ira's chest rise then fall in a smooth sustained rhythm for a few minutes. He then moves closer and sets the bag down on the bed. He has plans for this boy and he decides it's time to set things in motion.

Ira opens his eyes and he blinks, startled to find Diego looking down at him, his expression sober and edgy. Ira sits up in an instant. He's sleepy, uncertain, and troubled. He rubs his eyes, wiping the sleep. It's still dark and he wonders why Diego is standing by his bed. There's something about this situation that for the first time makes Ira feel uneasy with Diego. After a few uncomfortable moments of silence, Ira speaks. "What are you doing here?"

This seems to perturb Diego. "I live here, this is my house. The question is. What are you doing here? We know that you're not doing anything to earn your keep."

Ira lowers his chin, avoiding Diego's glare. He doesn't know what to say. Diego's rapid change of character renders Ira speechless.

Diego unbuckles his belt, then he slides it out of the loops of his pants.

Ira's eyes grow wide and he stiffens. Diego's eyes are filled with menace and in one quick move, he lifts the belt and strikes Ira with it.

Ira flinches as the strap hits the side of his face. Then Diego lets go of the belt, and it lands in Ira's lap.

"You stopped wearing your agave rope that holds your pants up. You're getting fat on my food and now you got my belt, too. You act like you own the place." He sneers, then picks up the bag with a new pair of work pants in it and he tosses it at Ira, "So dress like it. Put some work pants on. Get up now, you're gonna start working off what you owe me."

Ira's never been lazy, he has always worked hard at everything he has ever done. It's just that before this Diego has never asked him to do anything. He looks at Diego confused. "What do you want me to do?"

Diego curls his lips, then snaps back at him. "After all I've done for you, and you talk to me that way? You ungrateful punk, get your lazy ass out of bed, you'll start working it off today." Diego turns to leave the room, then stops at the door. "Get dressed and get downstairs, you got two minutes." He slams the door behind him.

Ira is caught off guard. He has never seen this side of Diego before. Something must have happened to set him off. Maybe one of the servants did something bad. He decides that he'll work extra hard at doing whatever it takes to please Diego today, so that things can get back to the way they were.

When Ira arrives downstairs at the breakfast table, the table is set in a formal manner and Diego seems to be fine. He acts as if nothing's happened. When the servant comes in to bring Ira his breakfast, Ira notices that Diego is almost finished with his. This surprises him since they've always eaten together. He sits down without mentioning it and begins to eat.

Diego stares at him for a moment. "Your new pants and belt fit okay, boy?"

Ira nods and continues to eat.

"You like 'em?"

Ira nods again, afraid to say anything.

"Wouldn't have guessed it, since you didn't thank me, but then, you've never thanked me for anything. An ingrate, I guess that's what you are, an ingrate."

Ira looks up at Diego through baffled and timid eyes. "Thank you."

"You know it doesn't mean much if you gotta pry it outta someone." Diego pushes his plate away and stands up, "You hurt my feelings, boy. I don't know anyone else who'd treat someone like you better than I have."

"Nobody has. I'm sorry, Diego." Ira hopes he can change Diego's bad mood with a compliment. "This is the best house in the world and you're the best man in the world."

"It's too late, boy, just finish your food." Then his voice softens. "I'm taking you to one of my clubs today. You gotta start doing some work. A man works for a living and you're a man, right? You wanna job, don't you?"

Ira nods.

"Good, then finish up."

As they drive along Ira tries the best he can to lighten Diego's mood by chattering about everything from the weather to the amount of people out today, but Diego isn't talking much.

They round the corner and enter the street where he first met Diego and stop in front of a nightclub with two men standing outside the door. Diego gets out and motions for the two men to come to the car. He opens the door and lets Ira out of the back seat. He tells the men that this is the new person who starts working here today. The henchmen nod, Diego gets back into the car and rolls down the window. "Teach him well." He taps the roof of the car with his hand and the driver takes off.

Ira stands watching Diego leave, confused as to why he left so fast without explaining anything and not even saying goodbye. Ira's been sheltered by Diego's companionship for weeks and is now dazed that everything has changed.

The pair of men usher Ira inside Diego's club. What a contrast to the beautiful house that Ira just left. The club is dingy and dirty and stinks of smoke and stale booze. Oh, well, he thinks, at least it's just during the day, then he can go back to the comfort of home.

Once they're inside the club, one of the men introduces himself, "I'm Cruze and this here's Taco." Ira smiles and tries to shake Taco's hand, but Cruze steps in between them and gives Ira an abrupt rundown of his situation.

"Don't bother talking to him unless you speak Spanish, 'cause he don't speak no English. He's under me so he does what I tell 'im to do. His brain is fried, that's why we call him Taco. Too much nose candy too young, so he's a bit crazy. He don't say much, but if he gets pissed, watch out."

Ira has no idea what nose candy is, and just stands there with a blank stare.

Cruze immediately begins to ridicule Ira, calling him stupid and making a couple of nasty jokes about him being Indian. Then he grabs Ira by the back of his collar and pulls it so tight that it makes him gag, "This is where we gonna start." He shoves Ira's head into a can of garbage, "I hear you're the son of a whore and you've been mooching off'n Diego for the past few weeks without doing any work." He pulls Ira's head back out of the can and looks him up and down, "Hell, I bet you ain't paid him for that brand new belt and pants your wearing yet, didja? It's gonna take you a lifetime to work off what you owe him, you lazy dirtball. From now on you'll stay here at the club. We got a room that's just your style right upstairs here. It's made especially for lazy dirtballs. Now go through that trash. Make sure that it is all garbage."

Ira stands petrified, at a complete loss, he can't believe what's happening.

Cruze and Taco don't leave his side for one minute throughout the rest of the day. After everything is done downstairs in the barroom, they force him to start cleaning the rooms above the club which is one of Diego's several brothels.

The rooms are filthy, some have puke and pee on the floor, and sometimes there's blood or feces on the mattresses, sometimes both. After spending his first day cleaning up from the night before, Cruze and Taco take him to a room no bigger than a walk-in closet for the night. Cruze shoves him in and after they leave they lock the door from the outside. Ira is bewildered, it's all happened so fast that it seems like a bad dream. His mind whirls out of control. He's been through some bad stuff, but nothing like this. As he looks around, he sees nothing except a bare twin mattress on the floor and one ragged blanket. He'd rather be out in the desert alone.

Ira sits in the tiny room for what seems like hours. He has never been to school, but he's smart enough to realize that this is wrong. He's been locked away like a criminal, but he hasn't committed a crime. He needs to talk to Diego, to apologize again for not being thankful enough and to tell him that he will work harder than anyone if he just gives him another chance to come back to his house to live. He hears the lock turn and Taco pushes the door open with his foot. He sets a paper plate of refried beans and a tortilla down on the floor along with a plastic cup of water, then closes the door and locks it. Ira ignores the food and water, he's too miserable to eat. There's nothing else to do but lie down, curl up with the blanket, and drift off to sleep.

The door slams shut and Ira springs up, he's sweating and his head is throbbing. He looks around, hoping that it was all a dream, but the only thing that is different is that the plate and cup are gone. The room is stale, his throat is dry and he wishes he had drunk some of the water or at least put it in his thermos. Then it dawns on him. His thermos is in his duffle bag and his duffle bag is in the closet at Diego's house. Everything he owns is in that bag. It isn't much, but it links him to his people, his past and to who he is. It's like his foundation. He has to get back to Diego's house. He lies back down, staring at the ceiling as he waits for someone to come. The hours pass by and he has plenty of time to think.

At dawn, the door opens and Taco fills its frame. He motions his hand at Ira to follow him. He gives Ira a few pieces of toilet paper and a frayed old towel then leads him to a bathroom with a toilet and a sink, and he stands outside the door waiting for Ira to finish his morning business. After a few minutes he starts banging on the door.

*"Date prisa, acelerale ahora!"*

Ira rushes to emerge and they put him to work doing whatever needs to be done, working for fourteen days straight. Every day is the same routine, except Taco seems to start banging every day a bit earlier until Ira gets accustomed to having just three or four minutes to do everything he needs to do in the morning. Day after day they condition Ira like he's one of Pavlov's dogs. After a couple weeks and a few beatings, Ira learns to live by their exact timeline and their exact rules.

When they first locked Ira away and turned him into a slave, Ira tried to get them to let him talk to Diego, but Cruze sneered, telling him, "Diego thinks you ran away, you stupid fool, he thinks you hate him, because that's what we told him. So don't even begin to think he's gonna ride in and rescue you."

Six months pass and Cruze and Taco still haven't let Ira out of their sight. They lock him in his room every night with a meager ration of food and a cup of water. They remind him every day that if he ever tries to leave, they will find him and torture him to death.

Ira has become their personal slave. He starts his day by shining their shoes while they laugh and spit on him. Then he cleans, scrubs, scours, hauls garbage, and stocks booze all day long. The last thing that he has to do at the end of every day is to dig through every piece of garbage in the trash bin. He's been instructed to look for money or notes or anything suspicious, but he's beginning to believe that it's just another way to make him feel bad about himself, because he never finds anything.

Every night Ira thinks about the life he had with Diego, and vows he will someday see him again. He will tell Diego what these men have done to him and Diego will turn them into to the police for punishment. Then Diego will bring him back to his house and shower him with beautiful food and let him live in comfortable surroundings again and Ira won't ever have to work in a dirty job as long as he lives.

Another four months go by and one day as Ira is washing glasses behind the bar he overhears Taco talking to Cruze in Spanish. They're trying to get a tired old ice machine back up and running, and Ira's within earshot. Ira had not spoken to Cruze very much and when he did it was in English, so neither Taco nor Cruze knows he understands and speaks pretty good Spanish thanks to Pela.

Ira has learned a lot about Taco, he learned that Taco doesn't get paid in money. That he had an absent father and that his mother was forced into prostitution to feed him and his younger sister. Diego bought his mother and his sister was sent away when she was seven. His mother watched, helpless, crying and begging Diego not to sell her, but Diego didn't care how much she begged. Taco was forced to work hard every day to be able to stay with his mother, who is now one of Diego's servants.

He also hears them discussing Diego's plans for him. Taco and Cruze reveal that Diego plans to turn Ira into a smuggler, not of drugs, but because he is so good-looking, into kidnapping and smuggling young girls.

Ira is fuming. Besides Diego's horrifying plan to start slave trafficking, it is clear that Diego has included Ira in his plans which means Diego's known all along that he didn't run away, so Diego must know how he's being treated. Blood rises to his face, hot and burning, prickling his skin. It takes all he's got to stop himself from hurling a glass into the side of their heads. He can't ever remember being so angry. He manages to hide it, though, and stay low key. He's been through a lot in his life and he'll get out of this. He has no reason to doubt these men are capable of murder, so he has to be careful.

As Ira dunks a glass to rinse it, *steam begins to rise and it roils round the sink; a thick cloud of it hovers about his hands. His mother appears, her face framed by a rectangular window. She reaches through and stirs the water with a stick. A tall man dressed in black appears; he holds the duffle bag in the air, wine spills out and pours to the ground. The water turns red and a feather floats to the surface.*

"Ouch!" Ira breaks the glass and cuts himself. A tinge of pink begins to trail through the water. Ira watches as it grows darker and thicker. Then it hits him, he knows what he should do. He squeezes his hand hard and the blood flows heavy. Taco and Cruze look at him. He lifts his hand out of the water, dripping with blood.

Cruze wrinkles his nose; he can't stand the sight of blood. "What didja do, worm! Stupid idiot. You broke a glass! Well, it's just more work you'll have ta do ta pay for it, that's all."

Ira discreetly squeezes harder, and blood gushes out. Cruze looks at Taco and throws his head to the side. *"Llevalo at bano."*

Taco gives Ira a disgusted look and escorts him to the washroom. Ira knows there's a rectangular window high up on the wall, he's looked up at it and sized it up many times. He's pretty sure he can fit through it.

Ira walks into the restroom and closes the door while Taco waits outside. He turns the faucet on full blast and turns the waste can upside down, setting it under the window. He's never tried to open it before and he's hoping it's not nailed shut. He turns the handle and pushes, but it doesn't open. He shifts his weight for a better angle and tries again. It moves a fraction; he pushes once more and it opens. He lifts it up as high as it will go, fresh air fills his senses and he's surprised. He climbs out with relative ease. He hesitates for a second, just long enough to get his bearings and figure out where he is. Okay, he recognizes this alley.

He's been up and down these streets in happier times with Diego and that's where he's heading, straight to Diego's house. He knows the way from here, including all the back roads, and he knows every inch of the route that goes into and out of Diego's property. He's had plenty of spare time to explore. Now is his chance to outsmart Diego. He'll sneak in, get his duffle bag, and maybe some supplies, too. After all the work he's done, Diego owes him. He ducks into the alley and dashes off in the direction of Diego's house.

Crouching like a cat, he roves quietly through the weeds and crawls under a chain-link fence where a dog dug a hole underneath and loosened the links. Ira found this weak spot in the fence many, many months ago. He's glad now that he never said anything, back then he hadn't wanted the guard dogs to be punished.

He slips under the fence and into the yard, he keeps low and moves fast. He passes through the scruffy bracken behind the servant's quarters and hustles down the gulch leading to the wine cellar door. Ira remembers, oddly enough, that it has a lock on the outside of it.

He slides the bolt across, opens the door, and steps down into the cool dark room lined with racks holding hundreds of bottles of expensive wine. Running fast, he climbs the dimly lit wooden stairs that lead up into the house. This is where it gets tricky. Diego has many servants and they're always hustling and bustling around, but Ira's an expert at eluding them, something he practiced time and time again when he lived here, entertaining himself while waiting for Diego to get home. He knows the route to his bedroom from here and all the places to hide on the way.

As the cellar door cracks open, Ira listens for footsteps or voices and he hears none. By his estimates, most of the servants will either be working in the garden or working in the kitchen. At any rate, the bed-making should be done by now. He peeks out and looks around. Seeing no one, he sprints to the trickling fountain at the bottom of the stairs next to the kitchen door. He ducks behind it. This is one of his favorite places to hide because he can hear what the servants are saying in the kitchen, watch as they come and go and nobody knows he's there. He waits for a minute as Diego's driver passes the fountain and hurries into the kitchen. Ira hears keys jingling, then the driver rushes out of the kitchen, charging for the front door.

Once he's gone, Ira ascends the stairs two at a time and ducks behind a grandiose, one-of-a-kind vase standing outside of Diego's bedroom door. He stops for a moment and listens. Nope, Diego is not in there, just as he hoped he wouldn't be. Ira crosses the hall and glides into his bedroom like he's done hundreds of times before. He opens the closet and there it is, his link to his past, the Padres duffle bag.

He sighs with relief, sits down on his bed and opens it up, he pushes aside the poncho, thermos, rocks, shells, and a few brass casings from his days at the shooting range; things he'd collected. Yep, there it is, still here, his prized possession; the eagle feather. As he sits staring at the noble memento, he thinks how shameful it is that he was fooled by Diego so easily. He promises himself he will never let it happen again. He looks around the room and he can't help but remember all the good times he had here. He was surrounded by beauty and abundance, something he'd never had before, but like everything else it has turned to pain and sorrow. These last eighteen months have been hard, and he feels much older than his thirteen years. He wonders what lies ahead. Where will he go? Maybe he'll try to cross the border into the United States.

Loud voices outside interrupt his thoughts, a commotion that is not normal. He stuffs the feather in the bag and races for the door. He takes the same route going out as he did coming in. He flies down the main stairs and through the foyer. He slips through the door to the cellar just in time.

He hears Diego's voice entering the foyer. "I know you're here, boy, you left a bit of a blood trail in the alley. I'm glad you came home. I heard they mistreated you. Nothin' to be scared of now, come on out."

Diego heads up the stairs to Ira's room. Ira rushes down the stairs into the dark cellar.

"Where are you, boy? I've missed you! They told me you ran away."

Ira pauses on the bottom step, just beneath the dingy bulb that dangles overhead. He hears Diego calling out to him. He looks up, ignoring his calls and selects a medium-bodied merlot off the rack. "Hmmm, this one's well rounded, with a clean fruity finish." He smiles and stuffs the dusty bottle into his bag.

He crashes through the cellar door, sliding the dead bolt behind him, then runs up the slope to the back yard. He races past the garden, watching the servants' jaws drop as he slips away. He dives under the fence and runs toward the train tracks. He hears a gunshot. He leaps and bounces through the field like a deer until he approaches the train. None of the box cars are open, and it's too long a train to run around, so he bows his head, bends over and scurries across the tracks underneath it. He hears another shot just as he reaches the other side. Pain sears the back of his shoulder, and blood oozes through the hole in his shirt.

As he emerges on the other side of the train, he straightens and grabs his shoulder. It's throbbing and feels sticky. *At least now*, he thinks, I'm hidden by the train, *they'll have to aim for my legs*, and he makes a dash for a bright pink building. He slings his duffle bag onto his good shoulder and sprints as fast as he can, though, fatigue overcomes him fast. He manages to reach the side of the building, but trips on a cluster of terra cotta planters and crashes to the ground, landing on his side. He sits up, then slumps back down next to the wall. He's so very tired, and weak, he thinks he'll just sit there for a moment and catch his breath. He closes his eyes as blood begins to soak through his shirt and a red stain pools around his body.

# CHAPTER SEVEN

## Daughters, Weep for Yourselves

Father Lelo awakens in a sweat. The dream seemed so real. It is frightening to think of Ira in so much danger. It was a disjointed dream, a collage of men with guns, of muffled cries from hidden people, of smoky haze, of white dust as lethal as gun powder and venom swirling in goblets shaped like fangs. Then the ending, the thing that disturbed him the most. The sight of young Ira sitting slumped on the ground, his shirt soaked in blood, the walkway littered with brass casings.

Father Lelo has been traveling with Ira's picture for a year now and just one person had said he recognized the boy. He was a smug, intoxicated tourist, peering at Father Lelo's white collar with hateful defiance, then, after looking Father Lelo's tall frame up and down, becoming confrontational. He staggered closer to Father Lelo. He pointed his finger at the picture slurring poor English mixed with bad Spanish while swaying back and forth.

"Oh, fur sure, I just saw him five minutes ago. He's the kid that walked on the ocean to bring water to my table at the *Ladridos De Pez Café*. About *veinte kilometeros directo porta culo en Crucecita*." Sneering, he puts his middle finger to his chin, "I think that means twenty miles straight south of Crucecita, yes?"

Father Lelo studies him for a moment. He makes his assessment, then speaks. "Correction, sir, fish don't bark. I think you must mean Ladridos Perro Café. *Gracias,* I will drive three thousand kilometers to Crucecita in five minutes and when I reach the shore, I will launch my truck into the ocean and sail twenty kilometers south, until I find The Barking Dog." Then he adds in Spanish. "*Adios, usted gran idiota*!" He takes his hat off, nods and says with sophistication "I think that means 'Goodbye with huge appreciation.'" Father Lelo puts his hat back on and walks away, grinning.

As he continues south to Santo Tomas, Father Lelo stops at every area that has even the slightest bit of a population. The days are dusty, dry and tiresome, seeming to last forever, but Father Lelo will not give up. He presses on without much luck and even though he didn't really expect people to recognize the four-year-old in the picture, he did think that someone would have at least remembered seeing a young boy traveling alone.

Though he hopes it's not the case, he begins to think, *What if Chief Dewey is right*? What if Ira has been lured into what Father Lelo refers to as the lairs of vice; the seedy bars and clubs that he, himself, prefers not to enter?

He is weary. He rises before dawn every day and sets out to search for Ira before sunrise. Today has been a long day and the day was mighty hot for this time of year. The sun is starting to sink and he decides to stop and find a place to settle in for the night. Most often, he camps in his truck, but this evening he decides to get a room. He's out of water and needs other supplies. He pulls up to a dusty roadside hotel named *Los Viajero Serenata*. He leaves his belongings in the truck and walks into the small lobby.

The walls are plastered with old-time family pictures and the room is vacuous and scanty, with just a few pieces of furniture. There's an antique television sporting rabbit ears bridged with a piece of tin foil in the corner and a couple of wooden chairs with a table between them covered with a thick layer of dust. The male desk clerk has shiny black hair; he's young and of average height, but he greets Father Lelo with a huge welcoming smile. He speaks no English so Father Lelo indulges him with good Spanish. He asks if he has a vacancy and where he can go to buy supplies.

After settling on a price he walks back outside to his truck to get his bag, and notices he's already parked in front of his room. He turns the key, pushes the door open, and looks around. Though not lavish in furnishings, and lacking in decor, the room is accommodating enough. The faucet in the bathroom has a perpetual drip, its left a permanent rust stain in the sink and the toilet gurgles on occasion, but it's clean and uncluttered and the price is right for a *peso*-pinching *padre*.

The desk clerk told him that there is a fiesta on the edge of town where tourists come from miles around to dance and listen to the music of the *Foot-Stompers of Baja* every Saturday night. It's a big deal for these parts and Father Lelo will take advantage of its crowd of people. He washes his face and runs his comb through his hair, then he sets out for supplies.

After he's purchased all that he needs and fills the tank with gas, he drives to the edge of town to the festival. He parks the truck and gets out. The atmosphere is joyous, full of noise, brightly colored costumes and a smorgasbord of smells. Firecrackers pop like corn in the evening air and curly puffs of smoke float like flags across the sky. Mexican gauchos with guitars serenade pretty women bedecked in dresses with bright ruffles and ribbon, their black hair adorned with fresh flowers and vivid colored bows.

A young girl dressed in a white shirt with poufy sleeves and a red-white-and green ruffled skirt approaches Father Lelo. She's holding a puppy that's playfully biting at the silver cross around her neck. She pushes some strands of hair from her eyes and looks up at Father. *"Es usted un Cura?"*

Father Lelo bends and scratches the puppy under the chin. *"Si, Senorita. Es usted creyenta?"*

*"Si, mucho. y tambien mi perrita; Rosa Flor."* She pulls the cross from the puppy's mouth and holds it up proudly to show Father Lelo that both her and the puppy are believers.

He begins to laugh, when suddenly he is overcome by an intense image.

*A woman arcs her body over a man covered in crisp white linen as mist sprays cool and clean into the man's nostrils. Milky gray-green vines travel across his chest, weaving their way into his mouth and through his nasal passages. The vines intertwine and spread as gentle as a mother's caress, covering his entire body like a protective shield as a radiant form rises above him, spreads open like wings and swaddles the man in muted light.*

He senses profoundness in this image, but as quick as it came, it leaves.

The young girl is tugging on Father Lelo's sleeve. She's speaking, frustrated that he hasn't answered her.

*"Dios ta ha enviado para salvar a la nina?"* She points her tiny finger across the street into the crowd.

Father Lelo looks at her, puzzled, wondering who she wants saved. *"Dios salvar a todos, mi querida paque nita."*

The look on the young girl's face has switched to sadness. *"Mama dice que dios tiene que enviar alguien especial para que salve a la chica. Crei que ese eres tu."*

Father Lelo's expression changes to concern as he senses distress in her voice and realizes that she is talking about someone specific. *"De quien estás hablando?"*

The young girl points her finger across the street at a cantina, *"Alla en la cantina. ella solo tien diez."*

Father Lelo thinking the ten year old she's talking about must live over there looks down at the young girl and her puppy, confused *"Vive elle alli?"*

*"Que ella trabaja ahi!"*

Father Lelo twists his neck towards the *cantina,* eyebrows scrunched, eyes drilling, "She works there?" he blurts out in English. The girl stiffens. He repeats his words in Spanish, *"Que ella trabaja ahi?"*

*"Si, señor."*

*"Que hace ella?"* He waits for her to answer, but as she looks down, shrinking, Father Lelo is fraught with deep concern. He begins to have an idea of what the ten year old might be doing. *"No te preocup, quedate aqui yo mi encargare de esto."*

And telling the girl with the puppy to stay where she is, Father Lelo takes off like a major leaguer stealing home plate. He reaches the *cantina* in seconds and flings open the door. He looks around the dingy room. It's filled with men along with smoke from their tobacco. A makeshift stage fashioned like a wedding cake is positioned across the room. Each tier is lined along the bottom with a white dust ruffle and at the top is a giant red balloon representing a cherry. A young, frail girl lies across the bottom layer propped up on her elbow in a seductive pose and even though she is not fully developed, she is nearly naked. Her eyes tell a tale of extreme sadness and shame. The men walk past her crooning and whispering; a fat, white haired man throws a peso in her direction while another man standing off to the side yells to her in English to get up and dance.

Father Lelo's stomach churns at the sight and he doesn't linger. His monumental frame is intimidating and his military fatigues are forbidding. He tears away the ruffle from the bottom of the stage then steps up and wraps the perverted audience's prey in the white ruffled cloth, picks her up and leaps off the stage, heading for the door. The men in the room are caught off guard and for a moment are silent. But the owner of the *cantina* starts shouting in English and crosses the room in a flash, blocking Father Lelo's path.

"What you think you're doing? That's my property. You want 'er, you gotta pay for 'er."

"She's not your property! She's a member of the human race and you're violating her human rights by depriving her of her dignity and worth as a human being. What relation is she to you?"

"Not that it's any of your business, but she's my brother's daughter. He can't afford her so I feed her and keep her alive. This is how she earns her keep." He eyes the white collar on the priest's neck, "Who are you, anyway?"

"I'm Reverend Colonel Lelonis, Kendall of the United States Marine Corps and I'm taking this child to a safe haven."

The *cantina* owner puts his hands on his hips. "Well you got some balls man, but being a priest ain't gonna stop me and my boys from ripping you a new one."

Father Lelo, who towers above him, bends down, putting his face in front of him. "Rip away. Last I checked, which wasn't long ago, I have a soul that you can't hurt. On the contrary, you may want to put some effort into looking for your soul." Father Lelo turns to the crowd and shouts out in English. "The sexual exploitation of a human being is sinful. It breaks international law and is punishable by up to thirty years in prison. If there's anyone in this room who doesn't understand English, I'm sure this girl's perverted uncle can interpret it for you." The room remains silent. "Good, now is there anyone else who wants to rip me apart before I leave with this child?" Nobody moves a muscle. Father Lelo turns back to the *cantina* owner. "See what happened to your brave cohorts now? It takes just one voice filled with decency to stop a mob of impiety, even in a language that is foreign to them. Step aside. I'm leaving and I'm taking this child into protective custody." Father Lelo passes him and tramps to the door.

A stream of profanity using God's name and wielded like a knife blade slices through Father Lelo's back as the *cantina* owner follows behind him, shouting, "You ain't seen the last of me!"

Without missing a stride Father Lelo turns his head and shouts over his shoulder, "You better pray that I have!"

Father Lelo pounds down the narrow sidewalk in full stride, heading straight for his truck. Pedestrians hop out of his way, annoyed at first, but then their glances change to curiosity. Not one of them says a word. As he reaches the truck he unlocks the door and sets the girl on the seat, then scoots her to the other side.

*"No te preocupes Chiquita, estas a salvo conmigo."* He assures the girl that she is safe as he speeds away. When they hit the edge of town, he stops at a stand selling tourist's clothing and buys a child's T-shirt, shorts and a pair of flip flops and gives them to the girl. She crouches on the floor of the truck and begins dressing herself with her back turned to Father Lelo.

He drives to Los Viajero Serenata, he is tempted to stay the night, he's already paid for the room and he's over-tired, but he figures it's better to vamoose and take the girl to the authorities right away rather than to risk a confrontation. It changes his plans and delays his efforts to find Ira, but the safety of this child and reporting of this incident must be taken care of. Besides, he believes everything happens for the best, even if it doesn't seem like it at the time. He leaves the girl, still dressing on the floor of the truck and dashes to the room to grab his bag.

Once the girl has dressed, he buckles her up in the seatbelt and gives her a military blanket for cover. She pulls the blanket up and curls up as far away from him as possible. He asks her what her name is, but she doesn't answer, and they travel in silence.

Father Lelo's been driving north all night and the sun is beginning to peek above the horizon. Except for stopping to gas up and the half hour he spent at La Viajeros Serenata before finding the girl, he hasn't had a break in thirty-six hours. He is so tired he's hallucinating. The child hasn't stirred once.

He passes a sign for Ensenada, a heavy populated commercialized tourist town that he knows from experience has a decent non-corrupt police force, a place he can trust where he can get help for the girl. The sign said twenty miles, but he can't wait, he is in need of a restroom, so he pulls into the parking lot of what appears to be a coffee shop. A good strong cup of coffee will do him wonders, and there's a sign outside the building, though missing some letters that reads EXPRESSO KITCHEN, then below it, SPECIALTY: CUSTO BI NETS. He's never had Custo coffee with beignets before, just chicory in the French Quarter in New Orleans. He is pleasantly surprised that it's not just wine, but beignets that is part of the French influence in Mexico and he's looking forward to having one of the famous pastries again.

He pulls up next to the building and parks the truck in front of the window. He taps the child on the shoulder. She peeks out at him with groggy eyes, then buries herself back in the blanket. Her eyes are bloodshot and Father Lelo realizes that she may very well have been drugged. The owners might get the wrong idea about him if they see her in this condition and Ensenada is less than a half hour away, so he decides it's better to leave her in the truck for a few minutes while he's in the shop. He leaves the air on low and the truck running, takes his spare keys and locks the doors. He'll bring her back a beignet and some milk.

The aroma of fresh morning coffee permeates his nostrils as he walks into the shop. The place is devoid of customers, but he's surprised to see a creative layout of five or six miniature kitchens. He assumes the idea is to choose one to sit and enjoy your coffee and pastry in. As he leans on the counter waiting for service he looks around, thinking how clever an idea this is.

A young woman emerges from the back room along with the waft of coffee and cinnamon rolls clinging to her blouse. Father Lelo isn't surprised to see she's an American, the store signage is all in English.

"Good morning," she says with a bright smile, while checking out his collar.

Father Lelo smiles back and pulls out his wallet. "Good morning, are you the owner?"

"Yes, my husband and I own this place. We moved down here three years ago from San Diego."

Father Lelo smiles and nods. "I'll have a large Custo coffee and two orders of beignets, and also a large milk. Make it to go, please."

The woman seems to be at a loss for words. Father Lelo senses that something's wrong with this picture and for a minute they just stand there and stare at each other, both of them trying to grasp where the confusion lies.

Then Father Lelo speaks up, "This is a coffee shop right? Don't you have any milk?"

The woman smiles and her eyes twinkle, but she covers her mouth and sighs. "I'm sorry, I meant to get to it yesterday, but time got away from me. The sign outside is missing some letters."

Father Lelo shifts his stance. "I realize that. You're missing the 'E' and 'G' in beignets."

"No sir, the 'M' in CUSTOM, and the 'C' and 'A' in CABINETS. The sign is supposed to say 'Custom Cabinets.'"

"Oh, for the love of mercy, you've got to be kidding me. Wow. I guess I'm way past spent; my mind is playing tricks on me. I thought this was a coffee shop, or should I say, I needed it to be." Father Lelo shakes his head in disbelief.

The owner apologizes, but she can't overcome the giggle in her voice as she offers to give him a cup of coffee from the private stash in the back office.

Father Lelo looks at her and begins to chuckle himself. "That would be terrific, I accept. I'm just going to use your restroom quick okay?"

"Of course, it's right over there." She points to the back where a sign on a door reads, MEN.

Father Lelo walks to the door, fixing his eyes on the sign. He hesitates for a moment, then turning back to the owner, he clears his throat. "Hmmm, this sign wouldn't be missing a 'W' and an 'O', would it?"

She breaks out laughing and points across the room, "No, the WOMEN's room is over there."

Father Lelo nods with a wink and a smile, "Just checking."

When Father Lelo comes back to the counter, the woman has a Styrofoam cup filled with coffee for him and a cinnamon roll wrapped in a napkin. He thanks her, but before he leaves, without knowing why, he opens up to her. He explains why he is so tired and describes the scene at the *cantina* concerning the child. She is appalled and yet grateful that he brought the girl with him. They discuss the situation further and she looks up an address. Then she wraps up another cinnamon roll and puts it in a bag, along with a doll that her daughter left at the store yesterday. She hands him the package and wishes him luck. He thanks her and leaves.

As he walks to his truck checking the directions she wrote down, she walks to the phone on the counter and dials the number for Social Services in Ensenada. She calls to inform them that Father Lelo will be arriving soon with a child in need of help. She waves to him through the window as he climbs into the truck.

He looks toward the girl. She's hiding beneath the blanket, he sets the bag on the seat. The sun is rising and it's beginning to get warmer. Father Lelo turns the air up a notch and then pulls the blanket away from the girl. She's still curled up in the corner half asleep. Father Lelo brushes the hair from her eyes.

*"Tienes Hambre, hija?"* She doesn't answer, but he knows she must be hungry. *"Tengo un pan de dulce para ti."* He pulls a cinnamon roll out of the bag, unwraps the napkin and hands it to her, but she refuses it. He tries again; he holds the pastry to her nose. *"Usted necesita comer, hija."* She turns her face away, refusing to eat. He pulls the cinnamon roll back and takes a bite himself. "Mmmm, *muy, muy bueno*!"

He devours the cinnamon roll and digs in the bag for the other one, but first he pulls out the doll the store owner gave him and lays it on the seat next to him, then he takes out the other pastry. He offers it to her again, trying hard to get her to eat, but she draws back under the blanket. He decides not to try to force her and starts to chow down on the roll himself. When he is almost finished he notices two brown eyes peeking out at him, she looks vexed.

He puts the last bite in his mouth and glances at her with a guilty look. *"Que? Yo te lo Ofreci. Lo siento."* He apologies and wipes his mouth with the napkin, watching as the girl takes her hands out from under the blanket and sets them in her lap. She twiddles her fingers while looking around everywhere except for at him. After a few moments Father Lelo catches her looking at the doll next to him and he picks it up and offers it to her. *"Es esto lo que quieres?"*

She disappears beneath the blanket.

Father Lelo sets the doll back down. *"Tu la puedas tener."* He slides the toy closer to her, then turns his attention back to the steering wheel. As he drives, he ponders the events of the past night and even though he has seen more iniquity in his life than most people, especially during times of war, he still can't believe that there are some human beings who will sell their children or others into sex slavery. To him it's the same as murder.

The exit sign says Ensenada. He takes the next right to Avenida Refoma. He digs in his pocket for the address of Mexico's Integral Family Development and notices that the doll is no longer on the seat. He smiles. He takes a right at the end of the ramp onto Floresta Entr then drives for a mile or so until he notices an old pickup truck ahead. The truck is pulled alongside the road and loaded down with squash, zucchini, and corn and the truck is lopsided from two flat tires on the same side. The driver is alone and in desperate need of some help.

The temperature is climbing and the man is standing outside the truck, dabbing the sweat from his forehead as the cars on the busy road zoom by. As Father Lelo passes him he checks his mirror and feels a twinge of guilt, knowing that it could be hours before the man gets any help and if he can't get his produce to shade in this heat, he'll lose the entire load to spoilage and a weeks' income.

Father Lelo puts his flashers on and pulls off to the side of the road. Just as he stops the vehicle the girl makes a gagging sound and throws up. Father looks at her and sees beads of sweat around her hair line. He can see she's ill. It is obvious that she has never been properly cared for. She has been drugged, malnourished and is dehydrated and he knows he has to get her help now. He gets out of the truck and unzips one of his bags in the back. He pulls out a towel and a washcloth and pours some water on both. He cleans up the mess with the towel and wipes the girl's face with the washcloth then he puts the washcloth in her hand and closes her fist around it.

*"Estare de Vuelta pronto."* Promising to be back soon he walks back to the broken-down truck and asks the driver what happened. The driver tells him that he heard two loud bangs and then both his tires went flat. Father Lelo explains that he has a sick child in his truck, but that he will send someone back here to help. The man has a worried look on his face. *"Por favor, señor, tengo que entregar esto a Tijuana antes del mediodia."*

Father Lelo promises the driver he will send help to get him to the city by noon and gets back in his truck and looks at the girl. She is once again sleeping and holding the doll tight against her chest. To Father Lelo she is as helpless as a human being can be and his heart is heavy with concern for her and for all the cruelty found in this world. He prays as he pulls back onto the highway and makes his way to the Family Development facility.

The woman in the reception area smiles warmly at him as he walks in the door, carrying the child in his arms.

"We've been expecting you, please follow me." Father Lelo follows her to a private room in the back of the building decorated in a manner comforting to a child. The color of the carpet and curtains are of pastel green, pink, blue, and yellow. There is a toy-box in the corner overflowing with dolls, toy trucks, and building blocks. All the furniture in the room is miniature-sized, built to accommodate children; Father Lelo is a tower in the midst of them.

He walks to a sofa and sets the girl down. He wipes the hair from her eyes, then touches her cheek with tenderness and again assures her of her safety. *"Usted esta seguro aqui, angelito."*

The child reaches out her arms and hugs Father Lelo's neck, clinging to him tightly. He's taken aback for a moment, then is so moved by the child's raw hunger for kindness that his eyes fill with tears. He frames her cheeks with his hands, but she will not look into his eyes.

*"Tu tendras una buena casa pronto."* He strokes the girl's hair and kisses the top of her head. He turns to the woman standing in the room and holds out his hand.

*"Hola, mi nombre es Padre Lelonis Kendall,"* Father Lelo introduces himself.

*Hola, yo soy la Doctora Rodriguez, Juanita.*

Father nods and shakes her hand. *"Por favor, cuidela muy bien."*

*"Lo Haremos."*

Having been assured that they will take good care of the child he leaves her in the care of the doctor who will begin a long process of psychological and medical treatment. He follows the receptionist to another room where he's handed some paperwork and is questioned by a bilingual investigator with a stocky build, glasses, and gray hair. Father Lelo interrupts him just for a moment.

"I need to find someone to help a man I met on my way here. I promised him I would send help. He has two flat tires and a truck full of produce that he's delivering to Tijuana. He must be there by noon. Do you know anyone who can go help him?"

"I can have someone call the nearest service station to see if they can send someone."

Father nods and thanks him.

After forty-five minutes of discussion, Father Lelo gives the investigator his signed statement and leaves. Just before he opens the door, he stops and turns around, "I almost forgot, did your people make the call to the service station and did they send someone to help the man with the flat tires?"

The investigator picks up the phone and calls the receptionist. He nods, then in a sheepish tone tells Father Lelo, "She said that she called four different places and none of them had the personnel to do that sort of thing."

Father Lelo lets out a long sigh, "Please take good care of the child; she's been through a lot in her short life. I'm going back to help the man with his tires." He tips his hat and walks out the door.

After he drives back several miles down the highway he sees that the truck is still there and is glad he didn't assume that help for the farmer had come. He pulls over, waits for traffic to pass, then swings a U-turn to pull up behind the produce truck. Father Lelo spends the next hour waiting at a gas station for the attendant to fix the two flat tires. Then he helped the driver put them back on.

Father Lelo learns while fixing the tires that the produce driver makes a trip from south of Punta Banyo to Tijuana with a load of vegetables from his farm every week and has been making the trip for twenty years. He has a wife, five children and his mother, all back at the farm. They are strict churchgoers and his youngest will be taking her first communion this year.

Father Lelo is pleased at the chit chat and he smiles and nods as he listens. Once they've finished up, he walks to his pickup truck, drenches another towel with water, cleans his hands with it, and offers it to the truck driver.

The truck driver has no time to spare and after he wipes his hands he thanks Father Lelo and blesses him, jumps in his truck and prepares to drive away. Father Lelo lifts his hand to wave, but at the same moment remembers the snapshot of Ira. He shouts to the driver to wait. He pulls the picture out of his wallet and asks the driver if he has ever seen this young boy traveling alone along this route. He holds out the picture and tells him the photograph is old, taken when the boy was only four. The driver shrugs and says he doesn't recognize the boy. Though Father Lelo is not surprised, his hopes are once again dashed.

Then the driver taps on the picture and tells him that although he doesn't recognize the boy in the picture he does recognize the Padres duffle bag, said he was a fan himself, and that he gave a ride to an Indian boy carrying a bag just like that a long time ago. He dropped him off on a street corner in Tijuana.

Father Lelo's blood is pressurized and his mind is racing as he follows behind the produce truck with a heart more hopeful than it's been in years. Could this have been Ira? It must have been. The other lone explanation would be if Ira's duffle bag had been stolen. But then, it seems unlikely that it could have been stolen by another boy of Indian heritage? It is certainly more probable that it's Ira. Father Lelo is so anxious to get to Tijuana he can hardly contain his excitement.

As they round the corner entering the narrow street where the produce driver first dropped the boy off, the driver points his finger to the sidewalk, then waves goodbye, hollering out the window. "*Buena suerte*!"

Father Lelo waves back, and desperately hoping that he does have good luck, he drives his truck to a side lot where he parks and walks to the train station, hoping to get information or at the very least a city map. As he walks down the street he is struck by the sight of a miniature donkey painted like a zebra hitched to a cart. A strange thought, almost a picture, passes through his mind and he's certain that Ira saw the same scene that he is looking at now.

As he gets nearer the train station he sees a person slumped alongside a building among some broken terra cotta pots. At first he thinks it might be a drunk sleeping it off, but as he gets closer he notices that it's a boy holding his left shoulder, slouched in what appears to be a pool of blood. His eyes are closed.

Father Lelo is shaken to the core when he notices a duffle bag lying beside him and an assortment of brass casings littering the ground around him. It is the Padres bag and the young boy is Indian. What a horrible twist of fate to have searched for the boy for years, then to come upon him riddled with bullets and covered in blood. Father Lelo prays as he reaches out to touch the boy with hands that are shaking, "Please Lord, don't let him be dead."

"Ira. Ira."

The boy opens his eyes, blinking, straining to focus, surprised to hear his name. Nobody has called him by that name since he left Ruby Dix's place. He doesn't recognize the face of the man kneeling in front of him, but he does recognize the white collar from his dreams.

Ira takes a labored breath. "Who are you?"

Father Lelo's eyes fill with tears and he blinks them away. "Is your name Ira?"

"Please don't take me back to Diego; he will kill me. He's already shot at me twice."

"I won't take you back there. Is your name Ira?"

"Yes."

Father Lelo grabs hold of him and hugs him close for a long moment, thanking God. He pulls Ira's hand away from his shoulder to inspect his wound. It looks as though his shoulder has a deep, nasty gouge, dirty and caked with rust, but it doesn't appear to be a gunshot wound. He looks around at the ground and touches the red stain that he thought was blood. It smells like wine and it's leaking from his duffle bag.

Ira quickly explains to Father Lelo what just happened to him, the shooting and how he ducked under a train to escape the gunshots. He tells Father that the man he once lived with is dangerous. That he buys and sells people, making them slaves.

Father nods. "You're coming home with me. I knew your mother and grandparents and they wanted me to raise you."

"Where are we going?"

"Back to the U.S.A., where you belong, we have a lot to talk about."

# CHAPTER EIGHT

## The Commencement:

## On The Road to Reckoning

Father Lelo, dressed in his military fatigues, checks his watch as he approaches the coffee-maker. It's not yet 0600, but he's already in the office at Camp Pendleton. He just returned home from Afghanistan. It should have been his last tour, but, as with priests everywhere he's spread thin, and even though he wants to retire, he can't. The country is involved in simultaneous wars and the Corps is in desperate need of his clergy qualifications, so the Archbishop of the U.S Military Ordinariate asked for him to remain in the military and his bishop agreed. He is over tired from the long trip back, and at the moment he is feeling irritable.

He slides the pot back under the filter, then uses a paper towel to wipe up the sizzling dribble, thinking about how he wishes the church would move forward into the 21th century and start ordaining women instead of oppressing them. If so there would be enough priests to cover the world because there are plenty of women who want the job. Unfortunately oppression blinds and the Vatican can't see that our omnipotent God is powerful enough to work through a woman's hands, just as well as a man's.

He walks back to his desk pushing the thoughts out of his head. He has something better to do than noodle those thoughts around again. He's been waiting for the sun's rays to dismiss the darkness so that he can call Ira and Rosa to say hello, and tell them he's back without that grating tin-can echo of 11,000 miles between them.

It's hard for Father Lelo to believe that sixteen years have passed and Ira is twenty-nine years old now, with many responsibilities. Ira has a house of his own, Rosa under his roof and a serious career with the U.S. Border Patrol. Time has flown, yet it seems like forever since he found Ira ravaged, bleeding and almost dead on the streets of Tijuana. He remembers Rosa telling him that she was in the kitchen of the rectory that day when she heard truck tires rolling across the gravel out in front of the tiny house. When she looked out the screen door she saw him walk around the back of his pickup, carrying a duffle bag that she'd recognized, but hadn't seen in many years. Memories of the day that she and Raina had bought it for her three-year-old grandson had flooded her mind and her heart skipped a beat as she zeroed in on the bag's intact, but faded, Padres emblem. Then she watched as he'd opened the passenger door of the truck and saw an adolescent boy with long black hair sit up. He'd rubbed his eyes and blinked several times as he twisted and turned stretching his neck, looking out the windows of the truck, disoriented.

When Rosa saw his face she knew it was Ira and her heart leaped with joy. He looked so much like Raina that the old memories almost swamped her. It was as if Raina had returned home. Tears spilled down her cheeks as she studied his straight, prominent nose, high cheekbones and the thick, dark lashes that were without a doubt Raina's DNA. Her heart had pounded hard, thumping her chest like a sledgehammer. Emotions swelled like a massive ocean wave and she'd had all she could do to stay grounded and stop the surge from sweeping the earth from beneath her feet.

Father Lelo had handed Ira the duffle bag; then coaxed him out of the truck. He was tall and gangly, clearly malnourished. His blue-and-gray flannel shirt was worn thin. His jeans, baggy and stained, held up by a belt, buckled on its last notch. His shoulders were slumped forward, his head lowered and his hair was hanging in his eyes.

Father had stood behind Ira with one hand on each shoulder while they both stared at the tiny, pitched-roof rectory in front of them. Ira hadn't showed any emotion as Father then put one arm around him and walked him to the house. The last time he'd been there was when he was three years old, and he had no recollection of it.

Father Lelo, sits down at his desk, picks up the phone and dials Ira's number.

Ira is sitting at his kitchen table eating breakfast. He pulls his phone out of his pocket. He looks at it and smiles.

Rosa has just come up from behind him with the coffee pot, she's still in her black and gray paisley robe. Her silver hair is pulled back into one long, thick braid trailing down to her waist. She offers Ira a warm up. He pushes his cup toward her while looking up at her smiling from ear to ear.

"It's Father Lelo, he's back."

Rosa sighs with relief, and puts one hand over her heart. They've been waiting on pins and needles for this call since long before they went to bed last night.

"Hey, it's great you're back! We've been waiting. How was your flight?"

"Hi, son, tiring of course; it takes a lot out of you."

"We're glad you're home safe. What time did your plane land?"

"It was around 0200 hours when she touched American soil. You know, there're two good things about leaving this country. The first is coming back, and the other is the reminder of the blessings that we have here; it keeps one humble."

Ira puts his hand on his forehead. "I know. I'm fighting to preserve it every day."

"I know you are. What's going on? You said that you had something important to tell me when I got back."

"I wanted to let you know that I've been assigned to an undercover operation in the field. The investigation is still in its infant stage, and I can't say much except that it involves a banker and some pricey real-estate development going on at a site behind his home. The banker coincidently hired a grounds-keeping company to do some work in his backyard, and the Border Patrol jumped at the opportunity to send me over there undercover as a landscaper. They've been working on busting a certain drug smuggling ring that's been working the border around San Diego and they stumbled upon a connection between this man's bank and a mob boss. It was significant enough so that they turned the information over to the Feds and now the FBI, SDPD and the BP are going to be investigating the situation expansively. I don't know who the San Diego Police Department has working the case, but the Border Patrol has assigned one aspect of the operation to me. I'm leading it, covert, from the field."

"Congratulations, I think. Sounds pretty dangerous."

Ira looks down into his coffee cup. "They say I'm ready to lead. I've passed all the written exams and I've been shooting in the top percent of all agents. I won the over-all High Master in the President's shooting match for the third year in a row last week. They've promoted me to Chief Patrol Agent. I have two stars now."

Father Lelo closes his eyes while pride seeps in. "I'm proud of you, son, you've always been a high-achiever. How does your grandmother feel about this?"

Ira looks at Rosa again. "She says it's my destiny, but that she'll never get used to it."

Rosa can hear Father Lelo let out a laugh on the other end of the phone. She sits down, and wraps her hands around her tea cup. "Tell him supper will be on the table at six-thirty tonight. Tell him we're having his favorite: baked chicken, dressing, mashed potatoes and gravy and lemon pie with fresh whipped cream for dessert. Tell him I can't wait to see him."

Ira smiles as he relays the message. With cheery eyes, Rosa takes a sip of her Toyon tea. She can hear Father Lelo say he can't wait, either, and that his stomach is already growling. Ira laughs and adds that his is, too. After they chat for a few minutes about Afghanistan, Ira tells Father Lelo that he has to get going, because he has to be at work early this morning, but that he'll see him tonight at supper.

Rosa starts to clear the breakfast dishes and Ira grabs his denim shirt off the back of the chair. He throws it across his shoulder, cuts through the kitchen and reaches for the doorknob. He stops for a moment, turns, and gives Rosa a wily grin. “Later, Gramosa. I got a country to save.”

“Yeah, yeah, okay, okay,” she waves him off, “Just be careful, Super Ira.”

He laughs, grabs his lunch cooler off the counter, and walks out.

As Rosa watches him through the kitchen window, Ira drives away. Suddenly she feels a pull. She sits down at the table, raises her fingers to her temples and massages. She squeezes her eyes closed, then relaxes them. She sees images that are indistinct, but some aspects of the images are certain. They form within the realm of her collective unconscious, a depth untapped by most, but where Rosa can connect with Raina. She sits quiet and still, allowing the experience of time to just be, to flow naturally. She’s clear, listening, and patient, open to perception. Her senses begin to receive.

*She sways back and forth in a trance. She’s forced into inescapable duress and robbed of her inherent role. Her skin becomes sensitive, her nerve endings seem tripled and agitation swells within her, forced into a status of no significance, and unable to comprehend her mesh prison. It’s dark, she’s frightened. She can’t see, nor is she able to understand why anybody would want to extinguish her light. The man bashes at her, slamming her skin with a stick, mauling her again and again. She’s oppressed, trammeled, desperate for a way out, but so suppressed she’s unable to stop it. The torment within is agonizing as her intrinsic being is stifled. If he weren't blind, he'd look into her eyes and see the Creator in her; in all.*

Rosa drops her shoulders as she lets go of the vision. She stands up and walks outside to the greenhouse in her backyard. She strolls between the rows, selecting specific herbs. As she cuts each one, she places it into her handmade basket, while humming the psalm of her soul. Then when she has harvested what she needs, she walks back to the house.

She prepares herself for meditation, sitting down in front of her home altar. Her spine is straight, shoulders relaxed and palms turned up. She holds her tranquil expression toward the heavens as white smoke rises from an abalone shell in front of her. She recites a mantra in her native tongue to the spirit of the eagle who soars the highest. Her eyelids are closed, but they flutter. Wavy echoing vibrations send forth a woman's voice resonating from beyond.

*The Earth feels pain within her; the raping and wickedness rage upon her. He suffers for all existence. Like the mother, his core becomes a sieve, filtering the deception and abominations against nature. Scathing infection will adhere. Know this truth; the eye of God watches.*

Rosa parts her lips and breathes in. She whispers. "Raina."

# CHAPTER NINE

## Bishop's Province

The sun peeks from behind the horizon in a golden-pink hue as Ira drives to work. He has been leaving earlier lately so he can first drop his white Chevy, Colorado off at the Border Patrol station and take an undercover truck to Land Performance, Inc., the landscaping company he's been assigned to.

As Ira had explained to Father Lelo earlier, Greg Bishop had hired Land Performance Inc., to overhaul his entire backyard and the authorities have positioned Ira there. The Feds are interested in the huge heavy equipment being used for the real-estate development on the site across the street behind Bishop's home. The Equipment is owned by the Dench Bros. Inc. a company which has suspected ties to the mafia, as well as Bishop's bank.

As Ira leaves the Border Patrol station his phone rings; he checks the caller ID and sees that it's his partner, Carlos Ramiraz. "'Morning, Carlos."

"'Morning. What's your position?"

"I'm on my way to pick up the truck at Land Performance, then I'm heading to the Bishop's place. ETA, about 15 minutes. You in place already?"

"Ten-four, parked down the street in a public works truck. I've got your back until 10:30 a.m., buddy."

"Got it. Any action?"

"Not unless you call his wife action. Greg Bishop left earlier this morning, but his wife's outside right now cutting some flowers in a pink satin robe. I got a visual. Man, she's a babe, long blonde hair down to her waist, drop-dead gorgeous. Whew."

Ira smiles. "Focus, dude. See ya in a few."

"I am, like a laser beam. I'm watching her walk into her house now."

Ira laughs out loud and hangs up.

The U.S. Border Patrol has been petitioned by the FBI, along with the SDPD, to help with an investigation into The Golden State Bank & Trust, where Greg Bishop is the Senior VP of Wealth Management. He started working for Ted Silar, the President of GSB&T, fresh out of high school, while he was going to college and worked his way up. He's become Ted's right hand man.

The Feds started watching Silar when some cell phone chatter from an organized crime family was traced to the bank. Authorities speculated that Silar might be involved with a local mob boss and a Mexican drug-smuggling ring. The Bishop's house is located in a posh community not yet fully developed. The chatter was vague but trigger words like shipment, bullet-proof, steel-plated, have the Feds speculating there might be some type of connection with the construction equipment on the development site behind the Bishop's home to the Mexican drug cartel and the mob. They may be using the equipment to move drugs or as a drop site and Bishop's bank holds the lien.

Julie Bishop hesitates on the steps for a moment, inhaling a breath of fresh morning air. She strolls back into her house, carrying an armful of fresh-cut flowers. As she goes into her kitchen, the sun's rays beam down through the eastern skylight, illuminating the kitchen table like a spotlight on a stage. The table is decorated with cheery, powder-blue placemats and pale yellow napkins rolled diagonally and placed in to white ceramic rings. In the center is a clear, empty vase; a pointless blank. Then Julie adds a draping bouquet of Canyon Sunflowers and *voila,* it's an aesthetic festival of shade.

Also to the east is a cornered glass casement with comfy window seats. The resident kitty cat, Miss Jingles, occupies a petite portion of the pillowed bench, bathing in the morning sun. The tiny bells on her collar jingle as she licks her paw and swipes it across her face again and again. Julie's residence is a poetic refuge, a sanctuary of harmony.

After she arranges the flowers in the vase, she goes upstairs to her bedroom and pulls on a pair of old jeans and tucks a white cotton T-shirt into them, appropriate clothing for this morning's work. She makes her way downstairs to her home studio, where she arranges the drop cloth beneath her easel, opens her paints and fills her pallet. She picks up where she left off yesterday, laboring to find the right combination of color. She uses the brush with skillful strokes, daubing, and blotting until she connects with what she's searching for; that precise emotional response within her that cries out. "Stop! That's it!"

At last, the thundery multifaceted sunset in the painting is almost finished, just a few more yielding strokes to the backdrop and the angry sky will give up her hero's spirit.

"Perfect," she whispers, then rinses her brush.

She checks her watch with anticipation, thinking *he should be here any minute*. She's feeling a tad strange about how eager she is for her new landscaper to arrive every morning now, but nevertheless is doing just that. It's unbelievable how timely it is to have such a poised and handsome Native American man working in her back yard. It's a genuine stroke of luck and one that she knows she has to take advantage of.

There's an art exhibit that's been in town for a couple weeks now that motivates her. It's been a huge success with its countless displays of Native American artistry. It's so successful in fact, that they are looking to add one new artist to expand their exhibit. They are having an open contest. All artists, amateur and professional, are encouraged to enter.

The contestants are to submit a sample of their work that would capture the theme: *The Spirit of the Native Southwest*. Julie hopes her piece will earn her the winning spot.

Her ancestors are from the Manzanita band of the Kumeyaay Nation. Her father's fifth great-grandfather was a tribal leader in the 1700s, a time of extreme pain and turbulence for the American Indian in their homeland. Julie's blood has been mixed but she feels a deep connection to her native people and she's been painting Native American scenes since early in her youth.

Ira pulls up outside her house in a white Ranger truck bearing the name Land Performance, Inc., in huge green letters on the sides. He rolls along the curb, slowing to a stop and puts it into park. He slides his cell phone into the pocket of his denim shirt and grabs his lunch cooler and a rolled-up set of landscape plans. The sky is misty and it's already seventy-seven degrees at six-thirty in the morning. It's going to be a hot one, but the tiny droplets of moisture floating in the air makes the early morning seem cool.

He puts his denim shirt on as he advances up the walk. This covert operation is the perfect fit for him, a natural choice since he helped put himself through college doing landscaping.

He appreciates the site of a flowery terrain mixed with an assortment of palm shrubs along the walk to the front of the house; he has to give credit where credit is due, the Bishops have impressive vision. There's an abundant trail of slate stone wandering throughout the plots of peachy orange Joseph's Coats and yellow cannas. Blackbearded Sugarbush blends with pale purple Yarrow and giant Papyrus plants enchant him as they lord over it all. Farther down, alongside the house, is the herb garden, teeming with the fragrances of purple Salvia, Bee Balm, Mint, Russian Sage and Cornflowers, an orchestrated opus of vines and spines, petals and stems, swaying like ballroom dancers in a clement breeze.

There's a drastic change in scenery as he rounds the corner to the backyard; it looks like a war zone. The yard's been demolished in order to add a waterfall and a pond. The backyard is not yet half done. It is littered with piles of rocks, heaps of debris and a horde of yard maintenance tools and equipment.

Wooden skids cast to the side in a heap, sojourn with a gathering of various-sized containers of sprouting plants and shrubs. Settled next to them is an oddball wooden crate with unfurled gunny sacks alongside. There must have been a couple deliveries made earlier this morning because the mayhem seems to spread everywhere.

Ira finds a place to set his lunch cooler down and glances at the house. This will be his fifth day here and he hasn't yet even gotten a glimpse of Bishop's wife. The Bishops aren't bothered with the day-to-day work; they've entrusted those details to their caretaker Tom, who handles all the direct contact with Land Performance.

Ira thinks about the comments that Carlos made about her, "Drop dead gorgeous," for starters and he wonders if she has any clue about her husband's dealings. Maybe she is involved in the whole thing. She keeps to herself, and most often keeps the shutters closed, so it's impossible to see what's going on inside. Yes, she could be involved, but Ira thinks it's more likely that she's just another one of those oblivious socialites who thinks she's better than everyone else, spending most of her life with blinders on, blocking out the rest of the world.

*What a waste,* he thinks, as he studies the plans for the layout, then picks up the shovel and begins digging a home for a Flowering Gooseberry.

Julie stirs her pallet as she peeks through the slats of her shutters. She stops for a moment, watching Ira work. She wanders to her desk positioned in front of a wall, lined ceiling to floor with French book cases. She picks up the phone and calls her friend, Linda Stevens. She had bumped into Linda at an art gallery years ago and they'd become friends almost instantly.

Linda's family lineage is embodied by self-made successes. She's the first-born in a well-to-do San Diego clan. Her great-grandfather was a railroad tycoon in the 1800s, her grandfather a bank owner and her father a prominent commercial architect, all known for their tenacity, toughness and ambition, all of which thrives in Linda's blood. She's practically royalty in Southern California. She has her own clothing design business, and she's toiled, pricking her fingers to the bone designing clothing to make it a success. She started from scratch selling couture in a trendy San Diego boutique, and after years of long hours and hard, demanding work she has made a name for herself as one of the hottest new designers in California. It didn't hurt that her family was rich and well known, but she worked unfaltering, providing high-end clothing to a network of California royalty. It's paid off; she's become San Diego's queen of fashion. She's just about to land a deal with a huge, high-end chain and is on the cusp of going national.

She is also the person who encouraged Julie to paint for this upcoming art competition.

Linda's been an art connoisseur as far back as she can remember and knows what Julie's capable of as an artist. She's ecstatic that Julie has decided to get into this competition, and is both surprised and delighted about the Native American man in Julie's backyard. Early in the week she told Julie; "If your inspiration sashays into your backyard again on Friday, call me, because I can squeeze in some free time for coffee, and I'd like to see him for myself."

Linda is standing in front of her mirror, choosing an outfit when her phone rings. She sees "Julie Bishop" pop up on the display and she answers it. "Jules, dear, good morning."

"Good morning. Do you remember telling me if my inspiration showed up today I should call because you'd squeeze in some coffee time this morning? Well, he just arrived."

Linda brushes her shoulder-length, honey-blond hair around her ears. "I'm almost dressed. As soon as I'm finished, I'll swing by."

"Okay, see you in a bit." Julie hangs up, walks back to her easel and picks up her pallet. She glances out into the backyard, concealed by half-closed shutters, her electric-blue eyes are captivated, concentrating, rapt in poetic imagination.

She imagines him as a hero, a young Indian brave sitting on the back of a splendid white stallion galloping beneath a stormy sunset.

*His quiver bounces on the back of his nape, long hair flies like a riders black cape. He holds his spear down at his side, then raises it up to a fiery sky. A thunder bolt collides, touching the tip, drops of blood silently drip. Red stains splatter the stallion's back, robbed of peace, he begins his attack. Hoofs gallantly dangle and pound at the air, noble nostrils alarmed and flared. Wild eyes reflect the scorching sky's blaze, red paint circles one eye's rage. A righteous steed festooned for battle, a brush sinks to its waiting young pallet. The warrior's horse, formed full term, she labors on, her thoughts confirmed.*

Julie is rudely summoned back to reality by the kitchen doorbell. *That must be Linda,* she thinks as she sets her brush down. She walks to the kitchen, turns the dead bolt, and opens the door.

Smoothing his perfect Clooney-like hair is her husband, the incomparable Greg Bishop. His eyes are Cambridge blue, his face is clean-shaven, he is wearing a flawless smile and he is dressed in a carbon-gray Armani.

"Greg." She looks around him. His Black Mercedes Maybach still running in the driveway, "What's wrong?"

He brushes past her, half-rolling his eyes, "I forgot my phone."

She watches him as he passes through the kitchen taking long strides, then he climbs the stairs two at a time, heading for their bedroom. He hurries into his huge walk-in closet, pausing for a moment to check if Julie's followed; she hasn't. He reaches for his Berluti Swann shoe kit that he keeps enshrined on the top shelf and pulls it down.

He raises the lid on the fragrant leather case and lifts the soft blue polishing cloths from the storage compartment in the center. He pulls out a Smith & Wesson .38 caliber pistol, holds it up, checking the load and then slides it down into the inside breast pocket of his suit coat.

Ira is lowering a gooseberry tree into its hole when he hears his phone ring once, then stop. It's his partner Carlos signaling him that there's activity going on. One ring means that Bishop came home and two rings means Bishop's wife has company.

Greg closes the extravagant Berluti box, and puts it back up on the shelf. He makes his way downstairs and into the kitchen. He stops at the door and turns to Julie. "Don't forget to pick up my Amosu suit. It's important that I look my absolute best this afternoon for that new client." He checks his watch. "Christ, I'm late. That suit should have been cleaned last week already."

Julie had dropped it off at *Dirty, Suits Us* dry cleaning late yesterday, and he needs her to pick it up later this morning and drop it off at the bank by noon today.

Julie nods, pecks him on the cheek and reaches up to straighten the Lapis blue silk tie she got him for his birthday. "Don't worry, Greg. You've only reminded me now a half dozen times. I'll have it there by noon."

Greg grabs her hands before she touches his tie to protect his inside breast pocket. He squeezes her hands lightly and gives her a peck on the forehead. Then he straightens the tie himself. "I know you will, sweetheart. It's just that you have other errands to do this morning and you also have an appointment for your car to be serviced. I'm just making sure you don't forget." He turns to leave, but then turns back around. "Oh, and also, make sure the doors are locked and keep the shutters closed. They sent that other landscaper again and you just never know these days; you can't trust just anyone."

"Greg, I know what you mean by that, stop obsessing. Just because he's not white doesn't mean he's a criminal. I'll be fine, and you'll have your suit at the bank on time."

Greg turns the doorknob. "I'm serious, Jules. Indulge me for safety's sake, make sure everything's closed and locked."

Ira walks across the yard to the back of the house where a hose lies under the window. He picks up the end of the hose and pretends to examine it as he strains to peek through the shutters. He knows Bishop's home, but he can't see anyone inside. He walks back to the gooseberry tree, pulls the trigger on the hose, and waters it. His phone begins to ring, but this time twice, the signal meaning company. Linda has just arrived in her black cherry XLR Cadillac, a convertible. It's not that she would be caught dead with the top down; she just likes the look of it. She pulls into the driveway and puts the car in park. She's wearing one of her own creations, a brilliant coral-colored silk blouse, sleeveless and high-collared, tucked into a calf-length white skirt, accessorized with a green-jade colored, leather sash, adorned with a platinum and green-jade buckle. Her shoes are two-toned white and coral, divided by a swirl of tiny green-jade poppers. Her matching platinum jewelry shimmers in the sunlight.

She slides one leg out of her car with stylish grace, and draws the brim of her white hat to the side, occluding the sun's rays. She steps out and covers her shoulders with a white, light-weight sweater and saunters to the door. She skims her sunglasses down on her nose and reaches for the doorbell.

As she presses it, Greg swings open the door at the same time.

"Oh, my!" She gasps, hand flattened to her chest. "You startled me. What are you doing here?"

Greg eyes her with amusement. "I live here, remember? I'm married to Julie."

She lifts her chin, eyeing him from beneath the brim of her hat. "Yes, I remember," she says, with a banal tone, "but that's not what I meant."

Greg chuckles, then nods at her. "I forgot my phone. How about you, did your husband, the good doctor, give you the day off?" he asks, teasing.

She observes him coolly with her deep green eyes for a moment. “Greg, I think we both know that I haven’t worked at Lee’s practice since our daughter Sarita took over the books. I have a rare and precious few minutes this morning, so I’ve chosen to have a cup of coffee with Julie.”

Greg sweeps his hand toward the kitchen and steps to the side. “Don’t let me stop you. As much as I’d like to stay here and amuse myself at a coffee klatch with the girls, I can’t; I’m running late, but you two have fun.” He says with a jeering grin.

Julie and Linda watch Greg get into his Mercedes, and accelerate down the street through a neighborhood of elegant homes and well-manicured lawns.

Julie gives Linda an apologetic glance. “Please, come in.” Linda takes her hat and sunglasses off, and sets them on the table while Julie pours two cups of coffee. She hands one to Linda. “I’m glad you’re here. Come with me.”

Linda follows Julie to her studio, a spacious, bright-white room, illuminated with tracks of full-spectrum lighting that shine in every direction on walls teeming with paintings of every size and shape. Once inside she puts her hand to her mouth as she spots the easel where Julie’s newest creation rests.

“That’s exquisite!” she says in a breathy tone. “The hues of oranges and reds in the sunset make the black thunderheads look as though their edges are on fire.” She admires if for a long moment, absorbing its power. “The white stallion is enchanting, Julie. It modifies the dark clouds yet maintains their integrity.” She leans in for a closer look, one hand fondling her necklace, “Oh, how superb, you’ve got the glowing edges of the black clouds reflected in the horse's eyes like flames. Julie, its genius! So natural and real, yet with a hint of the abstract. It's absolutely divine!"

Julie's smile is reserved. "Thanks. It isn't finished yet, I still have to mount my hero on the charging steed."

Linda steps closer to the window and folds her arms across her chest. She peers through the shutter slats. Her keen green eyes fixed on Ira. She brings her hand to her chin and watches in silence for a moment, then without taking her eyes off Ira, "So that's him. You're right. He's intriguing." Her eyes linger for a moment longer. She turns. "As odd as this may sound he looks familiar to me. It must be because he's so quintessential. I have no doubt that if you capture his essence you'll win the competition." She turns her attention back to Ira and he looks up at the same time, squinting in their direction. It is as if he senses that someone's watching him.

He's tall, standing in a wide stance with intense dark eyes probing in their direction. His features are precise, high cheekbones and a straight, stern nose. His hair is black like a raven's feathers, long, pulled back and held in place by a turquoise headband. He takes his denim shirt off and tosses it to the side. He bends down to pick up a mattock, exposing a feather-shaped scar that his white muscle-shirt can't hide, and begins picking at the earth with the end of the ax, loosening the rocky soil snarled with roots. He wipes his brow.

Linda looks at Julie. "He's hot."

Julie flushes. "Well, Yes, I know. I know he's very handsome, I've told you that."

Linda smiles. "No, I mean his actual temperature. It's hot out there. It's a perfect excuse to invite him in for a spell, to get him out of the heat, find out more about him. You can ask him about his background so you can better understand the essence of the man. Then you can do what you do best; paint him in body, mind and spirit."

Julie draws back. "No, I don't think so, Linda. Greg wouldn't like it. He's a tad suspicious of the guy as it is; it just wouldn't fly with him. C'mon into the kitchen and I'll pour you another cup of coffee."

Linda slides into the booth next to Miss Jingles. She places a napkin on her lap then picks up the kitty and sets her on it while caressing her thick gray fur.

Julie comes to the booth with the coffee pot and pours some fresh steamy brew into Linda's cup. "How's your team doing on the new collection?"

Linda sighs. "It's been a monumental undertaking that seems never-ending, but we're coming along with the negotiations and have come to an agreement on some changes." She leans forward. "At least that's finished, now the lawyers have to draw up the contract and my new line should go national in the spring. This project has consumed my every waking hour, I've been breathing it, Jules, but it's coming to fruition soon."

Julie smiles, "Wow, I'm so excited for you." She takes a sip of coffee. "How are Lee and Sarita, by the way?"

"Well, Lee's still a workaholic, still keeping long, late hours. His famous words are, 'I must continue to wine and dine clients so that my business remains prosperous.'" She shifts her eyes toward the window for a moment in deep thought, then looks back at Julie. "As far as Sarita goes," Linda tugs at her earring, "she is wonderful. Lee tells me she hasn't missed a step in the last couple years. She's handling her orthodontist tech duties, along with school and adopting Lee's bookwork and banking from me surprisingly well."

She moves her hand to her chest and takes a deep breath. "And words just can't express enough what a great pleasure it was to unload that responsibility from my plate. Although I do stop in from time to time when I have a chance, but my stops are just for a few minutes now." Linda smoothed her hair around her ear and looked down at Miss Jingles while petting her. "You know," she says, glancing back up at Julie, "People think that success is something that just happens to you overnight. It's not. It takes long, hard hours and lots of sacrifice to make it to the top and stay there. Lee's business was chewing up valuable time from my business and it made traveling to fashions shows and shoots next to impossible to do."

Linda takes a sip of coffee while contemplating. "When I think back, it was a miracle that I even got my business off the ground. Between Lee's company and mine, I no more than had time to breathe. Then on top of it, we adopted Sarita when I was just twenty-four, which added an overload to the pressure in my life. I had no idea how much work children could be. Yes, we had a housekeeper, and I'm grateful that Lee saw to it that Sarita's homework got done every night and that she got to school every morning and back again, because God knows as often as I was gone, I couldn't do it. But it turns out, that even after all the added stress that bringing a child into the house carries, she grew up and became a godsend to me when she was at last able to take over Lee's bookwork and banking. It's hard to believe she's in college now."

Julie looks down into her coffee cup. She knows Linda doesn't mean it the way it sounds. Julie lets out a long, thoughtful sigh. Linda lifts her cup with both hands curled around it. She takes a sip, reflecting again on Sarita's childhood and how fast the years flew by. "Her childhood was such a blur," she tells Julie, "It's hard to remember her when she was a young girl. I wish I could have been in two places at once. I would have gone to all Sarita's piano recitals, and parent-teacher conferences."

Julie senses Linda's guilt and tries to make her feel better. "But just imagine being Sarita, imagine your entire family being wiped out. For Sarita it couldn't have turned out any better. I can't imagine her having a better life with more opportunity anywhere than with you. You've given her everything, every opportunity she could want is hers for the taking. Thank *God* Greg's boss told Lee about her when she was eleven years old."

Linda closes her eyes for a second, and nods; then in a soft voice confesses, "I admit I hadn't thought things through when Lee first told me about her and I insisted we take her and raise her. I knew both of us were career-focused, but we had enough resources to give her everything she needed to grow up healthy and with a bright future. It just seemed selfish not to take her and look at her now; she's running the office by herself. Oh, darn, that reminds me," she checks her watch, "I've got to run." She moves Miss Jingles back down onto the cushion and walks to the sink with her coffee cup. She turns to Julie. "Take my advice and get to know that man in your back yard. He could be the key that opens a brand new door for you. At the very least, offer him something cold to drink, it's hot out there."

Julie nodded reluctantly and walks to the door. "Maybe you're right, maybe I'll make some fresh lemonade and take it out to him, at least talk to him for a minute or two."

Linda nods. "I think it'll make a world difference, Jules."

Julie smiles. "I'll call to let you know what happens."

Linda gives her a brush with her cheek. "Splendid. Talk to you later."

Julie waves to Linda as she gets into her car, then walks back into the house to her studio. She stands, watching Ira as he works, moving around the pond area, digging holes for the new shrubs and trees, jabbing at the ground with his shovel, lifting heap after heap of dirt and wiping his brow. She admires his impressive physical fitness as she puts her brush to work, creating her hero strong and poised, mounted on a noble steed.

Rosa's visions had been intense that morning and now she is thinking about Ira as she puts the last vines of the Desert Sage that she'd harvested into a soft, white leather satchel, closes the flap and ties it shut. She looks around her Oceanside home, thinking that a person never knows what's in her future.

*We're all dangling*, she thinks. Like bats in a cave, highly social beings spinning on a planet suspended in organized chaos. We all lose our grip and fall from time to time, but flap our wings back to the surface and cling to a new venue. A learning process renewed until the spirit leaves the body.

At Rosa's insistence there was to be no phone, no radio, or television in her new home. She prefers it this way. Her life consists of growing medicinal herbs, reading, and basket-weaving. She moved in with Ira at his insistence after he graduated from college and began his career with the Border Patrol. He used his landscaping money for a down payment and signed the papers for a three-bedroom stucco home with a terracotta roof, about one half mile off El Camino Real, east of Oceanside. The landscaping Ira designed is extraordinary. The rocky paths and mineral formations placed among flowering plants and herbs are bewitching. His entire yard radiates with mineral energies and haunting fragrances so fundamental and it stimulates the spirit.

Of course the house has modern electricity and plumbing, but the thing that Rosa likes most is that it has a greenhouse in the backyard. The previous owners had won it at a game show in Beverly Hills and they left it behind. She remembers how happy she was when Ira told her it came with the house. She believes in her heart that it was the sole reason that Ira bought the place. He wanted her to have a place to grow her herbs year around. He said it's what his mother would have wanted and he even expanded it for her.

Rosa's been thwarted all morning by troubled feelings, spurred by the vision she had earlier. It was a warning, she knows it, an unpleasant and menacing danger is surely near, but no matter how much warning she has, she can't stop the future from happening. She believes it has everything to do with Ira, and it's larger than the foothills that surround them, so she sits at the kitchen table, doing the one thing she can do to help. She weaves together a medicine wheel from a willow branch, creating a representation of the sacred circle of life.

Julie sits in front of her easel creating what she hopes will be her masterpiece and with a light feathery spin of her brush she puts the last details in the stallion's mane, then she dips into her red and puts the finishing touches to the sunset. She looks out the window and sees that Ira is walking toward a new batch of plants and shrubs that Julie doesn't remember being there yesterday. She checks her watch. It's late morning and getting warmer outside. This would be a good time to stop and make some fresh lemonade; she has to pick up Greg's suit and deliver it anyway.

She gets up and goes upstairs to change her shirt. When she walks into the bedroom she notices one of Greg's shoe polishing cloths lying on the white carpet of his walk-in closet. The bright blue material stands out like a Beverly Hills swimming pool in Siberia. She picks it up and puts it back in its leather case. *How strange*, she thinks, it wasn't there this morning.

She changes into a bright yellow satin camisole with crossed straps in the back and a pair of white cotton capris. She goes back downstairs to her kitchen and opens the fridge. She loads a pile of lemons onto her arms and balances them until she gets to her counter, then lets them roll onto her cutting board. She takes her crystal pitcher down from the cabinet, fills it half full of water and adds a packet of sweetener. She cuts the lemons and squeezes the juice from each half, then she cuts the last one into slices and floats them on top. She decides to add ice and let the concoction cool for a few minutes while she takes another look at her painting. She adds a whole tray of ice cubes to the pitcher and they clink against the glass as she carries it to the fridge.

When she walks back into her study she can see Ira is still at work with his shovel. Even though she's already changed her clothes she dips into her red oil paints, being careful not to drip and swirls a thick crimson circle around the stallion's left eye. She looks up once again and sees Ira fly backward then fall forward onto his knees. Instantly, she jumps up from her stool. Her knee catches the corner of her easel, sending it crashing to the floor. She lets out a gasp as she watches red paint splatter across the temple-white marble tile. A rush of energy surges through her like voltage and she bolts for the back door. She reaches for the handle, shouting to Ira. "Are you all right?"

By the time Linda stops in at her husband's orthodontic clinic it's just past noon. She'd put in tremendous hours here earlier in their marriage to help him build his business. She had changed the office environment from antiquated to high-tech. She set up the computer network and implemented all the newest software, allowing Lee to triple his business. Without Linda's brainpower and effort, Lee would not have been half as successful.

When she walks into the building, the place looks deserted and quiet. She checks her watch and imagines Lee must be in his office eating lunch. Lee's receptionist, Tiffany, a pale blonde, with a Barbie Doll tan who always wears her hair pulled tight in a ponytail is not at the front desk. In fact, the whole office seems abandoned.

Linda hears the faint ringing of a phone that's barely audible, but she can tell it's coming from Lee's office. She opens his door, expecting to see Lee sitting at his desk, but his chair is empty. She peeks in his bathroom; not there, either. The low-key ringing continues and it's coming from Lee's top desk drawer. She walks to his desk and pulls on the handle of the drawer; maybe he put his phone in his desk drawer by mistake. She has to rustle through papers, software discs, envelopes, and a stapler, but finally finds a phone at the bottom of the drawer wrapped in bubble plastic.

She arches her eyebrows, opening her eyes wide, she stares at the phone thinking about the absurdity of keeping it wrapped in bubble plastic in your desk drawer and even more baffling to her is the fact that it's one of those cheap disposable cell phones. She unwraps it and holds it out in front of her with two fingers as if it's contagious, as if it is infected with a virus.

She stands there looking at it while trying to form a logical explanation for wrapping a phone in bubble wrap and tucking it into a desk drawer. The one logical explanation is that it's purposely been hidden there, but why? She wraps the phone back up and puts it back in the drawer, but not before she writes the incoming caller ID number on a sticky note.

She hears Lee's voice somewhere down the hall, stuffs the sticky note with the phone number into her purse and walks out of his office, closing the door.

Seconds later she sees her husband emerge from the operatory in his doctor's coat and mask. He pulls the mask off and with his fingers smoothes his mousy brown hair. Lee has pale baby soft skin that makes him look years younger and his soft blue eyes emulate both sheepishness and haughtiness.

Their daughter Sarita walks out behind him. She is the complete contrast to Lee's pale complexion. Sarita is tall and slender, with cocoa-colored skin and dark-chocolate-colored hair. Her bangs are brushed to one side and her long locks are held behind her ears with a thick black velvet headband.

Lee looks at Linda with absolute surprise. "Linda! I thought you weren't stopping in until after one today?"

"I wasn't going to, but it turns out my meeting today with Harper's chief editor had to be rescheduled for Monday, so I'm running early." She steps past Lee to Sarita to give her a kiss on the cheek. "Hi, sweetie, I'll have time for a light dinner after work tonight. I haven't eaten lunch, and I'll be starving by then; would you like to join me?"

Sarita displays a genuine look of disappointment and sighs, but before she can reply, Lee puts his hands on his hips. "She can't, she has a class at six-thirty on Fridays, but my guess is that you didn't even know that, did you?"

A pang of guilt flashes in Linda's eyes and Lee knows he hit a bull's-eye. If there's one thing that he is good at, it's making Linda feel guilty about her regular deficiencies when it comes to Sarita's life.

Linda swipes her hair to one side with her pinky and then folds her arms across her chest, eyeing Lee up and down. "Yes, of course I knew, it escaped me for a moment." She takes a step towards Sarita. "How about if I free myself for lunch tomorrow, then?"

Sarita nods. "Okay, I'd like that."

"Do you need any help with anything here?"

Sarita smiles. "No, but thank you."

Linda puts one hand on her hip and turns to Lee. She eyes him for a moment, thinking about the phone, but decides not to ask about it yet. "It's quiet in here. Where is everyone?"

"In the lunch room. You're just not used to being here during lunch, that's all." He shrugs his shoulders. "This is the way it is here at lunch hour, the crew eats, and we keep working." He knows he's riled Linda, and tries to lighten it a bit. "Wasn't it your dad that said 'all work and no play, keeps the loan officer away?' or something like that?"

Linda throws her hair back and gives him half a smile.

He brushes past her and she watches him from the corner of her eyes.

He reaches back for Sarita's arm and pulls her toward the operatory. "Come on, we have Judge Thomas' kid to finish up. "See you later, Linda. Don't wait up. I have some networking to do tonight; a high stakes, no-limit game of Omaha at Barona."

Linda turns and watches him walk away. She hates it when he does that to Sarita, pulling her along like that. She's not a kid anymore and besides, he shouldn't be making her work through her lunch with him. The next time they get some time alone, she'll have a strong word with him about that.

Sarita looks back at Linda and waves goodbye. "See you tomorrow, Mom."

Linda watches her walk away, remembering what Julie had said about her being a lucky girl who has everything. Linda folds her arms across her chest as Sarita and Lee disappear into the operatory, thinking how much it baffles her that Sarita insists that she wants to be in the orthodontic profession. If that's so, why does she seem so uninspired by it? After a moment of standing there wishing as she often does that Sarita would change her mind and join her design team, she shakes it off and walks into the vacant office that used to be hers.

She sits down at her former office desk and logs into the accounting software. Everything appears to be in order, except when she decides to make a quick scan of the inventory, the part of the business that Sarita's responsible for, she notices something that catches her eye. She clicks on the details for two different controlled product accounts. She sits back and stares at the information for a moment while tapping her finger on the mouse.

Her phone in her purse rings. It must be at the bottom of her purse because the sound is muffled. It prompts her to think about the mysterious phone hidden in Lee's desk drawer. She lets the call roll into voice mail.

She puts her hand to her chin deliberating, studying the inflated inventory figures, then she thinks about the mysterious phone. An unaccustomed feeling of uncertainty creeps into her thoughts and makes her uneasy.

She knows Lee is way too busy at the office to have an affair and anyway he's not the type. He shows no interest in relationships other than with business associates. His emotions are primitive and habitual. He never ventures far from his territory and he is not interested in, or any good, at romance. He's bold, egocentric and controlling at times and even though he'd be considered a heavy drinker and gambler, he's still obligatory and regimented. He holds in high esteem a picture of himself keeping up the appearance of a good family man. He is single-minded, confident and glib. That's why she fell in love with him, marrying him over the shock and disapproval of her parents, who couldn't see past Lee's pomposity even though he had a highly esteemed up-bringing.

Her curiosity is piqued though and it doesn't look like it's going to be something that's going to roll off her back any time soon. A secret telephone along with overages of inventory items that are federally controlled and restricted raised questions in her mind. She reaches for her hat and purse and leaves the office. She runs into Tiffany the receptionist, who's just back from lunch.

"Hi, Ms. Stevens, I have some messages for you on my desk. Your assistant Alexandria called a zillion times and Julie Bishop called once."

Linda situates her white floppy hat on her head, slides her sun glasses on and then lowers them to the end of her nose. "Thank you. Tell Doctor Lee and Sarita that I've gone back to my company."

Tiffany smiles, holding the sticky notes out for her to take. "Okay, Ms. Stevens, I will."

Linda turns and walks out the door, leaving Tiffany still holding the notes. She crosses the parking lot to her car. She takes her cell phone out and tries to call Julie, but reaches her voice mail and hangs up. Next she calls her assistant and tells her how to put out the fires that she's called about. She drives out of the parking lot, thinking about the mysterious concealed phone and the inventory. Lee has always been somewhat reticent and aloof; she knew that when she married him, but that phone wrapped in bubble plastic and the overages of a controlled substance bothers her.

She wonders if she's distanced herself from her family through building her own career so much that she's carved a canyon between them. Even if that's true, she still has the right to know what's going on with him and his business. After all, he is her husband and her name is on the company's legal documents. She has to ask herself that if he has a disposable phone wrapped in bubble plastic buried in his desk drawer and a stockpile of controlled substances masked in his chart of accounts, could he be concealing other things, too? Maybe it's nothing, just bookkeeping errors, but what about the phone? Maybe it is something, and her reputation is worth a closer look.

As she drives back to her company, *Lines of L'Attitude,* she presses the button for the radio and catches the last of an animated weatherman's forecast.

"So folks, it looks like it is gonna be another hot one tomorrow and straight on through next week. In other news today . . . What! Are you kidding? Listen to this folks, just in. A report filed by the San Diego Wild Animal Park this morning says that some deadly reptiles are missing. It hasn't been determined yet if the cages were accidentally left open or if they were purposely left open and the reptiles stolen." The pitch of his voice rises. "Stolen! Now I've heard everything folks. Tell me, just who with a sane mind would go through the trouble of pilfering some deadly reptiles? I mean, really, folks, wouldn't it be easier to just pick one up at your local or state bar? I'm not talking tavern association here, folks."

Linda smirks and switches the station to some soothing music.

As she drives down I-5 she spots a sign that intrigues her. She takes the next exit and rolls the car along a strip mall parking lot. "There it is," she whispers. She stops the car in front of Radio World Electronics and reads the litany on the front window. Wireless Phones, Plans and Accessories, child tracking devices and other covert electronic devices. She stops reading, parks the car and walks into the store.

A sharp young salesman calls out. "Hi, can I help you find something?"

Linda eyes him thoughtfully, rather smugly appraising his fashion style and in an inquisitive tone she answers him. "Yes, I have some questions about GPS tracking devices."

"Okay, I can answer any question you have. Shoot."

Linda gazes over the top of her sunglasses, then takes them off. "I've heard about a device that you can stick to just about anything and it will track its movement. Is this true?"

The clerk nods with enthusiasm, knowing what she's talking about. "Yes, ma'am, it's true."

"Tell me how it works."

"Well, we have a couple to choose from; both use military satellite signals for positioning. One of them, called LEA, for Land, Earth, and Air, receives signals twenty-four hours a day and its internal computer displays the location within two point five meters or eight feet of accuracy."

Linda tilts her head, "Hmmm."

The clerk continues. "Its recorded data can be displayed with Google Earth. It comes with all the software you need and has two megs of flash memory." Linda nods and the clerk continues his pitch. "We also have the Super Sticker." He pulls one off the rack. "This little baby has all the same features as the LEA but in addition it has four megs of memory, and vibration detection."

Linda leans in for a closer look. The clerk pauses.

"And here's the biggy; it has its own built-in voice recorder, so it monitors conversation, too."

Linda arches one of her brows, looks up at the salesman. "A covert data and voice recorder in one, how resourceful." She doesn't hesitate, she tells the man she'll take it.

The salesman rings up her purchase, drops the tracking device in a bag and gives her a serious look. "It's my responsibility to tell you that the store does not sell this product with the intent that it be used to violate the privacy rights of others, and it shouldn't be used in this manner."

Linda picks up her keys and the bag from the counter, tosses her hair and whispers "Yeah, right." She turns to leave, but stops in contemplation. "May I use your phone? It's a local call."

The salesman hands her the store's cordless phone. "Sure."

She retrieves the sticky note from her purse, and calls the number that showed up on the caller ID of Lee's disposable phone. It rings eight times before a voice pierces the air waves, its Greg Bishop's voice. He sounds perturbed. "This is a private number! Who is this?" Linda is caught off guard; she hangs up.

She furrows her brows remembering that Greg's name didn't come up on the caller ID at Lee's office, so he must have a disposable phone, too. She stands at the counter processing the information; for Linda everything is methodical, she hands him the phone back. "I'll need one more of these devices. "She hands him some money. He nods, rings another one up, and deposits it in her bag.

She walks out to her car and tries Julie's number again. She needs to find out if Julie knows anything about this mystery phone. Julies telephone rings and rings. Linda hangs up when she gets a recorded message.

# CHAPTER TEN

## Getting Intimate

Julie dashes through the back door just in time to see a thick snake slithering sideways across her backyard. Ira is on his knees holding his elbow with two streams of bright red trickling down his arm.

The snake had launched itself three feet into the air, and sunk its fangs into him at lightning speed with such force that it thrust him off the ground, knocked him staggering backward then, trying to regain his balance, he'd stumbled forward and fell to his knees. It appears there were a couple of snakes, because he had been bitten in the leg by a different snake just a few minutes before and he is beginning to feel the effects of the first bite.

Julie is running across the yard, still holding her artist's brush dripping with red paint. She is pointing the brush back at the house while yelling something, but Ira can't make out what she is saying.

Ira's ears are ringing, his sight is bleary and he's dizzy and weak. He closes his eyes and sways backward, catching himself before he falls. He is seized by a vision.

*She is running fast; her long black hair is trailing behind her. She's frightened but focused. She sees a glimmer of light ahead of her, and she's sprinting as fast as she can. She's going to make it, she knows she will. She will find a way to tell everyone what they are planning to do. It's not far now. She is calling his name; his mother is calling his name, "Ira, my son, Ira, I'm here with you, trust me. Trust her."*

*He opens his eyes, a shimmering golden shield is spinning toward him. His mother's long black hair turns golden, her glimmering shield, once spinning is now stalled. It's tranquil, floating above him and two columns of white stand in front of him. A visage of a peaceful woman appears holding a red-tipped stick. A frenzied voice inconsistent with the apparition shatters the image, she's shouting at him, stunning him back to full consciousness.*

"Oh my god, oh my god! I saw it through the window, I saw it jump; we've got to get you to a hospital."

Ira opens his eyes and stays fixed like a statue. He's kneeling on the ground, glaring up at her, warning her to stay away.

She stops in her tracks. He shifts his eyes downward and to his right. Julie follows his eyes. She gasps and stiffens. There's another snake; thick, muscular, coiled a foot away. They both remain frozen in place.

The blaring sound, a sound like pressurized steam spews through the air. The snake lifts its fat triangular head, stretching its thin neck. Its vertical black pupils are alert and focused, waiting for Julie to move. It sizzles while its split tongue flickers in the air, checking her scent.

Julie stares into its lidless eyes, trying not to blink. The snake is in striking position and can have its fangs in and out of her in a split second. Her heart is racing making it difficult for her to hold her breath, but if she moves the snake will strike.

Ira is kneeling as still as possible. He can see the snake from the corner of his eye, he knows the other snakes were Mojave Rattlesnakes, dangerous, aggressive, venomously potent, the type of snake that will strike repeatedly when feeling threatened.

Julie stands still, but she's frantic inside. She slowly moves her eyes back toward Ira and for what seems like an eternity their eyes are locked; like two forlorn lovers aching for an escape from their torment.

She wants to help him. He's already been bitten and time is of the essence. The venom traveling through his veins will soon reach his nervous system. First it will affect his vision, then his swallowing. Within minutes, every muscle in his body will become so weak that he will not be able to breathe.

Her nerves are frayed, her mind is a whirlwind and her most basic thoughts seem to take forever to manifest. She eases her attention back on the snake.

Its sharp cryptic pupils are fastened onto her like a National Football League offensive tackle waiting for his opponent to flinch. It takes a swipe forward, trying to draw her off sides so it can deliver its poison. She remains disciplined; not moving a muscle, praying the snake will give up and crawl away.

Ira's sight is worsening; his focus is slowing, everything's wavy and he's losing perception. His throat is closing, his saliva is thick and tastes like tin, but he doesn't dare swallow.

The tension is building. He knows that he has to do something before his body submits to the poison. The shovel is within reach, but if he moves to grab it the snake will strike and most likely it will strike Julie first.

Seconds are ticking fast as the poison makes its way through his veins.

He watches Julie holding her breath; she's frightened, but remains brave. He can tell from the corner of his eye that the snake is creeping forward. She could turn and run, but that would direct its wrath on him and he's impressed that she stays.

Time has run out, he must decide what to do this instant, so without warning he lunges forward, crashing into her. Her paint brush flies into the air and she falls backward, slamming her head onto a pile of jagged rocks.

She is dizzy and confused. Her mind whirls trying to get a grip on what happened. Then at once, she comprehends that Ira's full weight is on her, his warm breath in her face. At the same time, the snake sinks its fangs into Ira's back, he jerks and clutches the back of his shoulder shouting. "Call nine-one-one!" His voice is raspy and strained. He rolls off her and slams his back down onto the snake, protecting her from its attack. Then once again his back arches, his chest heaves, and he winces in pain as the snake sends its venom smoldering through his back for the second time. He closes his eyes tight, then opens them. His lids flutter and roll to the back of their sockets while he releases a long, haunting groan.

He looks up through what appears to be a tunnel, the sun's rays stabbing his retinas. His eyes sting and everything's closing in around him. He fights to focus, yelling at her again. "Run! Call nine-one-one!" He feels the snake trying to coil beneath his back. Its jaw is still wide open with its fangs embedded in his flesh. He tries to subdue it by grinding his back into to the earth, pressing down with his full weight. The snake struggles, twisting beneath him trying to free itself, but it can't. It's trapped beneath his back, its fangs unsheathed and embedded in Ira's flesh.

Julie staggers to her feet and scrambles to the house, half running and half crawling. She flings open the door and grabs the phone in the laundry room. Her fingers, eyes and brain aren't cooperating so she struggles to pull it together.

She fumbles around the key pad of her phone, hunting for the numbers which seem to take forever to find. At last, her senses align and she locates the numbers.

She pushes the nine, then the one, then one again. She waits for an eternity for the phone to ring. "C'mon, c'mon. Hurry!" She waits hearing only hollow static, finally she hears the ringing. "C'mon!"

At last, a woman's voice. "Nine-one-one. What's your emergency?"

Julie's short of breath, huffing between words. "Snakes, rattlesnakes, huge ones. He's been bitten by snakes! Help us! Please hurry!"

"What is your location, ma'am?"

Julie puts her hand to her forehead and squeezes her eyes shut trying to think of her address; it takes a moment, but it comes to her. "It's forty-eight eleven Cardinal Flower Drive, Oceanside. Please hurry."

She tries to catch her breath, while the dispatcher repeats the address back into her ear. Julie nods. "Yes, yes, correct. Hurry, please, hurry!"

"Stay on the line, ma'am, while I try to reach someone who can help you."

Julie waits again in static, a period of time that seems like forever. "C'mon, hurry," she whispers.

The dispatcher breaks the static. "Okay, ma'am, there's an ambulance on its way. Keep the victim calm and lying down until the medics arrive."

Julie nods and hangs up. As she turns to run out the door, on impulse she grabs a bottle of paint thinner that's within her reach, and makes a mad dash back out into her yard.

As she runs toward Ira she sees him still lying on his back with his knees up, pressing himself into the dirt. His breathing is labored in quick short gasps.

He looks up at her, saliva trickles from the corner of his mouth. His voice is weak, barely audible. "The snake is stuck in me; I need your help to move it."

She looks into his eyes; they are deep pools of pain. She knows she has no choice. He points a shaking finger at the long handle of the shovel, "Use the shovel."

Julie looks at it, there's a hacked-up snake lying close by. She realizes now that there were more than two snakes which explains why Ira had been attacking the earth with such force. He must have been bitten before the one she saw through the window. *Oh, my, god, this is even worse than I thought.*

She swallows hard and zeroes in on the shovel. She knows she has to do it, and she has to do it now, but she's nervous about her surroundings. She wonders how many snakes might be in the area. So in slow delicate steps, she tiptoes sideways to the shovel. When she's close enough, she turns, inspecting the entire area for more snakes.

When she deems it safe, she reaches down to pick up the shovel. Then she runs back to Ira's side.

"Okay, I'm ready." She swings her long blond hair behind her back.

Ira looks into her eyes, his vision is dim, but her aura is calming. She's different from what he expected her to be. For a second he thinks about his partner Carlos's words, "drop dead gorgeous," and she is, but she's more, she's valiant and intelligent. He is thankful for her. His vision is wavy and he blinks, trying hard to keep her straight. Something about her gives him strength. He musters the breath to verbalize his words and he closes his eyes, still imaging her.

"On three, I'm going to roll over." *You're lovely.* "Scrape it off of me." *I've never seen such beauty.* "I've been bitten, hit it hard the first try ok?" *Love at first sight.*

Ira's voice trails off and he lies there gasping for air. Julie readies herself with the shovel. With his last ounce of strength he starts to count through clenched teeth. "One, two, three," and with a deep forceful groan he rolls onto his stomach.

Julie's eyes grow wide. She can't believe what she's seeing. The snake's belly is sliced open. She throws her hand to her mouth in horror, it's pregnant, the snake's offspring squirming inside a gaping wound. Julie begins to gag at the site of the squirming braid, she vomits.

"Now!" Ira shouts in a raspy tone, stunning Julie back to her wits. She wipes her mouth and jabs the shovel hard into his back. She scrapes the snake off gaging. Ira lets out a roar as the shovel sends surging pain through his nerves. His body goes limp as he passes out.

The mother snake tumbles along the ground, landing on its back, its intertwined offspring flopping alongside her. Julie runs, shovel in hand, and with all her strength she jabs at its head severing it from its body. One of the offspring squirms free, slithering across her foot, sinking its tiny fangs into her skin. She jumps, then she drives the spade into it, too. She runs to get the paint thinner, opens it and dumps it on the squirming tangle of snakes.

She hurries back to Ira's side and rolls him onto his back. His breathing is faint.

She pulls his boots and socks off, she begins CPR. She sticks her fingers into his mouth, clearing thick saliva from his throat. She covers his mouth with hers and with vomit mixing with saliva, she breathes life into him. She places her hands on his chest and pushes with all her strength, pumping and counting the thrusts while huffing in between. It seems like hours since she's called 911. She is tired, but she doesn't give up.

At last she hears the siren coming closer, the ambulance stopping in front of her house and she begins to scream. "Help us! Back here! Help us!" She breathes another breath into Ira, and continues to pump. Within seconds, three paramedics are running across the yard toward her and before she knows it they're all stooping beside her and she pulls away, holding her chest, and gasping for breath.

Julie stands up. She stares down at Ira in a daze. How could this have happened? Where did all those snakes come from? She watches one of the paramedic's inspect the bite on Ira's arm as warm tears stream down her cheeks. She shouts at them. "He has bites on his back, too."

A woman paramedic is searching for a vein to start an IV, as another paramedic prepares a tube to intubate. A man cuts off Ira's shirt and rolls him onto his side to examine the wounds on his back, he notices there's also one on his thigh; he does not know it's the first bite. He cuts into Ira's jeans and tears off his pant leg. The site of the puncture is swollen, and it's blistering. He reaches for his radio while staring at Ira. He calls for someone at the University of California/San Diego Medical Center. He holds the radio to his mouth while surveying the yard.

"We have a Native American male approximately 30 years of age. He has multiple puncture wounds from multiple snake bites, the snakes look to be Mojaves. The victim is unconscious with four puncture wounds on his back. There are also punctures on his lower left arm, and one on his left thigh, all of them bleeding. Swelling and blistering has progressed beyond the site of the puncture on his thigh. He shows signs of systemic shutdown. His vitals are: pulse 58, pressure 72 over 50, and dropping. Upon our arrival his wife was administering CPR. Due to severe pulmonary edema we are intubating. Over."

A women's voice breaks over the radio. "Roger that. We acknowledge. If there's no doubt it's a pit viper proceed with the first vial of CroFab. Over."

"Ten four. Over."

The attendant reaches in his bag and pulls out a vial of anti-venom. By now Ira's veins are so constricted they have to stick him with the needle four times before they can get the IV flowing. His esophagus is engorged, and the tube that they use to intubate scrapes his trachea. As it forces open his throat his mouth fills with blood, it gushes past his lips, and flows down his chin onto his neck.

Once again a voice breaks out from the radio telling the crew that they are standing by and to transport the victim as soon as the patient is stable.

One of the paramedics walks to Julie. She's staring in a trance and her body is trembling. The attendant touches her shoulder. She flinches.

"We'll be transporting him to the Medical Center." He bends down to look closer into her eyes. "Ma'am? There are more than 8,000 venomous snake bites treated every year in this country and the UC, San Diego Medical Center/Division of Toxicology is responsible for treating a high percentage of those bites. Their ER stockpiles anti-venom. He'll be in the best of hands. What about you, are you all right?"

Julie's eyes are red and swollen from her tears. She doesn't know what to say. She is much better off than her landscaper and she feels foolish to complain about a tiny snake bite on her foot, though she figures she better speak up. She tells him that one of the offspring may have bitten her ankle, but that she thinks it's a dry bite. The paramedic advises her to have it checked out at the hospital, offering her a ride with her husband in the ambulance. Julie's taken aback, for a moment she stares at him. "He's not my husband, he's my landscaper."

"Do you have any way of reaching his next of kin?"

Julie gazes into the distance, thinking about what Ira just did for her. How she's never even met him before today, but that now somehow, she's sure she knows his soul. She looks down at Ira. Then she answers the attendant in a whisper. "I'm sorry, I don't even know his name."

One of the paramedics pulls out a camera and begins taking pictures of the snakes. He asks Julie if she has any information about the victim at all. Julie touches the back of her head and realizes that she has a sticky gash where she bumped it on the ground.

She tells him that he's a landscaper from Land Performance. She pulls her hand away and finds her fingers smeared with blood. She hadn't realize she'd smacked her head so hard. She tells the attendant that she'll go with them to the hospital. She just needs a minute to grab her purse and the number for Land Performance from the house.

While waiting for the paramedics to stabilize Ira, preparing him for transport, she looks at her watch and remembers Greg's suit. She tries to call him to tell him what's happened, but he's in a meeting with a client and can't be disturbed. So she makes a call to the dry cleaners telling them to deliver her husband's suit to the bank before noon. She also tries to call Linda, but has to leave a message on Linda's answering machine.

She hangs up as the paramedics strap Ira to a gurney and begin loading him into the ambulance. When they have a spot situated for her, she climbs in herself. She rides along, praying that everything will be okay, while she holds Ira's hand, trying to reassure him, to let him know that he's not alone.

Ira's vitals are volatile. His mind drifts as he slips in and out of consciousness.

*The lights of the police car are flashing, blinding him, and the shouting of the people is deafening. He covers his ears as he bounces up and down in the back seat of the squad car. A woman runs crying out in her native tongue. She stumbles and falls. His back arches, and he cries out in pain, his voice turns into sirens. Straining, he tries to hear, but his ears are hollow. A woman appears, holding a red-tipped stick, her arms reach out, a cool spray fills his nostrils. He's fatigued, feels heavy, no strength to sit up. His chest heaves, a loud crack, a straight line forms, gathering women and children march to the trees. A wolf circles, flowing robes, rolling, falling, wailing, turning to vapor, everything goes black.*

The doors of the ambulance burst open. The stretcher scrapes along the bottom, and the first set of legs drop to the pavement. The wheels clatter as they race toward the emergency room doors.

There's a lot of commotion at the ER entrance. There are nurses, EMTs, and a doctor in a white coat. Julie's shivering in shock without even noticing it. An attendant throws a blanket onto her shoulders. She looks at him with worry in her eyes. The ER people have crowded around her, firing questions at her one after another. What size? How many? How long since the first bite?

Julie swallows and tries to speak. At last she manages a few words through her chattering teeth, "About an hour."

One of the EMTs interrupts, answering the questions for Julie.

They lead Julie into the hospital, to a space where curtains are used for walls, and the bed wears a crown of machines at its head. The funny thing is, she notices the light-blue curtains have tiny black dots that are arranged in a pattern of squares running diagonally. She groans, oh dear god how her mind wants to escape.

She lies down on the mattress feeling heavy, like she is water-logged. Her head and shoulders hit the pillow like a bowling ball. One of the nurses brings her a vomit basin, one is swabbing her ankle and a PA is shining a tiny light into her eyes.

"Look left. Right, now up, down."

Voices in the background are chattering about shock and concussion. They tell her to close her eyes, to just relax, an ER doctor will be in to check on her in a few minutes and someone will come in to let her know how her husband's doing. Julie's exhausted, her nerves are shattered but she manages to mumble.

"He's not my husband."

She starts thinking about Ira. Her mind rewinds to her backyard, she shivers as she imagines the snakes coiled up; striking bold patterns on thick muscular bodies, angry and defensive. She wonders where they all came from and why so many. She closes her eyes, shaking away the image. It's just not normal, something is wrong. Snakes don't form a detail to attack people.

The nurse turns and looks down at her. "What did you say, dear?"

"He's not my husband. He's a landscaper doing some work in our backyard."

Julie is on edge, jumpy, flinching when the curtain rolls open and two men appear in front of her. The graying older man is wearing a San Diego Police Department uniform. The other one is thirtyish, dressed in khakis and a polo shirt, but good looking and dark-skinned.

As Julie contemplates the police uniform and zeros in on his badge, the first thing that comes to her mind is that Greg's intuition about Ira might be right, could he be wanted by the law for something? But then why did he risk himself for her?

The police officer asks the nurses if they can talk to Julie for a couple of minutes. The nurses oblige, they leave.

"Good afternoon. Mrs.?"

"Bishop. Julie Bishop."

The police officer nods and lowers his voice. "How do you do, Julie. I'm Officer Randy Beck with the San Diego Police Department and this is a colleague of mine, Carlos Ramirez. He's with the United States Border Patrol. We have a couple of questions. Do you feel up to talking?"

Julie's not in the mood to talk, not wanting to get involved especially since the man they want to cross examine her about saved her from the sinking fangs of a venomous snake. She feels a bit protective of him, no matter what he may have done in his past. Although reluctant she figures she'd better answer their questions, but she remains reserved.

"Yes, it's fine."

"Can you tell us how many there were?"

She blinks her eyes with indifference, looking at Carlos and answering with a frigid tone. "Just one, and I doubt that he's here illegally."

The officers look at each other, then Carlos speaks up. "We mean the snakes."

Julie wriggles herself into an upright position while struggling to keep her composure. *Snakes*, she thinks. What do the police and the Border Patrol care about snakes? With all the robberies, rapes and murders going on, don't they have anything better to do? And that good-looking one who's supposed to be with the Border Patrol, he's not even wearing a uniform. What a joke this is, our hard-earned tax dollars at work.

She's exhausted, her brain feels like mush, and her emotions are over inflated, like helium balloons tugging at the end of a string, tense and straining, ready to pop. *This is nonsense*. She crosses her arms tight against her chest. She just can't help herself. She tosses her hair back and turns up her chin. She throws an insolent scoff at Carlos.

"What's wrong? Did the snakes cross the border illegally?"

The two men stand like statues, staring at her. Neither of the men so much as even crack a smile.

Carlos can't help but think that somehow this gorgeous woman that he saw outside of her house picking flowers this morning has turned out to be not so beautiful after all. It figures though, living in a lavish home like hers, of course she's a snob.

After a few moments though, Julie's disdain begins to fade away, but Carlos, who's already suspicious of Julie's husband, striving not to get personal about his friend, Ira, drills his dark-brown eyes into hers, suspicious of her, too, now and annoyed. He repeats the question.

"How many were there, Mrs. Bishop?"

Julie softens a bit as she picks up on his tension, thinking back, trying to remember the pieces of snakes that she saw before picking up the shovel. A quick shiver ripples through her body while she thinks about the scene in her yard. She puts her face in her hands and rubs her temples while she counts in her mind. She looks back up. "Four."

As she delivers her audible, she realizes in that very moment just how dubious it is. One snake in the backyard on a hot day is not so unusual, as they will seek shelter from the sweltering heat of the Santa Ana's, two could be a normal number, but four?

Officer Beck looks up from his pad of paper, not able to hide his shock. Carlos closes his eyes for a moment in disbelief. Beck flips the page of his notebook.

"Did you notice anything else peculiar in your neighborhood early this morning or late last night, like strange cars or people?"

"No, nothing."

"Where were you and your husband yesterday?"

"I was home all day, and Greg came back home around 8:30 p.m.; he had a business meeting."

"Do you have children or pets?"

"We have a cat, Miss Jingles."

"Was anyone else home when this happened?"

"No."

"Did any neighbors come out to help?"

"No, everyone was at work."

"What time does your husband typically leave for work?"

Julie loses her patience. "What's going on here? My husband doesn't even know about the snakes yet. Or even that I'm here."

Officer Beck squints, and with a level tone asks. "What time, ma'am?"

Julie shrinks down in her bed. "Six-thirty, but this morning he came back because he had forgotten his phone." As soon as she says it, the image of the blue polishing cloth pops in and out of her mind.

Beck nods, pulls a business card from his shirt pocket. "We don't have any further questions at this time, but I'll leave you with this card. If you think of anything else that may have been out of the ordinary, give me a call."

Julie nods, they thank her and leave. She lies back down and closes her eyes, trying to remember the events of the morning and the night before. She tries to relive it again. She can't think of anything out of the ordinary other than the number of snakes, which is itself out of the ordinary.

Down the hall in the emergency room, Ira's life is drifting in the shadows between this world and the next. Monitors are keeping rhythm with the swishing and sucking sound of his ventilator. As he lies immobile on a gurney, a team of nurses and a dark haired woman wearing a white coat and a pair of small binocular glasses are bent over him.

Doctor Issac shakes her head. "We need a CBC with a diff. A Chem Pan, Coag, Albumin, BUN, PT, PTT and Creat for starters. Sweet Jesus, I've never seen anything like this, we're on the fifteenth vial of CroFab, and he's not responding. Make sure he gets a dose of tetanus, and start him on some steroids, along with antihistamines."

"Yes, Doctor."

"Order a CT scan, and have them stand by. Damn, he's starting to bleed from the nose and gums. Get me one milligram of Benefics coagulant, start him on morphine, and keep pumping him with CroFab. I can't wait for those test results; he's starting to hemorrhage. How the hell does a person get bitten by a snake on the thoracic region of his back? And not just once, but twice."

Doctor Issac pulls a piece of fang out of a black bubbling wound from Ira's back. She holds it up to the light and sees it's covered with dirt. She sizes it up with an intense stare, then she drops it into a metal dish. The nurse holding the dish looks down into it. She can't believe her eyes; she's never seen a fang from a snake pulled from human flesh.

"This is a mess." Doctor Issac says. "He has gravel and dirt ground into his skin." She checks his lymph nodes. "He needs to be watched for rhabdomyolysis, and compartment syndrome. I'm finished here. Wash him good and swab him again, then dress the wounds. Wrap him in gauze and send him to ICU." She peels off her gloves. "I don't know why this patient's not responding like he should. Those EMTs with the camera must be at the nurses' station by now. I'm going to hunt them down. I can't wait any longer; I need to see some pictures. Page me if he experiences any changes. Call the lab, and tell them I need the results STAT."

"Yes, Doctor."

Doctor Issac is an expert in venom research, one of the best doctors in Southern California for treating venomous bites. She studied at UCSD; she's board certified in Toxicology and has been practicing medicine for eighteen years, including four years each in India and

Pakistan, two of the highest-ranked snakebite mortality countries in the world.

She leaves the emergency room with swift strides, moving straight to the admitting desk. She doesn't see any EMTs standing around so she calls out to a nurse, tapping her finger on the desk. "I don't know what's going on here, but I need snake pictures. Find the EMTs who brought the envenomation patient in and tell them to bring me that camera. I need pictures now!"

The nurse nods and scrambles for the phone.

Doctor Isaac's instincts are sharp and she knows where her patient is heading fast. She's seen the deadly destruction caused by venom on the human body and she's being proactive. She has just finished speaking when her pager goes off. She checks it and spins on her heels. "Here we go."

She dashes back to the ER like she's running a four-forty. The monitors are going crazy when she enters the room, each one beeping and flashing, sending out their warnings. She looks at the heart monitor first.

"His kidneys are failing." She tosses Ira's chart at the end of the gurney and the nurses drop the side rails.

Doctor Issac pulls a pair of latex gloves on, "Prepare to catheterize him for peritoneal dialysis." One of the nurses peals back Ira's gown and begins to swab his abdomen with iodine and gives him a local anesthetic. Another nurse yanks open the metal drawer of a cart filled with emergency instruments. She pulls out a scalpel and hands it to Issac.

Doctor Issac slices in and makes an incision on Ira's right side, just below his navel. She works fast and guides a tube through the slit into his peritoneal cavity. "Okay, now." She looks up at the monitors. "Start the flow." She watches. "Set up the CCPD to perform five exchanges over the next sixteen hours, then give him a dwell period of eight. We'll start with that. Also add an IV of antihypertensive at 50 milligrams every 10 minutes up to 300 milligrams and start a transfusion. Call doctors Larsen from Nephrology, and Kinny from Neurology and let them know what we have here. We need to prepare for tissue necrosis."

"Yes, Doctor."

Doctor Isaac turns to leave the room, but swings back around. "I want a piggyback of Vasopressin ready for septic shock, 40 IUs."

She leaves the room, and makes her way down the hall, stopping at the nurse's station for lab results. Then she walks to her office and sits down in front of her laptop. She types Pit Vipers into her browser, then changes the search to Asian Vipers.

She begins poring through her patient's lab results and cross-referencing it to a specific case that she remembers in Pakistan. She suspected, but is still astounded at the similarity of indications in this victim, compared with a victim of an Asian Russell's Viper that she'd worked on in Quetta.

The Mojave Pit Viper, native to North America, and the Russell 's Viper, native to Asia, would look somewhat similar to a lay person, but their venom is very different and must be treated with the correct serums or death is certain. If this is a Russell's bite, there isn't much time before cerebral hemorrhaging will begin. "Oh, my god," she gasps and closes her browser.

After Officers Randy Beck and Carlos Ramirez questioned Julie, they'd left the hospital and headed for the

Bishop's residence in Oceanside. A passionate young herpetologist by the name of Darren Wentz, from Oceanside Reptile Rescue and Control is arriving at the same time when they pull up to the house. Carlos and Randy introduce themselves and tell Darren they're also there to see the snakes.

When they walk into the back yard the men can't believe their eyes, it looks like a battle field. It's a gruesome sight whether you're a snake lover or not and Darren happens to love snakes. He's read every book he could get his hands on about snakes. He is an acknowledged expert, he has no fear of snakes, just respect for their graceful, agile, and sometimes ultra-dangerous nature. They are in fact very important to our ecosystem, especially to agriculture. Darren has been working as a licensed keeper for more than two years now.

He tilts his chin to his chest and swallows; the scene makes him queasy. He begins to survey the mess in the yard and he's disheartened. Among all the gardening debris lay hunks of diamond-patterned bodies. There are four adults, all of them thick and heavy, more than four feet long with wide girths. One of them has a tangled mess of babies sprawled alongside its body.

It's been a couple of hours since the incident happened so the snakes should no longer be a threat. However, one always needs to be careful around pit vipers; they've been known to bite even after being decapitated. Darren takes out a pair of collapsible tongs from his leather bag, and picks up pieces of the snakes, placing them into his metal box.

He turns and looks at the two officers, "You know, snakes don't attack people unless they feel threatened or they've been provoked, or encroached upon. They would rather crawl away. Every creature belonging to the mother Earth has a right to exist here. This is sick and to me it's sad. What happened?"

Randy Beck explains to him that a landscaper had happened across them as he was working in the yard, and that he must have stepped on one because he was bitten on the leg and arm. "He must have sliced at them with the shovel and before he knew it there was another snake within striking distance. He was bitten four times altogether."

Darren pinches the mother snake's triangular head with his tongs and lifts it up, squinting at it. "Wow! This is rare."

Carlos grimaces. "Yeah, and disgusting."

Darren moves in for closer look. "This is a viper, not a pit viper. I know this because it doesn't have heat-sensing pits on the sides of its face. The others do." Darren swings the snake's head closer to the officer's faces. "Look."

Both officers back away. Carlos nods while straining his neck as far away as possible. "Ah, yeah, we believe you; we'll take your word for it."

Darren shrugs and gives them a tolerant nod, then he continues to examine the snake. "You know, it's difficult to believe, but I'm sure this is an Asian Russell's Viper. Not only is its skin pattern more oval shaped, it's got huge nostrils and a triangular vertex between its eyes."

Darren puts the snake's head in the box, he looks around to locate the other half of the snake. He crouches down to examine it when he locates the body that matches it. He brushes the hair out of his eyes and sighs, "Damn, she was pregnant. And yeah, she doesn't have a rattle, instead her tail is thin and striped so I'm sure this is a Russell's Viper." He stands up and with heavy shoulders saunters back to his metal box and picks it up, walks back to the snake, scoops her up along with her babies, and puts them inside it.

He turns to the officers. "Just to give you some facts on the Russell's Viper. Its scientific name is *Daboia Russelli*, it's native to the continent of Asia and when a Russell's decides to tag you it's famous for holding on. Its fangs are longer than most, capable of delivering up to one hundred twelve milligrams of venom each time, though sixty-three mills is about average."

Carlos stares in stunned silence. He is horrified for his friend Ira.

Oblivious to what Carlos is feeling, Darren continues to churn out snake information. "Just to give you a comparison, a Cobra averages about fifty milligrams a bite and contrary to popular belief, snakes don't completely run out of venom. The Russell 's Viper is one of the deadliest snakes on earth; it's one of Asia's Big Four."

Beck's eyes grow intense.

Darren explains further as he collects the bodies and heads of the other snakes. "These here are Mojaves, they're cranky and deadly, too, but they're not foreign like the Russell 's Viper. Of all snakes, the Russell's has a reputation for being the most ill-tempered when threatened or provoked. They strike with such force they can throw a grown man into the air, and not just that, they may decide to hang on, too. Also, depending upon the snake's mood and the size of its prey, they have complete control over how much venom they inject. It can be nothing, which is a dry bite or it could be a full load. Their fangs are sheathed and retractable and they have independent control of the expulsion on either side."

Carlos blinks, as he takes in Darren's words. It's almost too much for his brain to comprehend.

Officer Beck drops his jaw in disbelief. "What?"

"Yeah, they have complete control of the discharge of their venom. They can discharge from one fang at a time, or both, or discharge from a sheathed dry bite. It's amazing, isn't it? It's proof they have a thought process."

Carlos' face is pale, looking past Darren, thinking about getting back to the hospital as fast as he can. Randy is a statue, his eyes hard.

Darren shuts the lid on the metal box and locks it.

Neither Ramirez nor Beck asks how it's possible that a foreign snake like a Russell's Viper could be found in the back yard of an upscale neighborhood in America. They already have a good idea and they know it's not because it's the Bishop's household pet. Darren holds the metal box out in front of him and Beck takes it into his custody. "I'll be taking the snakes as evidence to the station; we appreciate your help, and the information."

Darren holds out his hand, and shakes both of theirs. "You're welcome. If there's anything else that I can do, just call. It's a shame about the landscaper. I feel bad for him, especially if both a Mojave and a Russell's tagged him. The bill for the anti-venom alone is going to be in the hundreds of thousands, not to mention the trauma to his body, but I feel for the snakes, too. It's another bum rap for them."

The officers turn and walk to their cars, both of them on pins and needles for Ira.

Darren lets out a huff and shouts after them. "They do have redeeming qualities, you know."

The officers stop and turn around, eyeing Darren with skepticism.

He reaffirms with a nod. “The Russell’s Viper venom is used in diagnostic lab testing to detect diseases like Lupus, and as a diagnostic agent to determine deficiencies in blood clotting like in hemophilia. Viper venom is, in general, used for all kinds of treatments from cancer to stroke to pain killer for leprosy and all snakes keep the rodent population in check. You remember learning about the Bubonic plague in grade school, right? We need both cats and snakes on this planet to keep that from happening again. But it’s a thankless job, and most people don’t understand them.”

The officers wave without comment and retreat to their cars.

Beck looks at Ramirez. “Snakes just aren’t my thing.”

He nods. “Mine, either. I’ve gotta get back the hospital, pronto.”

Beck puts his hand on Carlos’s shoulder stopping him at the front of the car. “I sure hope your partner Ira pulls through; this undercover operation has turned into a hellish nightmare for him. He’s in my prayers.”

Carlos nods and lets out a huge breath. “I’m praying, too. I’m going back to the hospital to let Ira’s doctor know about the foreign snake and at the same time make sure this undercover operation remains top secret.”

Beck pats Carlos’s shoulder. “We’ll get the sons of bitches that did this to him, Carlos. We’ll get ‘em.” They lock eyes for a moment. “I’m pretty sure those snakes were stolen from the Wild Animal Park. I have to get this evidence back to HQ and start working on when and how they were stolen. Talk to you later.”

Carlos has all he can do to keep his composure. Before he pulls his car away from the curb he’s on the phone, calling the hospital. He's in deep thought about Ira. The snake incident must have happened just after Ira took over for him after he left the stakeout late this morning, and now that he has learned one of the snakes is a deadly foreign viper, his stomach is tied in knots.

# CHAPTER ELEVEN
## Railroaded

Greg Bishop sits at his desk in downtown San Diego staring out the windows that glaze the entire west wall of his office. The Pacific Ocean shimmers on the horizon. The Coronado Bridge that stretches across the warm turquoise swells of Mission Bay is his footstool. Silhouetted against the Bay's radiant scribbles is the haunting whitewashed palace, the Hotel Del Coronado, crowned with conical ruby towers and high flying flags flapping in a warm, saline breeze.

The view from Greg's office is breathtaking, a fairytale kingdom. Greg lives in a world of beauty, power and risk. His job is to use money to make money, as of late, however, he's had to stretch his financial prowess beyond reason to meet the bank Board's new income expectations. After being saddled with some new, near impossible loan goals he has had two huge deals go bad. After the first six months of not meeting his goals, the Board members' nerves were rubbed raw and they put immense pressure on Greg, threatening his career at the bank.

Then Greg's boss, Ted Silar, gave him a lead, and recommended that he do a financial deal that was not in his area of expertise, but that would help him meet the Boards' demands. Greg had started his career in Commercial Real Estate, but moved into Wealth Management soon after and his expertise is in Securities Investment. The deal that Ted pressured him into doing was a long-term leasing investment, a whole different animal.

The lead came from one of Ted's acquaintances in the commercial construction industry who wanted to invest in some heavy equipment; then lease out the equipment for residual cash flow. Greg spent countless hours over many weeks scrounging up every last resource he could find to help him put together a complicated multi-party contract; a leveraged forty million dollar leasing deal for Ted's acquaintance who borrowed fifty percent of the total cost from the bank.

Greg's new client did in fact lease the equipment out to a wholly-owned subsidiary of a multi-level conglomerate, but the parent company was not party to the deal. Six months ago Greg learned that the lessee was in trouble, hadn't been making his rent payments from the start. And, to top it off, they'd turned the lease obligations along with the big-ticket equipment over to one of their affiliates without prior notice and without providing any credit information on that affiliate. This created a huge headache for Greg. The lessee claimed he was in compliance with the terms of the lease, but Greg's client claimed the affiliate company didn't meet the requirements to assume the lease and they wanted out of the deal. So the bank's twenty million dollars got sandwiched in the middle of a fierce court battle.

Greg had spent numerous hours of backroom squabbling trying to mediate underlying issues and agendas with these two parties to make sure the loan was paid back. He'd been within inches of saving the deal, but the bank Board slammed the hammer down on him, called in the legal department and declared default, after months of expensive litigation and precious time that he could have used on other prospects. The fate of the twenty million dollars that he was responsible for fell into the hands of people who didn't know a Leveraged Lease from a Simple Checking Account and the results ended up being a huge loss.

Plus, and it is a *huge* plus, the second deal involved union money. The union boss was another one of Ted's acquaintances; one of his leads, another prospect outside of Greg's expertise, but Ted insisted it would be an easy way for him to appease the Board for the twenty million dollar loss on the previous leasing deal. The thing he didn't tell Greg was that the union boss was Jimmy "the stick" Castello, and that the deal would be the cement that would seal Greg's fate, making him loyal to the bank board and Jimmy the Stick for as long as they wished.

Ted arranged a meeting between Greg and Castello, and before long Jimmy had Greg investing twenty million dollars of the union's money into a commercial real estate deal that Ted called, low-hanging fruit. It seemed like an answered prayer to Greg. He put together a loan for a manufacturing/real estate package for a company that would extrude steel that would double the value of the construction holding company, netting the union an ROI, of twenty percent annually on their money. This loan would get Greg back into the Board's good graces. Needless to say they were pleased as pudding; they said it was damn good juice for everyone. The problem was solved, the board was off his back and some of the pressure was off Greg. Unfortunately, the property turned out to be a hidden toxic waste dump, the real estate value slid off the charts and the capital disappeared. Now, "The Stick" has threatened Greg's life if the union doesn't get their money back. *Yesterday*!

Ted Silar, Greg's boss, was lured into Jimmy "the Stick's" lair years ago, by the bank's six member board when some of Ted's rigged deals went bad. To save his own life he ended up becoming an associate of the Castello crime family, working his way rapidly up to CEO of the bank. He has worked a deal out with Jimmy on Greg's behalf to pay the money back. The problem is that Greg doesn't understand the terms. Unknown to Greg, the bank Board and Ted have been laundering money for the Castello crime family for years, and now they've snared Greg, too. They saw immense potential in Greg, had designs on making him one of their "high" earners from early on, so when the time was right they put the wheels in motion entrapping him by using phony loan documents and creating bad deals. Deals that Greg did not know about. Deals, in fact, which did not really exist.

When Greg first found out about Ted's shady dealings, he got flaming pissed and they had a fire breathing argument. Greg ranted and raved at Ted and told him he was quitting his job at the bank. Ted had stood and listened, then moved over to a large cabinet, opened a file drawer, reached in and withdrew a good-sized metal box. He carried the box over to Greg with one hand and when Greg finished his rant and was about to leave, Ted reached in and pulled out a hand, it was black, caked with dried blood, wedding ring intact, and he held it in front of Greg's face. *It's too late. Here's what is left of the last guy that wanted to quit. There's just one way out with Jimmy. No joke, Greg, you do what The Stick wants or you die.*

The Stick, Ted, and the bank are now using the hypothetical millions lost as an excuse to force Greg into the dark underground world of trafficking. Or, as Jimmy said, *If he won't go along we cram Bishop's lungs full of cement and toss him in Mission Bay.* So Ted made an arrangement for Greg to do a onetime deal which required Greg to move a shipment of heroin to pay back the union's twenty million dollars. Ted reminded Greg that The Stick had ways of forcing him to do it, and asked, *how much do you value your wife?*

Greg was in shock, but he had no choice. With despair, and a tightness in his chest, he told Ted he would make the heroin delivery once and he did, but now they want him to continue until they decide that what would have been the expected juice from the money is also paid back in full.

Greg's phone rings. He stares out the window when he answers it. "Hello? . . . Right now?"

He hangs up and calls for his secretary, Dorothy Cache, a red-headed perfectionist with long, straight hair always wrapped in a tight, braided bun. She's wearing a pair of half frame cheaters at the end of her nose when she pops into the doorway. "Yes, Greg?"

"I have to go to the branch in Junction City and probably won't be back today. Just put my calls into voice mail. I'll have to get back to whoever calls. The cell service out there is very spotty."

"Will do, Greg."

"Thanks. If Julie calls, tell her I'll be home quite late tonight."

Dorothy nods, “Got it.”

Against Greg’s wishes, he had been assigned to oversee an insignificant branch in a tiny southern California outpost that was a lively boom town in the 1800s, called Junction City. The branch is housed inside Camp Corners, a dusty convenience store that serves as the town’s restaurant, gas station and church all in one. A historic railroad depot that had once served the gold and silver mining community is located behind it. Both are only about a football field through the desert away from the Mexican border. The assignment is beneath him; he is embarrassed to have anything to do with it. The bank board saw potential in the mine and the railroad. Greg didn’t see the potential but he did understand getting railroaded.

Greg will drive the bank-owned truck that’s been designated to make the harsh trip through the rough and arid back country to the branch. He grabs the keys and walks out.

Ted Silar, tall and lanky, in a dark suit, burgandy tie, and silver hair on his temples, a definite patriarch-type, is standing outside his office door down the hall. He motions Greg to him.

“You just told me I had to go to the branch in Junction City.”

“I know, but I need to talk to you first. Come in, Greg.” Greg walks into his office and stops in front of Ted’s desk.

Teds office is a prime corner office, one of the best in the building, with a continuous rampart of windows offering both a west and south view; if Greg’s office is a fairytale, then Ted’s is the castle in the kingdom. Looking out to the right are the giant concrete pillars of the Coronado Bridge a massive sweeping structure, looming two hundred feet above foamy swells dwarfing navy carriers as they glide beneath her. On the other side is a pristine landscape of velvety emerald green, speckled with white sand bunkers, tiny flags flapping in the breeze and a water hazard with a sparkling fountain bursting from the center.

His desk is made of pure Austrian crystal and is situated in the corner of the room.

This is an empire, Ted's empire.

It doesn't seem possible that a bank the size of Golden State Bank can afford to employ a man with Ted Silar's extravagant tastes. Except, Ted Siler is a special friend of Jimmy the Stick, so the board gives Ted the salary he demands.

Ted moves to his well-stocked, smooth-polished black granite wet bar, takes out a bottle of Macallan 1950 single malt from a mahogany cabinet and pours a dram into a thick, weighty crystal glass. He offers it to Greg.

"No, thanks, I have to drive."

Ted nods, lifts the glass in a polite toast and takes the golden liquid in one swallow. "Greg. According to my source in the hospital we may have accomplished our mission this morning, it's not certain yet, but there's been a bit of a mishap."

"What happened?"

Ted sets his glass down on his desk. "Your wife happened."

Greg, raises his voice. "My wife! What did she do?"

Ted grabs his shoulders. "Lower your tone."

Greg breaks into a sweat and reduces the volume. "Ted, we're talking about my wife here. What happened, tell me."

Ted points his finger at him. "You tell me. You said you had it all taken care of, that she'd never even know until it was too late."

"What does that mean?"

"She's the one who called the paramedics."

The confusion on Greg's face is obvious. "I had her running errands this morning, how could she have?"

Ted interrupts and picks up a dry-cleaned suit still in its bag, off a rich tufted leather chair, and holds it up. "Is this the errand? I just happened to see it hanging by the temp's desk, so I inquired about it. It seems, Greg, that while you and Laura were busy in your meeting this morning, your wife was busy, too. So busy, in fact, that she didn't have time to drop this suit off herself; instead, she had it delivered. You wanna know why, Greg? Because she went to the hospital, instead."

Greg realizes that Julie must have been hurt, he opens his mouth but Ted interrupts.

"No, Greg. I know what you're thinking and you can't call her. You can't let on that you know about this." Ted tosses the suit back on the chair. "It'll blow this action like a Cardiff Whale. You are not to call the hospital nor say a word to her or anyone else about this. As far as you're concerned, it didn't happen. You will go about the business assigned to you and that's the end of it. I need that shipment back here tonight." He walks back to his desk. "You can assume she's fine, one of our scouts followed them to the hospital, and saw her walk in."

Greg strains for a reasonable tone between clenched teeth. "*Assume* she's fine? Don't call the hospital? Ted, do you have any idea how this feels to me? She's my wife for Christ's sake, I'm worried about her."

Ted snaps. "You got yourself into this mess, Greg, you put together a risky deal and you backed it, I might add, with money that wasn't yours and you lost. I offered you a way to save your ass and now you want to make a phone call that will take us all down."

"You approved the deal, Ted. Jimmy and the union had cash they wanted to invest, and we put a deal together; you said it was solid."

Ted jabs his finger at Greg. "*You* put the deal together; we trusted that you did a title search for discovery." Ted throws his hands into the air. "Property Buying 101."

"Ted, *you* told me the deed came back clean."

Ted waves his hand at him as if he were a fly. "I'm not going to argue with you about this. It's obvious it wasn't clean."

Greg feels his blood rising to the surface and he wipes the sweat from his brow, but he knows he has to hold his temper. Julie is what's most important right now and he tries to reason with Ted about calling her again. He knows the degree of danger that was in his back yard and he needs to hear her voice.

Ted steps forward and puts his hands on his hips, "Did I not make myself clear the first time? If you call her, there'll be consequences for the both of you. *For all of us.*" Ted's eyes declare a warning, and the two men stare in confrontational silence. After a minute, Ted's tone darkens. "Am I understood?"

Greg's fists are clenched, his armpits hot and sticky. He knows he can't change things, *I'm trapped, I'm fucked.* "Yes." He says, his tone like ice.

"Good, this delivery is different this time, I need you to follow directions to the letter." Ted walks to the door making sure it's closed tight. "You're running a shipment from the branch in Junction City back to San Diego."

Greg's jaw drops. "What?"

"Listen up, our guys will be waiting for you outside the bank at 5:55 p.m., leave the truck unlocked with the keys in it. Go into the bank and say hello to the teller like always, then explain you'll be in the restroom for a few minutes and she's to lock the door when she leaves. Go into the restroom, exchange the bag of money you'll have with you for the bag left in the garbage receptacle. There's a uniform jacket and a holster in it. Put them on, and stay in the restroom until the teller has locked up for the day." Ted pours himself another drink. "Once she's out of sight, an armored truck will pull up and you'll change places with the driver. That's why I asked you to bring your gun today."

Greg arches both eyebrows and starts to protest, but Ted throws up a hand to silence him. "I said, *listen*! There'll be an address written in green ink on a piece of paper that will be tucked into the front passenger's seat. Don't worry about any checkpoints on the route back, the guards are greased. Drive the armored truck back here and pull it into the back alley behind the bank. There'll be a cabby waiting; he'll have a new suit jacket for you to put on. Don't worry about the cargo, just get into the cab. Change jackets and give the cabby your gun. He'll drive you around the block to the bank parking lot and let you out there. Get in your car and head to our dinner meeting."

"This is impossible, Ted. How the hell did you convince an armored truck company to hand a truck over to me? Their security's not penetrable."

"We didn't."

"Just what the fuck is going on here? No way am I stealing an armored truck.

Ted curls the corner of his lip upward, but doesn't answer.

Greg squints. "What's the street value of this load; it better be enough to pay off my debt."

"Fuck, no. They've increased the interest rate."

"What! They can't just increase –"

Ted interrupts. "They can and they have. As a banker you should know how it's done. Jimmy the Stick, hell, organized crime in general, has found the financial crisis to be an opportunity to try out their banking shoes."

Greg sidles to one of Ted's huge leather chairs and collapses in it. He sits with his elbows on his knees, his face buried in his hands. Then he looks up at Ted with disgust. "How stupid! Of all the stupid fucking shit you could get involved with, really, Ted."

Ted pushes his suit coat back, placing his hands on his hip. "You still don't get it do you?"

Greg stares at him, no answer.

Ted huffs. "You're pathetic. They set us up! Hell, they set a lot of banks up. Who didn't get greedy? They pumped just enough money into a feeding frenzy of high-risk real estate to turn the entire financial industry into a house of cards and I have to say, that toxic waste dump scheme was a beaut. Now that the industry has collapsed banks are too busy working out bad loans to make good ones. So now, The Stick and the entire Castello crime family are loaning money to huge corporations so that they can stay afloat through the recession. Now they own the banks and the bank's customers, too. Including ours."

Greg's brows are knitted together. "What the *fuck* are we going to do?" He rubs his hands through his hair. "I'm not going to let this become a career. I agreed to making a few deliveries, just enough to pay off my debt. This is the last one I'm doing Ted, I'm done after this."

He stands up to leave, but Ted grabs him by the arm. "Do you know how Jimmy Castello got his nickname?" Greg pauses, staring at Ted. "Jimmy Castello grew up on the rough side of Vegas. Both his parents were addicts. Hell, it's a wonder the kid survived his childhood. His parents had him on the streets scoring coke and other drugs for them by the time he was ten. They never sent him out with any money, so you can imagine what he had to do to get the drugs, but if he didn't bring back the goods they taught him a lesson by beating the snot out of the kid with a broom stick. The only lesson it taught him was how to inflict pain." Ted squeezes Greg's arm tighter, then let's go. He walks to his desk.

"When Jimmy turned eighteen he took a job dealing craps at a podunk casino on the backstreets of Vegas; his position was stickman. Let's just say he had a nurtured knack for keeping the roughnecks and the cheats in line. When you get whapped upside the face with a craps stick it hurts, even the hard core drunks and cheats learned not to fuck with Jimmy. It wasn't long before some murderous scum, a small-time mob faction, noticed his toughness and recruited him to be an enforcer. His weapon of choice is the craps stickman's stick. After his thugs beat you toothless with their fists, Jimmy takes pleasure in ramming the end of his stick into every orifice you have, starting from the bottom up until you're either unconscious or dead. It's painful and I mean painful. I'm not joking. It's his signature, *capiche*?"

Greg swallows hard and long. He can't believe this is happening to him and he wants out. "How do we get out of this?"

"I've been working on that. This border run will be a down payment. I'm working on getting some stuff so pure that I guarantee when they find out how much money they can make on it our debt with them will be satisfied a hundred fold. The money we'll be making once we get this operation off the ground will make our salaries look like minimum wage."

Greg's unimpressed. "When my debt is paid, I'm done. I'll be out of this shit for good."

Ted scoffs. "There'll be a huge bonus for you come February, Greg. Since you've grown accustomed to money, you'll do whatever it takes to keep living a lavish lifestyle, of that I'm certain."

Greg stands up. "When the debt is paid, Ted, I'm done." He storms to the door. "Later."

Ted calls after him. "One more thing Greg. The Stick wants you to call the doctor and tell him we need more of his stuff." He raises his glass to Greg and sits down at his desk. "You'll be rewarded plenty, you watch and see. You'll be able to take your wife on a long relaxing trip to Venice and you'll be able to spend a mint on her; women love it when you spend money on them."

Greg stops in his tracks and turns around in mid-thought. "The armored truck? How *did* you manage that?"

Ted pushes back in his chair and puts his hands behind his head. "It's a fake. We put it together using an old Hummer body and a lot of sheet metal. It won't stand up to a strict scrutiny, but it won't have to."

“Are you fucking serious? This is *unbelievable,* Ted.” Greg points his finger at him. “One more shipment, that’s all I’m doing, you understand?” He turns and leaves.

Ted follows him to the door and closes it after him. He sighs while running his fingers through his hair, then walks to his desk and dials the phone; it rings until the voicemail picks up. He leaves a message.

“Yeah, it’s me, I need you tonight. Be here at six sharp and bring some flashy shoes. You know the address.” He hangs up the phone, puts his glasses on, and resumes analyzing the banks Q10s.

Greg storms down the marble-tiled hall and chases down an elevator. He slams his hand against the door to stop it from closing and then punches, G for ground. He rides to the lower level alone, fuming, extra pissed now because he realizes what Ted’s plans were for him all along. All the pats on the back, the encouragement, the promises of a dream career, the money, the car, the ridiculous low interest rate on his mortgage, they were all meant to get him addicted to a luxurious lifestyle. And right up until he met Jimmy Castello, he was a blind disciple.

Ted is a respected pillar in the financial community, a polished financial patriarch; actually, a wolf in sheep’s clothing who is leading Greg straight into a death sentence if he doesn’t continue to commit these felonies and now Ted’s got him involved in an armored truck crime to boot. It doesn’t take a genius to figure out that they've targeted him to continue to do these jobs until he's dead or rotting in some crumbling, leaky, cell block somewhere. For Greg, death would be a better option. And the worst part about the whole thing is if he doesn't comply with everything they tell him to do, Julie's life is in danger. There's no way he can go to her or her parents. Doing so would risk their lives, it's just not an option. He is on his own, and he has to figure out a way to get out of this while keeping Julie safe.

These shipments must be getting substantial in order for Ted to go through the expense of building a fake armored truck. It can mean just one thing. That this is going to be an ongoing method of delivery.

Greg unlocks the truck and climbs in, stewing, wondering how he got up to his eyeballs in this mess of trouble. He jabs the key into the ignition, thinking about what his father would say, or do, if he knew about this. He'd *disown* him, that's what he'd do. God knows his own old man was never the supportive helpful type of father, hard-working and successful, yes, but someone he could talk to, hell no. He was the most self-absorbed self-centered man on the planet and it's no wonder both of his wives left him. His mind wanders back to Julie. He wonders what it would have been like to have had parents like hers. Even though she's a military brat, her clan is close-knit, her parents are supportive and have managed to stay together. Then he takes a deep breath, so stressed that he can't slow his thoughts down. They keep looping like the Tatzu at Six Flags. He's starts worrying about Julie again. He hopes Ted was telling the truth about Julie not being hurt.

# CHAPTER TWELVE

## Identification Relay

No emergency room was designed for the impatient and it has been a very long afternoon for Julie. Ever since the moment she'd arrived at the hospital she's been lying on a cold, narrow, perfunctory bed, waiting to hear some news about her landscaper and since her injuries do not constitute an emergency for herself, she's just a prisoner being observed. She's been serving out her time staring at the ceiling while the same monotonous thought spirals through her mind again and again; someone has got to be coming back any minute now.

Finally, she hears casters clacking close by. Then a bright coppery-haired RN in pale pink scrubs, with heavy arms, and a ton of freckles slides the curtain open. She's as short as a whiskey barrel, wide as an ax handle, and she has an IV pole in tow.

Riding along in the basket attached to the pole is a digital thermometer and a blood pressure cuff. She stops at the end of the bed, perusing Julie up and down. Her cheeks are chubby. She has dark pigmentation around eyes that are tiny, set close together and seem out of proportion to her face. She reminds Julie of a pink panda bear.

To the nurse, Julie looks like a vision of a summer's day. Notwithstanding the blood and dirt from her morning adventure, she seems fresh and pleasant, upright in her shimmering yellow satin camisole top, once crisp, but now dirty, white Capri slacks, with a three carat round diamond draped around her neck.

The nurse smiles at Julie, then in a deep, robust, but kindly German accent introduces herself, "Mein name ist Helga." Then after a heavy exhale she looks down at Julie's feet.

"Vich vun is it, liebchen?" Julie points to her left foot. "It's my left one." With her landscaper still heavy on her mind, she wastes no time inquiring about Ira. "The man that was with me, my landscaper, how is he?"

Helga hobbles herself around the bed wheeling the IV pole behind her. She sticks the tip of the thermometer into Julie's mouth without warning, then reaches around the back of Julie's head to feel the injured spot. She examines Julie's foot, turning it from side to side while she answers Julie in her husky German accent. "He ist not respondink vell to treatment, liebchen."

Julie mumbles through the thermometer. "He's not going to die, is he?"

Helga attaches the blood pressure cuff, and pushes the button to inflate it. While the cuff fills with air, she reaches with short pudgy arms and places her fingers beneath Julie's ears. As she checks her glands, Julie falls victim to the rich libation of dark Columbian roast that lingers on Helga's breath. "Ninety-nine percent ov 'zem don't, liebchen, but two oft his vunds are in closs proximity to vital organs, and by zee looks of 'zem, I'd say he vas bitten by *ein pissed schlange.*" Helga steps back and looks at Julie apologetically, but with a twinkle in her eye. "Mein gott, do forgive *mien* langvich, liebchen."

Julie is relieved by the space between them once again and mumbles through the thermometer. "It's okay."

The thermometer beeps and Helga pulls it out and reads it. Then she puts her index finger to her lips while she places the stethoscope on Julie's heart. "You haben here vor long time, ja?" Julie looks down at her watch and then back at Helga with poignant blue eyes, nodding. Her smooth complexion and the nimbus of light dancing off her blond hair gives her the appearance of a distressed angel. Helga's sorry she wasn't more tactful with her answers about the man that came with her and she gives her a pat on her shoulder trying to undo the damage. "Don't vorry, liebchen, he haas zee besten toxicology doktors in dem land vorkink on him. Time ist critical, zough, und she's tryink to find zee pictures of zee schlange, so she kann treat im koorektly, but zee EMT forgot to dropen camera oft at za nurses' station."

A puff of air hisses then resonates through the curtains as the pressure cuff deflates. Helga peals the Velcro apart, and slides the cuff off her. Julie tilts to the side, and looks up at Helga puzzled. "She? The doctor's a woman?"

"*Ja*, she iss, Doktor Jeanette Issac. Vhy does that surprise you?"

"Because," Julie points to the window, "when we first got here, I saw the EMT hand the camera to a man in a white coat. I assumed *he* was the doctor."

Helga furrows her brows and squints. She puckers her mouth, changing her eyes into mere slits above her chubby cheeks. "Ist you sure 'bout diss?"

"Yes. I didn't get to see the doctor's name because his tag was flipped over and I was being led away through the emergency room doors."

Helga clicks her tongue on the roof of her mouth several times. "I vell have to let zee doktor in on ziss. Zee fitals are backen to normal, liebchen, but you look sickly to me. There vell be somvone in to dischargen you schoon. In zee meantime zough, here's little schomethink' to lift zee blood sugar." Helga reaches into her pocket, and pulls out an individually wrapped Star Crunch cookie. She gives it to Julie, and puts her finger to her lips, indicating it is a secret. She hands Julie the bed remote and pats her hand. "Put zee veet up and layen back in zee lap of luxurvy fur avhile, liebchen." She winks, nudging her head toward the cookie. "Zoes are deliceeous." Then she waddles away, closing the curtain, pulling the clacking pole behind her.

Julie looks down at the cookie, deep in thought. She's got nothing to do but think and think she does. She knows Greg well so she can predict his reaction to the whole scene. Once he's certain that she's okay, he'll have more concern for what their neighbors are thinking than how their landscaper is. He'll condemn Ira as if it's his fault and when the neighbors call to inquire about the commotion and they will no doubt hear about it, she knows he'll act blasé about it to them. He'll say something like. "I can't believe that company even hired a guy like that. Everyone knows it's typical of someone like him to come to work bagged up and high. I suppose when he saw the snakes he started messing with them; who knows what goes through the minds of people like him. Maybe now we'll get someone decent over here." Decent to Greg would be white, clean-shaven, salon hair, no tattoos.

Greg hadn't hid his racist feelings about the landscaper from the start, mentioning it to her on several occasions this past week. For a cavalier guy like Greg, it's out of character. It's just plain beneath him to give the landscaper that much thought. But, now that she's thinking about it, Greg's been acting different since, well, she can't quite pinpoint an exact time though it seems to have started months before he decided to level the back yard, changing it from the desert southwest into an elaborate tropical garden. She'd suspected it was his insecurity about the market decline and loss of money. To Greg, money is a personal thing; losing it is a loss of his identity and dropping a few hundred thousand into a new back yard is his way of showing the neighborhood that the country's financial problems haven't hurt him. Nothing has changed in his world; he's still a rich man. Greg has the need to appear as if he's always in control and on top, no matter what.

Even so, he is acting different now than he did before the recession hit. The stress in the financial industry has taken its toll. He's been working harder and longer hours but it never seems to be enough, and he's been withdrawn and distant for many months. She tries to make sure they spend quality time together as often as they can, but with his crazy schedule it's been difficult to make happen.

She's busy, too, absorbed in a program that she spearheaded at the YWCA that fosters healing through artwork for victims of domestic violence, especially children. The recession has without a doubt increased domestic abuse issues. The "Y" is at its capacity.

She plops back against the pillow, exhausted. She'll be sleeping by the time he gets home tonight anyway so she can wait until morning to deal with him, but what about the police officer and border patrol guy that questioned her earlier? Why were they here and why was the border patrol guy in plainclothes on a work day in the middle of day shift hours? Vacation day? It's possible, but a real stretch of a coincidence, them being here together at the same time.

It's baffling, but now that she's past the initial shock of the snakes and back to thinking clearly again, she rationalizes that it could only mean one thing. He is working undercover. Why would a Border Patrol officer waste his time investigating a Native American man? Native being the operative word. It just seems wrong. It makes as much sense as noodles in a birthday cake, ridiculous. Then there are the snakes, the sheer number of them alone stimulates a curious imagination.

Julie folds hers arms in an "L" across her chest, resting her chin in her hand, contemplating the events evolving around her. If nothing else the hours that she's spent in the hospital today have slowed her life down enough to put some serious thought into the day's events.

A strapping, late-twenties-something male nurse by the name of Luke, with black curly hair, wearing navy blue scrubs, is the only person at the ICU desk when Officer Carlos Ramirez hustles from the elevator to the nurses' station in his mountain khakis and burnt orange polo shirt.

He stops at the desk, runs his fingers through his dark brown hair, leaving it slightly mussed. With beads of perspiration forming on his temples and in a troubled tone of voice, he tells Luke that he needs to see the doctor who's taking care of Ira Notah ASAP. He tells him that he can't stress how urgent the matter is, because he has pertinent information to tell her about the snakes that bit Ira. He explains that he's called several times on his way to the hospital, but he was told that the doctor was in an emergency and could not be distracted at that time. Luke tells him that he will try to page her, though it may take her a few minutes for her to wrap things up with whomever she's with and get back to him.

Carlos is so intent on telling the doctor about the foreign snake this very minute, that for a moment he thinks about tracking her down himself. It's not a rational thought; for god's sakes, he doesn't even know what she looks like, but there's so much voltage running through his body that he could take the gold in a hundred meter sprint. It's hard to remain calm when his friend's life is on the line. He'll have to wait, though. Struggling to maintain his composure he asks permission to see Ira. Luke tells him he was just about to check on Ira's IVs, motioning Carlos to come with him to Ira's room.

They talk about Ira's condition on the way. Luke tries to prepare Carlos for what he's about to see. They stop just outside the doorway and Carlos takes a deep breath; he's stunned by what he sees across the sterile ICU room.

Most of Ira's body is wrapped in white gauze to slow the circulation of toxins traveling through him. He lies in the prison of his hospital bed beneath a rectangular window silhouetting the tubes, lines, bags, and monitors to which he is hooked. There's also a convoy of mobile diagnostic equipment lined up along the walls, along with a crash cart that stands at the foot of his bed ready to be charged should the graphic blips on his heart monitor change to one steady flat-line.

Thick tubes protrude out of both sides of his mouth. One is a ventilator for his lungs; the other is an electric sucking tube to remove secretions being produced by the poison. What skin Carlos can see has turned a sickening yellowish red because the toxin is destroying plasma membranes and capillaries. Suspended alongside the bed are a Foley's and a Dialysis Catheter bag collecting bloody fluids. Ira's sitting in an upright position, bent to one side. To Carlos, Ira looks incredibly uncomfortable, but he's on his side to keep him off his wounds and to help him breathe.

Carlos knew it would be bad, but he's still shocked and surprised that Ira has deteriorated to this point so fast. He is in critical condition and while Carlos digests his friend's state he contemplates the evil of the men who did this to him. He wants to talk to Ira; to hear what happened, but Ira's not awake and because of the tubes in his mouth he wouldn't be able to talk even if he were.

As he watches Ira's chest rise and fall beneath the ventilator, he gets steadily pissed off, and he can feel his temperature rising. He thinks about how snide, downright snooty, Julie Bishop was with him. Her attitude was culpable and after a few more seconds of watching Ira, he hits his boiling point. He can't stop himself; he's driven to having a few more words with that highbrow woman. He decides he'll find out if she's still in the hospital and pay her another visit. He's determined to find out what she knows about this. He tells Luke he needs to leave for a few minutes, but he'll come right back and wait for the doctor.

Luke nods. "If she comes before you get back, I'll tell her you need to talk to her about the snakes."

Carlos nods. "Thanks."

He leaves Ira's room, heading straight for the observation area where he and Officer Beck had talked to Bishop's wife earlier. He learns from one of the nurses' Julie's still here and she points to the same spot where he visited her earlier. As he stands in front of the curtain he closes his eyes for a moment before pulling it open, preparing himself to not act like an undercover agent, so that there's no suspicion raised about Ira being undercover too. He takes a cleansing breath before stepping into her curtain cube.

Julie is startled when the curtain swings open. She'd just pushed the last bite of her Star Crunch cookie into her mouth. Their eyes lock. Julie recognizes him and she holds one finger up as she pulls a Kleenex tissue out of a box, and finishes chewing the cookie.

She has a smear of chocolate, and a piece of crispy crunch stuck to her bottom lip, but even so, Carlos is struck by her flawless skin. She's beautiful on the outside, he thinks, there's no doubt about that, it's just too bad she's so hollow.

She swallows her last bite then wipes her fingers and her lips with the tissue. She extends her hand out to him. "Hello, again. It's Carlos, right?"

He's caught off guard by her warmth this time around, but he remains reserved, cautious about getting caught up in this beautiful woman's charm. He has a job to do, and he stands rigid. "Hello, Mrs. Bishop. I'm going to get right to the point." He doesn't shake her hand.

Julie's smile fades away; she recognizes irritation in his voice. She lowers her hand back down to her side.

He's direct, detached and stern. "I'm very concerned about the man who was working in your back yard. He's my best friend. I'm looking for answers about what happened to him."

She stammers for words. "I – I am, too. I don't know him on a personal level like you, but what he did for me was – well, I don't know how I will ever be able to thank him enough."

Carlos contemplates her. She's coming off like she's innocent, but he's cynical, she's holding something back. God help her if Ira dies, because he will spend the rest of his life proving that her and her husband had something to do with it, and he will make sure they're both locked away in a cold cement cell.

He gives her a cool nod, "If you want to do something for him, why don't you tell me why there were four dangerous snakes in your back yard?"

Julie looks at him like he's crazy. How would she know that? It's a question she's been asking herself. "I don't know, I'm wondering the same thing."

Carlos reads her expression; again she seems innocent. It's hard to believe, so even though he knows the snakes were stolen, he tests her once again. "As I'm sure you can imagine it's impossible for me to believe that four of the same deadly poisonous snakes would show up in the same back yard by sheer coincidence unless, of course, they were pet snakes that escaped."

She straightens herself up in the bed. "I can assure you, Carlos, that I don't know anything about anyone in the neighborhood having pet snakes and I know I'd remember if I owned some. I don't, although if I did, I would care for them better than that. They were not my snakes and they were obviously mistreated because they were furious and aggressive. As I said, I don't know why they were there, but you're giving me the impression that you suspect me of something."

Carlos's investigative nature, mixed with his personal emotions has him in overdrive. He decides he better change gears and back it down a notch so he doesn't blow his or Ira's cover. He relaxes his stiff shoulders, loosens his lips, smiles slightly, and starts again. "Excuse me, Mrs. Bishop, I didn't mean to make you feel that way. It's just that I'm afraid for Ira's life.

"Ira? Is that his name?

"Yes, and he's like a brother to me, like family. We crossed paths in college, and discovered that we were both orphaned young and lived a similar ugly childhood. We grew very close in college. I'm just making some inquiries on my own about all this, making sure there isn't something that you may have forgotten to tell the police."

Julie stares at Carlos, somewhat floored. She's wondering what Ira was studying in college when he met Carlos there. He's a landscaper, but could it be possible that he and Carlos were both studying the same thing, Criminal Justice for example? Carlos's words echo in her mind. They sound like the words of a soldier, *like a brother to me,* of course it's possible. Julie's eyes' narrow.

Carlos reads her expression; he knows she's getting suspicious. He couldn't trip her up, couldn't get her to say anything about the snakes, for example that one of them was exotic. So he believes she's innocent, just caught in the vats of sewage brewing in the underworld with no clue that her husband's deceiving her. Carlos' feelings soften toward her. He realizes that they are going to have to think about some type of protection for her in the near future. But, for right now, for her own safety, she needs to be kept ignorant about her husband's activities. In fact, he needs to come up with something to lesson her suspicions about Ira fast.

"Ira was in one of my psych classes in college; that's how we met and we hit it off right away."

This time it's Julie's demeanor that softens. There is something about this guy she likes, even though he's fishing for information that she just doesn't have. He's protective of his friend, rightfully so, but more than that he's intense about it. There's definitely more to this visit then meets the eye. He is hiding something, she senses it.

"Well, as I said before, I don't have any idea why the snakes were in my back yard, but it would have to be a freak of nature. I just can't think of any other explanation." She tilts her head to the side, now testing him "Can you?" Even though she can't think of any other explanation, it doesn't mean there isn't one, and she's betting that he's got some answers.

Carlos decides to end the conversation. Enough has been said, he has learned what he needed to learn and she is starting to ask questions. "No, I can't either, but I intend to make it my business to make sure the police stay on this. Like I said, he's like a brother to me. Now, if you'll excuse me, I think I'll go to his room to check on him." He offers his hand while looking into her eyes. Julie takes his hand and shakes it. He nods, then disappears behind the curtain.

As he walks back to the ICU, he is in deep thought about Julie. She has a quality about her that appeals to him. Her temperament reminds him of his girlfriend, Nola's. It's too bad she's married to Greg Bishop; he suspects there's going to be deep heartache for her in the near future. He thinks there's a good possibility that he'll be present when she learns with whom her husband has been consorting. It's something he's suddenly not looking forward to.

The doctor is bending over Ira when Carlos gets to Ira's room. She's a petite woman with dark shoulder-length hair, fastened at the back of her neck with a pearl hair clip. She is wearing her doctor's coat, black slacks, and a kaleidoscope red-silk blouse, and listening to Ira's heartbeat.

Luke is changing one of Ira's IV bags when he sees Carlos walk in.

Doctor Issac doesn't hear him come into the room, so Luke clears his throat and points. She takes her stethoscope out of her ears and looks toward the door.

Luke introduces Carlos to her. "This is Carlos Ramirez. He's the fellow I told you about that said he needed to speak with you about this patient's snake bites."

When Luke announces Carlos's name, Ira groans. Even though it's a weak groan, it is apparent to Doctor Issac that her patient knows Carlos and he might have information about the whole situation.

She looks Carlos up and down, then nods, "Okay."

Just as Carlos begins to ask Doctor Issac if he may speak with her in private, Helga barges through the door, barreling her charisma into the room with her arms flailing back and forth. "Schkuse me, schkuse me Liebsters," she acknowledges Carlos and Luke, then looks at Doctor Issac. "I haben looking for you, Doktor Issac." She stops and puts her hands on her rotund hips. "Zee woman who camen with zis patient said she saw zee EMT give zee camera with pictures of schlanges to man in a vhite coat outside."

Doctor Issac straightens her petite frame, meeting Helga's gaze. She crosses her arms and squints her eyes, clearly incensed. "There was someone with him when he came in?"

Helga nods. "*Ja*, dere vas."

"Why didn't someone tell me that in the emergency room? Where is she, in the waiting room?"

"Nien, in Observation, bed eight. She vosn't an emergency, but she banged ihr head hard." She points her finger at Ira. "Zis patient is ihr landscaper."

"Well I need to talk to her, now!" Doctor Issac moves toward the door.

Carlos stops her. "Doctor, I need to speak with you now. In private, please. It's urgent." He pressed.

Doctor Issac nods, and indicates the two nurses should leave. When they're gone, she looks up at Carlos. "So what can you tell me about this man and what happened to him?"

Carlos wastes no time. "Ira Notah is an undercover border patrol agent posing as a landscaper. He's in charge of a covert operation in its infant stages, I'm his partner. The operation is sensitive, just a handful of FBI, BP, and SDPD members know about it."

Doctor Issac is taken by surprise, but she regains her composure fast and focuses, listening, attentive.

"I believe the snakes were planted. One of them was a foreign snake that from a distance could be mistaken for a domestic Mojave; it's called a Russell's Viper. I think it was thrown in with the others to make sure Ira would die from the poison. I heard the snakes were stolen from the Wild Animal Park early this morning. Officer Beck from SDPD, who was with me this morning after Ira was attacked, is investigating the theft."

"Russell's Viper" rings out loud and clear in Doctor Isaac's ears. Carlos tries to give her more information, but Doctor Issac interrupts him. "How do you know for sure it was a Russell's Viper?"

"Because Beck and I went to the scene in the back yard where he had been working as a landscaper and a herpetologist by the name of Darren Wentz was there. He pointed out the differences in the snakes. The Mojaves of course are very dangerous, but the Russell's is more dangerous. To tell you the truth, without Wentz there, I wouldn't have been able to tell the difference, I wouldn't have wanted to get that close."

Doctor Issac's eyes go vague as she begins to unravel in her mind what is ahead of her. The scenario she is grappling with, is two different poisonous snakes, from two different continents, requiring two different anti-venoms. It's the reason the Cro-fab isn't working. The Asian anti-venom is not stockpiled in U.S. hospitals and will be challenging to come by. She's never been up against anything like this before. It certainly is plausible that someone wanted to kill her patient by surrounding him with four deadly snakes. All it would take was one slight move and all four would strike and the fact that one of the snakes was a foreign viper makes the prognosis of survival low. This is critical information. Time is crucial and too much time has passed.

Doctor Issac starts for the door. "I have to work on getting the correct anti-venom here in time to save his life. My God, this is going to be tough."

Carlos flashes her a look of pain, mixed with confusion. Doctor Issac can see the agony and question in his eyes so she tries to explain. "In a nutshell, anti-venom is pharmacopeia controlled by the World Health Organization, and we need Asian anti-venom. There's just a few places in the United States that may have some."

"What about the Wild Animal Park, wouldn't they have some on site in case of an accidental bite?"

"Yes, of course, they would, but if they have another Russell's on site, they won't release it. In that case, we'll have to get it from the Miami Dade/Venom Response Bank in Florida."

Carlos looks up at the ceiling, panic sweeping through him "Is there anything that I can do to help?"

Doctor Issac rushes for the door. "Pray that his will is strong enough to keep him alive long enough for the anti-venom to get here."

Carlos moves to Ira's bedside. "Hold on, buddy. I've called Rosa and Father Lelo. They're on their way. You're going to survive this, buddy, and then we're going to bust up that drug ring for good. Hang on."

Carlos hears a soft groan and sees Ira twitch his fingers. He clutches Ira's hand, closes his eyes giving Ira's hand a gentle squeeze. He knows it's going to take everything Ira's got to survive.

**Down in emergency** observation, Julie has just finished signing the paper work for her release, feeling happy to be a free woman again. She pulls her rugged leather hobo bag onto her shoulder, then brushes the Star Crunch remnants off her white slacks. She hurries down the hall to the emergency entrance waiting area, anxious to call Linda. She looks around for a good spot where she can have some privacy, choosing a chair in the far corner along the windows. She plops herself down, trying to make herself as comfortable as is possible in her uncomfortable situation.

She opens her purse, poking through it looking for her phone. After she turns it back on she checks her calls. She's surprised to see that Greg hasn't tried calling her at all, but in a way she's glad. She's too drained to answer his line of questioning right now anyway.

She looks through her other calls, noticing one from the car service about the appointment she missed. Also she has missed calls from Bently's Art Gallery, Land Performance Landscaping, and Linda. She's been longing to tell Linda what happened since she arrived at the hospital. Deciding to ask Linda if she can come to pick her up, she scrolls down to Linda's name and calls her.

After Linda left Radio World Electronics with her tracking devices, she decided to make a quick stop downtown at the Golden State Bank and Trust where she and her husband Lee both do their business banking. She went inside and asked for copies of the last six months of the bank statements for Stevens Orthodontics LLC. Since her name is on the account the statements were handed to her no questions asked.

Linda hasn't looked at the books in quite some time, she hasn't had to. Lee informed her that she didn't need to concern herself with them anymore, so she hasn't.

That was before finding the mystery phone hidden in his office. It's hard to explain exactly what it feels like when you find out that your husband of more than ten years has a secret he's hiding from you, but Linda would describe it like this; it's like sitting in front of the air horn when a chukker ends in a polo match, if that doesn't wake you, either you don't care or you're dead.

Linda's not dead and she does care. She's tolerant of Lee's long hours and late nights, but she's not going to tolerate this mystery phone incident; it's eating at her, and she will satisfy her need to investigate. The logical place to start looking for other possible secrets is within the business.

She is sitting in her Cadillac in the parking lot of The Golden State Bank & Trust with the tips of her Versace sunglasses between her teeth, scrutinizing the bank statements. Her eyes pop like champagne corks as she reads the numbers. There's been a substantial increase of payments being made to RX Oxy and Phyax Pharma; they've doubled and what's even more glaring is that the cash flow being pumped into the business is more than the receivables. She looks up and stares out the window. So where is the extra cash coming from? She's not making contributions to his business, his business is doing well enough without owners' contributions. Also, why hasn't the bank alerted them to the discrepancies? Or maybe it has. In any case, something's not right.

She folds the statements up, and shoves them into her glove compartment while thinking about Sarita. Her first instinct is to protect her daughter, but then she speculates about how much Sarita knows about the extra money that's funneling through Lee's business. She purses her lips tight, and puts her sunglasses back on. She feels like she's been catapulted into a spy movie, like this whole thing is surreal. She looks outside the car window at her surroundings; people are going about their business oblivious to the fact that the well-oiled world that she once knew has ceased. There are secrets being kept from her. The proof is in the pudding, or in this case, the glove box.

She begins to contemplate the ramifications for Sarita if Lee is involved in something illegal. It's very possible that Sarita knows nothing at all, but she could be implicated by association in money laundering or tax evasion, or whatever it is that Lee's gotten himself into. At times he's been obsessive about his gambling, could that be it? Maybe he hit the big time and he's trying to evade the IRS, or maybe he's filtering the money through his business bit by bit, but what about the surplus of inventory? He could lose his license. What the hell is going on here?

Linda's train of thought is interrupted by her phone ringing. She looks down at the caller ID. It's Julie.

"Hello?"

"Linda! Thank God I got hold of you. I tried earlier today but you didn't answer. I've been stuck at the UC San Diego Medical Center all day. Something terrible has happened. I need you to come here and pick me up if you would?"

"Oh my god, Julie! Are you all right? Oh my god, this is my fault. What did he do to you?"

"I'm all right, Linda. If you're talking about my landscaper, nothing, he didn't do anything. I'm all right, I promise. It's a long story and I'll explain everything when I see you. How soon can you get here?"

Linda checks her dash "I'm about a half hour away. I can be there around five-thirty, if the traffic is not too bad."

Julie's wiped-out, she's resting her forehead in her hand. Her voice is remote. "Please come to the emergency entrance. I'll be in the waiting area."

"The emergency entrance! I'll be right there."

Linda ends the call, tosses her phone into her purse and peels out of the bank parking lot. As she drives she thinks about Sarita and Julie. Things have come unglued in her ship-shape world and she feels as though her intuition is overpowering her with signals.

While walking to the emergency entrance after finding a parking spot, a gust of wind kicks up, lifting Linda's hat off; she grabs it in mid-air, then holds it in place as she crosses the no-parking zone and enters the building. She stops for a moment, scanning the waiting area for Julie. When she spots her, she turns to hurry across the room and almost knocks down a priest in her path. He is tall and distinguished-looking; she looks up at him and apologizes, then pushes past him, rushing to Julie.

"Julie, what's going on?" She tosses her hat on a chair.

Julie stands up. "You're not going to believe this, but my landscaper, his name is Ira by the way, is in ICU upstairs and he's in critical condition."

Linda's voice is breathy. "What happened?"

Julie tells her the entire story, the facts blowing Linda's mind.

"Oh, no! Is he going to be okay?"

"God, I hope so. Linda, he can't die. I would feel so awful, it would be my fault. It was me he was protecting."

"Where's Greg?" Have you told him about this?

"I tried to call him a couple times, but he's been in meetings all day."

"You mean he doesn't know?" Linda stares at Julie for a moment thinking about Greg answering the call she made from Radio World, but pushes the thought away for now. "You've been through a lot today. There's nothing more that we can do here. Come on, I'm taking you home." Linda grabs for her hat and knocks it off the seat of the chair. It slides down behind onto the floor underneath. They both try to retrieve it at the same time.

While they're bent down, a petite, elderly, gray-haired woman glides through the emergency entrance doors to the elevators. Neither Julie nor Linda notice her, but if they did they would know just by looking at her that she was there to see Ira. Rosa moves through the waiting area so smooth and quiet, it's as if she's a ghost. She has been informed of Ira's condition by Father Lelo and she's come prepared for a healing ceremony. She pushes the button for the elevator door and steps in, the door slides closed.

Linda dusts her hat off as she and Julie make their way through the emergency doors into the parking lot.

Julie lets out a huge sigh as she sinks into the maroon leather seat of Linda's Cadillac. "God, I'm beat. This is such a disaster."

Linda is thinking about Greg and the phone number that he answered. Why did he answer that number, but not Julie's calls? Now would be the time to find out if Julie knows about the other phone that Greg has.

"Did you try calling all of Greg's numbers?"

Julie lets out another deep sigh. "Yes, I called his cell phone and his direct number at the bank which rolled over to Dorothy, his assistant. She always knows where Greg is. In fact every time I have lunch with her she seems to know more about him then I do. I'm sorry, I don't mean to sound like that, I'm just irritable that's all, Dorothy's a friend as well as Greg's assistant. She told me that he was out making rounds at some of the other branches."

"Does he have any other numbers you can try?"

Julie searches for the seatbelt and buckles herself in. "No, just the bank's main number and they'd just transfer me to his direct line anyway."

Linda wonders if she should tell Julie about the lies that she's uncovered today, including the fact that Greg does have another phone, or if she should give Julie some time to rest. She decides against telling her now; it can wait until morning.

Julie also has something on her mind. "Linda, there's something strange about this whole snake scenario. I mean, even more so than the snakes themselves. A cop and a border patrol guy visited me in the hospital today to question me. The border patrol guy wasn't wearing his uniform, but he came back a second time, said he was a friend of Ira's, but it just seemed out of sorts to me."

This brings Linda an unsettled sense of foreboding and she turns away from Julie to hide her thoughts while digging for her keys. Julie's words are one more reason to believe that something really serious is going on. She suspects that Greg and Lee are up to their eyeballs in trouble and they may have dragged Sarita in, too.

What will Julie think? Will she agree or will she think that Linda has lost her mind? Should she say something or wait? Are the phones and bank statements enough to make Julie suspicious, too? *No, not enough information, not enough solid facts yet, not fair to upset Julie today.* For right now she'll keep her mouth shut.

She puts the car into gear, backs out of her space and drives through the parking lot to the hospital's exit.

# CHAPTER THIRTEEN

## My Shoes

Lee snaps his gloves off and pulls down his mask, its five-thirty in the afternoon and he's just finishing up with his last orthodontic patient of the day.

Sarita's already finished, she's down the hall in Lee's private bathroom adjacent to his office. She pushes the door shut tight and pulls at the mirror on the wall; hidden behind it is a safe. She turns the dial to the left, stopping at 28 then to the right at 13 then back to the left again until she hits the combination and hears it click.

She opens the door as wide as it will open. Inside the safe is a pile of invoices, stacks of cash, and a bank bag. She opens the bag and slides the cash and papers into it. She zips it up, closes the safe, and twirls the dial.

Her heart is pounding as she puts her ear up to the bathroom door making sure Lee isn't on the other side in his office yet. Her palms are warm and moist as she pulls a phone from her purse to check it for messages. Ted Silar gave her the phone, no one else, not even Lee, knows about it.

It was Ted Silar who put up the money to have Sarita smuggled in from Mexico when she was eight. He'd met her parents while he was on a fishing trip. They were impoverished, desperate, wretched people who, with no regard for Sarita's safety or feelings, sold her to an equally appalling Ted Silar. He in turn gave her to a crooked judge to use as a servant and sexual partner at his sprawling seven-bedroom ranch on the secluded outskirts of Bonita, California as a payoff in order to keep his good banking client and buddy, Jimmy Castello, out of prison years ago.

After three years, the cold-blooded judge had tired of Sarita and told Ted to get rid of her somehow; he didn't care how. "Give her back to Castello's men or whatever," he said, but instead, Ted saw a chance to set another hook. He talked the judge into drawing up some adoption papers and approve an adoption to a couple who Greg Bishop and his wife Julie had introduced him to at a swanky dinner party, Lee and Linda Stevens.

Lee Stevens and Ted Siler clicked on the spot. They set each other in motion like the steel balls on a Newton's Cradle. They hung together all night long, knocking around ideas one after another like they had been swinging together all their lives. Ted made mention to Lee about a homeless little girl and after an almost immediate nod and pat on the back, Ted was offering to introduce Lee to a judge who could push an adoption through the court system lightning fast.

When Lee told Linda about an orphaned eleven-year-old girl, her heart broke. Lee, above anything else, is a very convincing liar, telling Linda that the child's parents were both Mexican American citizens who died in a horrible car accident, leaving her with no one in this country to care for her. Linda believed him, desperately wanting to take this poor helpless child into their home. Her motives were altruistic. She wanted to, *needed to,* rescue this poor child from despair so she played right into Lee's hands. Almost immediately, she insisted on taking Sarita in and adopting her.

Lee of course already had Ted's crooked judge friend waiting in the wings with the papers. Lee knew the judge was corrupt. The judge quickly approved the adoption. The adoption papers were contrived for Linda's sake. She still doesn't know that Sarita was smuggled into the country or that the adoption was fraudulent.

In order to make the adoption seem more legit, Lee let Linda see that they paid a hefty adoption fee for Sarita which the judge and Ted Silar split. What it all meant was that Sarita was bought and sold like a slave, a victim of human-trafficking. To Lee's paltry way of thinking, he was saving the child from a ruthless subjection from a pack of heartless men. She would be much better off enslaved to just one man, himself.

Linda had other ideas. She adored Sarita, showering her with gifts and sparkly, little-girl things and enrolling her in the best private school in all of San Diego County. She had every intention of turning Sarita into an independent successful business woman someday.

Lee took on the fatherly role of provider and protector. Linda was surprised by Lee's paternal instincts. On the surface, they were the ideal family.

After a couple of years, Sarita began to blossom, and Lee began to take full notice. Soon he was indoctrinating the vulnerable thirteen-year-old girl on how to act, dress, and behave.

He used Linda's type-A personality against her. While Linda was submerged in modernizing his office and launching her own fashion design business, Lee was spending more and more time with Sarita. He began using the traditional psychological reward and punishment technique on her slowly molding her into his own personal slave.

His punishment technique was to threaten that he would send her back to the mob, or that he would tell Linda that she'd been seducing him. He reminded her every day about her life on the streets of Mexico. He forced her to remember what was expected of her at the judge's ranch, the horrifying details enough to make a lizard's blood curdle. He pounded it into her that it couldn't get any better than this for her, that it was because of him that she was alive in a warm safe home showered with everything that money can buy.

The intimidation was slow and restrained at first, but after months of subjugating Sarita while Linda was not around, he conditioned her into believing that she was safe as long as she did exactly what he told her to do. She understood that she would die if she did not align with him in accordance with his every wish. After months of subjugation, she developed Stockholm syndrome.

It was a scheme contrived to satisfy Lee's sexual needs, an unvarying pattern of selfish psychotic manipulation that played out for the next eight years right under Linda's nose, yet deeply hidden. A secret and desperate life that created a living nightmare for Sarita. She loved Linda and was scared to death of the things that Lee said he would tell Linda if she didn't obey his orders.

She was not allowed to make friends at school. He picked her up and dropped her off every day, starting in grammar school and continuing all the way through high school. When she was with Linda she was not to discuss or communicate to her anything that would arouse any suspicion that there was anything other than a normal father-daughter relationship between them.

Lee still questions Sarita on a regular basis and checks on her often throughout the day. He even has her phone calls forwarded to his phone so he knows who, if anyone, calls her.

He sometimes creates fictitious scenarios to set her up and test her loyalty to him. She never knows when he's testing her. She's always on edge, worrying if she's doing and saying the right things, or making the correct decisions. She fears how Lee is going to react; he flies off in a tyrant about the smallest things. She lives in constant dread. Yet when she is around Linda, she has to act smart and independent, but not too smart, because that makes Lee angry.

Sarita's daily life is like walking a tight rope above a swamp of jaw snapping alligators. It's a nerve-racking, high-tension act knowing that at any given moment her life support could snap and she'll fall into the jaws of death.

She is not allowed to do anything without Lee's permission, and of course he has forced her to tell Linda that she has no interest in clothing design and instead her desire is to work in the orthodontics profession. It makes her sick to her stomach just thinking about it. She loves color, fabric and style, and so wants to follow in Linda's footsteps. It would have been a way out for her, but he made sure that her future was in his prison.

Then on the day Sarita registered for college, Linda insisted that Sarita move into a condo of her own. Linda thought an apartment of her own was best in order for Sarita to acquire independence, a trait Linda thought necessary for Sarita to have a successful life.

Of course, Lee couldn't put a stop to the move without a heated discussion with Linda that might arouse questioning, so reluctantly, he went along with the plan and joined with Linda and Sarita in condo-hunting. They found the perfect condominium in a safe neighborhood in the suburbs, yet close to the college. They completely furnished the apartment and moved Sarita to her new home.

As any young person would be, Sarita was ecstatic about her new place, but additionally she was ecstatic about her new freedom from Lee. She was certain that he would back off after she moved away.

Lee was irate about the whole thing at first, but then he came to realize the situation could work to his advantage. Like whipped sugar on a stick he came out smelling like cotton candy. Now he actually had more privacy to control Sarita. Without Linda being in the same house he no longer had to worry about her influencing Sarita.

What was even worse for Sarita, was that as soon as Ted Silar learned that she had gotten a place of her own he slunk back into her life, too. Ted was in possession of a video of Lee and Sarita together. Lee had set up a video camera when Sarita was thirteen and he taped his first time with her to use as a hold over her. He put it in a safety deposit box at Ted's bank, but because Ted's the chairman of the bank he had access to everything, including Lee's safety deposit box. So he too has been blackmailing Sarita.

Unknown to Lee, Ted has forced Sarita into doing some illegal bank work for him on the side. She is caught between a utilitarian sadist, and a wealthy affluent sociopath, batted back and forth like a ping pong ball to satisfy their hideous needs.

Now, Sarita finishes listening to Ted's telephone message as she closes the office down for the night. He wants her to hide in the alley parking lot behind the bank to record Greg Bishop driving a counterfeit armored truck loaded with smuggled goods, an insurance policy designed to keep Greg as one of his pawns. He wants her to be there by six-fifteen that evening.

She'll have to think fast and come up with some believable excuse to tell Lee why she won't be going right home after work. She breathes deep while sliding the phone into a hidden pocket inside her purse. Ted had warned her beforehand that it may come down to getting some pictures of Greg to keep him under control. He bought her a pen-sized camcorder to use when the time came. She keeps it hidden at her condo.

Sarita closes her eyes, letting out a long stream of air. She is worn-out and overwrought from these games. All she has ever wanted was to be able to live a decent life helping Linda with her design business, but instead her life is mandated by Lee and Ted. They are the ultimate law, representing a law that she dare not disobey. Day in and day out, she lives her life in unmitigated dread.

She feels like waste material wrapped in a pretty package, anguished inside because of the things she's forced to do. They make her writhe in agony when they remind her about her smiles in the videos, forced smiles, of course. It is humiliating, filling her with guilt and shame. The one bright thing, the one good thing about her life, is her love and respect for Linda. Sarita will do anything to protect that one good thing despite Lee's demand that she keep the relationship shallow.

She knows that neither Ted nor Lee can ever bring the video of her and Lee to the surface. It would have dire consequences for both of them. They would never subject themselves to that, but even so, she's certain they wouldn't hesitate to arrange for her to disappear into a depraved world of sexual torture.

She takes off her scrubs and folds them neatly, laying them in a pile next to the sink. She steps into a pair of sporty khaki hipsters and pulls a red crisscross tank top over her head, tucks it in and snaps the button shut on her shorts. She is young and beautiful, yet full of anguish.

She closes the lid on the commode and sits down to change her shoes. As she ties the laces on her Prada's, she stops and stares down at them for a moment, it dawns on her how much the shoes are like her; a walking contradiction of red and ivory; high-heeled, yet sneakers, high priced, yet the soles thoroughly trampled on.

Sniffle drips from her nose, and she chokes back her tears. She wipes them away, driving her emotions back into her aching chest, burying them deep within her. It would make Lee angry to think she's not appreciative of everything that he does for her. She doesn't want Lee catching the slightest hint of her feelings. By now, able to read him like a book, she knows how to handle him.

She finishes tying her shoelaces and wraps things up in the bathroom, freshening up her makeup and changing her headband from black to ivory. Then she walks into the front office to make sure everyone is gone so she can lock up. She closes the blinds and snaps off the overhead lights, but as she turns around, she can see Lee coming toward her in the dim glow of the security light.

"Is the door locked?" It's his way of asking if everyone else is gone. Sarita nods and tries to walk around him, but he takes hold of her arm.

"You need to get rid of the invoices and get that money to the bank before they close." He pulls her closer and plants his nose in her hair. "Mm. You look and smell delicious; I'll meet you at your condo at six-thirty tonight."

Sarita is caught between two pillars of evil, both pulling her in different directions and both having the power to extinguish her.

She swallows and smiles at him "Would it be okay if you let yourself in tonight? I was hoping to go downtown for just a few minutes. I'd like to be home around six forty-five if it's okay with you?"

Lee drops his hand and backs away, wondering what she's up to. He's always suspicious and his eyes grow dark and intense as they always do just before his mood changes to one of displeasure.

"Are you putting me off, Sarita, 'cause if you are, I'm going to?"

Sarita interrupts him as she steps forward and maneuvers her hands around his back, pulling him closer just to pacify him. "No, it's just that I have my eyes on some new shoes. They're so sexy and they match the leathers you bought me. I thought I could wear them tonight."

He grabs hold of both her arms and squeezes. "Why you little nymph, you're trying to make me bust right here, aren't you?"

She smiles coyly. "No, Doctor, I just want to please you, that's all."

His eyes light up. “Yes, of course you do. You horny troublemaker, you always do. I’ll have to teach you a good lesson about being disobedient later.” He gives her a swat on her behind. “Go ahead, then. Just make sure you get rid of everything in the bank bag first. I’ll see you at six forty-five sharp. No later, you hear me?”

“Yes, okay. Thank you.” She winks, then blows him a light kiss. She grabs her purse and walks out the door.

Lee walks to his office deep in thought, smiling triumphantly; he finds the psychological and physical control he has over Sarita both rousing and amusing. He pulls a bottle of aged single malt from his desk drawer and pours himself a glass. He turns toward the window as she walks through the parking lot. To him she’s an instrument; a conduit for him to release sexual energy. She belongs exclusively to him, he’s trained her and she’s at his command. As he watches her, all he sees is flesh bouncing and swaying across the parking lot. To him she’s as stimulating as a conductor’s baton keeping time during the William Tell Overture.

When Sarita reaches her bright-red Maserati she keys in the lock code, opens the door, and settles her hips into the creamy white-leather buckets. She pushes the button to lower the top down, then cranks the AC, and her Eagles CD.

Lee stands in the window and lifts his glass in a toast toward her. “What am I going to do with you? I turned you into a fucking siren; I can’t quit you.” He gulps the scotch down in one swallow, then pours himself another.

Sarita doesn’t have to look back to know that he’s watching her, he is always watching her. She knows that he’ll think she’s trying to turn him on when she peels out of the parking lot, laying rubber behind her, making him believe that she's in a rush to get back to him. Sarita drives in the direction of downtown to fool him, but once she knows she's out of Lee's sight she turns off onto a side street.

She enjoys the feeling of the wind in her hair and the scarce few minutes of freedom that she has; it's exhilarating and she takes a deep breath, acknowledging all of her senses, not taking any of them for granted. These free moments are few and far between and she takes full advantage of them. She'd decided months ago to search her mind and look for any plausible resources for planning an escape from this noxious prison. She dreams of escape every chance she gets.

As she drives back to her condo she thinks about the other stops she'll be making, certain that it is going to be close as to whether she will get back home in time to obey Lee's orders, but then she lets out a huff and murmurs. "It's a good thing, like in the words of Joe Walsh. 'My Maserati does 185."' Her left foot trounces the accelerator.

"The wheel's wobbling, something's wrong." Linda looks at Julie then stops her car near the exit to the hospital parking lot. "I hope I'm wrong, but I think we have a flat tire."

Julie rolls her eyes. She's worn out, exhausted. "You're kidding, right?"

"I'm sorry, Julie. I'll get out and check for sure." When Linda steps out, the Santa Ana winds rush her, and her clothing flattens hard against her body.

"Geez," she mumbles, "Not exactly a day for a stroll in the park." She walks around the vehicle to check the tires. Sure enough, someone must have broken a bottle and left shards of glass lying in the parking lot because a hunk of it is stuck in her rear passenger side tire. She puts her hand to her forehead and looks up at the sky. "Why me? Why now?" She walks back to the driver's side and gets in. "Well, it's for real, we have a flat. I'll have to call my dealership for help."

Julie lets out a tired sigh and turns to the window. "Just wonderful."

Linda pulls out her phone and calls her dealer. They tell her it'll be at least a half hour before they can get there. Linda makes no apology for being annoyed. "A half hour! You're ten minutes from here, are you coming by horse and buggy? It's a 120 degrees outside. We'll be cooked by then! Let me talk to the manager."

Julie listens as Linda eventually negotiates the time down to 15 minutes. Then they sit with the car running and the air cranked up, waiting as a throng of vehicles pass by in the parking lot; first waiting behind them, then maneuvering around them.

Linda sulks as she looks around Julie out the passenger's window. "Jeez Louise, that guy could fit my entire car in the bed of his pickup truck."

Julie stares in a daze, preoccupied; the Dually Bighorn's wheels pass by inches from her window. They sit stranded in the hospital parking lot, Julie wondering if it's possible for a day to get any worse, and Linda wondering about the bank statements.

Rosa darts her four foot ten inch frame out of the ICU elevator wearing a knitted shawl decorated with owl feathers, ceremonial beads, and sacred shells. She dashes to the nurses' station in her simple agave sandals with a buckskin satchel hanging on her shoulder. She sprints through one of the most advanced ICUs in the country dressed in ritual armor, ready to harness the power of natural holistic healing, looking as much like she belongs as a Shetland pony charging from the gate at the Kentucky Derby.

Father Lelo is already in Ira's room. He can see Rosa across the hall, through the glass. She approaches the nurses' station looking distressed and when all the nurses behind the desk spot her coming they become edgy. He crosses the corridor to where Rosa is and they embrace in a much needed therapeutic hug. The tension in the nurses' station eases.

"Rosa, so good you're here."

"Thank you for sending Sheriff Dewey to pick me up."

"You're welcome." Father Lelo points the way to Ira's room, "I wish I could have gotten here sooner, but I just got the message myself. I was at Camp Pendleton's Naval Hospital making rounds and giving last rites to a dying patient."

Rosa nods and as she walks through the threshold of the ICU room, she grabs her mouth and gasps at the site of Ira's bulgy face jammed with tubes and his body covered in muslin gauze. She's overcome with anguish and her expression stiffens. "It's worse than I imagined," she whispers, reaching out to caress Ira's cheek. "I'm here now, son, it's all right, I'm here now." The monitors quicken and Rosa's features soften. "I'm going to help you to heal, my son. We must get your spirit restored to its state before the snakes wounded you."

Rosa wastes no time, she pulls her satchel off her shoulder and begins rummaging through its contents. She pulls out a bundle of white sage and a pouch of fermented vanilla bean powder. She rummages some more and removes a container of ointment made of olive oil and a strong astringent boiled from the miraculous perennial Yerba Mansa. "I need to remove the bandages so that I can wash and anoint the wounds."

Father takes hold of the sage and puts it back in the bag. He lays his hands on top of hers. "We have to get permission from the doctor first, Rosa."

She looks up at him. "Then we must do it now. My grandson is in grave danger, and time is of the essence. I can't stop his blood cells from being devoured and his kidneys from failing if I don't begin now."

Father Lelo walks out of the room with a reassuring nod and goes to the nurse's station. He has faith in Rosa's abilities in natural healing, healing intrinsic to Ira's people, the healing of the whole person: body, mind and spirit. To the Kumeyaay, if whole healing is not achieved it will leave open wounds in the mind and spirit. It would be like sending a shell-shocked shrapnel victim to a psychiatrist, but not a medical doctor, leaving open wounds in the flesh which would be an invitation for disease.

Father Lelo steps up to the nurse's desk and asks for the doctor in charge of Ira's case. The nurse tells him that her name is Doctor Issac. "I'll page her for you. She'll be glad to know that family members have arrived."

Father Lelo walks back to Ira's room and sits down in the chair in the corner. He watches Rosa as she hangs a medicine hoop on his IV pole. She takes a ceremonial rattle from her satchel and lays it on the bed alongside

Ira and begins to pray. When Doctor Issac walks into the room Rosa has her back turned to the door.

Father Lelo stands up and extends his hand out to her, "I'm Father Lelo, Colonel in the USMC."

Doctor Issac looks up at him and shakes his hand, "Jeanette Issac."

Then she glances across the room at Ira, parting her lips at the site of a tiny woman with a long gray braid, dressed in a shawl decorated with feathers, standing at his bedside. Above her is some sort hoop dangling from her patient's IV pole. It's crossed with leather straps dividing it into four quadrants and attached to the middle is a cluster of polished stones and shells. Doctor Issac has no clue what it's used for, but supposes it's some type of medicinal relic.

Father can read Doctor Issac's expression. "This is Rosa Notah, Ira's grandmother. She's a tribal medicine woman; a holy woman who's come to help Ira heal."

Doctor Issac shifts her eyes back to Ira and walks to his monitors. His vitals are elevated and unstable. "I have to say, this is a first for me; I've never experienced a tribal medicine woman making a hospital call before today."

Father Lelo looks at Rosa, but she hasn't looked up yet, her eyes are closed and her lips are moving without sound, she's silently chanting a prayer while holding Ira's hand.

He moves to her side and leans down to whisper, "Rosa, this is Doctor Issac, Ira's medical doctor."

Rosa opens her eyes; they're warm and kind. She smiles a faint smile and nods in support. "You've kept my grandson alive. I'm dearly indebted to you."

Doctor Issac is surprised by Rosa's congenial personality at a time of such anguish. She smiles back and takes a stab at some doctor humor, "Don't worry. Dearly will be paid by the insurance company."

Rosa looks at Doctor Issac with a blank stare.

Father Lelo clears his throat. "Rosa is wondering if you'll be changing his bandages soon. She would like to anoint his wounds."

Doctor Issac is taken aback and she searches for a way to tell this kindly priest and holy woman that herbal medicine isn't protocol in her ICU. Although she's been studying natural herbs and plants that heal for quite some time, she's not going give up on conventional medicine anytime soon and she can't let this go any farther. Hospital administration would come down on her like the winter rains and she'd disappear down a gully before she could even explain the circumstances. She walks around the bed to where Rosa stands, and the contrast between her symbolic white coat and Rosa's owl feather shawl, makes a compelling combination. Doctor Issac knows nothing of Rosa's capabilities as a healer; her major concern is her patient will die if she doesn't get her hands on the specific anti-venom she needs.

She looks at Rosa in a sympathetic manner, but without meaning to, she speaks to her in a patronizing manner. "Rosa, this is one of the best hospitals in the entire country; our doctors and drugs are better than you can imagine. We are just waiting for a call back about the correct anti-venom. Meanwhile, we have Ira on steroids, antihistamines, antibiotics, and coagulants, I don't expect you to understand all of this, but I assure you that they are working in unison,"

Rosa steps forward and interrupts in a soft, but confident voice. "All of which are synthetic pharmaceuticals. They deplete nutrients and suppress the immune system. They interfere with the natural process of the absorption of minerals; obstructing digestion, excretion and transport."

Father Lelo rubs his chin trying to hide his smile.

Rosa continues. "Just for example, antibiotics alone deplete biotin, folic acid, niacin, vitamins B2, C, D, calcium, iron, magnesium, potassium, zinc, and probiotics and that's just one mild example. This can leave a human body vulnerable to cancers. I'm sure that you can understand my concerns, Doctor."

Doctor Issac looks at Rosa as if she's just raised the dead. "Forgive me, I didn't realize."

Rosa again interrupting. "I'm well educated, Doctor, not formally like you, of course, but my knowledge has been handed down through many generations of wisdom, and my daughter was a medical student. She and I were working on mingling the best of conventional and natural medicines together. That was before she was killed."

Doctor Issac is intrigued by her words and wants to ask questions, but Helga bursts into the room at that moment, and in her burly, matter-of-fact voice interrupts. "Doktor, Miami/Dade ist on zee phone askink fur you."

Doctor Issac shifts her focus to Helga and rushes for the door. "Excuse me, please don't go anywhere. I'll be right back." She maneuvers a gurney and a cart out of her way as she dashes to the nurse's desk and grabs the phone out of a nurse's hand. "This is Doctor Jeanette Issac, to whom am I speaking?" She motions for the nurse to write down the name. "Okay, Tom Lampert, I have a patient who's been bitten multiple times by a pregnant Russell's Viper. I need an Asian Polyvalent STAT and I need you to check your database to find where the closest serum is, Yes, I'll hold, thank you."

While she's on hold, the nurse answers another line. "One moment please. Cindy O'Connell from the San Diego Zoo is returning your call. She's on line eight."

"Tell her to hold."

Tom Lampert comes back on the line. "Okay, looks like there's some Asian Polyvalent in your neck of the woods right now. It's at the San Diego Zoo's Research Department. Plus, there's some at Reptile World in Atlanta and the Brookfield Zoo in Chicago, which means all three zoos have Asian vipers on site. We have some here in Miami, too, but that's it for the United States right now."

"Okay, do you have a direct line in case I need to reach you again?" She repeats the number out loud for the nurse to write down, thanks him, and then punches line eight. "This is Doctor Jeanette Issac, Cindy O'Connell? . . . How do you do? We called earlier because it's come to our attention that some snakes were stolen from the Wild Animal Park's lab last night and I've been told that one of them was an exotic. I have an envenomation victim here that's been bitten multiple times and according to the herpetologist and police officer handling the case of your missing Russell's Viper, the snake that bit my patient has been identified as one and the same. . . . Yes, that's right, it was pregnant and very aggressive. I don't have to tell you how serious this is. If I don't get my hands on some Asian Polyvalent fast, I'm going to lose this patient. I'm hoping you can send it here STAT, and

I'll have Miami/Dade replace it as soon as possible if you have other Asian Vipers on site." Doctor Issac nods. "I'll hold." She covers the phone with her hand and looks at Helga who's made her way to the nurse's station. "Cindy O'Connell is the director of research at the lab and she's double-checking that the Asian Polyvalent is there. It'll take a minute to confirm it."

When Cindy O'Connell returns to the other end of the phone, Doctor Issac's face becomes calcified, her expression frozen with alarm. "Oh, my lord," she whispers.

Helga squints her eyes. "Vhat?"

Issac looks up at the clock, a knot in her chest tightens, she lets go of her breath, "Damn!" she whispers.

Sarita swoops into her driveway, leaves the car running and rushes into her condo. She grabs two pen-sized camcorders out of a drawer and stuffs them into her purse. Then she takes an empty shoe box and tosses a pair of her shoes in it. He'll never even notice that he's seen these shoes on me before she thinks, but I'll pretend they're new and have them in my hands when I get home, just in case he gets here before I get back. She tries to never give him reason to have any added suspicion; he's relentless when he's pissed at her about something.

Sarita sprints out the door and jumps into her car, she throws it into reverse and almost backs into her neighbor Riel Marquez.

He's a slender, average height, young Mexican-American man around her age who lives next door. He's working an internship while studying for a graduate degree in Structural Geology. He's wearing his usual chinos and a plaid shirt, and he's always pleasant and chatty with Sarita. He jumps out of the way with a dramatic hop and grins.

"Hey, Sarita, you trying to kill me?" he teases.

Sarita turns to see Riel standing next to her car with his hands in his pockets, smiling. She covers her mouth. "Oh my gosh! Riel, I'm sorry, I'm so sorry, I didn't see you there."

He chuckles. "I know, I'm kidding. Where you going so fast chica?"

"I can't talk now, Riel. I'm in a huge hurry." Sarita continues to back down the driveway.

Riel calls out to her. "I just wanted to let you know that there's a special on the History Channel tonight about Florence Bascom. I thought you might want to watch it, it's on tonight at eleven."

Sarita waves her hand shouting. "Thanks!" She puts the car in forward and drives off.

Riel stands with his hands in his pockets watching her drive away, wondering what a beautiful girl with so much potential like her sees in that possessive idiot she calls her boyfriend. He's got to be twice her age, he thinks. He's never met the jerk, but he doesn't like the feeling he gets when he sees him with Sarita from across the driveway. He can't quite put his finger on it, but something about that guy is off, lacking, just plain old wierd. He shakes his head and walks back to his Condo.

As Sarita drives away she's thinking about how she has never done anything like this behind Lee's back before, wondering how he will feel if he finds out. As vicious as he is, she worries that he might actually have her killed, setting up an accident of some sort. What if he followed her? Her heart starts to pound hard and fast like it always does when she thinks about Lee being angry with her. She tries to calm her fears. No way, he would have stopped me as soon as he saw Riel.

She starts to think about Riel. He's such a gentle soul, so patient and genuine. He's the complete opposite of Lee and though she's had a sparse few minutes alone with him here and there, those usually spent just standing in the driveway or on the bench under the huge Magnolia trees, she's grown very fond of him. She tries to keep her distance because she would never want him to know the truth about her. Even though it would be nice, there isn't a lamb's chance in a lion's lair that they could ever have a relationship. Yet he's given her something that nobody else has, something to open her mind and for whatever reason, because of that, she has had a shift in her consciousness.

One day Riel was sitting under one of the magnolias reading a book about the healing power of stones and crystals and she questioned him about it. She, almost immediately became fascinated when he began to explain to her that the DNA molecule that is present in every single cell of every living thing, is itself a hexagonal crystal structure, and that biophysicists are now suggesting that our physical bodies may, in fact, be liquid crystal. The whole thing sounded fascinating to Sarita and she indulged herself by looking into the intricacies of the study of crystals. She hides her interest from Lee, of course, but she's read as much as she could get her hands on about stones and crystals. The more she reads about the scientific properties of crystals and their usefulness in so many communication devices, like LCD televisions, lasers and especially the phenomenon of crystal radios, the more it seems plausible that energy from a crystal could be received by her own body in the same manner a crystal radio receives a broadcast from a tower. She opened her mind, started fine-tuning her electrolyte energy and began receiving. For the first time in her life she felt protected and began to believe she could change her future.

Sarita reaches down and turns her music off. She slows the car to a crawl and rolls into the deserted parking lot of the neighborhood post office about one half mile from the bank, a quick added stop that no one else knows about.

She spots the perfect parking space next to a row of lemon trees. She pulls alongside a particular tree and steps out of her car, sets the timer on one of her pen-sized recorders, and clips it to one of the branches. She makes sure that it's aimed in the right direction, but that it's not noticeable in the tree. Her plan is to make a recording of Silar meeting her here after she completes this assignment. She is heart pounding scared, but she's ready to change her life. She gets back into her car and drives to the cul-de-sac behind Ted's bank.

When she turns into the alleyway she sees the semi-truck that Ted told her would be waiting there. It is parked in the cul-de-sac for, as he said, "practical purposes." Anyway, it gives her something to hide behind. She drives around to the other side of the rig, parking her car behind a row of dumpsters.

When she approaches the shiny black chromed-up Kenworth she hyper-extends her neck to look up at the top of the giant bullhorn stack. She looks back down at her camera and turns around, aiming the micro-sized gadget at the dark, empty entrance of a vacant building behind her. She clicks record for a couple of seconds, rewinds, then plays it back to check if it's working. Setting her recorder down, she leans her body against the chrome fuel tank on the passenger's side of the truck.

She is stressed out and trembling, but with the jaws of the damned snapping at her Prada's she has no choice. In her life there are no choices. With shaky fingers she rubs her temples, then feels something moist and sticky trickle down her elbow. She swipes at it and when she pulls her fingers away she finds them smudged with grease. She crinkles her nose, sighs as she brushes her forehead with her wrist, leaving her bangs messed, with oily sweat. After several minutes, a taxi rolls into the alley, the driver glides around the perimeter of the cul-de-sac, then comes to a stop on the opposite side of the eighteen wheeler.

Sarita's heart begins racing, and she crouches down behind the huge front wheel. The taxi rolls to a stop and the door opens. She watches from underneath the truck as a pair of wing-tipped shoes shuffle onto the pavement and the smell of fresh nicotine wafts through the air.

The cab driver is Pakistani, or Arab, she thinks, of medium height, dark, rugged skin and a thick bristly beard. He's dressed in a traditional Salwar Kameez, white pajama-like bottoms with a long white tunic, and a black vest. He checks his watch, then he pulls in a long drag from his cigarette, exhaling the smoke through his nose. He glances at the impressive rig, admiring it from a distance, then decides to check it out.

Ted, is lurking from his hide-a-way in the abandoned building doing what he calls, "a double insurance policy," by recording Sarita and the cab driver. He is thinking now, though, that he shouldn't have picked such a flashy semi; it was meant to distract not attract. He unsnaps the holster of his gun, while the, "Poppy Bopper," as he calls all middle-eastern traffickers, makes his way closer to the semi.

Sarita tries to sneak up onto the running board of the truck, but she slips. She squeezes her eyes shut, and on the verge of tears she grabs hold of the side bar, pulling herself up. Then she holds her breath as she leans her back against the wheel well and squats down, flattening herself as much as possible. She covers her mouth when she hears the cab driver's footsteps crossing the blacktop in front of the truck. She can feel her blood pulsing in her neck, while beads of perspiration roll down the side of her cheek.

He stops to admire the gleaming vertical grill for a moment, drawing another deep pull of nicotine into his lungs, then exhaling in a long stream. To kill some time he starts to walk around to the other side, just to have a look. Sarita sits with her mouth covered and her lids squeezed shut. She hears his footsteps closing in on her, he's at the edge, just about to come around the truck. Her ears are ringing; her mouth feels like it's stuffed with cotton. Tears seep from her eyes as she clenches her jaw tight. She knows what's coming next. She's petrified, her heart's pumping blood so hard her veins are showing through her skin, and her temples feel like they're going to explode from the pressure. She covers her head.

Then, as if an angel has trumpeted its horn, the whining sound of a down-shifting motor slices through the air and Greg turns the heavy armored truck around the tight corner and coasts into the alley. A puff of diesel blows from the exhaust pipe as he drops a gear, then the powerful engine roars as it accelerates again, hauling its six tons of steel into the cul-de-sac.

The sound of the armored truck stops the cab driver in his tracks and he turns to look at it.

Sarita eases the air from her lungs in short, silent increments.

The cabby moves toward the armored truck with his arms stretched out like a Dutch windmill. The sun is cast behind the buildings but while turning the corner Greg could have sworn that for a brief second he saw a figure standing in the doorway of the vacant building just ahead of him. He curls forward over the steering wheeling, squinting, but all he sees is the cab driver waving his arms like a member of the ground crew at LAX.

Sarita, flattened alongside the wheel well of the semi, thought she saw the same thing, it was just a flash of metal or something just for a second, now it's gone. As the armored truck rolls in, Sarita steps down from the running board with wobbly legs, and crouches on the ground. She lies flat on her stomach behind the tire, her heart pounding like a jackhammer into the pavement. Doing her best to try to keep it steady, she aims her pen-recorder in the direction of the license plate of the armored truck, and then at Greg in the driver's side window.

Greg brings the armored security truck to a grinding halt, hurriedly shifting it into park before he turns the key off. He climbs out and wastes no time getting into the back seat of the taxi. Wanting to get this done with as fast as possible, he removes the fake security company jacket that he's wearing, along with his gun and holster and slides them over the top of the front seat.

The cabby smashes his cigarette into the asphalt with his foot and climbs in, lifts a fresh suit coat from the front seat and hands it back to Greg.

"Here's dee jacket I'm to give. You got special meeting tonight or so, ha?"

Greg nods and puts the coat on. The cabby conceals Greg's gun under the crumpled security jacket and makes small talk while driving out of the alley.

Greg watches as they pass the dark doorway of the abandoned building, sensing that something just doesn't feel right, but he is unable to put his finger on it. He turns to glance out the back window as they drive out of the alley. He sees the semi and the armored truck, nothing more.

It ended up being an easy switch. *Maybe too easy*. As the cabby turns the corner and Greg loses sight of the scene, he ponders the menacing feeling he got from that vacant building.

Sarita watches as the cab pulls out of site from her vantage point on the ground behind the tire. She stands up, brushing pebbles off of her skin and clothes, disgusted at the smudge of grease on the side of her shoe. She tries to catch her breath and slow the trembling in her body, thankful that they're gone. She gets into her car and drives back to the post office parking lot where she'll meet up with Ted and his men to give them the one recorder, while unbeknownst to them, they were being recorded with the other recorder she'd placed in the lemon tree earlier. She pulls into the parking lot, and backs her car into the space she scoped out earlier alongside the lemon trees.

After the coast is clear, Ted and two of his bank guards step out from the abandoned building. Ted stops for a moment to video the license plate on the armored truck, then continues to follow one of the guards around to the back. The other guard jumps up into the cab, and pushes the button for the electronic door to open. Once they hear the lock click, Ted makes a motion and the guard pulls the lever, swinging the heavy door open. Ted stands ready behind the truck with one hand on his gun. Once the door is open wide, he takes a video of the costly cargo inside.

# CHAPTER FOURTEEN

## A Step Closer

Helga takes a step closer as Doctor Issac sets the phone down and gazes at the clock on the wall, her color fading away. "Vhat iss vong, Doktor?"

"We're running out of time. According to Miami/Dade's data search, the Asian polyvalent can be located in just four places in this entire country and the one that we have the best chance of getting it from is the farthest away at Miami/Dade."

"Miami/Dade!" Helga blurts out, "Zhat's seven hours from ere. Forgiven mien bluntness, Doktor, but zee poor man vell never make it zat long. Vhat about zee serum at zee Zan Diego lab?"

Doctor Issac turns without answering her question. "I'll be right back." She dashes down the hall toward the administrative offices. She has an idea, and needs to talk to Doctor Mike Marlon, the hospital's CEO. She stops at his Secretary Nancy's desk and asks to see him.

"Doctor Marlon's in a meeting now and can't be disturbed," Nancy tells her with a frown, reading Doctor Issac's expression. "Is there something wrong? I can give him a message as soon as he's out."

"Yes, please, tell him that I need to speak with him in person, right away."

Nancy is a gentle, matronly woman. She's been at the hospital for as long as Doctor Marlon's been around, and she quickly realizes when a person is operating under extreme pressure. "I'll tell him the minute I see him."

"Have him page me." Nancy takes notice of her tone and writes URGENT on a pad.

Doctor Issac hurries back to the nurses' station and as she approaches she waves one of the nurses down. "Get Tom Lampert from Miami/Dade back on the line for me. Tell him to start working on sending 100 ampoules of the Asian Polyvalent STAT."

The nurse drops what she's doing and picks up the phone and starts dialing. "One hundred! Whew! I hope he's got good insurance," she whispers. Then she looks up at Doctor Issac. "I don't see why the San Diego lab won't let us use their serum."

Issac has her hand on her chin, preoccupied, her thoughts a million miles away, but still answers the nurse. "Because, they still have a Saw Scale Viper and some Common Kraits at the lab, so they're taking precautionary measures, and there's not a campfire's chance in a hurricane that Chicago or Atlanta will act any different about it."

The nurses' expression is dismal. They both know the situation for Ira is dire.

As worried as Doctor Issac is about losing Ira, she manages to resume composure. "Let me know when you've spoken to Miami/Dade." She walks across the hall to Ira's room.

When she enters, she stops for a moment, observing Rosa in deep meditation while Father is standing on the other side of the bed, also in prayer. She shifts her glance to Ira and his monitors. They're a bit more stable, but his color is bad and the catheters hanging on the side of his bed are full of dark fluid.

She steps into the room and clears her throat. Father Lelo makes the sign of the cross and looks up.

"Doctor, any news about the anti-venom?"

Issac's expression tells the story. "I'm afraid we're still working on it. We have a problem and it's a serious one."

"What's the problem?"

"It's complicated and even if we get permission it may take up to seven hours or more to get the anti-venom here. It's in Miami."

Rosa looks up in dismay.

Father Lelo's tone is curt. "Tell them to step it up, this is a deadly circumstance, a Border Patrol officer's life is at stake here."

"I'm doing my best, Father, but the air ambulance alone could take up to five hours and there's a lot of red tape to go through before that."

Father Lelo can't believe his ears, his facial expression turns hard, he begins pacing at the foot of Ira's bed, mind racing about the severity of the matter. *Ira's been bitten by a deadly Asian snake, tissues are breaking down fast, anti-venom is light years away.* He racks his brain trying to come up with ideas, with anything he can do to help.

Rosa steps forward, pleading with Doctor Issac. "It'll be too late! The poison will spread and he'll be devoured alive. Please, Doctor, I appeal to your mercy, let me buy some time by calming him with the smells of white sage and vanilla bean. Let me salve his wounds with my ointment. It will relax him and slow the poison from spreading through his tissues until you can get the serum here."

"Rosa, I honestly wouldn't mind doing that, but there are rules and regulations that we have to abide by here, certain steps that have to be taken. We need to bring it before the ethics committee and the hospital administrators first."

Rosa looks as if she's swallowed a sword and it's piercing her heart.

All three of them know that without the Asian anti-venom there's no doubt that Ira will go into septic shock and die. Doctor Issac's mind is reeling and she wishes Doctor Marlon would call her, but she doesn't have the luxury of time. She has to make a decision now.

Father Lelo's normally serene accord is tense, and he stops pacing as a thought occurs to him. "What about the San Diego Zoo?" He says in a prickly tone. "They must have some of this special anti-venom there?"

"They still have Asian Viper's on site, so they aren't willing to release any. We're working on that, but in the meantime, I will appeal to the ethics committee and ask them for permission for Rosa to use her medicines, but even before we do that, I have to write an order for Ira to be put into a negative pressure room."

Rosa's eyes grow wide, and for the first time *she* uses a curt tone. "Negative! No, no, not negative, nothing negative."

"Rosa, I'm talking about a room that has a controlled environment," Issac reassures her. "Where the ventilation generates negative pressure allowing air to flow into the room but not out. It protects the rest of the hospital from room to room contamination. You've probably heard it called isolation."

"But what does that have to do with my grandson? He's not contagious."

"The herbs that you brought are harvested from the earth and carry with them microorganisms from the soil. We need to protect the hospital from airborne fungus like *coccidioides immitis,* for example, which causes *coccidiomycosis,* Desert Fever."

Father Lelo nods, but Rosa's expression changes to one of defensiveness, and she folds her arms across her chest. "No! There's not even a remote chance that my herbs carry soil contaminations; it's not possible."

Doctor Issac is surprised by her sudden stubbornness. "Rosa, I'm not trying to offend you. It's conclusive, an absolute, all soil has bacteria and fungus. It's impossible for it not to."

"Mine doesn't. I know it for a fact."

Doctor Issac's expression changes from surprise to impatience and she wonders if she'd misread this woman's common sense and wisdom. "We're wasting valuable time here. I have to protect the hospital."

Rosa takes a step forward. "My daughter was an outstanding chemist, she excelled at it and together we grew herbs hydroponically to produce my medicine. I use the same method today. It's free of soil contamination."

Doctor Issac breathes a sigh, thankful she hadn't misread Rosa after all. "I believe you, Rosa, but they'll want proof of that nonetheless, and besides that, they'll never approve of you using anything even if it's just ceremonial, unless it's in a negative pressure room and then *only* after I convince them that it's a last rite type of ritual. I'm going to write the order for Ira to be moved at once.

I'll be back as soon as I'm finished." Father Lelo nods, he pulls out his phone, he has an idea. It's a long shot, but he has to try, he calls the number of an old Marine buddy of his.

Doctor Issac approaches an LPN across the hall named Kathy, a tall brunette with an excellent nursing reputation who's just started her shift.

"Kathy, I'm writing an order for the patient in room three to be moved to isolation room nine. He's a Native American male who's been bitten by an exotic viper. His grandmother is a tribal medicine woman and she's here to help him heal spiritually. We're moving him so that she can administer her tribe's rituals and possible last rites. She'll be using natural herbs. I want you to allow her to use topical treatments, but nothing oral or intravenous. I need you to coordinate this. Please don't ask any questions now. I'm waiting to hear from Doctor Marlon about getting a recommendation for granting an exception for this by the hospital administrators."

Kathy looks at her with surprise, but nods. "Okay."

Doctor Issac turns to leave, determined to do everything she can think of to save Ira's life. Then she stops. "Stay with them in isolation until I get back. I'm going to my office to check on something."

Again Kathy nods and walks across the hall to check on her new patient and get him ready for the move. When she walks into the room she sees Ira covered in bandages, his face is ruddy and swollen, his mouth and nose burdened with tubes. He has a medicine wheel dangling from his IV tree. He's unresponsive except for the flashes and bleeps that cross his monitors. She looks at the petite grandmother standing alongside his bed clothed in a peculiar way, then across the bed from her at the tall priest standing with his prayer book open. She's unsure about how to handle this, but she has been trained to respect the practices of all cultures and religions.

Kathy announces herself with a light rap on the door and introduces herself. "My name is Kathy, I'm the nurse on duty with Doctor Issac now." She rubs sanitizer into her hands. "We'll be moving your grandson to another room so that you may hold your spiritual ceremony. For now I need to turn him."

Rosa nods, she helps Kathy roll Ira on to his other side. He lets out a groan of relief, and he's conscious for a few seconds, aware of Rosa and Father Lelo's presence.

When Father Lelo hears the deep groan of Ira's voice, the vision he had in Mexico of a man draped in white and covered with green vines flashes through his mind and his tension lessens. *A warm floating energy fills the room, and a filmy halo of faint light drifts in unnoticed, and lingers above Ira's bed.*

Father Lelo moves to Ira's side and takes his hand. "Ira, my son. Everything will be fine, I had a premonition of this day. The Great Spirit has sent us help. Its energy is with us now." Ira moans again, and his lids flutter. Father bends down and whispers in his ear. "Stay calm, son, trust in God. Things are working toward the higher good." Ira can only think about the steady throbbing racking his entire body, intense pain not completely deadened by the morphine.

As she waits for her browser to pop up, Doctor Issac checks the clock on her computer, she types in the word Carnitine. She knows that while they are waiting for the anti-venom, Ira's heart will gradually starve for oxygen because his blood cells are breaking down. Once he deteriorates to a certain point, septic shock will set in.

She remembers a study done on L-Carnitine by some Vietnam army officers during the war. The study was never recognized by the FDA, but it seemed conclusive that L-Carnitine had a dramatic effect on venom. She begins to pour through the information on her computer in double-time. She's certain that she read about it, but she wants to make absolute sure of what it said. As she scrolls down the list of different studies, she clicks and opens each one, skimming through the findings of the effects of L-Carnitine on septic shock.

"Where is it?" she whispers, and continues to scan page after page of information. Her lips are mumbling a mile a minute, her eyes rolling side to side as she speed reads the documents. She leans into the screen closer, and begins to read out loud.

"'*L-Carnitine, when given as treatment after the toxicity process was in full swing, reversed the toxicity of Russell's Viper venom.*' That's it!" She says out loud, and at the same time her pager vibrates. She checks it, and finds that it's Doctor Marlon. "Perfect timing," she mumbles and turns the pager off as she rushes out of her office.

When she enters Nancy's office, Nancy stands up and opens Doctor Marlon's door for her. "Go right in, Doctor Issac, he's waiting for you."

Marlon's been a senior executive of the hospital for three decades. He's a distinguished-looking man, fit for his age, with bright silver hair and a commanding presence. He looks up over the top of his glasses as Issac walks in. "Jeanette, what's the urgency?"

"You're probably aware we have an exotic snakebite victim in ICU; a rare circumstance. The Asian Polyvalent that is at the Conservation Research Lab can't be made available to us because there are other vipers on the premises. The nearest place to get Asian anti-venom right now is the Miami/Dade Anti-venom Bank which will take seven hours to get here. I need to buy some time. I need you to back me with the board on some tribal ceremonial, herbal treatments."

Doctor Marlon's expression changes from concentration to surprise. He removes his glasses at lightning speed. "Ceremonial and herbal what?"

"Treatments."

"You want me to talk to the board about treating a lethal venomous bite from an Asian viper with folk remedies in my hospital? Come on now, Jeanette. I know that your vast knowledge and studies of snake envenomation does not include magic chants and potions."

"No, of course not, Doctor Marlon, but while I studied in India in the nineties, herbs were gaining esteem throughout the World Health Organization in reputation, regarding their ability to strengthen the body's organs and stimulate normal function in a gentle manner without leaving a body susceptible to other illnesses. I'm hoping you will see eye-to-eye with me on this."

"I understand that herbs have an important natural role in healing, but this is a weighty case that will be scrutinized hard. My jurisdiction is conventional medicine, and the board would have my license if they heard that we are administering herbs to treat a patient in critical condition, circling the drain, to be exact. Besides that, what will the press write when the story breaks about the Asian viper bite patient at UCSD/MC? That the hospital is treating the victim with the most advanced herbs you can get anywhere? Do you see what I'm getting at here?"

Doctor Issac puts her hands on her hips. "As opposed to what? We're waiting for treatment to arrive from Miami Florida?"

"Jeanette, you know very well that the press would have a field day with this."

"Doctor Marlon, think about it from my standpoint. Put yourself in my position. I need your help on this. I wouldn't be asking if it weren't imperative. My patient is dying; he needs every bit of help he can get. It may not cure him, but it might bring him one step closer. I've already ordered that the patient be moved to a negative pressure room and his grandmother is a medicine woman, quiet, and holy, and quite good at it, I suspect. She grows everything hydroponically. I believe her contribution will be beneficial here."

Marlon rubs his chin while looking down for a moment. Then he gets up and moves to within earshot of his door, volume slightly raised. "I would never advise an order for herbal treatments as a cure for a critical patient, but if he has a grandmother who would like to practice her tribe's ceremonial unction, it's within her rights to do so."

Doctor Issac is relieved, "Thank you and also, I'm thinking about using L-Carnitine on him. Any thoughts?"

Marlon walks back to his desk and then turns his gaze on her. His eyes linger in deep thought for a moment, then he runs his fingers through his silver hair. "There are no substantive medical studies to demonstrate that L-Carnitine neutralizes the effects of snake venom, and you know that. So ordering it for that purpose would be controversial." Issac starts to butt in, but Marlon throws his hand up to stop her and sits down. "However, it was FDA approved for Carnitine deficiencies, and it's proven to be effective in the protection against Cardiac Ischemia and PAD."

Doctor Issac nods. "That's exactly what I've been thinking and it's not been substantiated to have any adverse side effects when used in a controlled dose, except acting as a mild laxative."

Marlon leans back in his chair. "It's one natural substance that I'm not averse to using, but keep your Vasopressin handy."

Doctor Issac sighs with relief; it's at the very least something for now. "I will. Thank you for your time."

Marlon nods, "Keep me posted on this case, Jeanette, and I'll take care of things with the ethics committee for you. As you know, my son, Charles, is on the Board. I'll call him and ask him to expedite things. I also know Ms. O'Connell from the Research Lab; I'll give her a call and see what I can do about getting them to release the anti-venom. We'll have Miami/Dade deliver our order to them to replace it." Issac nods and walks towards the door. Marlon stops her, "One more thing."

"What?" She turns.

"Make sure only the people who have to know about this know about it, and keep the blinds closed in that room. I don't need tourists coming up here for Native American sightseeing."

Doctor Issac nods, "I will, Doctor, thank you again."

"Thank goodness." Linda points her finger down the road. "That looks like it could be the dealership's utility truck coming now." She strains her neck for a better look as it turns into the hospital parking lot. "Yes, it is. Good."

Julie checks her watch as a young bushy-haired man pulls up alongside them, hops down from the service truck and bounces toward them. By the looks of him, Linda would bet he's an avid surfer. She rolls her window down. It is like opening an oven door. The heat from the desert rushes in, stifles her breath and she turns away.

The young man bends down and sticks his face and bushy blond mane halfway in. "Yo, dudette, you the caddy with the flat?"

Linda lurches backward and lowers her chin, peering above the rims of her Versace's, then in a slow, airless tone, says. "I suppose that would be me."

"I'll have it fixed for you in a jiffy, Mama." He gallivants back to his truck and begins digging through the drawers for the necessary tools.

Linda rolls her window up, turns to Julie, her forehead creased she mouths '*Yo, dudette*? *Mama?*' Julie smiles wearily even though she's drained. Then they sit in comfortable silence waiting for "Yo dudette" to finish fixing the tire.

After a couple minutes pass, Julie breaks the silence. "I'm sorry I've been such a bear. Thanks for coming to get me."

"You're welcome, I'm sorry about the flat."

The young mechanic comes back and taps on the window, speaking through the glass. "You ladies want to step out, please?"

Linda gives him a crazed look, then opens the window a fraction of an inch. "Are you kidding me?"

He puts his hands up and takes a step back. "It's for safety purposes. I have to jack the car up." He points to the service vehicle, "You can wait in my truck." The two ladies are reluctant, but have no choice. They leave the comfort of their climate-controlled car without enthusiasm and climb into the dealership's service truck. They watch as he works at loosening the lug nuts.

Julie crosses her arms. "Doesn't he have to jack the car up first?"

"No, I think you loosen the lug nuts first, while the tire's still on the ground."

"Oh, I guess that makes sense."

The young mechanic starts cranking on the last nut with his wrench. Suddenly, he takes a nosedive forward. The wrench flies through the air, his fist hits the ground, slicing his knuckles open and his other hand slides across the pavement, catching a handful of road rash.

Julie gasps. "What happened?"

"I don't know, but I'm sure we're not going to like it."

The young mechanic walks back to his truck picking gravel out of his palm and opens the door. "I'm sorry to say that your lug key broke."

The two women look at him like he is dinner.

He throws his bloody hands up as if in defense against their glare, hoping they will appreciate his sacrifice. "I can either give you a ride back to the dealership so they can loan you a car, or you can wait for a tow truck and ride back with him."

Linda grabs her forehead "Oh for the love of! What on earth did you do to my car? Never mind, we'll stick with the devil we know and ride with you. How are they going to get my tire off now?"

"Oh, they'll probably use a Gator Grip socket."

"Don't you have one?"

"Not with me."

Their silence says it all, Julie and Linda stare at each other for a long moment, their patience wearing thin.

They ride in uncomfortable silence the entire fifteen miles back to the dealership. Julie is so tired she's leaning against the door with her eyes closed. Linda is leaning on Julie, huddled as far away from the mechanic as possible, holding out hope that she won't end up with grease stains on her clothes.

The experience at the dealership goes smoother than anticipated for the women. The manager apologizes and in less than fifteen minutes she's signing for a brand new loaner; a loaded ebony XLR with dark gray leather and tinted windows. He tells Linda she can pick up her car first thing in the morning. "We get the show on the road early around here," he says, smiling and dangling a set of keys in front of her. They thank him, impressed that he dealt with things so fast and efficiently.

On the way out of the showroom, Linda checks her watch, then pulls out her phone and tries to call Sarita.

She turns to Julie. "I need Sarita to come pick me up in the morning before work so she can give me a ride back here to get my car. Lee will never be ready, his routine is to be in the shower at seven in the morning." Julie nods. Linda waits for Sarita to answer, but instead gets her voice mail so she hangs up.

"Julie, do you mind if I swing by Sarita's apartment quick since we're on her side of town? It'll just take a few minutes or so to get there, and a minute to run in."

Julie hasn't seen Sarita in a while and wouldn't mind saying hello even though she's tired, and can't wait to get home. "That's fine, I guess. I haven't seen her place anyway and I'd like to."

Linda smiles. "It's nice, she has a knock 'em dead style when it comes to decorating. So enchanting."

Julie shrugs her shoulders. "Well, what do you expect? She's your daughter, she takes after you."

"You think so?"

"Of course."

As Linda approaches Sarita's street, she remembers that Sarita has an evening class on Thursdays. "Oh, darn. I forgot Sarita has class tonight. That must be why she hasn't answered her phone."

Julie points out the windshield. "Isn't that her pulling into her driveway now?"

Linda slows down and watches as Sarita's garage door begins to slide up. She squints her eyes. "Yes," she says, as her pulse quickens. "That's her, but the real question is, what's Lee's car doing in her garage?" She pulls alongside the curb a few houses down, puts it in park and watches through the tinted glass with a fierce glare.

Sarita pulls into her garage, she steps out of her car with a shoe box under her arm. The inside garage door swings open and Lee is standing in the threshold. Sarita hits the button for the garage door and the last thing they see as the garage door slides down in slow motion is Lee opening the shoe box and looking inside.

Linda turns to Julie, her green eyes now full of hostility. "What the hell is going on here?"

Julie sits up in her seat, she has forgotten about how tired she is. "I don't know, but something is going on, that's for sure. Why did he park his car in her garage, and how did he know that she wasn't going to class, that she'd be coming home?"

"It's obvious, they've made arrangements to meet here, but for what? When I saw them at lunch today, I asked her to join me for dinner tonight. It was Lee who reminded her that she had an evening class."

Julie shifts in her seat uneasy with the situation. "Well, either something's changed since lunch, or they have some sort of a secret going on."

Linda's brows crease together tight. "Secret?" she almost hisses.

"Yeah, like maybe they're planning a surprise party or something."

The word *secret* makes the hair on Linda's neck stand on end. She thinks about finding the phone buried in Lee's desk drawer, then the bank statements and now this. She decides it's time to tell Julie about the phone and the tracking devices. "I have a confession to make."

"What?" Julie says apprehensive, not certain she wants to know.

"I didn't tell you this before now because I wanted to have more information, but I'm just going to come right out and say it. Greg and Lee both have secret cell phones."

This turns Julie's expression from questioning to shock.

"It's true. They have those cheap prepaid phones. I heard Lee's ringing in his office and found it in his desk drawer buried under a bunch of stuff and wrapped in bubble plastic."

"What? When?"

"When I was at his office today."

"How do you know Greg has one?"

"Well, the more I thought about it, like a good mystery novel that you can't put down, I wanted answers. I figured that where there's one secret there must be more, so I wrote down the number on the caller ID, called it later and Greg answered." Julie tries to interject, but Linda holds up an index finger. "Wait, there's more. I started looking through Lee's accounting books, and I came across some things that don't add up. So I went to the bank and retrieved some past bank statements and my suspicions were confirmed. Lee's got something going on with his business that looks iffy, and somehow it's connected to Greg. *And,* now here's Lee at Sarita's tonight when Sarita is supposed to be in school. I hate to even think this, but he may be teaching Sarita something crooked, like how to cook the books."

It's hard for Julie to swallow this information. Linda waits in silence for her to digest the facts. "Lee banks with Greg; he's one of Greg's clients. The cop and the Border Patrol officer, Carlos, at the hospital today asked me specific questions about Greg that I thought were out of line; irrelevant even."

"Like what?"

"Where he works. What time he leaves in the morning. What time he gets home."

"Hmm, the police and the border patrol making a hospital visit to you, that's peculiar, don't you think?"

"Yes, and it's getting stranger and stranger by the minute."

Linda puts the car in gear. "Strange enough for you to want to find out what our husbands are up to?"

"Yes."

"Good, because I bought a tracking device with a voice recorder."

"A tracking device! You didn't."

"Yes, I did, and after Greg answered the mystery number, I took the liberty of buying one for you, too."

"Oh, my God!" She stares at Linda. "You're serious, aren't you?"

"Very and since Lee and Sarita didn't notice us in this car, I'm not going to go in there and confront them. Instead, I'm going to plant a device in his car to see where else he goes and what his conversations are about."

Julie puts her elbow on the ledge of the door and rests her head in her hand for a moment. Then she releases a huge breath and stares out the window. She thinks about the snakes, about Ira, about Greg's acrimonious feelings toward him and how Greg's been so different these past months, so edgy and short with her. She thinks about her questioning by Carlos and the cop. Now she finds out that he has a phone that she doesn't know about and from Linda's description it appears Greg doesn't *want* her to know about. She can't believe he'd be involved in something shady, no way, not Mr. Flawless, but she needs to know one way or another and even though it feels a little on the sinister side, she turns to Linda. "I'll do it, I'll use one of those things."

"Oh, shoot! I forgot."

"What?"

"I left the tracking devices in my glove box."

Julie waves her hand, "Fine. You'll get'em in the morning when you pick up your car."

Later as Linda pulls her car into Julie's driveway, she tells her. "Julie, remember to make sure everything looks normal in the house and in the back yard so Greg doesn't get suspicious. If he asks you about the snakes, as far as you know, it was no big deal, just another run-of-the-mill snake bite."

"I'm on board, Linda, but I hope we don't regret this spying. I'll talk to you in the morning." She gets out of her car and walks into her house, relieved to be home and looking forward to a nice long soak in the tub.

Dressed in gowns, booties, and masks, Rosa and Kathy pull the bandages away from Ira's blistered lesions with extreme care, and daub at his wounds. If Ira could move he'd wince in pain, his mind is clouded, but he knows that Rosa's doing what is necessary and he tries to think positively about survival as often as he is conscious. Kathy helps Rosa bathe Ira's flesh in Swamp Root astringent, and smooth yerba oil on his back. Rosa reaches for her amulet and sprinkles some powder above his wounds as she chants a prayer.

Kathy's watching her. "What is that?"

"It's bark from an oak tree, sterilized by baking it, then ground into a fine powder It will help his tissue bind together and reduce swelling." Rosa takes out a pouch of chaparral and mixes it together with a few drops of fresh palm oil, making a rich balm that has a repugnant fragrance.

Kathy wrinkles her nose at the smell. "What is that?"

Rosa smiles. "It's chaparral, better known as the Creosote Bush. Even though it smells like creosote, it doesn't contain creosote. It is a potent antioxidant that reduces inflammation. When my grandson is well enough to drink it, I will make strong tea of it for him. Our ancestors have used chaparral for thousands of years."

Kathy looks up at the hoop on the IV pole. "What do you use that for?"

"It's a sacred medicine wheel wrapped in cord that I braided from dog's hair. The raw stones in the center have the earth's energy and healing power. The feather is an eagle's, the rattle from a snake's tail, the tooth from a bear and the amulet holds a shard of dear antler. This wheel will protect him from the snake's poison, slow his metabolism and send a message to the Great Spirit, to restore harmony and bring balance to his body, mind, and spirit."

Kathy nods, fascinated. "I like the smell of the vines; what are they?"

"Mescaha, known as Desert Sage. I mingled it with vanilla bean powder for growth and energy. Mescaha has many uses. I am using it here for purification and to steady and strengthen the mind and the nerves."

Kathy shifts her eyes to the corner of the bed. "What's that?"

"It's my ceremonial rattle, made from a turtle's shell. Inside it is the smoothest and largest pebbles that I could find from the very top of an ant hill. Rhythmic sound is good spirit medicine and has an enormous effect on altering consciousness. I handpicked the pebbles to be uniform in size so they will make the sound of a continuous flow of cooperation throughout the spirit world and ours."

"When will you use it?"

"When we've finished wrapping his wounds and have placed the sage vines on his body."

Father Lelo sits in a chair waiting for a return call from his buddy and watching as Rosa and Kathy lay sprigs of

Desert Sage around Ira's nose and mouth, and across his torso. Summoned to mind once again is the vision he had while talking to the young girl on the streets of that tiny town in Mexico years ago, and assurance washes over him that everything will be okay.

Rosa picks up her rattle and shakes it in a rhythmic, rolling motion while chanting prayers. Ira's heart monitor stabilizes and his breathing slows.

Father Lelo's cell phone vibrates. He steps out to answer it.

# CHAPTER FIFTEEN

## The Sound Barrier

Julie drops her purse on the kitchen counter and walks into her study. The easel is tipped on its side and there's a splotch of red paint on the carpet that missed the drop cloth. Miss Jingles jumps down from Julie's desk and comes to nuzzle up against her leg. Julie picks the blue-eyed gray-haired tiger up and strokes her thick coat as Jingles purrs. "How's my pretty girl today? Oops, where's your collar, sweetie?" She looks around but doesn't see it. She figures it must have slipped off somehow. It's happened before. She'll come across it somewhere.

After Julie takes Miss Jingles into the kitchen and feeds her dinner she goes back into the study and tidies up. She stands the easel up and pulls an area rug over to cover the red paint stain on the tile. She'll try using some paint thinner on it tomorrow. She's had it for today and she climbs the stairs for a soak in the tub.

As she walks into her bedroom she stops in front of Greg's closet. She is struck by a strange sensation as she stands and stares at the Berluti Swann shoebox high on the shelf. She thinks about the blue polishing cloth from this morning and an impulse hits her. Curiosity strikes her like a spring-loaded firing pin and without hesitation she bolts forward into the closet wondering if this might be where he keeps his secret phone. She grabs the leather case and pulls it down from the shelf, certain she's on to something.

She opens the lid and rummages deep into the box looking for clues. She finds a soft bristled brush, tins of polish and buffing cloths. *That's it?* Frustrated she rolls her eyes. She is so exhausted even her normally good intuition has taken leave. She puts the box back up on the shelf. *God*, she needs to unwind. She lumbers to the bathroom and pulls her tank top over her head. She unbuttons her white capris and they drop to the floor while her mind is elsewhere. She lifts a pale-blue plush robe from its hook, slides her arms in, then sits on the ledge of her marble soaking tub and turns the water on.

She is adding some lavender and mineral salts when her cell phone rings. She turns around and looks at her nightstand with a sigh; the last thing she wants is to answer a line of questioning from Greg right now, but she turns the water off and goes to the phone. She is relieved to see that it's Linda. When she says hello, her ear drum is assaulted by Linda breathing fire through the airwaves.

"Julie! If you're not sitting down, sit down, 'cause you're not going to believe this!"

"What's wrong, are you okay?"

"Are you sitting down?"

Julie sits down on her bed. "Yes."

"After I got home, I tried both Lee and Sarita's numbers and neither of them answered. That bothered me. So I started thinking about Sarita's classes. She told me her evening class started at six-thirty and it was at least six forty-five when we saw her with Lee. I know she was going to class tonight because she specifically told me she was when we were talking at the office today."

"Maybe she had to run an errand for Lee and she went late."

"No, she didn't."

Julie's silent for a moment. "How do you know?"

"Because I checked."

"What do you mean, you checked?"

"I know the class runs until eight so I looked up who the evening instructor is, waited until a few minutes past eight, then called his office and he answered his phone."

Julie cradles the receiver on her shoulder and folds her arms across her chest. "And?"

"I told him that I had a family emergency. That I was looking for my daughter Sarita Stevens and asked him if she had been in class tonight. He told me he didn't have a student by that name."

Julie's voice is breathy. "What? Are you sure?"

"Yes. I asked him if he was sure about that, and he said absolutely. He said it's a name he would remember."

Julie closes her eyes and takes a deep breath. There is a pause before she exhales.

Linda's voice breaks the silence. "She's been lying to me, Julie! They both have!"

Another pause, a moment of disbelief as Julie wrestles with her own thoughts, then puts her hand to her forehead, almost afraid to ask. "What do you think Sarita's doing?"

"I don't know, Julie, but it makes me sick to my stomach. Since I looked through Lee's bank statements today I've been worried. Knowing she's doing both his books and his banking has my imagination running wild."

Julie can't believe what she's hearing, *Greg, the snakes, the bank, Lee, Sarita. Is it all coincidence, or is it tied together*? "None of this makes any sense. Why would Sarita lie to you about school?"

"I haven't the foggiest, but I will get to the bottom of this. What if Lee has Sarita doing something illegal with currency at the office and Greg's using the bank to launder the money? It all seems impossible, crazy, *preposterous* even, I know, but I can't let this go on, my reputation is at stake, my name is on his company, too. I'm going to check with the college tomorrow about Sarita's student status and so help me God, if I find out she's never been enrolled there I don't know what I'll do, but I'm sure it won't be pleasant."

"Are you going to ask Sarita?"

"Not yet, we both need to do some more discreet digging just in case there is a chance I'm over-reacting. I hope so, but my intuition tells me I'm not."

"I agree with you about not calling Sarita, your tone will give you away. I'll pick you up in the morning and take you to your car."

"Can you be here by seven?"

"Yes, and Linda, I'm sorry about Sarita, I know it's breaking your heart, but maybe there's a good explanation."

"I sure hope so."

"Goodnight, Linda."

"Goodnight."

Julie walks back into the bathroom. She adds another scoop of mineral salt to the water and finishes drawing herself a therapeutic bath. She loosens the sash on her robe, lets it fall to the floor and climbs into the soothing violet pool. She leans back and relishes the feeling of the soft warm water as she soaks, while her mind floods with the events of the day.

Her thoughts linger on Ira. She closes her eyes as she remembers him, recalling the moment his warm breath fell on her face as he jumped in the path of the snake. Absently she stirs in the water in response to the memory of the weight of his body on hers, protecting her. For a moment their eyes had met and then a whirlwind took him away as he rolled on his back to squash the snake.

She places her hand on her heart because she feels terrible, even somewhat responsible for his predicament. She decides she'll pay him a visit in the hospital after she drops Linda off in the morning. Even though rattlesnake bites are common and the hospitals stock anti-venom, he was bitten a couple times so he'll probably have to be there for at least twenty-four hours. She needs to see him again. Even though it is not her fault she wants to apologize for the snakes in her back yard.

Linda slides her phone shut, tilts her head back, and lets out a deep sigh. She walks to her dresser and picks up a family portrait of Lee, Sarita, and herself taken a few weeks after Sarita came to live with them.

She recalls the first day she'd met Sarita. She was drawn to her huge brown eyes, so dark, she couldn't distinguish the iris from the pupil; beautiful, yet anguished. She felt protective of her and took her under her wing, determined she was going to give the bereaved, orphaned child the best life that she could give her. As tears pool in Linda's intense green eyes, she touches the picture and whispers. “My precious girl, what is going on with you?” She stares for a while then sets the picture down.

She changes into a cream satin nightgown and climbs into bed. Pulling the covers up to her chin, she rolls onto her side.

Still awake at ten forty-five, she hears the garage door open, then close. She hears Lee rummage around in his office. After a few minutes he walks into the bedroom. She can hear his belt buckle and slacks hit the floor, then he crawls into bed. He rolls onto his side without waking her. Some nights he’ll reach out and caress her hair, but tonight’s not one of them. She listens to him breathe for a while, smelling the faint, but peaty scent of scotch lingering in the air. Before long he’s sound asleep.

How odd, she thinks, that she’d never noticed before tonight how much the whole thing bothers her, the smell of alcohol, the late-night business dinners and the attempts to arouse her at his whim. Somehow she managed to submerge herself so deeply in her design business that she repressed the resentment that was building for years from their lackluster relationship. But things changed today and something is burning deep within her. She curls up as far as she can on her side of the bed. Her mind is reeling and her back is to him. She peeks through one eye and looks at the clock on her nightstand. It’s a quarter after eleven, in truth, a bit of an early night for him.

Ira’s isolation room is lit up like a ballroom and the chair that Father Lelo was sitting in earlier is empty. Nurse Kathy is rolling the medicine rattle in a gentle, soothing tempo while Rosa chants prayers. Doctor Issac explores the dark wounds beneath Ira's bandages and the catheter on the bedside looks like it is a red Boudreaux versus a Chardonnay. The blinking lights of his monitors are keeping rhythm with the other machines and they are all the life of the party. At least his vitals are somewhat stable.

It is certain that Rosa's healing has calmed her grandson's body, but Doctor Issac is still administering her conventional care when Doctor Marlon walks into the room. She looks up at him with hope and anticipation, waiting for the good news that the research lab has released the anti-venom. Doctor Marlon crosses the room, then stops at the foot of the bed. He looks disturbed. "Jeanette, I'm afraid I don't have good news."

She straightens, and releases a stress-induced breath. She looks at Ira, the trunk of his body is a swollen and angry purple. She shifts her gaze back to Doctor Marlon, waiting for the hammer to fall.

"I got a call back from the Conservation Research Lab." He hesitates for a moment as the three women stare at him. "The anti-venom isn't there."

Issac's expression changes to alarm. "What?"

Rosa steps forward and covers her mouth. "No," she whispers.

Doctor Marlon feels terrible; he holds his arms out to his sides. "I tried, I did all I could. I pleaded with Christine Brokaw—a past colleague of mine who's on the Board over there—about finagling things around for an early release and swap. They'd decided to go ahead with it, but when they went to the cooler for the serum it wasn't there. It's feasible that it was stolen with the snakes. They've checked everywhere to make sure it wasn't misplaced, but it's gone. I don't know what to say, sorry seems so inadequate." He looks at Ira, knowing the man is battling for his life. "It appears there's nothing random about this young man's tragedy; he must have powerful enemies. The lab's notified the police."

Father Lelo steps in from the corridor and stands behind Doctor Marlon; he's heard what was just said.

Doctor Issac turns to Rosa. "We're in for a long night, but we won't give up."

Rosa blinks away tears, nothing could have prepared her for this. She feels the despair welling up inside her, then feels pangs of guilt for exiling herself. Those thoughts tear open the gates. The flood of lost time flows, time she could have given to Ira when he was a child. He's the last of her blood and like a once-rolling ocean wave now expired on shore, she can feel him disappearing.

Memories engulf her, beginning with memories of her daughter Raina placing her newborn son into her arms, only minutes old at the hospital, while Grandpa Samuel quietly beamed with pride at his newborn grandson. Her mind flashes back to her life prior to Raina's disappearance, to birthdays and holidays, picnics and evenings when all of them gathered on the porch.

Her mind retraces her life after she returned from exile. How she became part of Ira's life from the moment Father Lelo first brought him home. She remembers how her spirit soared, rejoicing at the sight of him. He was malnourished and demure, but she recognized him as he walked with slumped shoulders through the rectory door. She remembers the many hours she devoted to helping him heal his mind and spirit with blessing rituals, smudging him with white sage, sweet grass, and frankincense. She brewed strong teas made with special herbs, and they meditated in stone caves on the mountain, pounded drums and chanted in their native tongue. They prayed to the Creator and called upon the eagle's spirit for help.

She thinks about how Father Lelo spent every moment of his spare time teaching Ira academics so that he could catch up and attend school with the kids his own age. She recalls the high school baseball games she attended, the trophies proudly displayed on his dresser alongside his eagle feather, then she thinks about his college graduation, how she arose and stood as he was handed his diploma.

Now although he is only twenty-nine years old, she fears she will lose him again. This time, as with Raina, there will be no hope of him returning. The one physical lifeline to her husband and daughter will vanish. It will leave her empty, like an abalone shell in the sand on the shore, once filled with life, but no more. Her entire family will have been swept away; she drops her head into her trembling hands barely able to whisper. "No, please, Great Spirit, no."

Father Lelo steps farther into the room and walks to Rosa. She doesn't look up when he puts his hands on her shoulders. "Rosa, I made a phone call earlier to an old colleague of mine. I just got off the phone with him a few minutes ago. It appears that the USMC and the U.S. Navy may be able to help us out with this matter." She wipes her eyes, looks up at him wounded, but still with hope.

Father Lelo smiles at her, "My colleague is an old buddy from aviation school by the name of Joe Hayes. He and I met way back, I mean way back in Introductory Flight Screening School. We were Velcroed at the hip back then, so to speak. That is until I was selected for training in the Rotary Winged pipeline, and he was sent down the Advanced Strike pipeline. I remember he slapped me on the back and laughed when he heard I was sent to Roto. He said. 'Choppers are just your style, preacher boy, they're loud and bulky.' Anyway even though we were sent our separate ways, we've remained in close contact. He's an Air Boss in the Navy now and in charge of some Super Hornets, an F-18E squadron, called 'The Nighthawks.' If we can get Miami/Dade to release the serum to the military, they can have it here in a couple of hours."

There is absolute silence in the room. They eye Father Lelo with a mixture of perplexity and hostility. It's almost as they think he is playing a cruel prank. Father Lelo extends his arms out to his sides. "What? Where's your faith?"

"There's no way," Doctor Marlon says, "it's impossible, the military won't just send out a $60 million aircraft to make a hospital delivery. Forgive my bluntness, Father, but it's not only impossible, it's preposterous."

Father Lelo nods, "True, but it's not just *for* us. I heard about a slight flaw in the F-18's design, so I called Joe to ask him about it. As fate has it, the under wing pylons are faulty, reducing the aircraft's service life significantly unless repaired. The Navy started recalling them into the Marine Corps Air Station at Miramar for maintenance a few weeks ago. They can't afford not to."

Everyone in the room is waiting with baited breath, except Father Lelo. He takes a deep one and continues. "So here's what I've been able to obtain. The USS *Nimitz* left Pensacola's port not long ago. It's floating about 250 miles north of Havana and it's carrying a couple of Super Hornet's still in need of repair. The Navy sent orders late this afternoon for the fighter jets to fly ferry to the Flight Readiness Center at Miramar to be repaired tomorrow. They're scheduled for a night flight this evening."

Doctor Marlon's eyes light up, astonished. "Miramar! It's only fifteen minutes from here."

Father Lelo nods, "If we can get a puddle jumper out to the *Nimitz* with the serum before the jets take off for the west coast, we're in luck. They'll be flying just under Mach 2 empty, and from where they're floating right now the jets are within range to make it to San Diego without refueling in less than two hours. It couldn't be more perfect."

Kathy drops the rattle to her side. "Holy shit!" They all turn and look at her. Her cheeks turn pink. "I'm sorry, Father, I didn't mean to."

Interrupting, Father Lelo smiles and nods. "It's quite all right. My first thoughts were somewhat similar."

Doctor Issac looks at Doctor Marlon. "How can we get Miami/Dade to expedite this?"

"I'll work on that end of it, the theft has left the Zoo's research lab with an urgent need for anti-venom, too. You just concentrate on keeping this young man alive; someone upstairs seems to be watching over him." He looks across the room. "Father, if you don't mind, I could use your assistance, please."

"Certainly." Father Lelo follows Doctor Marlon out the door.

Rosa turns and walks back to Ira's side. She takes his hand in one of hers and wipes the tears from her face with the other. "Hold on, my son, your mother has given the eagle our prayers, flown them to the Great Spirit and they're being answered. Hold on, son, use your mind and fight the poison."

Though Ira can't move, he can hear, and he thinks, *I'm giving it all I got, Gramosa.*

Sarita curls up in her fluffy white robe on a soft sofa upholstered in pure linen. In her ethereal living room she stares down at the flickering candles gathered on her mirrored coffee table. It's odd she thinks, how the reflection of the candles in the glass seem to be looking up from underneath, straining to be authentic.

She thinks about Linda and their relationship. There's no doubt that Linda's tried to be a good mother, even though she was absent most of the time. Sarita never doubted her love and god knows Linda's not at fault for what Lee does. She's the one mother Sarita's ever known. If it weren't for Lee and Ted, she and Linda would be even closer. As it is right now, though, their relationship is like the reflection of these candles, it's truly there, but can't be grasped and Lee is like this mirror, he splits reality.

She has no feelings except numbness when it comes to Lee, but she loves and admires Linda. She hopes that the day never comes when Lee tells Linda that she has been seducing him, like he's threatened to many times throughout the years. The thought of it turns her stomach. It's worse than the threat of being sent back to Mexico to live on the streets.

She tilts back, staring at the ceiling. She's been living like this since she was a child and she can't stand to live in this nightmare any longer.

She knows what she has to do, but doesn't know who she can trust. Tiffany, the receptionist from the office seems to have befriended her. Lee doesn't seem to mind when she and Tiffany chat and laugh together. So maybe Tiffany's the one she can confide in, the one who can help her get out of this, but then again she thinks, it's too good to be true and maybe Tiffany has been planted there to spy on her.

It's late, but she decides it's time to put Tiffany to the test. She picks up her land line and dials. As the phone rings in her ear, she thinks how exhausting this whole thing is. When Tiffany finally answers, Sarita is battered with an assault of brain-throbbing music. At first it sounds as if Tiffany's at a party, but then the volume fades into the background and she answers. "Hello?"

"Tiffany, it's Sarita, I'm sorry to call so late. Am I interrupting anything?"

Tiffany pulls the phone away from her ear and holds it outward. Ted Silar is there with her. He is Tiffany's lover, and he wants to hear the conversation, too.

Tiffany rolls her eyes. "Sarita, hi, no, not at all. What's going on?"

Sarita apologizes again, "I'm sorry to bother you. If now's not a good time, it's okay."

"No, no, it's fine, I was just vegging out and listening to some favorite tunes."

Ted has his ear to the phone, listening close. Tiffany acts as natural as can be. "What's wrong?"

"Oh, it's silly, really. I had a bad dream, and I woke up shaking."

Tiffany looks at Ted, they both roll their eyes. She pretends to sympathize. "You poor thing, what was the dream about?"

"I dreamt that I was standing on this long fence, and men in uniforms were shooting at me. It was scary. I was screaming and nobody could hear me. Men kept shooting their guns at me, but no sound came out of my mouth, nothing. I know it was just a dream, but it seemed so real. I just needed to hear somebody else's voice and I knew you would be up."

"It's okay, Sarita, I understand, dreams can be creepy sometimes. Do you want me to come over or something?"

"No, but thanks for offering, like I said, I just wanted to be able to hear someone's voice and to know that someone could hear me, that's all I needed. I'm thankful that you answered your phone. I'll let you get back to your music now."

"Are you sure, 'cause I can come over or talk for a while if you want."

"No, no, I'm fine now, really, I don't want to bother you anymore than I already have, thanks though. Goodnight."

"Goodnight, Sarita, take care, I'll see you tomorrow."

After Sarita hangs up, she pulls the bath towel off her head and rubs her fingers through her long damp hair, thinking that by morning she'll know if Tiffany can be trusted to help or not. She has watched Lee most of her life, and she knows him inside and out. This is an advantage she can use to stay one step ahead of him. He's a control freak and he may be spying on her through Tiffany. If so, then Tiffany will tell Lee about the phone call and Lee will bring it up to her tomorrow, testing to see if she will lie to him about it. Of this she's positive.

She gets up and walks to her bathroom. Stopping in front of the mirror, she observes her image for a long moment in contemplation. It seems as though her reflection is more real than she is. She thinks about the reflection of the candles in her coffee table and vows in this very moment that she'll shatter this illusion and destroy this twisted façade. *Soon, the real me will be free. Free to be myself, free to have my own job, my own money, make my own decisions and never be kept as a man's slave ever again.*

Lee has no idea that Sarita is struggling to become liberated. Lee did achieve his goal of complete control over Sarita, but his one mistake was allowing her to have her own condo after she turned eighteen. Of course the only reason he had let that happen was because Linda insisted. Thank God for Linda.

Lee still keeps close tabs on Sarita, but there are two things he's no longer able to do since she's moved out. One is, enforcing his damned rules on her twenty-four hours a day and seven days a week and the other is interrupting her private thoughts every waking moment.

Slowly but surely, Sarita began destroying the barriers that kept her from realizing the truth and it started after she had met and spent some scarce, but quality, time with Riel from next door. He taught her about the power of meditation and she liked the clarity it provided her mind. So she had begun a regimen of daily contemplation before bed while holding some healing stones that Riel had given her when they met under the magnolia tree. She's been meditating every night since and has been experiencing a new sense of self and perception of the world around her growing stronger every day.

She leaves her reflection in the mirror and walks back to her living room, stopping in front of a 17th century foyer desk staring down at the phone beneath an exquisite crystal pendant lamp.

*It's time.* She picks up the receiver. She swallows hard at the sudden dryness in her throat, then wrestles with an urgent sense of panic rising to the surface. She begins dialing the phone number she had seen on a storefront poster long ago for the "National Tipster" hotline. Remembering their motto, *making America safer one call at a time."* She taps out the number with her well-manicured fingertip, almost like a wartime spy tapping out Morse code to betray enemy secrets.

What she's doing terrifies her like nothing else she's ever done. Panic is swirling in her stomach as she struggles to maintain her composure. She knows she's gambling with her life, but she can't live in this hell on Earth any longer. She pushes her French tip down on the last number. She hopes this call will cause all hell to break loose. As she waits for someone to answer, she feels as though the air is disappearing from her lungs.

When a voice on the other end answers, it is a woman's voice. Sarita covers both her mouth and the receiver and begins to speak Spanish in a low pitch, knowing that the walls have ears. She tells the operator on the other end of the phone that she's been kidnapped from Mexico, and is in the U.S. without legal documentation.

The operator takes note that the kidnapped victim is from another country, and recognizes it as an international matter. This alone is enough to get the operator's full attention. Then Sarita tells her that she's been held against her will in sexual servitude since she was eight years old and stresses that she fears for her life because she's made recordings of her captors' illegal connections with a Mexican crime gang and some board members of the Golden State Bank and Trust in San Diego.

After a moment of silence while the woman on the other end of the phone decides this sounds like it might be a sophisticated crime ring. So sophisticated in fact, that it may well require the attention of international law enforcement. She tells Sarita that an investigator will need to verify the allegations and that because this is a rare circumstance where the victim is calling in a tip about herself, she will need to give her some personal information.

Once the operator has taken down all the information she needs, she tells Sarita that someone will reach her in an indirect manner to tell her what the next move will be. After they hang up, she conveys Sarita's information to the USNCB, U.S. National Crime Bureau, the official U.S. representative in INTERPOL.

Despite INTERPOL's portrayal in the movies as a bunch of bad ass undercover agents with complete international jurisdiction across the globe on the hunt for evil-doers, its primary purpose is not quite that sexy. In the real world, INTERPOL's purpose is to facilitate the exchange of information between law enforcement authorities from its 188 member countries to identify and locate missing persons and crime suspects. INTERPOL has the tools and services to enable them to send out alerts and to share information from an enormous global database that can make connections between seemingly unrelated crimes and link common threads in even the smallest investigations.

Sarita sets the phone down and draws in a long breath, then exhales. Tonight she has set the ball in motion, a moment she both anticipated and feared. A search of her name will start an investigation of a missing person and at some point spark the FBI's interest. She has no idea how large the investigation might be.

She bends down and blows out the candles one by one on her coffee table and stands watching as the ghostly gray smoke curls and scales the lunar beam shining through her bay window. She closes the blinds, and turns to leave. She reaches into the pocket of her robe and pulls out two stones. She takes a deep breath and squeezes her fist closed. She walks to her bedroom with a dichotomy of feelings swirling in her stomach of both hope and fear.

On the other side of town, Tiffany is lying in bed half asleep. She rolls on to her side when Ted's phone rings. It's a call he's been anticipating.

He answers, his voice rigid and stern. "Assad, I've been waiting, what's taken so long?"

"Eet take time to line up arrangements for transport, many times change hands. We will have them for you in less den two months. Eet is good payload, very young. Taliban take them from village while on way to school. They cull through them without burqa, take best, vill train dem and make obedient, by time vee deliver, dey be like sheep."

"How many?"

"Ten; trained for pleasure, but still virgin."

"You've kept this hidden right, nobody knows about them, right?"

"Correct, we keep our part of bargain, but boss, Daboia, has question. He vaunts to know, if your transport and bunker is good enough so dat dey never be found? If not he has a safe place for dem. He been working on a place to store merchandize for years. Ever since he began trafficking between Mexico and the U. S. many years ago."

"Yes, it's taken care of, we have transportation so tight no one will question it. We just ran a cargo from the Philippines today and it went off without a hitch. Your shipment will be taken to a place so secluded no one will ever find them."

"Good, I be in touch den."

Ted slips out of bed and gets dressed, while thinking. *Maybe he'll get himself a little piece of that Afghani action; something different from Mexicans and Filipinos.* He leaves without saying a word. Tiffany hears the back door shut and the lock click. She reaches for the long, delicate stem of a crystal flute, swallows the last sip of her champagne, then nestles into her soothing and luxurious 1000-count percale sheets and falls asleep.

Tearing through the night sky is a ballistic thrusting growl and Father Lelo stands alone in the hospital window harkening to the snarling echo of the F-18 as it approaches overhead. He looks up into the celestial glitter as his thoughts provoke memories of wars gone by, then he whispers to himself. "If you've never had the opportunity of hearing an F-18 fly overhead you don't know what the privilege of freedom sounds like."

He turns to Rosa, who's sitting upright but sound asleep in her chair next to Ira. He turns back to the window and looks up to the heavens again. It's heartbreaking to think that human beings have to go to such extreme measures to protect their God given right to think freely, but ever since the dawn of time there have been forces waging war to crush what is sacred to others. It is good to know that protection is there when you need it.

By the time he walks from one side of the room to the other he knows that the jets have already lowered their landing gear and by the time he reaches to touch Rosa's shoulder they are descending. "Rosa," he half whispers, "it's landing, the anti-venom; it's here in San Diego."

Rosa flinches and blinks her eyes, she looks around. "What?"

Father Lelo smiles at her. "The jets, they're here, there's no mistaking that sound. The anti-venom is minutes away. The hospital's courier is at Miramar waiting for it. They'll have it back here in less than a half hour."

Rosa takes Father Lelo's hand and pats it while breathing deep.

Doctor Issac has stayed at the hospital. Enduring what seems like an eternity waiting for the air cavalry to land with the anti-venom, she vowed not to leave until the Asian Polyvalent was in her hands and Ira was on his way to recovery.

She is in her office now reading about L-Carnitine and the Vietnam studies on the effects it has on Russell's Viper venom. Her pager goes off, she checks the clock. She takes a deep breath then picks up the phone and calls. In just seconds she's heading down the hall to Ira's room, bursting through the door.

"I just got word they've landed." Father Lelo nods and Rosa rises from her chair. "How long does it take for this anti-venom to take effect?"

"It begins to help right away, but it's been more than ten hours since the bite, so I suspect it will take at least seventy-two hours to restore his coagulation and renal function."

Father Lelo steps forward. "Are you going to test him for an allergic reaction first?"

"He wasn't tested for the CroFab and I don't recommend testing now, the Asian polyvalent is overdue. The possibility of an anaphylactic reaction is not grounds to delay anti-venom when a patient's life hangs in the balance. I recommend we prepare, and stand by with medication to manage any adverse reactions." Father Lelo and Rosa both nod in agreement.

Issac directs her gaze at Rosa. "Rosa, you've done a fine job keeping your grandson calm and relaxed. I have no doubt that your medicine has helped to slow the toxin. I honestly believe his condition would be much worse without you're healing efforts."

"Thank you, I believe his situation would be much worse without yours, too."

"Doctor Issac's eyes linger on Rosa, she thinks that in another place and time they would have been friends. "I appreciate that."

She smiles, then excuses herself and leaves the room. She crosses the hall heading for the nurses' station and calls out to the RN on duty before she even gets to the desk. "I need forty milliliters of lactated ringers with a piggyback setup in nine STAT. Also have a standby of twenty milligrams of adrenaline and a hundred milligrams each of hydrocortisone and H1 Antihistamine ready." She plants herself in a random chair and taps her finger on the desk. "When the courier shows up, I'll be waiting right here for him."

"Yes, Doctor, we're on it."

Sarita rolls to her side, stretches her long, lean body, and looks at the clock on the nightstand, six in the morning. She fills her lungs with air and stretches some more. It's Saturday morning, the office is open for half a day. Lee will get there at seven-thirty and she and Tiffany are expected to be there by eight-thirty. Everyone else is off on the weekends.

She gets out of bed, dons her fluffy white robe and slippers and shuffles to the kitchen to start the coffee. As she watches the steamy dark brew flow into the pot, she hears her garage door open. The one other person that has a remote for her garage is Lee. She wonders what he's doing here so early, but then remembers the phone call she made to Tiffany last night. She takes a deep, cleansing breath and prepares for his outburst.

Lee turns the key in the lock, bellowing out to her as he opens the door, destroying the harmony that Sarita works so hard to achieve every night. "Are you up?" He hurls his assault through the room.

Sarita closes her eyes just for a moment to soothe her frayed nerves, then calls out. "I'm in here." She crosses the kitchen and stands in the doorway. "What a surprise, how nice to see you so early."

Lee crosses the room with quick strides, wraps his fingers around her throat firm enough to mean business, but careful not to leave marks and looks hard into her eyes. "Where were you last night? I tried to call you after I pulled into my driveway, but you didn't answer your phone." Sarita stiffens in his grip and softens her voice even more, trying to ease his aggression. She knows he

Greg is standing at the top of the open staircase. "What time are you coming back?"

Julie is startled, she stops in her tracks and turns fast. "Greg! I didn't see you there."

His tone is sarcastic, a stress "tell" in his character. "I figured as much," he says, nodding toward their bedroom, "or you might have sung me a lullaby, something to the tune of 'Kiss Me Goodbye' would have been nice."

"You looked so peaceful, Greg, I just figured I would let you sleep."

He walks downstairs toward her, reaches for the doorknob and opens it. He picks the morning newspaper up off the walk. "How much did that landscaper do yesterday? Is he finished?" She follows him as he walks to the kitchen, takes a coffee cup out of a cabinet and pours himself some coffee.

"I'm not sure, I was out most of the day yesterday."

Greg stares at Julie for a moment. Then he sets his coffee down and unrolls the paper. "Thanks for dropping my suit off yesterday." He watches for her reaction.

She smiles and nods while running her fingers through her long blond hair, then tries to change the subject. "That reminds me, how did that important meeting of yours go? Did you close the deal?"

Greg flips the paper open to the business section. "I think it's pretty safe to assume so, but you never know, things can always unravel at the last minute. We'll know for sure by Monday."

Julie smiles, and gives him a light peck on the cheek. "I'll be back around noon. I have some things to do after I drop Linda off; their anniversary is coming up, you know."

"Is it that epoch already? Time sure flies when you're having fun," he says dryly, before taking a sip. "I probably won't be here when you get back. I'm golfing with Ted and some of the board members and then attending a lunch meeting with them afterward. I won't be home 'til later this afternoon."

"Bourbon-crusted stuffed king crab for lunch?" she teases, as she opens the door.

Greg takes a sip of his coffee with mild amusement. He watches through the window as her SUV backs out of the driveway. He is glad she's okay, but wondering why she didn't mention the snake incident, or her visit to the hospital.

He decides to take a look in the yard, and makes his way to the back door, but as he passes Julie's study he notices the door is cracked open. He gives it a push and steps in, the shutters are half closed, but the sun is straining through the slats, leaving a striped patch of warm energy on Julie's desk. Miss Jingles is occupying the space.

Greg walks to the desk and reaches out to pet the kitty. Then he notices her collar lying on the floor. It's looped around the curled foot of Julie's pewter candlestand. He reaches down to pick it up and sees a thin red line trailing along the tile. He follows it all the way to the area rug. Grabbing and peeling the rug back exposes a red splotch of paint. He scratches his head.

"What the hell happened here?" he whispers.

He sets the kitty's collar down on Julie's desk and looks around at the perfection of her study. *Everything neat and in order, so what's up with the red paint stain?* He wonders. To satisfy his curiosity he ambles to her closet, not expecting to find any surprises, because in all the years he's known Julie, she's never kept anything hidden from him, but when he pulls open the closet door his jaw just about hits the floor. The light hits the canvas, illuminating a white stallion with two flaring nostrils, with one eye painted red, rearing up beneath a fiery sunset. Greg takes a step back as he recognizes the Native American warrior sitting on its back naked from the waist up, holding a spear high into the stormy sky.

Greg blinks his eyes in disbelief. "What the?" He stares at the painting in his wife's closet realizing that she's been watching the landscaper, the undercover Border Patrol agent and using him as a model. The same agent that Jimmy, "The Stick," Costello, has ordered killed.

"Son of a –" He stops in mid-sentence, staring at the painting. His thoughts swirl inside his head like plastic flecks in a snow globe, a paranoid kinetic whiteout. *Why didn't Julie tell him she was painting the landscaper? Why didn't she tell him she went to the hospital and since she went to the hospital, does she know that the guy's an undercover agent? Does she know the snakes were planted? Does she know about the bank and the mob and the drug-trafficking? Is she in on some kind of a sting with the border patrol? Is she working to bring them down? Does she know that Ted has gotten him involved in all this?*

He rubs his hands through his dark hair, and tries to calm his thoughts.

*No, impossible. Not like her, she's not involved, doesn't have the mettle. Knowing Julie, she hid the painting because she feels guilty about finding the Indian attractive, an exciting model for her canvas, and that's why she didn't say anything about going to the hospital yesterday. That's gotta be it, she doesn't know anything about this; she's too naïve, too benevolent, too wrapped up in her sheltered sphere of existence to know what's going on. She would never have the guts to be in the middle of a sting operation, nor the desire, for that matter. She's just a young, beautiful, bored housewife, who's in her late twenties and needs to play out her fantasies. Thank goodness she's doing it on canvas. Hopefully, she's had enough excitement for a while.*

He leaves Julie's study and ascends the stairs one by one while stroking his morning stubble. But this has hit way too close to home and he knows he has to end it with Ted and the mob straightaway and for good. He just has to figure out how to do it.

Julie presses the horn as she pulls into Linda's driveway and Linda wastes no time emerging from the house. She flattens her green silk tank top against herself before buckling the seat belt, after which she lays her cream cashmere sweater across her lap. "Good morning," she says. "Thanks for picking me up."

"It's no problem at all. After I drop you off, I'm going to the hospital."

"It's Saturday, won't Greg wonder where you are?"

"No, he's got golf this morning," then murmurs as she backs out, "and some stuffed crabs for lunch."

Linda curls her lips upward. "The bankers?"

Julie nods, and they both laugh.

As they drive to the dealership, Linda passes the time thinking about Lee, the bank statements and conversation with the college professor about Sarita. She stares out the window wondering why Lee left so early this morning, then allowing her mind to drift to Sarita. She feels a lump in her throat, enough to make her swallow hard.

Julie checks her passenger-side mirror while crossing three lanes of traffic to get to the exit ramp for Linda's dealership. "I'll wait while you grab one of those tracking devices from your glove box. Hopefully, I can put it in Greg's car early tomorrow morning while he's showering."

"I'll attach mine to Lee's car after he falls asleep tonight."

They pull into the parking lot surprised to see that Linda's car is already sitting in front of the showroom window, washed and polished, still dripping at the front bumper and glistening in the early morning sun. Julie pulls up behind it.

As Linda walks to the passenger side of her car she presses the numbers on her keyless remote then bends down, leans in, and opens the glove compartment.

Julie can see two men standing in the showroom window. They're sipping coffee, eating donuts, and gawking at Linda's backside. "It's a good thing Linda wore slacks today," she whispers.

Linda takes the bag, with the devices in it and walks back to Julie. She pulls one of the devices out of the bag and hands it to her.

"Thanks, I'm going to the hospital now. You want to follow me there?"

"No, I've got some calls to make to the college regarding Sarita, then I'm going to make a surprise visit to the office."

Julie puts her sunglasses on and pulls her visor down. "Okay, good luck, call me later."

"Thanks again for the ride, I'll talk to you soon." Linda closes the door and waves.

Doctor Issac is leaning in front of Ira, his eyes are closed, he's groggy and weak, but he understands. "Ira, can you move your fingers? Good, how about your toes?" Ira is wiggling his toes as Father Lelo and Rosa step into the room back from breakfast. It was a long night, but Ira showed signs of improvement from the anti-venom without any allergic reaction within an hour of his first vial.

Doctor Issac turns.

"How's he doing, Doctor?" Father Lelo asks.

"Well, he won't be doing cartwheels and backflips within the next twenty-four hours, but he's doing well considering what he's been through. With his willpower and attitude, I believe he'll be making a quick recovery. His kidneys have already taken a turn for the better and with the help of the exchange transfusion, his blood is getting back to normal. Thank you both again for donating your blood to the hospital."

Father Lelo nods and Rosa walks to Ira's side. She touches his forehead. "How long will he have to stay here?"

"I think no longer than four to seven days. Maybe less if he continues to improve the way he is." Ira's still incapacitated by tubes and bandages, he can't talk, and can only flutter his eyes, but he moans and tries to shift his body, impatient and already anxious to leave the hospital, so he can begin taking down that drug ring.

There's a gentle knock on the door and all three turn to see who it is.

When they see who it is the expression on their faces reflect both surprise and wonder. They see a vision of a woman with long blond hair, dressed in an ankle-length white cotton skirt, and a white pashmina shawl draped around a diamond shaped, turquoise halter top. Rosa looks as if she has seen a ghost.

Father Lelo steps forward. "Can we help you?"

Julie slides her bag up onto her shoulder and crosses her arms. She is nervous, but she smiles. "My name is Julie Bishop."

Dr. Issac walks around from the other side of the bed. "Yes, Julie, hello." She turns to Rosa and Father. "This is the woman who rode in the ambulance with Ira; it was her backyard where the snakes bit him."

Rosa stares at her and Father Lelo extends his hand.

Julie takes it then she looks at Rosa, "I'm so sorry about what happened to your son."

Rosa continues to stare, then finally she speaks. "I'm not his mother, his mother is."

Her voice trails off and Father Lelo finishes for her. "She's gone; his mother died many years ago. This is Rosa, his grandmother."

Julie extends her hand to Rosa. "It's a pleasure to meet you, Rosa. Your grandson is a very brave man."

Rosa smiles and for a moment they stand in awkward silence, then Rosa speaks. "Forgive me for staring, but you resemble her, my daughter. Your hair is pale, but your face reminds me of my people."

Julie looks Rosa in the eyes. "My great-great grandfather was Kumeyaay, but his daughters, my great aunts, were taken to camps and later sold and married off. I'm afraid that my Kumeyaay blood is somewhat washed out." Julie slides her hand through some strands of her hair. "Hence the color of my hair." They all chuckle, and the awkwardness dissolves. Julie points to the bed. "May I say hello?"

Rosa nods and steps to the side, sweeping her hand toward Ira. "Yes, of course."

When Julie approaches Ira's bed, his eyes flutter and the pace of his heart monitor quickens.

Doctor Issac smiles. "He remembers you."

Julie puts her hand to her chest. "Oh dear, I'm not so sure that's a good thing, I hope he doesn't think I had --" she stops in mid-sentence. Ira is frustrated, he tries to move his lips but he can't speak, he wants to tell her it's okay. He knows she had nothing to do with it.

Father Lelo clears his throat. "May I speak with you for a moment in private?"

Julie looks up at him. "Yes."

They excuse themselves and step into the hall. Father Lelo touches Julie's shoulder, guiding her away from the nurse's station for more privacy. "I don't know how to tell you this in any other way except to come right out and say it. There is reason to believe that the snakes were planted in your backyard to hurt Ira."

Confused, Julie looks as if she didn't hear him correctly. She is taken aback. Greg may have some faults, but hurt someone with rattlesnakes on purpose is ridiculous. People of Greg's prominence don't just round up rattlesnakes to hurt others with. Father Lelo can read her thoughts and he looks her in the eye. "I know it's hard to believe, and I can't say anything more about it, except this, one of the snakes was a foreign viper, think about that, and think about how many snakes there were."

She gasps in disbelief. "A viper." She looks down at his clerical collar for a moment, and back up to his eyes. She realizes he's serious, "Do the authorities believe my husband is involved? Where would he get a snake like that from? I don't understand. Why would my husband risk his reputation and possible legal action over a landscaping job? He's successful, he has everything he wants, why would he do that? It doesn't make any sense."

Father Lelo contemplates her in silence for a moment, then chooses his words with care. "There's much more going on here than you know about. I wish I could enlighten you, but I can't."

As they stare at each other, Julie feels as though she's in a soundproof booth, as though there's a thick plate of glass between them. *More secrets?* Her mind swirls in a riotous hush, searching for answers, for understanding, for any plausible reasoning, and it seems like forever passes before she breaks the silence, "What's going on Father? I have to know. Am I in danger, too?"

Father Lelo sighs, he agrees she should be told, but it's not his place to tell her. He has to wait for the authorities to make that decision, so again he speaks with caution. "I can tell you this much, that it's top secret, the feds are involved and somehow your husband is involved. I'm certain that the people who are in charge of this undercover operation will be in touch with you at some point, but your life is probably not in danger as long as you don't know anything. I suggest that you leave the hospital and not mention to anyone that you were here or about what I've told you. The perpetrators of this horrible act will no doubt be swarming this place when they hear Ira survived."

There's fear in Julie's eyes as the full realization hits her, that authorities are watching her husband and her home and that this dangerous snake incident is the result. She thinks about Greg's irritability and suspicious nature of late, the polishing cloth on the floor, the mystery phones, Lee and Sarita, Linda and the tracking devices, the police and the border patrol at the hospital and now a priest talking to her about a foreign viper and the FBI. The priest is serious and staring deep into her eyes.

She nods. "I'll leave now. Please give Rosa and Ira my best."

"I will, and remember you're safe as long as you don't know anything. I'm not sure to what extent your husband is involved, but it must be a serious situation or the authorities would not have started investigating it undercover. Silence is golden."

Julie's mind is a whirl wind, a tempest of speculation, but she manages to pull it together and nods at Father Lelo, walks to the elevator, pushes the button and waits for the elevator while their conversation rules her thoughts. When the door slides open, four men; suspicious looking characters, are standing inside. Julie steps aside to let them out, then steps in alone. Absorbed in Father Lelo's words and trying to hide her jitters, she watches the men cautiously until the door seals her view.

# CHAPTER SIXTEEN
## Awakening

Linda inches her way through Lunar Beans drive-thru waiting for her turn to instruct the electronic host on what she wants to drink. When it's her turn she slides her window down and commands the computerized box to produce a tall, skinny, French Toast Dolce Extreme and nothing more. She slips her phone to her other ear and cradles it there while she pulls out her wallet and drives around to the window. The attendant cranks open the glass and hands her the double-shot brew along with her change. "Thank you."

Linda drops the coins into the plastic tip cup and with the phone still glued to her ear she takes a sip of the Maple-flavored brew. "Mmm."

She is expecting to get an answering machine and is surprised when Anna Garcia, the university campus president answers in person. Linda sets her coffee in the cup holder and pulls into a parking spot.

"Hello, Ms. Garcia? My name is Linda Stevens. I'm so sorry to disturb you on a Saturday, but I'm the mother of a CSU student and a friend of Chancellor Oliver Reid. I need to check on the history of my daughter's enrollment; actually, her enrollment for the past three years. Oliver said that you could help me with that."

Linda hears a heavy sigh travel through the phone. "Well, Ms. Stevens, I'm not sure why he told you that I can help, we have strict privacy laws and I can't divulge a student's GPA to anyone, even a parent."

Linda changes ears again and shifts her car into park. "I think there's a misunderstanding here, Ms. Garcia. I need to confirm my daughter's enrollment, not get her grades. I know it's unusual, but although my daughter has been attending CSU, I've never seen a bill because they go to my husband's accountant and there was a semester back in the beginning that she missed, but I can't remember which one. I'm working on some back tax problems and I need to confirm the dates of the semesters that she's attended there."

There's a long pause. Ms. Garcia clears her throat. "I'm not at the office right now, Ms. Stevens. However I have a few things that need to be done there and plan on going in sometime this weekend. Would it be okay if I called back with that information later this morning?"

"Yes, that's fine."

"And what's your daughter's name?"

"Sarita Jolita Stevens."

There is a pause. "Okay, I'll have that information for you sometime before noon."

Linda smiles. "Thank you so much for your time and help. I appreciate it."

"You're welcome, Ms. Stevens."

Linda ends the call, then slides her phone into her purse. She pulls out of the parking lot and drives to the next stop on her list, her husband's accounting firm.

When she pulls into the accounting firm's lot, a city garbage truck is picking up the week's trash. She waits for a space while checking her manicure, she'll have to fit one in this week somehow; it seems to be getting harder and harder to find time for things like this. She looks up through the windshield again and watches as the man empties the containers into the truck. After he's finished, he climbs on the back and signals to the driver to move on, then waves Linda into the spot.

Once inside the office she stops at the reception desk, introduces herself, and asks for the CPA. He's not in on Saturdays they tell her, instead they send out a petite woman with short brown hair, wearing wire-rimmed specs and a tan shawl with long fringes. No doubt she is his assistant.

Linda introduces herself and then holds out a flash drive in front of her, explaining that she needs a copy of Stevens Orthodontics LLC's general accounting ledger and sub-ledgers transferred onto it. She tells her that they're having some computer problems at the office and she needs to access the company's books. The woman hesitates for a moment looking at her strangely. "I need to see some ID," she checks it, she tells Linda to wait. When she comes back, she's carrying a laptop. She sets it down on the reception desk, takes the flash drive from Linda's hand and slides it into the USB. When it's done transferring, she hands it back to Linda. Linda puts the flash drive into her purse and thanks her.

*Next stop, Lee's office.*

As she's driving, she turns on some soothing music to try to bring up some optimism. She sips her coffee while thinking about her relationship with her daughter, Sarita. It is complex for sure. She knows that Sarita loves her, but there's always been a slight disconnect with her. Sarita has a bit of a detached personality and Linda attributes it to the physical and emotional tragedy of Sarita's childhood, but now she wonders if her absence while Sarita was growing up has perpetuated it; a pang of guilt shoots through her. Of course the scars of Sarita losing her parents at a young age are the greater part of its basis. But for some reason, the accidental spotting of Sarita and Lee at Sarita's condo after finding the mysterious phone has brought to the surface, from deep within her, a sensation that she can't quite put her finger on. There's some sort of a secret between them and Linda believes it has something to do with Lee's business practices.

The jingling of her phone summons her back to frontal lobe consciousness. She pulls her phone out of her purse and looks at it. She's surprised to see its Julie, she turns her music down and answers it.

Julie's voice is fueled. "Linda, sit down!"

Linda furrows her brow. "I'm driving."

"Oh."

"You sound anxious, what's wrong?"

"You're not going to believe this. I just left the hospital and I'm down in the parking lot; it's more serious than we thought."

Linda lets out a huge sigh. "It doesn't surprise me from what you described yesterday. I knew it had to be bad. Is he going to live?"

Julie shakes her head. "No. I mean, yes, he's going to make it, but he's not the plain old gardener we thought he was."

Linda glances out her window with a slight grin. "Well, I would have bet odds he wasn't your plain old gardener variety type, so what is he?"

"He's an undercover agent."

Linda's smile fades away. Her mind starts spinning like a roulette wheel and her eyes dart to and fro while contemplating. As the marble bounces along the top of the pockets, she waits for her thoughts to sink in. "A what?"

Julie repeats herself. "An undercover agent, like for the FBI or something."

Linda arches both her brows. The marble drops into the slot, the chips scatter and the player's paid. "I have to pull over. Hold on a second." She swerves the car to the side of the road and a semi driver lays on his horn as he whizzes past, sending a heavy turbulence of wind against her car. She waits for the dust to settle and the noise to dissipate. "Did you say undercover or FBI?"

"Both! I was shocked by the information this morning by some Catholic priest at the hospital. He couldn't give me much more information than that, but we need to meet somewhere, now."

"A priest and the FBI? You're right. Where?"

"How about Chief Jomoka's Bean House on Calle Barcelona, just off Arcadia?"

Linda nods. "Okay, I can be there in about twenty minutes."

Julie pulls out of the hospital parking lot and loops around to the I-5 then north to Carlsbad. She thought she'd uncoiled herself in the tub last night, but after her conversation with the priest this morning, she's spring-loaded and ready to launch an investigation of her own.

Even though this whole thing is chilling and she would rather bury her head in the sand where she's safe, she knows she can't. Her dad always told her, if you bury your head in the sand, someone's sure to come along and cut you off at the neck. That is something she's never forgotten.

She is used to living a benign existence, but this is driving her to be vigilant and to seek the truth. She settles into the groove of the traffic and begins mentally scrutinizing every word the priest said.

She believes he is right about her not being in danger herself, because if that were the case Greg would have told her, she's sure of that. However, it's still unbelievable to hear that your straight-as-an-arrow banker husband may be implicated in some crooked financial scheme. The words hit her like a tidal wave. She is trying to put it all together, but it's like putting a screen door on a submarine expecting to keep the water out. She's having trouble believing Greg is implicated. Yet what about the viper the priest told her about? Even though she's never known a priest on a personal level, she can't believe that one would come up with some dramatic lie merely to stir up trouble. He seemed like a real priest and in her experience, real priests don't lie.

Maybe there's a mistake. It's just not in Greg's nature to be involved with something illegal. He has a squeaky clean record and he's particular about it. He has to be; his career depends on it. If he's caught up in something, it's by accident. But still, she's not going to take any chances by confronting him. She'll just go about her business and snoop in secret.

She exits the expressway, signals left at the top of the ramp, and turns. She should've taken an immediate left after leaving the ramp, but she's missed the driveway for Chief Jomoka's. She continues to the next intersection and makes a U-turn. When she pulls into the coffee shop's parking lot, she sees Linda's car is already there.

Linda is in the window, waving her arms. She grabs her purse and keys, and runs out the door.

Julie puts her car in park, and is sliding her leg out of the vehicle when she hears Linda shout to her, "Julie, don't get out, I just got a call from the school. My Johnny fell from the jungle gym on the playground and he bumped his head really hard. I'm too unglued to drive, I need you to take me to the school, hurry!"

The confused appearance of Julie's face is almost funny, and she wonders if Linda's the one who might have bumped her head. She squeezes her brows together. *What the devil is going on? Linda doesn't have a son.*

Linda winks as she gets closer, then rushes to the other side of the Land Rover. She hollers out across her shoulder. "I'll tell you all about it on the way to the elementary school." She opens the door, and through clenched teeth says, "leave now!"

Julie sees the seriousness in her eyes. She puts the SUV into motion, pulls out of the parking lot and back onto Arcadia Boulevard. She turns to Linda. "What on earth is going on?"

"Check your mirror. Do you see a dark Buick sedan behind us?"

"Yes, it's pulling out now."

"It's following us."

"How do you know?"

"Because I watched you miss Jomoka's driveway, go up a block and make a U-turn. That Buick followed your exact moves and now he's following you out again. What are the odds?"

"A lot of people miss that entrance and make U- turns, Linda."

"You think? Okay, then let's test it. Make a random turn somewhere, see if he follows."

"Okay, I'll stay on the freeway for a while then turn off."

As she drives, she reveals to Linda her conversation with the priest. She tells her about the foreign viper, wondering if it is possible that the snakes were planted there to hurt Ira. She knows that the priest couldn't tell her everything, but she is pretty certain that the FBI is watching Greg because somehow the bank might be mixed up in this whole thing.

Lind's rubbing her temples as she hangs on every word. It's becoming clearer to her that all of these particulars they're learning are proof that something shady is going on. She takes a deep breath and asks if the Buick is still following. Julie tells her that it is, but it's about four cars back in the center lane. After driving for a few more minutes Julie exits onto San Luis Rey Mission Expressway and crosses to the fast lane. She watches in her rearview mirror and sure enough the Buick follows.

"Oh, my God, Linda, they *are* following us!"

Linda doesn't turn around. "Do you think it's the FBI?"

"I don't know, but I'm not going to stop and ask. I have a better idea." She crosses traffic again, getting off at the next exit. She loops around and merges back onto North I-5 heading for Oceanside. She checks her mirror. The dark Buick that was once keeping some distance is now moving faster and is only a couple lengths behind her.

"He's gaining on us."

Linda looks at Julie, then down at Julie's foot, waiting for her to accelerate. "Well, aren't we going to try to lose him?"

"No, we're going to lure him in."

Linda peels off her sunglasses. "Lure him in! Are you crazy? What if it's not the FBI? What if it's some bad guy?"

"That's what we're about to find out. Hold on." Julie swerves and makes a quick lane change, Linda grabs the armrest on her door. The Land Rover swerves into the next lane and the Buick follows suit. Julie waits until the very last second, changes lanes again and quickly takes Exit 54B. She watches in her rearview mirror. The Buick almost misses, but makes the exit and slows to a crawl.

Linda looks up at the huge green highway sign, Camp Pendleton/ Harbor Drive. She looks at Julie, nodding. "Pendleton, very clever."

"You don't think I keep this visitor's decal in my window for artistic purposes, do you?" She pulls up to the base's main gate, takes an exasperated breath and rolls down her window.

The stoic Marine guard advances to her SUV. "I need to see your driver's license, registration and proof of insurance, ma'am." Linda opens the glove box for the papers, and Julie digs in her purse for her wallet, hands him the information. He unfolds the papers and peruses them, he looks at Julie. "What is the reason for your visit today, ma'am?"

"I'm here to visit my father, Colonel Raymond F. Price."

The sentry hands the papers back, but takes her driver's license to the guard shack with him. He punches her numbers into the computer, running her background. Julie checks her rearview mirror and sees that the Buick has pulled to the side of the road about fifty yards behind them.

The guard makes his way back to Julie and leans into her window, peering at her with all the intensity of a fearless Marine. "Are you carrying any firearms, explosives, or weapons on your person or in your vehicle, ma'am?"

Both women shake their heads, and Julie answers. "No, sir."

The Marine turns and glances into the back seat. He turns back to her meeting her eyes once again, for a moment his gaze lingers, he hands Julie her driver's license back.

"Proceed through, ma'am."

Julie drives away, checking her rearview mirror. She looks at Linda, pointing her thumb at the back window. "Check it out."

Linda turns in time to watch the wheels of the Buick make a U-turn and drive away. Linda turns back to Julie. "The FBI would have come to the gate, right?"

"That's what I'm thinking."

"So who was that?"

Julie shrugs her shoulders. "I don't know, but whoever it is probably followed me from the hospital."

"How can you be so nonchalant about this, Julie? These men don't seem to be taking this lightly. They know where you live."

"I've already thought about all of this, it's all I've been thinking about. It's my house and husband they've been watching, remember? I'm thinking that this must have something to do with regulators and bad loans; bundles of sub-primes participated by loan sharks through the bank, who didn't know what they were getting into, or something like that. No wonder Greg's been a bear of late. I don't believe they're all that interested in me, just keeping watch is all and as long as I react without fear and emotion, I'm not letting on that I know anything about this."

Linda's skeptical but she leans back and lays her throbbing cranium against the head rest. "What do we do now?"

"Let's get lost on base for an hour or so; there's no safer place for us to be right now. There's a new place at Maineside attached to Johnny Rocket's Grill, it's a coffee shop. We can perch there low-key and ease our headaches with some French roast. After things cool down, you should drop by the office like you planned. Given the mysterious phones, there's something to be looked into over there, for sure."

"I've already called the campus for information on Sarita, and picked up a copy of our business books. We'll get to the bottom of all this stuff and I'm thinking that you should let me plant that tracking device in Greg's car for you."

"Why?"

"Because they're watching *you* Julie, not me."

Julie turns to look out her window for a moment contemplating the wisdom of it. She nods. "Okay, it's in the glove box."

Ted is at the bank early this Saturday morning, at his desk finishing up a mango and coconut muffin. "Here, take this." He fusses, dusting the crumbs from his fingertips, then picks up the plate and hands it to the cleaning woman. She reaches for his coffee cup. "Not that, I'm not finished."

Early Saturday mornings are always quiet at the bank and he waves the cleaning woman out when his private cell phone rings. He gets up and walks to the door to make sure it's closed tight, then answers. "Yeah, what is it, Bruce?"

Bruce is a guard at Ted's bank, an over-grown man with light brown hair and ruddy skin, "We lost her."

The words strike a nerve. Ted goes cold as stone. "What do you mean you lost her? She's a broad; all they do is shop and sleep. Are you sure it was her?"

"Yeah, a blonde in a green sleeveless top and light-colored slacks, the maroon Cadillac was in the parking lot."

Ted wipes his mouth and sends a huge breath of air through the phone. "I find it absurd that you could lose track of a broad at a Bean Shack. Explain it to me, 'cause if I weren't so pissed it might be laughable."

"Whoa, just chill, Ted. This is what happened: We were behind a SUV on our way to Chief Jomoka's. We missed the entrance so we went to make a U-turn and so did the SUV. Then when the SUV pulled into the coffee shop parking lot, we watched the Stevens broad come running out of the building and get into it. We tailed 'em right up until they went through the gate at Camp Pendleton."

"Pendleton! Shit. Did the driver know you were following them?"

"Nah, I doubt it, just some dizzy blonde, probably in there cackling senseless like a couple of laying hens."

The stress is showing in the veins of Ted's neck. Lee Steven's accountant had called him earlier and told him that Doctor Stevens' wife had been there asking for a copy of the orthodontist's business books, but his assistant gave her the wrong set. She should have given Linda the cooked set, but she didn't. Now Linda has in her possession a copy of all the illegitimate transactions concerning the money he has been laundering through the bank.

Teds voice cracks like a whip. "I need that flash drive now! So get back to whatever donut dipping wigwam it was that she was slurping coffee at and wait for the dumb broad to come back for her car! All day if you have to and I don't care what you have to do to get it back, just get it! And find out who the bimbo was she was with! Got it?"

"We'll get it, Ted."

"Good, and don't tell anyone about this. I don't want anyone pushing the panic button. I have a golf date with the board and Castello this morning and the next time I hear from you it better be because you've got that flash or heads are gonna roll." There's a loud click in Ted's ear and he pulls the phone away and looks at it, C*all ended*. Ted hangs up. "Damn fool." He moves to his wet bar and pours himself a dram of scotch.

There's a light rap at his door, and Greg peeks in. Ted's taken by surprise, but motions him in. "We're supposed to meet at the club." He lifts his glass up and throws the scotch back in one swallow.

"Bit early for that, isn't it, Ted?"

"Not on a morning like this." He sets the glass down. "What's up?"

"I wanted to talk to you in private." Greg is stressed and it shows in his expression. "I need your help. I damn well want out of this smuggling business. I have a great wife and a great marriage; we're planning to have children in the not-so-distant future. It's the kind of life I want, Ted. I know I made some loan mistakes and I'm sorry, but I'm asking you on a personal level to loan me the money to pay Jimmy Castello back, so I can get out of this mess. I've already done a lot for you, Ted. You owe me that much."

"Loan you!" Ted pours himself another shot. "Loan you twenty million? Just like that, a twenty million dollar personal loan. Have you lost your mind? Better yet, have you checked your credit score as of late?"

"What about my credit score?"

"What I mean is, when was the last time that you applied to the bank for a loan? Nobody in their right mind is going to loan you a dime ever again."

Greg squints and his eyes glare like a rabid stray. He points his finger at Ted's face. "If you've tampered with my credit, I'll kill you, Ted."

Ted crosses the room like an offensive tackle and grabs hold of Greg's polo shirt, twisting the collar. "You listen to me, you sniveling bastard, I've had a bad morning and I'm in a foul mood. I'm not going to put up with threats from a greedy punk that can't even own up to his responsibilities. I owe you nothing. You're stuck in this like I am. There's no way out. You play by their rules for the rest of your life." Ted twists the collar tighter. "I'm giving you one warning Greg: get it through your thick skull or your wife might have a household accident of her own."

Ted lets go, and gives Greg a shove, sending him stumbling backward and clutching his throat. He stands frozen like a block of dry ice, burning holes into Ted's skull with his eyes. He knows he can't touch him, he knows Ted is serious and he knows what Jimmy and his men are capable of. So for Julie's sake he won't smash Ted's head into the corner of that thick crystal desk of his. Greg eyes are crazed. "You're stark raving mad, Ted!

You've lost your fucking mind! You know that? You've lost your fucking mind!"

"I haven't lost anything yet, and neither have you, but that could change in the blink of an eye if you know what I mean. Now, I recommend that you put on your happy face and get your ass out of my office and over to that golf course like a good employee. I'll be there shortly."

Greg points his finger at Ted. "They better not hurt –"

Ted casts his arm toward the door. "Get out. Now!"

Greg leers at Ted giving him a loathsome look, then leaves his office in a rage, slamming the door on his way out. He's trapped in a world he never meant to enter. He had everything going for him, he was a brilliant business student who graduated with honors from a prestigious college. A successful banker married to the ideal woman: young, beautiful, loyal and talented. He had the perfect future lined up. Now he's owned by the mob. Just the thought of it makes him feel as though he has a cement block tied around his neck. If he's going to fight them, he's going to need help from the authorities. He knows that if the mob finds out, they'll kill Julie and make him watch. Then they'll snuff him out, and not with the respect and courtesy of a quick gunshot to the back of the head, but with a slow and agonizing death. He has to think this through with careful deliberation.

Julie is standing at the counter in the coffee shop on Pendleton, ordering pastries and coffee for both her and Linda. Linda is saving a table for them and while waiting her phone rings. She sees it's Lee's accountant's office. "Hello?"

"Ms. Stevens, this is Sidney Johnson from Morgan & Anderson CPAs. You were just here not too long ago and I gave you some information that you requested."

"Yes?"

"I apologize, but I gave you someone else's information, so I'm sure you understand that we need that information back as soon as possible. *It's privileged,*" she stresses. "I hope you haven't opened the file."

"No, I haven't even had a chance to get to a computer yet."

"Oh, good. I wouldn't want to be in breach of any client's confidentiality. I'm terribly sorry about the inconvenience, how soon can you get it back to us?"

Linda is frustrated that she has to go back there, but she tells the woman that she'll bring the flash drive back as soon as she finishes her coffee.

"How long before we can expect you?"

"I should be there in an hour or so."

"Thank you for understanding."

"You're welcome." Linda hangs up the phone just as Julie's setting a black forest latte, and cherry puff pastry down in front of her, then she goes back to the counter and retrieves her own. Linda's phone rings again. It's the campus.

"Hello?"

"Hello, Ms. Stevens?"

"Yes?"

"This is Anna Garcia from the campus, I'm not sure how to tell you this, but I can't find any record of your daughter in our system anywhere."

Linda sits motionless for a long moment. "Are you sure you're not mistaken?"

"There's no mistake, Ms. Stevens? Hello? Hello? Ms. Stevens, are you there?"

# CHAPTER SEVENTEEN

## The Promise

All the blood drained from Linda's delicate features. Julie is standing next to her with a cup of coffee in one hand and a pastry in the other, staring down at her.

"Linda? What's happened? What's wrong?" She can hear a muffled voice coming through Linda's phone. *"Ms. Stevens are your there? Ms. Stevens?"*

Linda squints, staring straight ahead, ignoring the voice, her mind whirling. Then she pulls the phone away from her ear and holds it out to Julie. Julie sets her coffee and pastry down on the table.

"Hello?"

The voice on the other end sounds concerned. "Who is this? I was just talking to Ms. Stevens?"

"Umm, yes you were, but my name is Julie Bishop. I'm a friend of hers, we're having coffee."

"Oh, okay, this is Anna Garcia the university campus president. I'm afraid I didn't give Ms. Stevens good news, and I hope she's okay, but I'll let her tell you about it. Also, please tell her to make sure she's checking the correct university." Julie cringes as she imagines what the woman has just told Linda. *We don't have a Sarita Jolita Stevens enrolled here; we've never had a Sarita*

*Jolita Stevens enrolled here.* "Yes, I will. Thank you for your time and concern." Julie closes the phone in deep thought. Another lie, and this time it's not the size of a sand dune, but of Palomar Mountain and needs to be examined with the giant Hale Telescope.

Linda is staring out the window, replaying the conversation with Ms. Garcia in her mind.

*"Are you sure you're not mistaken?"*

*"It's no mistake, Ms. Stevens. Sarita Jolita Stevens has never been enrolled at this university."*

How could she have been so blind? On the other hand, why would she have any reason to doubt? Sarita talked about going to school there. She told her about her GPA after each semester, about her class schedule, about things that happened at college, even about a young man named Reil she'd met in one of her classes. Everybody knows Sarita's in college. All the grandparents knew it, Lee knew it, Julie and her other friends knew it. Everyone around them knew it, so why would Linda doubt it?

It's mind-blowing what you find when you start digging. Thick saliva forms in her mouth and she tries to swallow it down. "Julie, I need to use the restroom." She gets up from the table with poise, but it's obvious she's about to be sick.

Julie follows her. They lock the door and Linda bends down, clutching her chest for a moment, then she enters a stall and throws up in the commode.

Julie is mortified, she crosses her arms against her chest wondering what this means. Why has Sarita pretended to be taking classes at the university? Why has she gone to such lengths to lie about being enrolled in school? Her eyes narrow as she begins to think about Lee and Sarita, recalling again that Lee was with her yesterday when she was supposedly in class. He knows something, he must, but what on earth is going on?

Linda, still stooping next to the commode, steadies herself with one hand on the toilet paper-holder. She looks back at Julie, her green eyes red rimmed and smudged with black mascara, she wipes her mouth.

Julie pulls a piece of paper towel from the dispenser, dampens it with cool water and hands it to Linda, she covers her own mouth as tears saturate her eyes. "Linda, I'm so sorry. I don't know what to say."

Linda wipes her mouth, her green eyes penetrate Julie to the bone. "Lee was with her yesterday when she should have been at class; he knows about it. Promise me, Julie, promise me that you'll help me figure out what Lee has got Sarita involved in. Whatever it is I'm certain that it's not of her own doing. He's somehow manipulating her. He's good at influencing others, but never, not even in my wildest dreams did I think that he would manipulate his own child into doing something illegal." She puts her wrist on her forehead and looks up at the ceiling. "It's just incomprehensible."

Julie looks down at the floor and for a moment she stares at her white Tory Burch moccasins, not able to look Linda in the eye while the thought flows through her mind, *but she's not really his own chil*d. She looks at Linda. They stare at each other in silence

It's a long moment before Linda speaks again and not before her eyes turn to bitter contempt. *A*s if she'd read Julie's mind she puts her hand to her chest and with quiet sobs she tries to maintain her dignity as she cries, crouched down on the restroom floor.

It hurts Julie to see someone with so much grace and dignity wounded like this and of all places, on the floor of a public toilet. She stoops down next to her.

Linda is both sick for Sarita and ashamed that she allowed Lee to get away with this for so long. If he's managed to keep Sarita's college, or lack of college, a secret, what else is he capable of doing? Then like an iceberg in the dark of night, a thought appears. The bank statements float into her mind and the blood in her veins turns to ice water. *RX Oxy,* Lee's narcotics vendor pools into her brain and corks there like water restrained by a dam. If she pulls out the stopper the flood gates of hell will open. She whispers in a muddled tone. "The bank statements."

Julie wants to speak out; to express her thoughts, but a feeble hand held in the air interrupts.

Linda doesn't want to be indulged until she's had time to restore herself to a more composed frame of mind. She pulls herself up off of the floor and brushes the grout dust from her shoes, then smoothes her cream-colored slacks; an emblematic way of regaining her self-confidence. How could she have been so credulous? How long have they been deceiving her and what else is going on that they're keeping from her?

She looks at Julie again. "Julie, what the hell is going on here?" She rants with one hand on her forehead. "Why would they do something like this? It's absurd! My god, Julie." She stares for a moment. "I don't even know the man I've been married to all this time. I shared my life, my home, my bed with him and I find he's a total stranger. Why haven't I seen this before now? So help me God if Sarita ends up in prison for insurance fraud or for helping him launder money, I'll hang him by his ankles and drown him in a bucket of ice water! Why didn't I see this before now?"

Julie bends to swipe Linda's purse up off the floor, disgusted. "Don't blame yourself for not seeing this Linda, none of us did. He's a respected professional in the community, a highly regarded figurehead, a Doctor of Dental Medicine for god's sakes. It is his responsibility to be honorable and decent, but instead he's been deceitful and conniving. It's not just you he's been deceiving, it's everyone. We'll figure out what's going on and we'll right this wrong. I'll help you through this, no matter what it takes."

"I can't go to the office now. I'll never be able to hide my feelings; he'll notice a change in my attitude and so will Sarita." She looks down at the floor, trying to unscramble her thoughts. "Oh no, I just remembered that I told Sarita I'd have lunch with her today. I can't face her right now. I can't face either of them right now."

Julie nods and moves out of Linda's way as she brushes past her on her way to the sink. She turns the water on and cups her hands beneath it letting the cool water moisten her fingers, she pats her cheeks. She pauses for a moment while she stares at her frazzled reflection in the mirror. She pulls a paper towel down and wipes her hands with it. "There's no telling what Lee will do if he has something illegal going on and he finds me snooping into his business." She tosses the towel into the wastebasket. "I don't trust him now as far as I can throw him; I have no idea what else he's capable of. For Sarita's safety, I think I should disappear for a while. I do have that Textile Trade show coming up next week in New York and then the Printwear show in Dallas after that, but I need to go away now." She puts her hand to her forehead. “Maybe I can tell them I have an emergency with my mother in San Francisco; that she’s ill and I’m going to take the first flight out to be with her for the week, before I have to hit the textile circuit. Then I’ll get a hotel room in San Diego so we’ll have some time to sort this all out.”

Julie’s thinking about her own episode, the one in her back yard and how she can’t believe it’s come down to this, but she agrees it’s the one way to handle it and she nods. “Come on, let’s get out of here, we can pass some time by taking a short drive along the coast, it’ll help clear our minds. Then you can call Lee and Sarita and tell them you won’t be home for a couple days and make arrangements with your assistant to take charge of your company this week. I’m going to make a call to my dad. I want to find out if he knows of a priest by the name of Lelo. They’re both Colonels here on Pendleton so maybe my dad knows him. I want to see if I can arrange a private meeting with that priest. The more I think about this, the more it’s looking like the bank is the common denominator when it comes to the mysteries going on in both of our lives, and I know that priest knows more than he’s saying. If I can’t talk to him, then I’m going to go straight to Ira.”

Julie dispenses another paper towel and wets it with warm water and some soap; she hands it to Linda. Linda dabs at the dark smudges of mascara around her intense green eyes, and wipes them away.

Once Linda’s spruced herself up and they both regain their composure, Julie opens the door of the restroom. In front of them stands a short line of women who gawk with curiosity as they tread past single file. They walk out of the café, leaving their untouched coffee and pastries sitting on an abandoned table. Julie opens the door of the Land Rover for Linda and hands Linda, her purse. "I promise we'll figure this out."

Throughout a long night, and what seemed like endless hours of worry and waiting, Doctor Issac had administered ninety vials of Asian Anti-venom, into Ira's blood stream and ordered that he have an exchange transfusion. Even though the whole process seemed like an eternity, Ira showed signs of improvement almost immediately and by mid-morning his blood pressure had begun to normalize and his pulse rate began increasing. It wasn't long after Julie left that Ira became fully alert.

The treatments that Doctor Issac imposed on Ira prompted a fast reversal of the venom, particularly on the respiratory and the pharyngeal muscles, but perhaps the most dramatic change of all was in the reversal of his neurotoxaemia. He regained some of his strength. Later in the morning the tubes were removed from his throat and even though his voice was strained he went to the extent of telling Doctor Issac every last detail about the moment he was bitten, something not uncommon with venomous bite victims. As tired as she was, Doctor Issac stood there listening until he finished.

She ordered him to be moved from isolation to a private room at the end of the hall in ICU. It would be twenty-four hours before she could have his catheters and monitors removed, but she made sure he was resting comfortably before she slipped away in search of some rest for herself in the doctor's lounge. Though not required to sleep at the hospital she'd stayed there for the last thirty-six hours and now she's able to let her guard down enough about Ira's condition to sneak off and get a much needed twenty winks, but not before she treats herself to a slice of artichoke and mushroom flan, topped with broiled tomatoes and sprinkled with fresh parmesan from the cafeteria.

After she leaves, Ira is sitting in an upright position taking small sips of his restricted liquid diet of black coffee, apple juice, and broth. An undercover security officer is outside his door across the hall at the nurse's station; he has just given four undercover agents who've been waiting for Ira to be able to talk, the go ahead to enter Ira's room.

There's a light rap on Ira's door and he looks up. Rosa and Father Lelo both turn as Ira's best friend Carlos Ramirez walks in the room. Following behind him are bald-headed FBI agent Alan Herroso, affectionately nicknamed Hero, and huge Reggie Noble with bulging pipes and a direct line to ICE, Immigration & Customs Enforcement. Also, there's skinny, stringy-haired New Orleans-born Lucius Lastad, also from ICE, who's quiet and reserved, but speaks four languages, including French, Latin, Chinese and Arabic. Both Reggie and Lucius are underdressed in wide saggy jeans, and baggy T-shirts. Both have access to ICE's criminal database.

Special Agent Herroso stops and stands at the end of Ira's bed, wearing a pair of tan Dockers and an oversized polo shirt with a Home Depot emblem on it. Underneath it is a bulletproof vest. He asks Father Lelo and Rosa if they would step out for a few minutes and they oblige. As Rosa follows Father Lelo out, she's looking back at Ira, enjoying the blessing of seeing him without the tubes in his mouth and nose. She watches his face right up to the very moment that Herroso shuts the door.

Ira's still worn down, but, although weakened, his mind is clear and he's determined to get through this meeting without passing out from his infirmity. He looks up at the men, greeting them with a nod.

Once the door is closed the atmosphere turns intense, and the men begin to exchange information. The men are emotionless, frigid, and it seems as though Ira's dilemma is trivial to them. He can't help but wonder what's going on? He was certain that he had at the very least established a basic foundation for a polite working relationship. Yes, these agencies aren't known for their warmth, but would it kill them to at least congratulate him on pulling through this before they get down to business? It's not every day that someone survives a bite from a pregnant Russell's Viper. Not that he's a drama king about it, but would it be too much to ask for one of them to ask how he's feeling first? Some consideration would be nice here. Though what surprises him the most is that even his best friend Carlos hasn't commented on him surviving the deadly venom, or at the very least a *Good to see you pulled through, Bud,* leaving Ira a bit doleful.

Instead, the agents waste no time informing him that while he's been lying on his back in the hospital, there have been two different cell phone pings that may interest him. Both calls originated from the Golden State National Bank made by the chairman of the bank, Ted Silar, one to a cell phone with no name attached, a prepaid that was traced to 9872 Lavente Ave in Oceanside, an orthodontics professional building owned by Doctor Lee and Linda Stevens. They did some digging on Doctor Lee Stevens and found that he did his Business Banking at Ted Silar's bank, the same bank that employed Greg Bishop.

Carlos crosses his arms against his chest and his dark eyes meet Ira's, he's indifferent, all business-like. He steps forward. "The visitor that showed up at Bishop's house yesterday morning while you were in the backyard was a blond-haired woman driving a maroon Cadillac XLR with vanity plates stamped Stevens2."

Agent Lastad nods. "No coincidence. We traced it back to Doctor Lee Stevens' residence and established she's his wife. She is either a friend of Greg Bishop's wife, or she's involved, too. The second cell phone ping also originated from within Silar's office at the bank, but was made to the main number at Stevens Orthodontics LLC a few minutes after the call to the prepaid. So that's two calls in a matter of five minutes made by the bank chairman to Stevens' Orthodontics building, but to two different phones. Assuming that one of the calls was to Doctor Lee Stevens himself, who was the other call made to?"

Ira stares straight ahead for a long time in silence, as if he's in another world. The men watch him, doubting he's able to focus on what they're saying. Ira begins tapping his fingers on the top of his tray table; they continue to watch him. Then at last he looks up at them.

"When I was in the Bishop's backyard, I noticed they had shutters on all their windows, a good way to keep an eye on the construction equipment across the field, but I felt as though I was being watched instead. I'm certain it was the two women watching me, I could see the shadows behind the shutters in the window."

All four of the men look at each other, nodding and mumbling, they turn back to Ira and put their hands on their hips while giving him a *give us a break* look. Reggie steps forward, his biceps the size of bowling balls. "That's all you got? Sounds like one of those old diet coke commercials to me." Reggie pretends to fluff his hair up and raises the pitch of his voice. "Is it Diet Coke time, girls?"

Ira squints his eyes, he throws his arms out to his sides, IV tubes dangling. "Aw, c'mon guys. Cut me some slack here, would you?"

Special Agent Herroso stares into Ira's eyes, they lock onto each other for a jaw tightened moment, slowly a wide grin spreads across Hero's face. The rest of the guys can't hold back their laughter any longer and the room brightens with smiles. Ira slumps his shoulders and lets out a sigh then his expression turns stone-cold serious.

"Okay, you got me, quite the comedians you are, now knock it off. I'm not dead, so I'm still the one in charge and I'll have you all written up for insubordination." Then, after giving them a stern look, he changes *his* tone to a higher pitch. "Or at the very least, the lack of sensitivity to a co-worker."

The mood in the room lightens as they burst into laughter; it feels good to joke around a bit, to feel relief that Ira's going to survive this perilous ordeal.

Carlos is exceptionally glad to see Ira awake again. They've been thick as desert scrub for the last ten years and he can't imagine life without Ira. This whole circle of guys clicked with collective chemistry from the moment they were brought together on this undercover investigation. They may not have known each other for long, but they were worried about Ira, not just on a personal level, but because Ira is the one who has been designated to lead this investigation.

They take a few minutes to talk about the snake episode. Ira answers their questions and shares his story while the guys shake their heads in disbelief and pat him on the shoulder, congratulating him on having the strength to overcome the venom. Ira thanks them, but gives the credit to his grandmother, Doctor Issac, and Father Lelo, then he folds his arms across his chest and gets back down to business.

"Back to those two women. My instincts gave me every indication that they were hyper-curious about me. I'm pretty certain that Bishop's wife isn't involved because of her actions after the snakes bit me, but that leaves the Stevens woman and I'm wondering why she was there. I can't rule her out."

Carlos lifts his hand to his chin. "I agree about Bishop's wife, and I have reservations about the Stevens woman, too. You think she could be using Bishop's wife to get to you?"

"Anything's possible. Let's find out if she's listed on the formal financial documents of her husband's business as a member and see what else we can dig up on her. Also, let's pin a tail on her."

Agent Herroso steps forward. "I'm on it."

"Good, we want to know who her friends are, who she runs the borscht circuit with, where she gets her nails done, who her drycleaner is, we want everything on her, you know the drill. She may be playing a central part in this whole trafficking operation."

Herroso nods. "I'll get on her right away." Herroso's phone starts to vibrate and he steps aside to answer it while the other guys discuss a plan of action. Hero's expression turns to disbelief as he nestles the phone closer to one ear while plugging his other ear with his finger. "Gimme that again?" The other men stop what they're doing and wait for him to hang up and elaborate.

He has an odd look on his face. "What the? . . . You gotta be kidding, right?" He hangs up and looks around the room, running his hand across his bald head. "We're on to something boys. I just got word from HQ that Greg Bishop the banker is moonlighting as an armored truck driver for Guardit Security." The room is so quiet you can hear a feather drop. Hero nods. "It's legit, he was driving one of Guardit's trucks into the alley behind Golden State National Bank yesterday afternoon, around six."

The blackness of Ira's eyes seems to intensify as he squints with suspicion. "No way, you gotta be kidding. A rich genteel banker earning cash on the side as an armored truck driver? There's not a snowflake's chance in an August desert." He points to Noble. "Check it out. Call Guardit's HR department and verify that he's not on their payroll. Then verify that Guardit didn't have a legitimate pick up at the Golden State Bank and Trust yesterday afternoon; I got a hunch they didn't. And while you're at it, check to see if there was an interruption in their satellite tracking at around that same time." He turns to Carlos and the rest of the crew. "If Bishop was driving an armored truck, then we've just been tipped on how this drug and weapons ring is moving their goods. Think about it, guys. There isn't a more secure way to move goods then an armored truck. We're dealing with more than your run-of-the-mill criminals here. We need to do some deep diving into Guardit's transactions records."

Noble steps forward. "Consider it handled."

Carlos walks to Ira's side. "We should dig into Ted Silar's phone calls to Stevens Orthodontics LLC yesterday. I have a feeling there's more than meets the eye going on at that office and somehow it all ties in together."

"I think so, too. There's someone else there who's involved with Silar. Find out who it is."

"Will do."

Ira nods at Carlos, then turns to Lastad. "If there's an armored truck involved in any kind of trafficking at the bank there must be bank guards involved. Get a list of the bank's employees and their duties, then run a background check on its guards now and in the past. Also, since this is a crime involving an armored security truck, I'm sure the TSA will want to know about it, so start working on getting a roving bug on both Silar and Bishop's cell phones."

"Got it."

Ira leans back and takes a deep breath; he's exhausted and needs a rest. "I won't be going anywhere for a while. Call me on my cell. Don't come back to the hospital again. Call me with whatever you dig up. No matter how minuscule, it may be relevant."

The men nod and congratulate him one last time as they leave the room.

Carlos hangs back and once the others have gone, he looks him in the eyes. "Man, you had me worried. Glad you made it, buddy."

"Thanks, Carlos."

Carlos extends his hand out and they lock thumbs. "We're close to figuring this trafficking ring out."

Ira nods. "I know we are and Carlos, I saw things, I mean I had visions, while I was in and out of consciousness and time and time again they included my mother. I believe those visions have some relevance to this case, but they don't seem to have any logic behind them yet. I keep running through it in my mind; I know there's an answer, but I don't know what it is yet."

Carlos sits down on the chair next to Ira's bed. "Maybe Rosa can help. I know we can't discuss this operation with *anyone* including family members, but maybe you can talk to her about your visions and your mother and get her thoughts. Maybe she'd be able to shed some light on it."

"I hate to have to drag her into this, it's risky, dangerous."

"True, but if I know Rosa, she'd be interested in hearing about the visions you had."

Ira sits for a moment just staring straight ahead. After a moment he looks back at Carlos, his eyes anguished, but he doesn't say a word.

Carlos stands up. "You think about it, but first get some rest. You need to concentrate on getting out of here."

"Don't worry about me, I'll be out of here before you know it. You watch your own back, we're up against evil people with hair trigger tempers."

Carlos rests his hand on Ira's shoulder for a moment, then leaves the room.

Ira watches him walk away in deep thought oblivious to the hospital bustle going on in the hall outside his door. After a moment he pushes the button on his remote and reclines the top half of his bed. He closes his eyes for some rest.

Almost immediately the existence of a spiritual presence seems to slip its energy into his room.

*He feels the lightness of feathers brushing against his skin, reassuring him and filling him with trust. Then he begins to turn clammy, and hunger and thirst descend upon him like a sheet of rain in a washed-out gully, they speed through his body sweeping him to a window where he stares into the distance at a thicket of dense trees and scrub brush along a barbed-wire fence. In the haze, the form of a dog appears at its perimeter and as his vision clears he sees its Rocko. Ira feels a wave of sorrow pass through him and he's transported to his long ago lost pet and friend. Rocko circles around for a moment and then stops, sitting and facing Ira. He's on a swatch of darkened dirt.*

Father Lelo and Rosa step into Ira's room and see that his eyes are closed, they turn to leave him to rest, but stop to watch when they see Ira reach out as if someone is in front of him. Ira smoothes his hands through mid-air, then cups them as if he has them around someone's face.

*Ira cups his hands around Rocko's face and nuzzles his forehead into the dog's forehead, and rubs his ears. "Good boy, Rocko, you're a good dog. I missed you, Rocko, where have you been?" Ira pulls his face away and looks into Rocko's brown eyes. He can see the reflection of a winding dirt road lined with thick trees. Standing tall in the distance on the right side is an old fire tower with a small section of unshaded metal shimmering in the sunlight.*

*A fine mist swirls beneath the fire tower, it turns into a woman wearing a flowing white gown. Ira sees it's his mother, Raina, holding a stick, pointing it across the road. He reaches for her, and she hands him the stick, laying it across his palms. He looks down at his hands; the stick turns to liquid and begins to drip through his fingers like blood.*

He snaps out of the vision. He looks across the room and sees Rosa and Father Lelo standing there. His face is ashen white. "I was there." He flattens his back against the bed, and looks up at the ceiling, releasing a deep hard breath. "She showed me where she died."

Rosa covers her mouth with her hand and both she and Father Lelo walk to his side.

Ira looks at his hands, trying to relive the vision again in his mind. "The stick is the common aspect; I keep seeing her with a stick. It must be the source." He looks at Father Lelo and Rosa in absorbed thought. "I've been having strong visions of my mother ever since I took on this assignment and the one thing that is always present is a stick. In fact, now that I think about it ever since I can remember having visions of her, there's always been a stick present. First it's in a dog's mouth and then it's in her hand. I believe it has something to do with this assignment, and I shouldn't be discussing this, but you happen to be here in the middle of a vision and something is telling me that it's no coincidence." He looks deep into Rosa's eyes. "Gramosa, do you have any idea why she would keep coming to me with a stick?"

Rosa's eyes pool with tears, time has not healed the wound of her daughter's disappearance and murder, a mystery still not solved. Her mind takes her back to that day when she had the most dreadful vision of her life, the vision of her daughter's ravaged body found by her husband, causing him to die of a massive heart attack on the very same day. Her shoulders grow heavy and slump forward as the vision flashes through her mind once again.

*Raina is sprawled face down in the desert, swirls of sand wisp around the matted mass of her thick black hair, caked with blood. Her feet are cracked with open wounds, and whip marks split her skin open from her ankles to her eye lids. A swarm of metallic greenish/ black blow flies swarm around a gaping wound in her back, exposing the larvae feeding on her lungs and the clotted blood on her shattered ribs. Her precious blood, smeared and dried, covers most of her torso. Her eyes are dead, but open, revealing a tale of unspeakable anguish. She's a daughter, a mother, a friend. A short branch from a tree covered in her blood is still clutched in her fingers, a memento of her last moments alive. Moments spent desperately in the pursuit of freedom. Freedom from evil, soulless men.*

A wave of agony washes through Rosa and she covers her face with her hands. Father Lelo puts his arms around her and holds her as she weeps. After a few moments she wipes the tears away and looks once again at Ira. "Your mother was found gripping a branch from a tree, that is what I heard, and also what I've seen in my vision."

Ira furrows his brows. "A branch? Why did she have a branch?"

The silence in the room is long, but then Father Lelo remembers the day he was at the police station on the reservation. "The evidence box!" he says, "There's an evidence box on the reservation. Sheriff Dewey showed it to me just before I went searching for you. When I examined the contents there was a branch in it. I didn't give any thought to it then. It was a stick smeared with," he can hardly say the words, "her blood. It may be what she's trying to lead you to."

Ira sits up straight. "There was an evidence box on the reservation?"

Father Lelo nods.

Rosa looks up at him, "Is it still there?"

"I don't know, but I think it's high time we find out."

# CHAPTER EIGHTEEN

## Exploding Indications

It has been a couple hours since the agents left the hospital and Agent Herroso has just been informed that the BOLO for Linda Stevens' vehicle has panned out. Her maroon XLR Cadillac tagged *Stevens2* is at Chief Jomoka's Bean Shack off Arcadia in Oceanside. *That tag is like a sitting duck.* He smiles, pleased to hear the news. He's on his way to the Bean Shack to check it out.

After driving for twenty minutes he pulls into the entrance of the coffee shop's drive-thru, orders coffee, black, then parks his car three spaces down from where Linda's Cadillac is parked and sits reading his paper while sipping the brew.

About ten minutes pass before the sound of car engine prompts him to slide the paper down past his nose just in time to see a white Land Rover drive by and stop at the rear of the Cadillac.

Inside the Rover two women converse for a couple minutes, the passenger gets out. She tosses her hair as she makes her way to the parked Cadillac. The woman behind the wheel of the Land Rover waves, then drives away. Agent Herroso runs her tags before she turns out of the parking lot. He learns that the vehicle belongs to

Julie Marie Bishop, address, 4811 Cardinal Flower Drive, Oceanside, the property where Ira was bitten by snakes. *Must be Bishop's wife.*

He turns his attention back to Linda Stevens. After making a few phone calls, she writes something down, looks up and stares out her window for a moment, then makes another phone call. After hanging up, she lowers her visor, freshens her lipstick and fluffs her hair, then drives away.

Agent Herroso tails her, staying behind her at a manageable distance on the express way all the way to the exit ramp for the Gas-lamp Quarters in downtown San Diego.

Linda holds a Black Level membership to the Omni Hotel, a swank thirty-two story, five-star in the heart of the city, overlooking San Diego Bay. She pulls up to the front of the building beneath the tinted glass awning and shows her membership card to the concierge. He opens her door and she hands him her service key.

Herroso parks his car along the curb and watches. He runs a quick background check on her and learns that she's a fashion designer and owns her own design business. Its name is *Lines of L' Attitude*. So he checks on the possibility that there may be a fashion convention at the hotel this week that she might be attending. Nope, no cigar, which of course makes Linda's behavior somewhat odd, but what's even more dubious is the fact that she's got spooks. In every move she's made since she's left Chief Jomoka's Bean Shack she has been followed by two other men. Others are watching her, too, but who? He checks with the CIA, and the Bureau's other local field offices and finds that none of them have a tail on her. This more than likely means the bad guys are keeping close tabs on her. It is plausible they don't trust her, so it's questionable whether she's in on whatever mobocracy they've got going on, but they're watching her for a reason. She must know something.

He becomes uneasy when the two men get out of the dark Buick Sedan and follow her into the hotel.

One of the spooks is a bank guard from Ted Silar's bank and the other is a mobster from Jimmy Castello's gang. They're after the flash drive in Linda's purse, the one she'd forgotten to take back to Lee's accountant. Herroso doesn't know anything about the flash drive, but he does recognize trouble when he sees it and he can't afford to let anything happen to the Stevens woman. If she's important to the perps, she's even more important to the Feds.

He doesn't want to lose sight of the two spooks, so he grabs his newspaper off the car seat and follows them, calling an FBI contact for help. Within minutes a tele-florist delivery truck is dispatched to the hotel. He walks into the hotel lobby, still dressed like a handyman clerk from the Home Depot. He feels like a lumberjack at a cotillion. He tries to keep a low profile, meandering to a chair in a distant corner of the vestibule. He chooses a seat next to a giant potted palm plant and spreads open his newspaper, holding it high enough to conceal the logo on his shirt and most of his face. He sits waiting for the flower delivery.

The two spooks haven't made a move yet. They're sitting at a grouping of sofas on the opposite end of the lobby waiting for word on how to handle Linda from the mob's *consigliere*. The *consigliere* has told the accounting office to try calling Linda one more time to remind her to bring the flash drive back, but in case she should refuse they've ordered the spooks to kidnap her and squeeze the flash out of her. In fact, the exact words were, "pry that fucking flash drive from those Prada prancing fingers, dead or alive."

Herroso keeps one eye on the spooks and the other eye on the sunny windows of the main lobby. He watches the florist van glide up the curved drive, custom-painted with bright pink, yellow and orange retro daises and the words *Dead Head Petal Pushers* written in fluorescent green on the side.

He folds his newspaper, placing it close to his chest as he gets up and saunters to a bank of elevators.

As he waits for the elevator to open he can see the florist walk around the front of the van and then roll open the door on the side exposing the traveling garden. Every inch of the van from floor to ceiling is covered with foliage and blooms. He lifts a whopping bouquet of brilliant red, yellow, and orange flowers out of its slot. It's wrapped in a bulky mass of green tissue twisted around the stems and tied with a huge purple ribbon. There's a balloon attached, floating above it that reads Happy Birthday.

As he watches the florist slide the door closed again, his elevator door opens and he steps inside thinking about the van. In a brow-raising moment, he pictures the Dead Head Petal Pushers van parked in front of a funeral home.

Agent Herroso knows that the florist company is a legitimate company. Their help is on occasion enlisted by the FBI. The florists have been chosen for their ostentatious ability to distract, but the man delivering the flowers is an undercover agent who had made a call to the hotel in advance for Linda's room number. The undercover florist will meet Herroso on the second floor and give him both Linda's room number and the flowers.

The huge mass of tissue paper the bouquet is wrapped in hides a shirt bearing the Omni Hotel's logo on it. From there, Agent Herroso will head to the restroom, ditch the flowers, change his shirt and make his way to Linda's room disguised as hotel staff. He'll knock on Linda's door and identify himself as a maintenance man, explaining that there has been complaints of the air conditioning not working in other suites on this floor and that he needs to check the thermostat. Once inside her suite, he'll plant tiny voice transmitters in various locations.

Meanwhile, Agent Carlos Ramirez has stopped off at Stevens Orthodontics LLC acting as a concerned parent and inquiring about the price of braces. He tells Tiffany who's on the phone at the front desk that he was passing by on his lunch break and decided to stop in because his eight-year-old needs braces. Tiffany holds one finger up as she writes something down, then tells him that she can be with him in a moment.

Carlos nods, passing the time by noting the layout of the office and watching the comings and goings.

Tiffany barely has a free moment, but in between the busyness she smiles at him. When she gets a few consecutive minutes she gives him a quick rundown, telling him that Doctor Lee is a hard-working board certified orthodontist. It's a family-owned business that Lee runs with eight employees. She's courteous, but explains that it's necessary to set up an appointment for a consultation with Doctor Lee in order to get the most beneficial information. Carlos declines making an appointment for now, citing that he's just begun his search, but that he would like a business card.

He realizes that even though Tiffany's narrative about the office was brief, she hadn't mentioned Linda, Doctor Stevens' wife, at all, which of course doesn't jive with their theory about her being a co-partner in the family business. Was it an oversight? He decides to inquire about it in an unassuming way. He segues the conversation back to the part about the family-owned business. He tells her that he's always admired mom and pop shops, he asks if Doctor Stevens' wife is an orthodontist, too.

Tiffany looks at him with a peculiar expression. "Oh, no, she's in the fashion business; his daughter Sarita is the one who works here." Then she goes onto explain that Mrs. Stevens used to work at the practice, but now their daughter Sarita does what Mrs. Stevens used to do, "You know, the banking and administrative things."

Bingo! In just a few seconds, he's uncovered an interesting fact about the Stevens couple, that they have a daughter named Sarita, whom the agents didn't even know existed and that the daughter does his business banking. As he stands listening to her, once again her phone begins to ring. He looks down at the business card in his hand and notices the web address.

"I can see you're busy," he says with a smile, "I'll check out your website." He slides the card into his wallet, then picks up a brochure from the counter and sticks it in his back pocket as he walks out the door.

Once outside the building, he settles into his car and downloads Stevens Orthodontics, LLC website onto his phone. After taking a virtual tour, he clicks Our Staff, he slides the cursor down the list of employee's names with their pictures next to it.

He clicks open some of their profiles, and finds them to be very vanilla; name, school attended, and so forth. When it comes to Sarita's name, he finds it a bit more interesting. He can see by her picture that she's Mexican-American, but her last name is Stevens. *Adopted?* He decides to dig further. He runs a general background check not expecting to find much and he doesn't. She has a driver's license, but no traffic tickets. Nor does she have any arrests, priors, or convictions. He digs further and finds she also has no credit, no car loan, no apartment, and has never had a utility bill. To Carlos, when an individual is that invisible red flags are immediately raised.

He decides to run a general check on Doctor Stevens, and the information that spews out is generally benign. Caucasian, forty-two, married and has resided at his current address for the last fourteen years. He'd purchased a condominium less than two years ago at an address close to the university. This would be an obvious place for his daughter. *What a lucky kid*, he thinks, never had a day of worry in her entire life.

Then Carlos decides to run a check on Linda Stevens and learns that she's Caucasian, thirty-four, married, has resided at the same address for the last fourteen years and is the owner of a fashion design business called *Lines of L'Attitude* which was formed ten years ago. She is also listed as a member of Stevens Orthodontics, LLC and her name appears on the official corporation documents.

Carlos leans back and thinks about that information. He decides that since both parents are Caucasian, he'll pull up the vital records database in California and find out when Sarita was adopted.

As he reads the information he finds that neither parent had any prior marriages, then finds the proof that the Stevens' did adopt a child. There's an amended birth certificate for a child named Sarita Jolita Stevens. There should be an original sealed birth certificate, too, but there isn't. So just in case there's a glitch, he tries running it again, nothing. It could be a database error, but he finds it to be an important lack of information. No doubt Ira will want someone from Homeland Security to dig into this further.

In the meantime, Agent Reggie Noble is in his office sitting at his desk. He's delved into the Guardit Armored Truck Corporation, making one phone call after another and after ending this last call he sits rubbing his forehead, perplexed, occupied in deep thought. *No trace of a barcode, no signatures, not even one bag number on record for a six p.m. delivery to the Golden State Bank yesterday. There's no audit trail for that truck. It's as if it were invisible. Was it a smoke screen, a false tip?*

He decides to call a personal friend of his who works for the Department of Justice's Financial Crime Enforcement Department. The man is an infiltration genius and Reggie hopes to get some help from him on how to penetrate Guardit's Reporting and Data Collection System. He picks up the phone to dial, but is interrupted by a light rap on his door. He looks up to see Agent Lucius Lastad standing there.

"You got a minute?"

Reggie sets the phone back down. "Yeah, Lu, what's up?"

"Well, let's start with Greg Bishop and Doctor Stevens. We already know that Stevens does his banking at Golden State Bank and that Greg Bishop works there. So like Ira said, I checked the bank's land-line records for yesterday's calls and they showed that Bishop got two calls from his wife within the time frame of the snake incident, which may or may not be of any relevance. But, here's the interesting thing: There was a call made from Bishop's private cell phone to an 888 number earlier this morning, which was interesting for a Saturday."

"Why, who's the number for?"

"The FBI tip line."

Reggie lets out a deliberate exhale. "You're kidding, right?"

"Nope, I'm not kidding."

"You mean to tell me Greg Bishop called in his own tip?"

"Yep, and that's not all. I checked the call records for Ted Silar's direct line from this morning. Turns out he's been a busy boy, starting very early. It's not so much who the calls were made to, and received from, that intrigue me, but the sequence and the timing of them. Ready for this?"

"Shoot."

"Early this morning, prior to Bishop making the phone call to the tip line, Silar received a call from an accounting firm by the name of Morgan & Anderson CPAs. Then after hanging up, he made a call to a bank guard. There was no phone action after that for about forty-five minutes, then Silar got a return call from that bank guard that lasted a few minutes. There was nothing for another twenty minutes, but then another interesting sequence occurred. The phone records show that Silar made a call to a board member almost simultaneously as Bishop called in the tip from his private cell phone. Then Silar received a call back from that same board member two minutes later. Within seconds following that call, Silar called a shady character named Robert Dench, a mechanic who owns an engine repair and tow truck shop on the south side of the city with known ties to a faction of mobsters out in Vegas. His brother's company is the one that owns the construction equipment Ira's been watching behind Bishop's house."

"Sounds like Bishop is getting cold feet in whatever he's doing. He put himself in jeopardy by calling the Feds so he must want out. The trouble is, Silar's playing for keeps. Something huge must be going down."

Lucius nods, "And there's another connection here."

"What's that?"

"I looked into Morgan & Anderson CPAs' office, the one Silar called this morning."

"And?"

"Stevens Orthodontics LLC, is on their clientele list. Stevens has his accounting done by them."

"So we have a triangle going on. Now why doesn't that surprise me?" Reggie folds his arms across his chest and leans back in his chair. "You wanna know what I found today? I found that it's possible for a heavy-duty armored truck to move undetected through this city, no radar, no satellite, no barcode. It's miraculous really, a six-ton, steel ghost."

"No records?"

"None. No trail of that six p.m. delivery at all." He looks out the window, reflecting for a moment. "Let's connect the dots here, Lu. We have an armored truck making deliveries to Silar's bank, yet not showing up on radar. And an accounting firm, a bank guard, someone from the bank board, and a shady mechanic with mob ties all in contact with Silar outside of banking hours. Not to mention that someone is making calls to Ted Silar's bank from Pakistan, which prompted the start of this whole investigation.

"We also have Stevens' wife Linda at the snake crime scene just before it happened, and the orthodontist himself doing business with both the bank and the accounting firm. All these things may appear to be a scattered skeleton when separated out, but when you start connecting the bones, it could hold the guts of an international money laundering scheme."

Lucius nods. "Yeah, at least, and I'll bet whether by hook or crook, Doctor Stevens is involved."

"Yeah. Me, too. With Silar's communications to Pakistan, and the bold warning of an *invisible* armored truck moving through the city, no telling what's about to go down. I think we have enough of a breakthrough to bend the attorney general's ear, at least give him a heads up. I'll give Ira a call, let him know what we've got and he can take it from there."

Father Lelo is working on some investigating of his own. He has just veered his truck off a dusty road into the gravel parking lot of the police station on the reservation from where Ira's family had roots and where Dewey is still the sheriff.

He rolls to a stop and the dust begins to settle on his windshield. He puts his vehicle in park and eyes the aged building for a moment. He notices how the white paint has all but worn away, leaving a ghostly gray appearance. It casts him back in time twenty years when he first saw the evidence from Raina's murder including the note from Rosa. It is also the place where he learned of young Ira's fate. He rests his arms on the steering wheel for a moment. *Time has stood still here,* he thinks.

As he steps out of the truck the soles of his shoes crackle on the stones beneath his feet and he considers that there's a real good chance that the evidence box concerning Raina's murder might very well still sit in the same musty old closet of this building. Right now, for him finding time at a stand-still is a fortunate thing.

He walks across the parking lot, climbs a series of eroded cast concrete stairs and reaches for the door knob. The rusty hinges squeak out an eerie welcome as he pulls the door open and steps into the dark hallway. He stops to tap the brim of his hat on his palm to shake the dust from it.

The sheriff's squad car is sitting alone in the parking lot and Father Lelo's hoping Dewey hasn't gone home for the day. As he stands in the hallway he looks to the right where Dewey's office used to be. There isn't a light on, but the door is open. He tried to call before driving here, but there was no answer so he left a message. Then he couldn't stand the anticipation of a call back, so he took a chance that Dewey would be in and he drove straight down.

When Father Lelo approaches the doorway of Dewey's office he sees him. The sheriff's back is turned and he's hanging his hat on a coat rack behind his desk. Dewey must have just gotten here a few seconds earlier, he thinks. He also notices that time has not stood still for Dewey. His hair is white, he's thicker around the middle and his posture is hunched.

Sheriff Dewey turns around to see Father Lelo's large frame filling the doorway, dressed in black from head to toe, holding his fedora next to his chest. Dewey pauses for a half second, waiting for recollection, then a wide smile. "Father Lelo." He hobbles toward him offering his hand. "It's good to see you, Father. What brings you down to these parts?"

Father Lelo smiles and stretches his arm to shake his hand. "Hello there, Dewey, good to see you, too. Thanks for getting Rosa to the hospital for me yesterday."

"Oh no, no need for thanks, wasn't a problem at all. I was happy you called." He points to a chair with his other hand gesturing for Father Lelo to sit down. "Ya know, I called Ira's room just before lunch and talked with him for a few minutes today. He's recovering fast for having wretched bites like that."

Father Lelo lets go of Dewey's hand and takes a seat. He leans back, crossing his long legs in a relaxed manner, he sets his hat on top of his knee. "Yes, he is. He's a strong young man, body, mind, and spirit. He'll be good as new in no time."

Dewey nods and limps to the light switch by the door, jiggling it from side to side until the light comes on. "Damned old building," he mutters as he ambles back to his desk. "I have to assume that you've come for a specific reason and I think it has something to do with Ira, but before you say anything I want you to know that I'll be happy to help in any way that I can."

Father Lelo smiles. "Thank you. Yes indeed, I've come on behalf of both Rosa and Ira. They're interested in a piece of evidence that was in with Raina's belongings. Do you still have that evidence box?"

Dewey lifts his hand to his chin, then he scratches his head. "Geez, I haven't even thought about that box in years, it should still be in the closet. That is if Laura hasn't cleaned it out and disposed of it yet." He moves to the closet, and begins rummaging through the clutter on the top shelf. He shoves aside stacks of papers and files. Then he stands on tiptoes and reaches in the back to where Raina's evidence box used to be. "Well, I'll be damned. Sure enough, it's still here."

He pulls the box from the back of the shelf, and sets it down on the corner of the desk. "It looks like Laura taped it up; sealed it pretty good, too." He pulls his pocketknife out, unfolds the blade and then zips it across the tape in several places. "Don't know how much use this stuff will be to you," he says, setting the knife down. "Geez. It's been perty neer twenty-five years since she was found in the desert, ain't it?" He looks down into the box. "It must be close to twenty years since you looked in here, but here it is, still packaged and marked the same. Nothin's changed; it's still all the same stuff." He takes a step back and looks at Father Lelo.

Father Lelo stands up and sets his hat down on the chair. As he approaches the box...*a light ambient breeze circulates around him, a heavy weight of solemnity penetrates through to the bone. A misty fusion of both sullen grief and triumphant faith swirls above the opening of the box. It unifies in equal balance and sends Father Lelo into another state, a hypnotic interval of separate awareness.*

Father Lelo takes a huge breath in acceptance of the rite, and gives thanks to his loving creator God for this blessing. He pauses for a moment, opening his heart, receptive to the Holy Spirit's energy flowing through him and prays for help in putting Raina's mysterious death to rest; a death gone unnoticed by the secular world.

Father Lelo closes his eyes, within moments he's mesmerized by a slow-moving vision.

*He sees a flimsy tail of soft mist drifting on the surface of a clear-running creek. Swaying above in a gentle breeze are whispers of ghostly lichen draping from the long limbs of trees. They drip their likeness beyond the water's soothing ripples. Like angels wings they descend to the river's bed where beneath the crystal cold they meet tender shoots of river-grass striving to reach the surface, submerged like a choir of children, they stretch and sway with up-swept arms, yearning to touch the warmth of the sun's rays.*

*Three horses drink from the creek, while nearby, a wolf with her nose to the earth circles the ground. The horses lift their heads and turn their ears. A hawk sitting on her perch watching from afar sends out a piercing shrill as a cougar digs her claws deep into the thick bark of an ancient pine. The wolf stops and waits... then in answer to a voiceless call, the wolf convenes to a precise patch of earth where first he sits, and then lays his body down.*

*A voice rolls through the mist.*

*"Observe the signs...make haste to free the spirit of virtue, for only then will light increase across this sphere. Upwards you will find what you are looking for. Harness as one your strengths to repeal the spread of darkness."*

The vision releases him and Father Lelo takes a step backward. He opens his eyes and for a moment he's stunned and he stares in silence. He draws a huge breath of air into his lungs, then reaches for his handkerchief.

He shakes the white cloth open and uses it to reach inside the box to pull out the stick. Once long ago this stick was soaked in Raina's freshly spilled blood, now all that remains of Raina is graced here. The stick is covered with dried earth and blood, and the wood is not recognizable. It's a wonder it was kept at all, it's the one article in the box not bagged or tagged.

Father Lelo turns and looks at Dewey. "What I'm in need of," he pulls out the stick, "is this stick. May I take it?"

Dewey gives him a strange look. "The stick?" He shrugs. "Well, yeah, I guess. It's against protocol, but nobody has ever so much as even inquired about this box before you did twenty years ago, or after you did, for that matter. You can have it, but I have to ask, what in tarnation do you want with a dirty ol' dried-up stick?"

"I want it for testing."

"Testing?"

"Do you have a bag I can put this in?"

Dewey opens his bottom desk drawer, and pulls out a plastic 12" x 18" evidence bag. "Yeah, here you go." He opens the bag and holds it out in front of Father Lelo. "DNA testing?"

Father Lelo wraps the stick in his white handkerchief and drops it in. "Yes, DNA testing. I'm taking this stick to the U.S. Forest Service to find out anything and everything I can about this wood."

Dewey sits down in his chair, and after a pause he nods. "Yeah, you're right, you should. They've come a long way with DNA testing since nineteen eighty-four. I guess there could be someone else's blood besides

Raina's on there, and no matter what Raina was up to, her kin is good people and they have the right to put it to rest."

Father Lelo gives Sheriff Dewey a scowl while he zips the baggie closed, "You know how I feel about you saying that, Dewey. There's no proof of her being a prostitute. She was a friend and her mother and son are still friends of mine. I'd appreciate you having respect for that." Father Lelo reaches for his hat.

Sheriff Dewey responds by asking a question. "Why the U.S. Forest service? Shouldn't you be sending it to the Crime Lab in San Diego?"

"We will, but since it's obvious her murderers were found dead in a car near her body, we're more interested in analyzing the DNA of the wood first."

Sheriff Dewey furrows his brow.

Father Lelo continues, "You remember how Rosa always had powerful visions? Well, so does Ira and they both believe that the stick may give us some answers as to where Raina's murder took place."

Sheriff Dewey pauses, his mind jostles back to the past, remembering Rosa's abilities as a medicine woman while she still lived on the reservation and he nods. "Yeah, it's true, there's no doubt that Rosa is an excellent visionary, the best I can ever remember. She must have passed the gift to Ira." He leans back, folding his arms across his chest for a moment. "Wish 'em luck for me and if you find anything out about that stick, let me know, would ya?"

Father Lelo gives him a nod and tips his hat. "Will do, Sheriff. Thanks for your help. Good day, now."

He leaves the sheriff's station carrying a mixed bag of emotions in his mind and the bag with the dried bloody stick in his hand. He crosses the gravel with long quick strides, opens his truck door and climbs inside. He puts the stick down on the seat next to him.

As he is driving, he thinks about the vision, pondering its meaning. He knows it's important to share the vision with Ira and Rosa as soon as possible. Between the three of them they will, no doubt, come to some sort of understanding.

He looks at the stick rolled in the cloth and he absently clenches his jaw while deep in thought about Raina's tragic ending, how it was treated with such disdain and indignity. The story of her life and death never made the papers, nor was it investigated in depth. He wonders about the stick, where it came from and if, or how, they will ever be able to find out.

Back in San Diego, Greg has just walked off the course, finishing his eighteen holes wishing he could feel good about his respectable score of seventy-two and just get in his car and go home, but as much as he's dreading it, hiding his fear as best he can, he is on his way into the Clubhouse Grille to choke down some brunch with board members and one of the banks clients, Jimmy Castello.

As they sit at a round table, cornered by windows, adorned with white linen and crystal stemware, Greg orders the Chorizo and Red Pepper Quesadillas along with a side order of fresh fruit, and a cup of coffee. He pretends to be connected with the rest of the group as they converse about some light business, but in his mind he's a million miles away.

Just hours ago he placed a call to the FBI tip line reporting a suspicious delivery by an armored truck. He gave his name as the driver of the truck, but did not divulge that the truck was a counterfeit because that is something that just the people seated at this table would know and he would be the first person that they would point their fingers at if the Feds reacted too fast. His intention was to get the FBI to start snooping around. But now that he's leaked the information, he'll be balancing on a very thin, tightrope without a net.

He had to hold the Feds back a bit, because after contemplating his conversation with Ted earlier, he's concluded that the safest way to handle this for both Julie's and his sake, is to pretend to have had a change of heart, to make sure that Ted understands that he is not ever going to give up his lifestyle. So if that means smuggling for the rest of his life, then so be it. It's the one thing Ted will accept. He remembered reading a wise quote by Sun Tzu. 'Keep your friends close, and your enemies closer.' He's decided to do some serious sucking up to his enemies in order to get them to trust him while he's ratting them out behind their backs. As the old saying goes, desperate times call for desperate measures, and after thinking about his situation he's come to the conclusion that it's his one chance of getting Julie and himself out of this mess alive.

As he sits across the table from Jimmy Castello, observing him, he decides that if Jimmy had a lookalike it would have to be a toad. Nothing against toads, Greg's certain that toads have better manners and are nicer creatures than Jimmy. It's just that Jimmy resembles one. He has brown spotty skin and a pointy nose and he has no neck at all. His cheeks always look like he's ready to belch and his voice is deep and croaky. Even as he sits right now, his husky shoulders are hunched above his plate and Greg can't help but think that if a fly flew over the table this very second, Jimmy's tongue would roll out and snatch it out of thin air.

Jimmy catches Greg looking at him, he stops chewing for a brief moment, his cheeks crammed with pastry, he nudges his chin up toward Greg with his mouth full. "How er things at the bank?" He takes a sip of water to wash down the pastry. "I mean, with the economy like it is, things gotta be nerve-wracking, you still faithful to your job, Greg?"

Greg scrapes the last strawberry from his dish, angst now churning in his stomach. He raises it to his mouth. He looks up to see the weight of everyone's eyes pressing for a prompt answer. He lowers his spoon and accidently clanks it against his coffee cup, sending the strawberry plopping onto the table. It splatters its scarlet juice and rolls across the white linen leaving a red trail before coming to a stop at the stem of his water goblet. Spooked, but trying not to let it show, Greg reaches for the strawberry, his heart thumping and sets it on his empty plate while forcing a smile.

"Things are going good." He glances around the table at everyone, lingering on Jimmy for a second, then turns to Ted. "Thanks for that pep talk this morning Ted, I needed it. It gave me a whole new perspective on ways to handle things and I already have some ideas on how to get the numbers up." He turns back to the others. "It's great to have someone as inspirational as Ted in charge of the bank; he's one of the best in the business. I see a lot of money being made by all of us in the future."

Greg sees signs that he has appeased the group by their thin smiles and bobbing heads. He has relieved some of the tension, at least for now. Ted takes a sip of his scotch while peering above the rim of his glass at Greg. He lifts his glass and makes a toast. "Here's to a brilliant next generation chairman who keeps his clients business practices to himself."

All eye's shift to Greg and they lift their glasses. Greg feels the hair on the back of his neck stand on end while they stare at him as if he were a trophy buck, stuffed and hung on the wall of a hunting lodge, but he manages to smile. He lifts his coffee cup up to reciprocate, while mentally cursing the day that he had ever met Ted Silar.

Later, after they've finished their meals and their business, Greg is the first to push his chair back and lay his napkin on the table. He stands up, excusing himself. "It's been a pleasure, gentleman, but my wife has some chores around the house for me to take care of, so if you'll excuse me I'll be on my way." He walks around the table, shaking everyone's hands, thinking what a stupid comment that was and how he could kick himself for having brought up his wife. When he offers his hand to Jimmy, Jimmy grabs hold and doesn't let go. "How's the little woman doing, Julie ain't it?" He squeezes Greg's hand like a vise grip. "I trust everything's fine at home, landscaping problems all taken care of?" Greg knows what he means. Jimmy knows every corrupt law enforcement officer in Southern California and he greases them for every bit of information relative to any of his businesses. He's the one that put a contract out on his landscaper's life. He knew the landscaper was working undercover for the Border Patrol and that they were keeping tabs on his heavy equipment and the transportation of it, back behind Greg's house.

Tiny beads of perspiration form on Greg's forehead, but he flashes Jimmy a wide smile, "She's doing great; no worries at home, everything's under control." Then patting Jimmy's hand with his free hand, he pulls away. "Thanks for asking."

When he gets to Ted, he sets his hand on his shoulder and tells him that he'll see him bright and early Monday morning, trying to remain calm and sound as cheerful as possible. He smiles at him, then turns for the door.

Once outside the building the mid-afternoon sun hits his face and he lets loose a long sigh of relief, thankful to be on the periphery of their presence. *Damn, I've got to get away from this pressure cooker. I'm so stressed, I feel like I'm going to explode.* He walks to his car, staring down at the herring-bone pattern of the red brick sidewalk, thinking about Julie. His eyes soften as he recalls her words from this morning. *Bourbon Crusted Stuffed King Crabs for lunch?* He can't wait until the FBI boils these king crabs. Her words calm him down. He is glad he called the tip line.

He's been preoccupied and irritable for months now. As a matter of fact, he's been downright hard to live with and he knows it. He realizes how much he misses Julie and the closeness they once shared and he's aching to feel that again.

As he approaches his car, he looks up to see a tow truck parked one space over from his Mercedes, an absolute oddity for a parking lot belonging to a distinguished country club. The driver is just getting in it and the name on the side panel says, *Southside Road King Robert Dench & Sons.*

Dench hops in his truck, and rolls his window down.

Greg is about to unlock his door, when Dench pops his head out. "Hey! What model is your Benz?"

A bit startled, Greg looks around to see if the guy might be talking to someone else, but there's nobody else around. "It's a Maybach."

"She's a beaut," Dench says, shaking his head with a toothy grin. "Car like thats gotta be worth $300k or more. He nods his head toward the high-end assortment of luxury automobiles. "When I first drove into this lot I felt like I was rollin into The Pismo Beach Classic or somethin. Anyways, nice car." He gives a thumbs up, then backs out and drives away, leaving Greg staring in wonderment.

*How strange,* he thinks. *There's something you don't see every day; a tow truck amidst Bentleys, Benz, Rolls, and Porsches. Friendly enough guy, though, wonder what he was doing here?*

He opens his door and slides into a world of high-quality surroundings. Reaching around his left shoulder, he fastens his seat belt, then just as he puts his finger on the ignition button his cell phone vibrates. He stops to answer it. "Hello."

"Yeah Greg, Ted here, I want to let you know I appreciate the attitude at lunch, but I want to make sure you are clear about something. We're watching both you and your wife. So don't try anything stupid, like going to the Feds, you understand what I'm saying, Greg?"

The air in Greg's windpipe disappeared, and he struggles to take a breath while the blood rushes to his face. He's fearful and angry at the same time. It feels like his head is going to explode, but as much as he wants to blow his stack at Ted for getting him mixed up in this mess, he knows he has to keep a lid on it. He fears for Julie's and his life, so he closes his eyes and calms himself, he musters up a soothing tone. "I understand, Ted, and my change of attitude is sincere. I have a lifestyle that I enjoy and after thinking about it, I realize that I can't live any other way. I intend to continue living the way I'm accustomed to, so I'll do anything you want me to."

"That's all I wanted to hear." Ted hangs up.

Greg lets out a deep growl, then tosses his phone on to the passenger seat, and reaches again for the ignition button. As he leaves the parking lot he is thinking how much he hates Ted Silar. He hates him even more than he did this morning, a fact which he never thought was possible. As he drives home, he thinks of Julie, about the painting he found and how he's been neglecting their marriage for too long. He decides he's going to start making it up to her this afternoon. He has a special pass to travel across Camp Pendleton as a short cut to and from work, compliments of Julie's dad, Colonel Price and he remembers at the intersection of Mission and Ammunition Road, just before the back gates, that there are roadside stands selling fruit, vegetables, flowers and fresh seafood. He decides that picking up some flowers for her would be a good start, maybe some fresh seafood, too, some crab legs to boil. He smiles thinking about the parody he and Julie shared.

Meanwhile, back at the club house, Ted excused himself from the table and walks toward the men's room. He stops in the hallway, looking refined in his navy colored Chapman's and white Polo shirt, his phone is ringing and he pulls it from his pocket. "Yeah, Dench."

# CHAPTER NINETEEN

## On the Horizon

After Julie dropped Linda off at Chief Jomoka's, she called her dad to find out if he'd ever heard of a priest by the name of Father Lelo, a colonel in the Marine Corps. He responded in the affirmative telling her that he'd served with Colonel Lelonis Kendall, better known as Father Lelo, aboard the USS *Maddox* off the north coast of Vietnam in '65. He also said that Father Lelo was first and foremost a respected man of God and secondly, a tough, gritty Marine with the miraculous energy level of someone half his age. He added that he bumped into Father Lelo from time to time through mutual friends.

Julie asked if he could find out what Father Lelo's cell phone number is, telling him she'd met him while visiting someone at the hospital and wanted to thank him for helping out with some spiritual matters. She wasn't about to tell him what happened in her back yard, or about Greg's troubles yet, it would do no good. It would cause him immediate distress and send her mother into a tailspin. *Besides,* she thinks, *I don't know anything except for what the priest told me, and that isn't much.* She's got more digging to do and she's not going to lose her cool, or as her Dad would say, *I'm not ready to flip the chicken switch just yet.*'"

She could almost hear her dad's wheels spinning through the phone. Then after a prolonged intuitive pause, instead of pushing the subject, he said that he would check the phone listings on base and get back to her.

She pulls her SUV into the garage and walks into the house toward the door of her study, she pushes it open and calls out for her kitty cat.

As she scans the room for Miss Jingles she notices the closet door is open. She crosses the studio to shut it and sees Miss Jingle's collar; pink with sparkling sequins and a tiny bell, lying on her desk. She picks it up, realizing that Greg must have come in here after she'd left this morning. She glances at the closet door again, realizing that he must have seen the painting.

*So, now he knows I've been watching the landscaper. I can assume he's no less than peeved about it. And, to top it off, it's just a matter of time before the neighbors ask him about the ambulance being here.* She lets out an unconscious sigh. *Now I have to bring up both the painting, and the hospital event. Great, my weekend's going to become a melodrama; a bristly colloquy, before I even have my facts from the priest yet.*

In the beginning she didn't tell Greg about the painting because she wanted the contest to be a surprise. Then after she'd already committed to painting the landscaper, Greg made it quite clear by innuendo that he was wary of the man. She rolls her eyes. Amazing how leaving something undisclosed could lead to so much aggravation. *I should have just told him in the first place.*

She finds Miss Jingles curled up in her basket next to the fireplace hearth. She fastens the collar around her neck and pets her for a few minutes before going upstairs to her bedroom.

She walks into Greg's closet, looks up at the shoe polishing box on the shelf and feels a tinge of guilt surface for what she's about to do. It's abnormal for her to snoop. It makes her feel awkward, but her curiosity's gotten the better of her.

Once again, she pulls the extravagant leather box down from the shelf, opens it expecting to find nothing at all. Instead, she gasps at the sight of a pistol, a cold, gray, barrel, with a warm walnut grip. Beneath it, a cheap prepaid phone, alongside it, a loaded magazine. She closes her eyes and reminds herself to breathe. *Oh my god,* she thinks, exhaling. *What is Greg doing with a gun? He's never owned a gun, never even fired a gun, he hates guns!*

Earlier in the day, before Father Lelo drove down to the reservation to talk to Sheriff Dewey, he had dropped Rosa off at home in Oceanside so she could catch up on household chores, and steep some fresh chaparral tea for Ira to sip while in the hospital. *"The tea's an infusion,"* she'd declared. *"It'll cure just about anything. Given in the correct dosage, that is."*

She's standing at her kitchen counter pouring the steaming concoction into a thermos just as Father Lelo is pulling into the driveway. She looks out the window, screws the cover onto the thermos, pulls her satchel off the counter and hikes it up on her shoulder, then walks out the door to his truck.

Father Lelo watches the petite grandmother dressed in a long-sleeved white button-down blouse, baggy, tan trousers and a brown vest, draw near to the truck. As she approaches her 4' 11" inch frame slowly disappears and her round face with its distinct curved eyebrows and her long gray braids are all he can see in the window. She opens the door smiling and Father Lelo can't help but notice that the seat of his truck is at chest level to her.

She lifts the stainless steel thermos up in front of him. "My tea just finished steeping before you pulled into the driveway so it's real fresh. I have it here in the thermos." She sets the thermos on the floorboard and starts to climb in.

Then she stops, remaining still, she senses Raina's essence. She looks across the seat to where Father put the stick wrapped in the white linen cloth and sealed in a baggie. She stares at it. Tears form in her eyes and she buries her face in her hands as the sensation of Raina's spirit flows through her. "Oh my beautiful daughter," she says. "I feel you."

Father Lelo furrows his brow with immense regret, realizing that he should have concealed the cherished remains somehow. "Rosa, I'm so sorry, I wasn't thinking, I should have put—"

Rosa lifts her hand stopping him and then places it on her forehead. "I'm all right, I'll be all right," she assures him, taking a deep breath. "The blood on that stick is the blood of my child. It's hallowed to me, I would have sensed it no matter what." She squeezes her lids shut, refusing to let her tears flow, after a few seconds she opens her eyes staring into his. "I would like to hold it in my hands."

Her gaze penetrates Father Lelo's soul. He nods, then offers his hand to help her climb up into the truck.

She takes the satchel off her shoulders and hands it to him, gives him her hand and he pulls her up. After she's settled she turns to him. Their eyes lock and they stare at each other in contemplation. For a prolonged period they remain indifferent to the demands of the outside world, sitting in stillness, their hands locked together and hovering above the stained piece of wood, the dried blood all that remains of the young woman. A shift from tension to inner balance transpires, seeping into them. They sit in silent unification, their intentions positive, their hearts open.

Father Lelo lets go of her hand. He picks up the stick and places it on her lap. He watches her expression change from calm to consecrated rapture.

It pleases him to see her look so blissful, though a practical thought surfaces and creates a bit of unease for him. How is he going to make her give up the remains of her daughter to the Forest Service? By the look of her countenance, it'll be nothing short of sacrilegious.

Rosa breathes deep and closes her eyes, *"Haa, Temeshaa,* Yes, Spirit," she says, then continues to chant in her native tongue.

The beautiful, ethereal tone of her voice sends an impulse through Father Lelo's spine. He lifts his face to the sky in solemnity, transported to a timeless space of reverent nothingness, yet fully aware of his every breath.

As Father Lelo's heightened consciousness begins to fade into the ordinary day, he again opens his eyes. He looks at Rosa. She's staring down at the stick wrapped in white linen. *In a moment of unexplainable phenomenon,* a *trace of red pigment has begun to seep into the cloth; leaving a stain in the center of the white cloth.*

Father Lelo arches his brows in amazement. As a feeling of pure love flows through his body he realizes the meaning of this miracle. "Praise to our loving creator God," he says looking at Rosa. "You will not have to part with Raina's blood again." Rosa folds her hands together and closes her eyes, venerating the Great Spirit.

After a long period of silence, his eyes moistened with tears, Father Lelo backs down the driveway. He listens to Rosa's chants all the way to the San Diego Forestry Service. Once they drop off the stick they'll go to the hospital to see Ira.

Long before daybreak on this Sunday morning Doctor Issac had written an order for Ira's catheter and mummifying bandages to be removed. He'd been restless all through the night so the nurses carried out the order fast, then Ira fell into a deep sleep. Doctor Issac had gone home to shower and change. When she came back she spent the early hours of the morning in her office putting the finishing details on a case report detailing Ira's one-of-a-kind event. Now she's on her way to his room to check on him.

The first light of day has just shone through the curtains of his room, but Ira's already been awake for a period, deep in concentration. His eyes are boring a hole into his notebook when Doctor Issac walks up to the end of his bed. Her black hair is up in a French twist, she is wearing navy slacks and a bold plum colored blouse unbuttoned enough to expose a single strand of pearls draped around her neck. Ira remains locked in concentration. She puts her glasses on and picks up his chart. "Well, good morning, Ira."

He jerks his head up and for a second their eyes meet.

She flips a page, looking through the chart. "The nurses tell me that you've used the restroom on your own already this morning. If your kidneys hold up for the next twenty-four hours, I won't have any excuse to keep you here." She meets his gaze again. "I'll have to release you by tomorrow afternoon."

Ira lets go of his notebook and cups his hand to his ear. "What's that? You're releasing me this afternoon?"

A delicate smile parts Doctor Issac's lips. "Don't push it, tomorrow is soon enough given all that you've been through." His expression turns humorless. She looks at the thermos bottle that Rosa had left yesterday, sitting on his tray and she lowers her chin, dark eyes peering at him above mahogany frames. "Would that be homemade chicken broth your grandmother brought for you to sip on?" she asks, reminding him of her tolerance thus far.

Ira's expression softens as he looks at the thermos.

"Low sodium, I hope," she says setting his chart down on the end of the bed.

Ira hesitates staring at the thermos for a moment, then picks it up and puts it in the nightstand drawer. "Sodium free," he murmurs, as he closes the drawer.

Doctor Issac slides her glasses off, and puts them in the pocket of her white coat. She steps around the bed to his side and puts her stethoscope to his chest. "Breathe deep," she tells him. Then she presses on both sides of his neck, examining his lymph nodes. "Your color is good, but I'm going to order some more blood work just to be on the safe side. I'm also going to change your diet to include some solids for lunch today, then for dinner you can have a full-blown meal." She puts her hands in her pockets. "Your fast recovery is quite remarkable given the types of snakes and the location and acuteness of the bites. I've done an extensive case report on your incident and included your grandmother's therapy in it. I'm quite impressed by it."

Ira doesn't say anything about Rosa's capabilities; he's not surprised by them, but he knows in the end the medical community will never authenticate her indigenous medicinal approach. Instead, he looks out the window in deep thought. He'd spent most of the afternoon and evening yesterday on the phone with his fellow agents talking about the information they've gathered and his mind is on the mission ahead of him. He turns back to Doctor Issac. "What's the earliest I can get out of here tomorrow?"

She hears the determination in his voice and in his eyes she is reminded of the stealth of a crouching leopard, stalking and anticipating the take down of its prey. She places her hand on his shoulder. "If all the tests come back satisfactory, I should think by late tomorrow morning."

"First thing in the morning, then." It's not a question.

Doctor Issac gives him a sympathetic pat. "We've already talked about this. I understand your eagerness to avenge whoever did this to you, but *my* concern is for your health. We must go about this one step at a time. I can't promise you anything, we'll see how things go." Then she starts walking to the door.

She is right about Ira's eagerness. He has an unbendable will, single-minded about getting out of the hospital early the next morning, but she has it all wrong about why. It's not about revenge, it runs much deeper than that. It's about justice.

He pushes himself up in his bed. "When will you be back?"

She doesn't bother to turn around, avoiding his gaze. "I'll be by to check on you after dinner," she throws the words back, knowing what he's thinking.

Ira watches her walk to the door. *I'll work on getting you to sign those papers when you come back here later.* "Thank you," he calls out. "I'm looking forward to the visit."

She acknowledges his thanks with a backward wave and pulls the door closed as she leaves.

Ira checks the clock on the wall, five-thirty in the morning. He pulls his cell phone out of the drawer of his nightstand and calls Carlos.

After spending the last five minutes in a warm invigorating shower, Carlos is just stepping out dripping wet when his phone begins to ring. He shivers as the cool air-conditioning envelops his skin. He picks up a towel to rub his hair dry, leaving it disheveled, then wraps the towel around his waist. He hustles to where he had peeled off his cargo pants the night before and begins groping the pockets in search of his phone. When he finds it, he checks to see who's calling. He answers, fast. "Ira! Wow, you're up early. I just got out of the shower. I'll be heading to the hospital as soon as I get dressed. How you feeling?"

"Good as new. I plan on being out of here tomorrow." Then getting down to business. "Listen, I know it's early, but I've been going through the debriefing notes from the others yesterday and I think there's more going on here then money laundering and weapons or drugs smuggling."

"Like what?"

"I've been torn, going back and forth on whether the orthodontist ties into this scheme or if he just happens to bank at the same place that Bishop works, but after Herroso reported back to me yesterday, I believe that Doctor Stevens, even though he keeps a low profile, is as much involved as Greg Bishop. He's the key to whatever it is the bankers have going down." Ira's voice cracks and he has to clear his throat, he continues. "Herroso told me that Linda Stevens took a room at the Omni Hotel yesterday. He planted some bugs in her room and the information he learned is eye-popping. Linda Stevens has spoken to just two people in the last eighteen hours, one of them being Julie Bishop and the other her secretary. She told her assistant that her mother has taken ill and she's going to San Francisco to be with her." He clears his throat and sips some ice water through a straw, then continues. "From her conversation with Julie Bishop, it's clear that she's been digging into her husband's bank statements, *and* she has a flash drive with his financials on it. The accounting firm Morgan & Anderson is pressing hard for her to return the flash drive to their office."

"You got my attention."

"And, here's some keg powder that'll knock you out of your shoes. Stevens' wife has someone else besides Herroso tailing her." Carlos raises both brows and Ira continues. "This coupled with the information that you gave me about an adopted daughter missing an original birth certificate who is responsible for Stevens' bookwork and banking, gives us cause for scrutiny of both him and the daughter."

"Do you think the doctor hired someone to follow his wife?"

"That was my question, but Herroso doesn't think so. He's got a keen sense for taped conversations and he said that judging by the wife's words and inflections, he guesses Stevens doesn't know that she's nosing around his financials. My opinion is that both she and Julie Bishop have stumbled on something that has made them both flip their vigilance switch, but they've just begun to scratch the surface and neither of them has the slightest clue yet as to the danger they might be in as a result of their curiosity."

Carlos runs his fingers through his damp hair. "Yeah, I get the same feeling."

"I'm not getting out of here until tomorrow morning, but things are starting to heat up fast." Once again he clears the phlegm from his throat. "I want that flash drive as much as Morgan & Anderson does, but we need the Stevens woman safe, too. Herroso's been on her for eighteen hours now. It's time I pull him off. I need you to replace him. I need someone fresh, someone to break the news to her about the danger she's in. I want you to copy that flash drive pronto, then get it back to the accounting firm and then get her to a safe place ASAP. I'll let you know where to take her once you have her in your custody. Don't let either her or that information out of your sight."

"I won't. What about Julie Bishop? What do we do about her?"

Ira pauses, picturing Julie in the back yard. His expression softens. "Linda Stevens disappeared on her own accord, making it convenient for us." He hesitates, staring down at his tray table for a moment, "but if we take Julie Bishop into protective custody as a precautionary measure right now it would lead to suspicion. As much as I hate to, we'll have to cool it with her for the time being." Ira senses a strong, *but what if,* reaction coming from Carlos through the telephone and his tone deepens. "I'll take full responsibility for her well-being," he says, before Carlos can get a word in edge-wise.

Carlos doesn't dispute Ira's reasoning, but wishes there was something more they could do to protect Julie. After all, the perps know she was with the Stevens woman who has the flash drive and anybody who's been within an arm's reach of that flash drive is most certainly being watched. After a moment's pause, he changes the subject. "Ira, you said you think there's more going on than weapons and drug-smuggling after gathering this new information, so what's your guess?"

"Once I concluded that Stevens is a piece of this puzzle, I asked myself, if I were a smuggler, what would I use an orthodontist for? And what seems to be the obvious answer, of course, is his power to write prescriptions for controlled substances. Then I wondered what controlled substance would *he* supply to the cartel that isn't accessible to them on the streets?"

Carlos lets out a sardonic laugh. "Uh, there's no drug you can't get on the street."

"Right, but doctors do use something else that's controlled." There is a long pause. Ira can almost hear Carlos' brain spinning.

Then the answer slams into Carlos. He sends a long forced breath of wind through the phone. "Medical Gases."

Ira nods. "Yeah."

Suddenly there's a lump in Carlos's throat and he swallows hard, then his thoughts roll off his tongue.

"They're using an armored truck to smuggle medical gases to make explosives with, but why. What are they planning to blow up?"

Ira narrows his eyes and shifts his gaze out the window, he stares, preoccupied, lost in thought for a long and frustrating half a minute.

Carlos can hear him breathing. "Why would wealthy bankers and an affluent doctor scheme to blow something up? These are people who have everything that money can buy, everything they need. What do they want?"

Ira's still in deep thought, staring out the window as he answers, "It's not about what they need or want anymore; it's about what they've acquired a taste for."

"What do you mean? What are you talking about?"

"Bear with me for now. I'm still figuring this out. It's the weekend so we have a slight window of opportunity here. We need that flash drive and every bit of information that Linda Stevens can give us. I need you to go to the Omni as soon as you can and take Linda into protective custody. Call me when you have her with you and I'll tell you where to take her. I want to meet with her first thing tomorrow morning. Remember, she's got a tail so be cautious. Lay low until the timing's right, then disappear with her."

Carlos nods, "I'm on it. Talk to you soon."

"Be careful," Ira warns, before he hangs up his phone.

When Julie found the gun and phone yesterday, she'd contemplated, then concluded that silence about the trip to the hospital and the painting would be okay, because now both her and her husband had a secret. The playing field was level. She'd decided to wait, instead, to see how Greg would act toward her when he got home after his stuffed crab luncheon. She'd wondered if he would broach the subject. Surprisingly, his mood was much better than it had been in a long time, both sweet and attentive.

After his golf game and business meeting, he'd brought home flowers, along with some fresh seafood that he cooked for dinner that evening.

Then once the sun had disappeared, allowing the appearance of the mystifying nuance of an inky backdrop, frosted with the glowing band of the Milky Way, they enjoyed a glass of wine on the patio in their Jacuzzi. It had been a long time since they'd spent any intimate time together and when Greg slipped his arm around her and there was nothing between their naked bodies except the softness of the warm water Julie could feel her heart pounding in her chest. They devoured each other in a long passionate kiss and all thoughts except for him left her mind. Then Greg got out to the Jacuzzi, donned his robe and lifted her from the water. Her wet, naked skin glistened as he kissed her everywhere, while carrying her all the way up the stairs. After he entered their bedroom, he laid her down on their king-size bed where he rekindled her fire over and over again. The fire that he had let burn out for so many months was once again blazing. Julie responded with fervor, teasing him with her passion until Greg was elevated to a place he had never been before. Then they collapsed in each other's arms, both of them floating on air, their nerve endings pulsating, suspended in a state of pure enjoyment.

She didn't want the night to end and even though there was a lot hanging over both their heads, it wasn't the right time to discuss her concerns. The right time would be after she had met and learned more from Father Lelo. He had returned her call before Greg came home with the seafood and flowers and she had arranged to meet the priest for breakfast in Oceanside on Monday morning.

Last night had been more than Julie could have hoped for. She lingers next to Greg for a while longer, snuggling close, and breathing in the masculine scent of his skin. When she peeks at the clock on the night stand, she sees it is only six in the morning, but the rumbling in her stomach makes her realize that she's famished. She kisses Greg's shoulder, then his cheek and makes her way downstairs to prepare a special Sunday morning breakfast. She smiles, certain he must be famished, too.

She brews a pot of coffee, after which she prepares a quiche of avocado, tomato, and cheddar and puts it in the oven to bake. Then she squeezes some fresh oranges, and puts the juice in the fridge. While the quiche is baking, she showers, then dresses in shorts and a tee. Rejuvenated from last night's love making, she's hoping Greg is game for a bike ride this morning.

The smell from the kitchen trails upstairs and entices Greg from his slumber. Overcome by his hunger, he quickly dons a robe and trudges down the stairs to the breakfast nook.

His eyes meet hers as she sets a plate of quiche on the table and he smiles, thinking of last night, the silkiness of her skin, her warm breath on his neck and the lovely tone of her passion as she reached ecstasy. With tenderness and the morning glow from the skylight in his eyes, he sits down across from her. He sips his coffee while watching Julie eat. He examines her features, thinking, *damn, she's beautiful. Even in shorts and a t-shirt, with her hair pulled back in a ponytail, she's radiant.* He picks up his mimosa and slides the orange rind round the rim of the glass, thinking of her some more as he takes a sip.

He had noticed her preoccupation of late and has interpreted it to be the secret about painting the landscaper that's vexing her. He considers telling her for a moment that he already knows she's been painting the guy, but that might lead to a conversation about the hospital and the snakes so he decides not to. Besides, he doesn't want to spoil the quality of this morning. He'll let her tell him about it in her own time.

Julie looks up from her plate and sees him staring at her. She tilts here head and smiles. "I have an idea. Why don't we take the bikes out and go for a ride along the coast this morning before the beaches get too busy and while the sea breeze is calm? We haven't done that in months."

Greg sets his glass down. "Okay," he says, sounding cheerful. "I can't remember the last time we did that. Let me get showered and dressed and then we can go."

Julie smiles, relishing the easiness of being together once again. She welcomes the chance at getting outdoors; it always clears her mind. Greg slides from the booth and walks to the stairs, turning back to look at her. "Have I told you lately how much I love you?" She smiles, a captivating smile that he hasn't seen in a long time and he's glad they have the entire day to spend together.

"I'll get the dishes cleared away and get the bikes ready for you to load on the Rover," she tells him.

When Julie steps into the garage, she sees that Greg has pulled the Maybach too far ahead and the bikes are sandwiched between the grill of the Mercedes and the wall of the garage. It would be impossible for Julie to roll the bikes out without taking a chance at nicking the car. The car doors are locked, and she'll have to get Greg's keys before she can back it up and make room.

Greg is already in the shower. She finds his keys on the dresser. As she descends the stairs, her cell phone starts to ring. It's at the bottom of her white Bottega on the kitchen counter. She fishes it out to check the caller ID, it's Linda.

Linda wasn't able to sleep at all last night and although it's quite early, she couldn't hold off any longer. She needed to talk to Julie. Julie had told her about finding the gun and the prepaid phone yesterday and she's calling to find out if Julie has said anything to Greg yet.

Julie answers the phone in a soft voice, aware that Greg could come downstairs any second.

"Good morning Linda."

"Forgive me for calling so early, Julie, but I couldn't wait any longer. Have you said anything to Greg yet?"

Julie turns to make sure Greg isn't within ear shot. "It's ok, I was already up and, no, I haven't. I made an appointment for tomorrow morning to talk to that priest I told you about. I want to hear what he has to say first."

Linda's voice is tired, she is run down. "Perhaps that's best. I spent the entire night agonizing about Lee and Sarita. I tossed and turned all night, haven't slept a wink."

"You need to take it easy and relax, try to catch up on some sleep."

"I agree I need to, but that being said, I have a deadline for an important shoot with *Vanity*." She lets out a breath. "At least I have my portfolio and laptop with me. Do you realize that it's been since yesterday around noon that I've been in this hotel room? I haven't left once and I'm going stir crazy." She sighs, "I don't even have a change of clothes with me, and the only place for me to get something is down in that dreary hotel boutique" She sweeps her hand across her forehead "If I shop there I'll have to purchase something off the rack to wear."

Julie understands Linda's frustration and predicament. She's exhausted, away from her home, her belongings, her office. She's had no sleep, has an important shoot coming up and she learned things yesterday that could make your blood boil. Then to top it off, she's a woman who never wears anything but *haute couture* and now she is going to have to dress in ready-made clothing. Julie guesses that Linda's about ready to unravel at the seams.

Then a partial solution pops into her head and she proposes it to Linda. "Maybe you can at least find something that's suitable for pool-side to study your portfolio options in."

Linda tosses her hair. "Maybe, as a rule, a poolside lounge chair beneath an unbrella does relax me," she says while checking her manicure. Then she tells Julie to call her after she talks to the priest Monday morning. After that they'll figure out whether or not it is time to confront their husbands.

Julie hangs up the phone and stands for a moment, thinking about the priest and then the gun she'd found, not aware that she's biting her lip.

She walks out to the garage and unlocks the driver's door of Greg's car. She slides in, pushes the ignition button and backs the car up. When she turns back around Greg is standing in the doorway dressed in a pair of navy blue, board shorts and a white zip up Jersey tee. He's holding two bike helmets under his arms.

"Where are you going?" He shouts above the engine.

She shuts the car off and gets out. "I had to move the car to get the bikes out without scratching it."

"Oh," he says.

As he steps through the doorway, he stubs his toe on the door jam. He drops one of the helmets and it bounces off the step, then wobbles to and fro until it's under the car and has stopped next to the front tire. He hands Julie the other helmet and bends down to retrieve it. He reaches under the car and after an initial look of confusion, his expression sours. "What's this?" He rolls the helmet out and looks at the back of his hand. He lifts it up to his nose and smells the thick, sticky grease on it, furrows his brow and shrugs. "Doesn't smell like oil or tranny fluid. It's tacky," he says, tapping his fingers together. "Some kind of sticky grease or something. Must be from when I had my brakes done. I'll have to have a word with that mechanic."

Julie wrinkles her nose. He gets up, finds a clean rag in the rag box, and then loads the bikes onto the bike rack of the Land Rover.

Thirty minutes later they're biking down the San Luis Rey River trail. They ride, wind in their hair, laughing and joking, racing and chasing each other along a river bed trail designed to give the illusion of privacy and isolation. They push thoughts of everything but each other out of their minds. Today is their day to recapture their love and their youth. It has been too long.

The morning is glorious and golden and the sights and sounds of nature are soothing. They stop for lunch at a sushi bar, spend some time window shopping at a plaza just a short distance off the trail and end up at Ye Ole Town Sweet Shoppe. While sitting at a wrought-iron bistro table for two, they share a hot fudge sundae with pecans, whipped cream and cherries and then they splurge, and share a fresh cream puff, too.

On the way back home the ride is quieter and their spirits a bit more subdued. They're both besieged by private thoughts about the uncertainties that life has thrown in their paths. By the time they arrive back at the Oceanside pier, the blood-red sun is just about to make its silent splash into the ocean.

They lean on the railing looking out on the ocean. Greg's arm is around Julie's shoulder, hers around his waist. They watch the seagulls gliding the zephyrs, silhouetted by the gigantic ball of fire on the horizon. They stand watching the majesty of the sun command awe, even as it does nothing except sink and fade.

At 7:30 a.m., after Linda had hung up after talking with Julie, there was a light rap on Linda's hotel door. She'd thought it was her paper and coffee that arrived, but when she checked the peephole she saw two men standing there and when she asked who they were, one of them introduced himself as the hotel manager. He said he needed to speak with her, then pulled out his hotel identification card and held it up in front of the peephole.

Linda is standing on her tiptoes wearing makeshift pajamas of workout shorts and a white tee from her gym bag, peeking through the peephole and wondering about the man standing next to the manager. He's a dark-haired man, polished yet rugged-looking, with a strong jawline, wide cheekbones and a wisp of a black curl on his forehead. She can't help but notice his attractiveness, but he's holding a breakfast tray and she didn't order breakfast. She realizes that whatever the manager wants, it must be important for him to be at the door of her suite so early, but why is he here with room service?

"Just a minute," she says. Then she goes to the bedroom, slips on the hotel's thick white terrycloth robe and goes back to the door. She turns the dead bolt and pulls the door open.

She looks at the man with the breakfast tray first. "That can't be mine, I ordered coffee." She says curtly. The hotel manager steps forward. "It's complimentary from the hotel, ma'am. May we speak with you?"

Linda folds her arms across her chest shifting her green eyes from the room service man to the manager. "What is it?" she asks, impatiently.

"May we speak in private? It's urgent, Ms. Stevens." After a moment of uncomfortable silence while she is staring into his eyes, she notes the weightiness of his mood. She relents and moves away from the door, motioning them in. As soon as the room service man is inside he closes the door and sets the tray down on the hall table. He pulls out his badge. "I'm Agent Carlos Ramirez, Field Officer with the United States Border Patrol."

Linda lifts her hand to her mouth in a gasp, frozen for a moment. Then she folds her arms again, as if she's just gotten a chill. "I'm Linda Stevens, but I suppose you know that," she says in a cool tone, not extending her hand.

Carlos shifts his gaze to the hotel manager and thanks him for his help. The manager nods and walks out, Linda and Carlos watch as he closes the door behind him. Carlos turns to Linda. "May I call you Linda?"

After seconds that seem like an hour, she approves. "Yes, go ahead."

Carlos looks at her with gentle, but serious brown eyes. "I have something to tell you Linda, and you may want to be sitting down when you hear it."

Her heart begins to beat faster, and her eyes are locked on his, then she motions for Carlos to follow her into the living room of the suite. She chooses a spot on the pastel print sofa along the wall and sits on the edge, crossing her legs and tucking the thick white robe around them. Carlos sits across from her on the ottoman of a matching pastel chair. Between them is a round coffee table of bleached oak, adorned with a bulbous, pink vase filled with fresh white roses resting on its lustrous sheen. The spectacular view out the balcony window between them, is of the bright blue sky and the white foam rolling across the top of the turquoise swells of the bay.

Carlos hesitates for a moment searching for the right words. "Linda, we have reason to believe that your husband is involved in some highly classified criminal activities."

*Highly classified criminal activity,* she thinks. *Since when is tax evasion a matter of classified undercover work? It's handled by the IRS.* Linda searches Carlos's body language for a hint of over-exaggeration, but there isn't any. *Unless this has something to do with offshore tax evasion,* she thinks. And, assuming she already has the answer to her next question she remains reserved. "What is it you suspect my husband of doing?"

Carlos looks down at his feet for a moment, noticing the bleached oak floor's impeccable shine – he looks up. "I can't give you any specifics. I can just tell you that you're being watched and that your life may be in danger."

Now that was something she wasn't expecting to hear. It throws her for a loop, and with her ears ringing, and mind whirling, she clenches her jaw trying to digest his words. *Your life may be in danger.* "What did you say?"

He looks deep into her dramatic green eyes, now wide with disbelief and this time he does not soften the words. "Your life is in danger. I've been sent here to make sure nothing happens to you and the best way to do that is to take you away to some place safe. I can't impress upon you enough the gravity of this situation."

Linda puts her hand on her chest, her heart pounding like a sledgehammer. "Are you serious?"

"Yes, your enemies know that you're here so we need to leave now."

"Enemies!" she says thunderstruck, her brain spinning like a cyclone. "Who are my enemies and how do I know I can trust *you*?"

"You don't, but I will tell you this, you have a flash drive that some very dangerous people *don't* want you to have. You need to get it back to your husband's accountant's office pronto *and* you have to be a good enough actress to sell it like you have no idea what's on it. I'm the one chance you have at this point of getting out of here safe. So you have to trust me and cooperate."

Linda stares into his eyes. There's honesty there and though her mind is whirling and she's cautious, she remains reasonable. He knows about the flash drive and about the pressure the accounting firm's been putting on her to bring it back. If he were a bad guy, she thinks, he would have made his move the moment he had her alone. She relents, and allows the urgency to sink in. She stands up numb, yet determined and tells him. "I'll get dressed."

Wasting no time, Carlos moves to the room service tray that he'd set on the entry table earlier. "There's no time for you to shower. I brought some things for you to wear. He lifts the steam cover off the tray, exposing a curly dark-haired wig and a rolled-up house-keeping uniform, along with a pocketed apron. He unrolls them and hands them to Linda. "They're not your style by a long shot, but they'll get you out of here safe through the service exit."

Linda stares at the uniform and wig, pursing her lips. She narrows her eyes thinking about Lee, about how's she's going to kill him for getting her mixed up in this. She holds the uniform out in front of her aghast. "This looks like a parachute. Who needs the service exit when I could jump from the window with this thing?" She flattens the uniform against her body. "And I just might, once I see myself in it." She looks at Carlos, he's holding the wig out to her with an apologetic look in his eyes. She takes it between her thumb and index finger displeased. "Is this necessary?" Carlos nods his head. She stares at him for a moment, then turns on her heels and starts for the bedroom.

"Just a minute, I need that flash drive. Do you have your laptop with you?"

Linda turns around, still holding the wig at arm's length in front of her as if it were about to bite her. "Yes." She says dryly, staring at the wig.

"I need to copy the files from the flash drive onto your laptop and then transfer it onto a flash drive that I've brought. I'll do it while you change."

Linda dresses as fast as she can. She and Carlos leave the suite and walk out of the hotel through a service door, both disguised as hotel employees.

While Carlos drives Linda calls and leaves a message on Morgan & Andersons' voice mail. In her most innocuous, convincing voice she apologizes for letting the flash drive slip her mind, but that her mother has taken seriously ill and she's leaving now to be with her, *but*, she explains, before leaving for the airport, she'd met with an important client for breakfast at the Omni Hotel and that she'd left the flash drive in the care of the hotel manager, who put it in a safety deposit box and they can pick it up anytime. After she hangs up she turns to Carlos. "I need to do one more thing."

Linda insists they stop at an out-of-the-way boutique at the edge of San Diego's city limits on their way to the reservation where they'll hide at the rectory, so she can purchase some suitable clothing to wear.

The first thing Malcolm Morgan does on Monday morning after listening to the voicemail from Linda is to call Lee Stevens, and the second thing he does is to call Ted Silar.

"Bullshit!" Ted yells into the phone. "I don't believe it."

"Calm down, Ted," Morgan tells him. "I'm sure she's telling the truth. I know both her and her husband inside and out and I know for certain that if it's not something that's relevant to fashion she won't allocate one moment of her time to it. We called her right away and told her that the files weren't the ones she was looking for. I'm surprised she didn't toss the flash in the garbage on the spot."

Ted lets out a growl through the phone and once again Malcolm reassures him. "Linda Stevens is not the type to waste her time, nor demean herself by looking at someone else's humdrum daily bookwork. Besides, I've already checked out her story; I talked to Lee Stevens before I called you, and he verified that his wife's mother is ill and that Linda's already left to be at her side. She had an early client appointment downtown at the Omni this morning so she stayed there last night to be able to make the meeting, before catching her flight. She's not going to be a problem."

Ted rubs his hand through his hair. "What about Lee Stevens? Shouldn't he know his wife's nosing around his financials?"

"No! Stevens would scurry to the border like a scared rat, and we need him. We remain calm, even if she comes back from her mother's and asks for the books again. There is just the one set at the office now and she'll find them to be in perfect order. In fact, I'll make a courtesy call to her next week and offer the books to her."

After Greg collects the Monday morning newspaper from the front steps, he lingers at home for an unusual amount of time. It's as if he doesn't want to leave Julie's side. He reads the paper at the table while sipping his coffee instead of taking it with him and a few times she's caught him staring at her.

When he's done reading the financials, he stands up and tells her he had a wonderful weekend and that he's going to miss her today. He gives her a hug, holding her tight as he kisses the top of her head. He closes his eyes, relishing the irresistible scent of her hair and tells her that he's thankful that he has someone like her at home. With one last look into her eyes, he says, "I can't wait to see you tonight." Then he turns and walks out the door.

At 7:30 a.m., she watches from the kitchen window as he drives out of sight, wondering about the dichotomy of his change of mood this weekend and the gun in his closet. She still needs to get to the bottom of this, no matter what his mood is.

She's meeting Father Lelo this morning and she dresses casually in a pair of sateen khaki roll-up pants, and a white poet's shirt that she belts with a brown, hemp sash. Then she weaves her hair into one long braid and slips on a pair of gladiator sandals. She puts her white visor on and grabs her purse. She's thinking that after she meets the priest she'll go to Linda's hotel room to discuss how they should proceed with the information that they've discovered.

At 7:55 a.m., Ted Silar receives a call from Dench telling him that the job's been executed. "It's finished, a successful hit." he says. "I heard and saw the explosion myself. It vaporized him, not a trace left. They'll never figure out what happened to Greg Bishop."

After a long moment of silence, Ted clears his throat. "Stand by, we may need you to take out his wife, too." Not waiting for an answer, Ted hangs up the phone. He shoves his chair back and tosses his pen on his desk. He stands up and walks to the window. He remains motionless, staring out at the horizon of the Pacific, wishing it could have turned out differently. He thinks about Greg's potential and what a shame it is to be snuffed out so young, but there's always someone waiting in the wings willing to do the job and this instance is no different. The back-up driver is already lined up and the show will go on, then under his breath he whispers. "It had to be done, it was him, or me."

At 8:00 a.m., Father Lelo sits down at a table for two at The Pier View Café. He orders coffee with cream and opens his newspaper, waiting for Julie to arrive.

At the same time, Ira has put his signature on the last piece of paper needed for his release and Doctor Issac, thinking about Ira's heavy persuasion, is just leaving his room.

Ira doesn't have to report to work this morning. He opens the bag of clothing that Father Lelo brought to the hospital yesterday. With his wounds still tender, he grapples with a pair of faded jeans and then pulls on a white, V-neck tunic. The tunic had been handweaved in Peru and around the neckline is an elaborate embroidered pattern of small red, yellow and black, crosses and diamonds. It was a birthday gift from Father Lelo.

Ira finishes dressing, thinking about Carlos and Linda's getaway progress yesterday morning. Everything went off without a hitch so far. Carlos has been with Linda since yesterday. He spent the night in the old rectory with her, questioning her, obtaining every piece of information that he could gather. She told him every fact that she knew about her husband Lee's business, emphasizing the outlandish circumstance of her daughter Sarita lying about her attendance at college.

At 8:30 a.m., Ira is just leaving the hospital when his phone vibrates in his pocket. He checks and sees that it is Herroso. "What's up, Hero?"

"Ira!" Herroso's voice is amplified. "There's been an explosion on Pendleton. The military reported it to the FBI because it happened seconds before a training maneuver got underway this morning. Shit is about to hit the fan with the top brass. They're about to pull the trigger on a full alert. And get this, the MPs who arrived on the scene found nothing of any consequence in the general area, but two hundred yards away smashed into the side of a boulder they found a charred, crinkled license plate. When I ran the plate numbers, they came up as Greg Bishop's."

"Damn, it's starting already. Hero, get yourself a prepaid phone. From now on call me from it, unless we stage a call."

"You think they're on to me?"

"Yeah. I don't think it's a coincidence that Silar's spooks knew that Linda Stevens was at Chief Jomoka's yesterday and I don't think it'll be long before they have you tapped. After you get that phone, go to Pendleton and spend some time talking with the MPs there. I want whoever's watching you to think we're distracted by the explosion on base."

"Got it."

Following Herroso's call, Ira calls Golden State Bank and asks for Greg Bishop. His assistant Dorothy apologizes, telling him that Greg is usually in before 8:00 a.m., but he's not in the office yet and that she's trying to reach him herself.

She's just confirmed what Ira fears. He hangs up thinking about the danger that lies ahead, not only for him and his team, but possibly for Julie. He feels anguish and anger at the same time and he knows there's no room for failure, he must stop this ring of thugs before they do something to Julie too. He remembers that Father Lelo had planned to meet with her this morning. He's somewhat relieved thinking, *She is in good hands with him, he'll protect her until they can get her someplace safe.* He calls Father Lelo's number.

Father Lelo is sitting across the table from Julie, enjoying his chat over coffee and a crescent roll. She arrived a few minutes ago and he's getting to know more about her. She's just told him who her parents are. Father Lelo nods with recognition, thinking, *I knew she reminded me of someone.* Julie is just about to try to change the subject to what Father may know about the snakes, when Father's phone rings. Pulling it from his pocket he sees that Ira's calling and holding one finger up he excuses himself for a moment, then answers it.

"Hello,"

Ira interrupts before Father can say his name. "Are you with Julie Bishop?"

Father Lelo hears the tension in Ira's voice. "Yes?" he says in a questioning tone.

"Brace yourself, try not to change your expression after I tell you what I called to tell you. "Okay?"

"Okay."

After another short pause, giving Father Lelo a moment to compose himself, Ira tells him about the explosion and the charred license plate belonging to Julie's husband. Father Lelo's looking at Julie when Ira tells him the news. As prepared as he thought he was, the news sends a shiver through his body and he tries to hide his reaction, but it's difficult, so he shifts his attention to the people at the table next to them for a minute, while he attempts to achieve a sense of composure.

Father Lelo does his best to remain impassive while Ira talks, he nods in agreement when Ira tells him that it would be a good idea to take Julie down to the old rectory where she'll be safe, where they've taken Linda Stevens. Ira wants Julie to be with Linda before she's told the shocking news about her husband.

# CHAPTER TWENTY

## Unraveling Fast

It is around 8:30 a.m., when Father Lelo hangs up the phone. He leans back in his chair, deliberating on this urgent and pressing situation.

It was moments ago that Julie told him who her parents were and he realized he knows them both, Ray and Lisa Price. Ray is a Marine he served with years ago and he's had the opportunity to meet Lisa on several occasions at the Marine Corps Ball. Now, implausible as it may seem, he's just been informed their daughter's husband has been murdered by a bomb detonated on Camp Pendleton.

He studies Julie's face for a moment, noting her keen, intuitive blue eyes. He senses that she gets the impression the phone call was somehow related to her and just as he is speculating, she says to him. "What is it, Father Lelo?"

Father Lelo has been caught off guard by the news of the explosion and is understandably unprepared to answer her. Nonetheless, he remains calm, looking her in the eyes. "That was Ira, he's getting out of the hospital this morning."

"That's wonderful!" Julie beams. "He's been on my mind and I was going to stop by the hospital today, now I won't have to." Father nods and rubs the bridge of his nose, wondering what to do next. Although he's no stranger to death and danger, for a moment he feels lost. He looks at Julie's hands wrapped around her coffee cup, her left finger sparkling with a platinum wedding set. *This is a tragedy*. She's young and vibrant, and in this moment so unaffected. He wishes he could stop time and lock her in this moment so she doesn't have to hear about her husband's death, but he can't.

He reaches for her hand with the tips of his fingers. "There's something else that you need to know, but I would like for you to hear about it someplace more private."

Julie is startled by the emotion in his voice and she glances down at his fingers touching hers. She looks back up at him, his bluish gray eyes full of concern. She searches for clues, but finds none. She shifts her glance to the window, taking in the Pacific's relative morning calm, yet for some reason she's sensing a perilous undertow. Her thoughts drift back to the conversation she had with Father Lelo at the hospital, then to the Feds watching her house and then she thinks about the men that followed her and Linda to Camp Pendleton. She glances back at Father Lelo, "Where should we go?"

Father folds his hands on top the table, "Ira would like to speak with both you and Linda Stevens. There's an old rectory off Highway 94 in an Indian village where he grew up. He has asked us to meet him there." Father Lelo is rubbing his thumbs together, preoccupied. "Your friend, Linda, is already there."

Julie scrunches her eyebrows together, she's puzzled and she murmurs. "Linda's already there? But how did she get there? Why is *she* there?" Then it hits her. "This has something to do with the secret phones and the gun I found in Greg's closet, doesn't it?"

This takes Father Lelo by surprise, the revelation of a gun in her husband's closet has him raising both his eyebrows. Soon his facial features fade to bleak and after he glances down at his coffee cup for a moment, he reaches into his pocket, takes some money from his wallet, and lays it down on the table. "We should get going," he says as he stands up. "I'll follow you to your house to drop off your car so you can ride to the village with me and I'll bring you back home, later."

At first, Julie is struck by confusion at his abrupt action and presumptive words, but then she thinks about the gun and the phones and she realizes he knew nothing about them. She senses the urgency in his voice, pushes her chair back and rises to her feet. She picks up her purse and follows him out the door.

After she drops her car off at home, she climbs into Father Lelo's truck and they start for the village on the reservation. The mood during the ride is quiet and low key. Although Julie tries questioning Father Lelo as to what this is all about, it is to no avail, he remains vague, not saying anything except that it's a serious situation that will be clarified once they are at the rectory.

Thinking that this is all about Linda and that Father is avoiding the subject until they've met up with her, Julie turns to the side and watches in silence as rocks and desert scrub zing past the window. She's anxious and worried about Linda. Her thoughts diverge to Lee; what has he done to warrant undercover agents bringing Linda out into the middle of the wilderness? And if it weren't for this priest who knows my parents, she thinks, I'd be terrified. God knows, Linda must be beside herself with fear.

When they pull into the dusty drive of the old rectory and park the truck, Julie sits staring for a moment at the worn, pitched-roof building, with its rectangular, box-shaped addition, not able to picture Linda inside there. After hesitating for a few seconds, she gets out and follows Father through the crunchy, dried grass of the yard, to the door.

When they step through the threshold into the tiny kitchen, there is a moment when she feels as though she's stepped back in time. She looks down at the green-speckled, linoleum floor and then at the pink, porcelain, one-basin sink.

Then she sees Linda from across the kitchen, sitting in the living-room on a brown, button-back sofa next to a woodstove. She's wearing a light, sleeveless safari jacket with a long khaki skirt and next to her on the end table is a canvas outback hat, with a leopard print sash. She's holding a tissue up to her nose and her eyes are red from crying.

Julie rushes to her and takes a seat next to her on the outdated sofa. She puts her arm around her. "Linda," she gasps, "what's happened? What's going on?"

Linda has heard from Agent Carlos about the explosion on base and that Greg's license plate was found crinkled and burned, but readable. She looks at Julie with puffy, red-rimmed eyes, then at Father Lelo and Carlos. She lowers her hands to her lap, and stares down at the mutilated tissue for a moment, she takes a deep breath. When she looks up again her expression is grim, and her voice cracks as she speaks. "She doesn't know?" She murmurs.

Father looks into her eyes, he shakes his head no.

Julie's shaken. She tightens her jaw and turns from Father Lelo to Linda. "Linda, what's happened, is Sarita okay?"

Linda sinks back on the couch and for a moment stares at the ceiling, tears streaming down her cheeks. She's in anguish, she's just spent the last twenty-four hours with Carlos talking about Lee and Sarita. He interrogated her on everything, the fishy bank accounts, the flash drive, the gun, the secret phones *and* he drilled her about Sarita's adoption. He hasn't given her detailed information about the undercover operation, but he has told her about Sarita's missing original birth certificate, hoping she could shed some light on it, but she knew nothing of it. Now this, Greg is dead and Julie's the one person in the room who doesn't know it. Things are unraveling so fast, it's difficult to comprehend.

Father Lelo sees Linda's torment, not just for herself, but for Julie. He knows both women are in peril, but at this very moment, more so Julie. He walks to the couch and stops in front of her. She looks up at him with questioning blue eyes. He sits down next to her. "Julie, there's been an explosion on base."

She shrugs her shoulders, "There's always explosions on base. What does that have to do with me or Linda?"

"It was a car that exploded." Julie narrows her eyes and Father continues, "There was a license plate." He looks down for a moment – then back at her. "It belonged to your husband, Greg."

Julie turns her entire upper body toward him and stares at him. It's a long moment before she blinks her eyes. A thick cloud has just clogged her brain, making her both deaf and mute and for a long moment she's stuck, baffled; there's nothing but a loud, hollow ringing happening between her ears. She turns around to look at Linda's tear-streaked face and swivels back to Father Lelo's solemn gray blue eyes.

Then she can hear herself shouting. "Oh, God, oh my God! Where is he, what hospital is he in, I have to go to him *now*! What are we doing *here?* We have to go to him now!" She tries to stand up, but Father Lelo puts one hand on her shoulder and looks into her eyes. "Julie," he says, "No one can find him."

Nothing could have prepared Julie for this moment. She knows in her heart what Father Lelo is telling her, but she refuses to accept it. "No! No! I don't believe it, No! It's not true. I was just with him, we just had breakfast together. It's a mistake, they're mistaken." Julie turns back to look at Linda once again. She waits for her to say something, to take sides with her, but Linda can only swallow, she covers her mouth, squeezing her tear-filled eyes shut. She hangs her head for a moment, then she opens her eyes and looks at Julie with deep compassion, whispering through her fingers. "I'm so sorry, Julie, I'm so very sorry."

Julie whirls around and looks at Father Lelo. She breaks the hold he has on her shoulder and stands up. She turns around and stares down at both of them unable to find any words. She steps away and starts for the kitchen door.

She reaches for the knob not knowing where she's going or how she'll get there; she's just compelled to escape what seems to be a warp of insanity. As she's about to take hold of the handle, the door swings open and she stumbles backward, dropping her purse, spilling the contents onto the floor. Her lipstick, compact, wallet, and loose change bounce onto the speckled linoleum, scattering about.

Ira steps into the kitchen, his raven black hair pulled back, his dark brown eyes responsive. He reaches out to her. "Whoa, are you okay?"

Even though the whole scene is surreal to Julie, for a moment she's stunned by his presence and how it fills the room. She stares at him, forgetting for an instant why she'd been rushing out the door. Then she stoops down and begins stuffing her scattered belongings back into her purse. He stoops to help, but she stands up quickly and brushes past him without saying a word. She slams the door behind her.

It all happened so fast that Ira had no time to react except as he did. He looks across the kitchen into the living room, first at Carlos, and then at Father Lelo and Linda. Their expressions say it all and he realizes that Julie's just been told about her husband. He rolls his eyes, and mocks himself, *"Are you okay?"* he repeats, then spins on his heels and follows her out the door.

"Julie!" he calls, but she doesn't turn, "Julie, wait!" She keeps walking. He rushes to catch up with her, and when he reaches her side he pleads for her to stop and listen to him. "Julie, please, you have to listen to me." When she doesn't stop, he walks alongside her, getting right to the point as gently as he can. "You're here for you own safety; your life is in danger, too."

She stops in her tracks and stares at him. Her bright blue eyes wet with tears, her thick black lashes saturated. "My life is in danger?" She scoffs. "My life is gone."

Ira plants his feet on the ground in front of her. "This is tragic and shocking, and I can't express in words how very sorry I am. I do understand how you feel and I want to help you, Julie."

She stops and glares at him. "How could you possibly presume to understand how I feel?"

Ira knows what it's like to lose your life in a figurative way, but he says nothing about his past. Instead, he focuses on the task at hand. He looks into her eyes, nods toward the rectory door where Linda is standing with her arms folded across her chest. "Your friend is waiting for you. She needs you; her life is in danger too. We believe the people who did this are after the flash-drive that Linda had, they saw you both together at Chief Jomoka's yesterday and they had her followed to the Omni. That's when we stepped in and that's why she's here. We're not taking this lightly; we need to protect both of you."

Julie's defiance diminishes, but she's confused, exasperated, wounded and scared all at the same time. She's aching for relief. She stands face-to-face with him, hoping to awaken from this nightmare, but time stands still and their eyes remain fixed in a heart-rending stare.

Suddenly feeling chilled, she pulls her sweater closed. Then with one hand she wipes at the tears on her cheek. With her shoulders hung low and in a voice soft and defeated, she surrenders. "Is there any chance that he is –" She stops, unable to finish the sentence.

Ira's mouth goes dry, he stares into her tear-filled eyes for a long moment . . . He whispers. "No."

The answer forces her to grapple with reality and she feels the final blow as her heart is gouged from her body. With her chest hollow and soul drowning in grief, she lowers her head into her hands and begins to sob, her lamenting uncontrollable.

Ira moves closer, feeling her pain, wanting to reach out and comfort her, but he hesitates. He'd felt a stirring deep inside from the first moment they'd met in her back yard and he wonders if his motives are truly selfless. Would holding her be inappropriate and unprofessional at a time like this? Would she pull back appalled at him, at the arms of a stranger? He stares for a moment longer. She's sobbing hard, her body's shaking. He can't stop himself; he reaches out, pulling her into him, wrapping himself around her, letting her tears soak into his tunic. He envelops her, biceps flexed; enclosing her in his protective arms, trying to ease her pain. "Julie," he whispers, his lips pressed to her hair. "I swear on all that is sacred, we'll find whoever did this and bring them to justice."

He stands holding her for a long time, then with one arm around her shoulder, he turns her around and leads her back to the rectory where Linda is standing at the door. She helps Julie inside, leading her to a chair at the kitchen table where Carlos is sitting and talking on the phone.

Father Lelo left for Camp Pendleton without either of them noticing while Ira and Julie were still in the yard. He had called after leaving the café to get a message to the Sergeant Major of the Commandant on Camp Pendleton telling him that he had pertinent information about the suspicious explosion on base this morning. Now he's hurrying to get there so he can tell them what he knows before the story breaks and hits the local news media creating an Orange County panic. It's a lucky thing for this undercover operation that news travels slow on a military base, when top officials want it to, that is.

Father Lelo knows what's going on behind the scenes at Camp Pendleton this very moment. It's like when a prankster pulls the fire alarm during Mass. A wave of panic moves through the inside while the outside world goes about their business in ignorant bliss.

If not by now, then real soon, the top brass will ascertain that the explosion was not orchestrated by a live-fire training that happened seconds ahead of schedule and they'll order all gates leading in and out of Pendleton to be on high alert. Because it was a vehicle laden with an explosive that breached the gates of a major military establishment of the United States of America, The President, along with the entire U.S. armed forces will be notified and put on full alert. One needs to just remember Hezbollah in '83, or 9/11 to realize that both the Marine Corps and the entire U.S. government have zero tolerance. They will no doubt investigate this to exhaustion and crush those deemed responsible for the breach. Father Lelo knows that when he tells the Marine Corps commanders what he knows about the explosion, they'll launch a covert military investigation as well. Not just because the safety of the country has been compromised, that's first and foremost, but also because the breach bruised the delicate egos of top-ranking officials and bruising a General's ego always means someone's head is going to be served on a platter!

While Father Lelo drives he's already on the phone with the Major General's secretary and Carlos is on the phone at the rectory making sure that all the departments involved in this undercover operation stay under the radar while investigating the explosion. They want it to appear to the perpetrators as though everyone believes it was a military exercise gone terribly wrong. Anything else would halt all illegal activities and it's a matter of public safety that they catch these guys red-handed. It's imperative they bust up this ring and put these criminals in a cage where they belong.

Ira hadn't gone inside the rectory. Instead, he watched outside the door as Linda helped Julie inside and then he retreated.

Feeling the need to be alone, he went to the old church and sat inside for a long while. Then he walked outside and entered the old cemetery next to the church, reflecting beside the graves of his mother and grandfather. His spirit is disturbed.

After an hour or so he walks to the ruins of what used to be Rosa's herb garden. Choosing his spot, under the wide spread of a Chestnut Tree, he sits in stillness with his eyes closed, calming the turmoil that filled him deep in his core. Once he has diffused the bad energy, he begins to meditate and after a while he starts to receive his heart's vision.

*A mist swirls in slow motion; it circles, and spirals around until it's formed the image of an expectant mother. Vulnerable and hopeless, she watches in despair as children appear one by one in a line. They're listless, filled with misery, their eyes blank.*

Ira is so haunted by the wretched feeling in his chest that he shifts his position. He is uncomfortable, but he knows he must go deeper and he resumes his meditative state and soon he's there.

*He's a young child and its dark; pitch black. He's cold and weak; he can't move his arms or legs. He's groggy and gagged, but a cool mist sprays into his nostrils. Then in an instant, tunnels of hot blinding light shoot from the darkness, stabbing his eyes, making it impossible to see, but he feels people watching... his body is pubescent, innocent, naked, with a long shiny blade resting on his neck. Then the vision shifts to a woman, sitting on a rearing white stallion, he recognizes her, sees her face plain as day and he realizes, she's the key. Then a voice from another dimension reverberates in his ears.*

*"The truth is beyond belief, difficult to comprehend, follow your heart my son, your path is right."*

Ira snaps out of the vision and for a moment he sits still while a shiver runs along his spine. He contemplates the meaning, letting it sink in. The vision was so offensive it's difficult for him to grasp; it oozed undiluted evil. It is hard to believe that humans can be so wicked. He knows what has to be done and he hastens back to the rectory.

Father Lelo just got back to the rectory from Pendleton. He is on the phone with Don McCreary of the U.S. Forest Service; the man who went into work this weekend to analyze the stick.

Father Lelo holds the phone close to his ear, and listens hard to what McCreary is saying.

"It's a rare type of cypress," Don tells him. "A Tecate Cypress. There are about fifteen known populations of them in this country, four of which are in Southern California. Although it's possible there's some scant isolated stands scattered as you go south toward the border, the four known stands are on the mountain ranges of Guatay, Otay and Tecate Peak."

Father Lelo raises his brows, impressed that this stick came from a type of tree that can be narrowed down to existing in so few places, with just four of the stands in Southern California. Just as he's thinking, *I have to tell Ira this,* Ira walks through the door, making tracks straight to Julie, who's still sitting at the kitchen table, wiped-out and hunched over, her hands folded around her coffee cup, staring down in it.

He stops in front of her, his dark brown eyes intense, but sympathetic. Then he sits down in the empty chair next to her. He puts his hand on top of hers. "Julie," he says in a gentle tone, "do you feel up to talking? I wouldn't ask if it weren't important."

For a moment, Julie stares mindlessly at the black mascara stain on the upper sleeve of Ira's tunic, she looks up at him, numb. She blinks her swollen, red-rimmed eyes; she's heart-sick and bereaved, but Greg's death has also made her angry and it springs forth in her tone. "If this has anything to do with finding out who did this to my husband, I'll go to the ends of the earth for that."

Ira understands what she's going through and decides it would be beneficial for her to know about his mother so he opens up and reveals his personal loss and the private details of his mother's kidnapping and details about the slavery and suffering he's seen her endure in his visions. Julie and Linda listen stone faced, engaged, and disturbed.

Later, around 2:00 p.m. on Monday, an attractive man by the name of Nick Collins walks into Stevens Orthodontics LLC.

Beneath his white sports blazer against his golden tan is a mango colored shirt peeled open at the top. His hair is disheveled, bleached and streaked by the intense California sun. If he were wearing board shorts you'd think he'd just ridden in on a wave. He looks around the office with garishly blue eyes. He sees Tiffany at the front desk on the phone, nods and gives her an easy smile. Then he spots the unisex restroom and she watches him disappear inside. A couple minutes later, he emerges and swaggers to the reception desk with a confidant air.

Tiffany looks up from her computer and smiles. "Can I help you?"

Nick begins to speak, but before he can get a full sentence out his phone rings. "Excuse me for just one second," he tells her and answers it. After a pause, with a tone of urgency in his voice, he tells Tiffany, "I'm sorry, but something pressing has come up and I'll have to come back later. I'll take a pamphlet and card, though." He turns for the door.

Tiffany shrugs her shoulders. "No problem. I'm here 'til five," she says in a mechanical tone, focused on her computer screen.

Nick Collins had been sent to investigate the validity of Sarita's hotline tip. She'd told them that she would hide some video footage in a flower vase in the restroom at Steven's Orthodontist office and Inspector Nick Collins from INTERPOL United States National Central Bureau, had been sent to retrieve it. Missing persons tips are taken seriously, and the first step is to pass the tip to USNCB so an investigation can be launched, a yellow alert sounded and INTERPOL's global database searched for any common threads.

Once outside, Collins slides his phone open and while walking to his car he puts a call into HQ. When he hears his superintendent answer the phone, he affirms. "It's me. The footage was where she said it would be."

After he slides his phone back into his pocket and before he drives away from Stevens' parking lot, he attaches a high speed USB cable to his laptop and begins downloading the information. As the video from the pen-recorder streams across the screen he pauses it, and stares at the picture of Asheed, the cab driver. "This is more than I expected," he whispers.

Inside, Sarita is struggling to remain calm while going about her usual daily tasks. She knows the authorities will come today to collect the recordings she'd made. She's well aware of the torture that Lee and Ted will put her through if they figure out what she's done. She's on the verge of a panic attack, her hands tremble while she works.

She had not just given them the recorder she'd put in the lemon tree, she'd also taken incriminating videos of the contents of a locked storage unit where Lee keeps an abundant cache of oxygen tanks and opioids, including opium suppositories, along with copies of invoices that don't show up on the legitimate books. She had videoed pages of names and phone numbers, including Lee's Pakistani contacts *and,* perhaps what will turn out to be the most helpful, the spare recorder she had while in the alley behind the bank and the footage of the armored truck and its license plate. Now she stands lost in thought, her hands shaking, a queasiness in her stomach, wondering what her future holds. Will she be a free woman? Or will she become nameless and naked, chained to a bed in a dark basement somewhere, tortured until she's dead and discarded like trash in a shallow grave?

Nick has streamed the recordings to the USNCB and is working with its team of experts identifying the characters. They establish that it's Ted Silar, Chairman of Golden State Bank & Trust in the lemon tree video. The two other men are Esteban Mercado, and Silvano Rodriguez, both thugs from the Castello gang. They establish that the driver of the cab in the recording behind the bank is Haji Asheed, a person who's been on their watch list for having suspected ties to an Afghan by the name of Abdullah Najibullah, AKA Daboia. Daboia fled the chaos of Soviet- invaded Afghanistan in the early eighties, straight into the arms of a Pakistan-based truck shipping mafia known as the, "Afghanistan Transit Trade, ATT." It was the ATT that helped train, arm, and finance the original mujahideen, militia fighters, now known as the Taliban, who drove the Soviets out of Afghanistan. Back then, Daboia was described as the most elusive operative of Operation Bear Trap. He was later alleged to have been playing both sides of the fence.

The driver of the armored truck was Gregory Andrew Bishop, a clean banker, no prior criminal record. They contact the FBI to see if the Feds have him on their watch list and they find out he is, but that he'd just died in his car in an explosion of unknown origins earlier that morning. USNCB decides that Bishop was somebody who had important information and that it's time to join forces with the FBI and let them in on the videos. After they do, they learn that the FBI, the Border Patrol, and the SDPD are already involved and now because of the explosion on base, the USMC is involved, too.

What started out many months ago as an investigation of the Golden State Bank and Trust's funding habits to questionable clientele, namely, the Castello gang and some of their affiliates from Vegas, who have joint ownership of the enormous construction site behind Greg Bishop's house, was just a scratch in the surface of what the authorities are now beginning to uncover.

The information that Sarita supplied to USNCB and the explosion on Camp Pendleton, prompted a quick alliance of the United States Marine Corps, with INTERPOL, the U.S. Border Patrol, and the FBI, and a council made up of leaders in each organization was appointed. A teleconference between them was scheduled for Monday at one o'clock in the afternoon.

When noon came around, Ira remained at his desk working through lunch, continuing his preparations for an intelligence dump and a lengthy discussion with the council members. The conference gets underway with military promptness at one o'clock sharp.

The council is made up of Camp Pendleton's Major General, Richard Weston, the FBI's Executive Assistant of National Security, Intelligence division, James Talbott, Inspector Nick Collins of INTERPOL, and of course Chief Patrol Agent, USBP Special Ops, Ira Notah.

Major General Weston is briefed during the meeting on the attempt on Ira's life and the undercover work that had prompted the attempt. Ira's assignment started out as an intelligence gathering mission on what was thought to be a cross-border drug trafficking and money-laundering operation executed from behind Greg Bishop's house and linked to the bank where he worked. "Bishop," Ira tells the Major General, "was the man who died in the explosion on Camp Pendleton."

When he tells him Bishop was videoed-taped driving an armored security truck that is an exact replica of a Guardit armored security truck, with a license plate that's a mock-up of a standard DMV plate, it would have been easy to hear a pin drop in any of the offices. A phony armored truck, able to move throughout the city without detection, beneath the radar, so to speak was an amazing fact. It didn't take a genius to figure out that the armored truck was moving something illegal and that the lengths to which the culprits have gone to transport whatever it is, makes it clear that it's a high-value target.

Their discussion turns to Sarita, the young woman held against her will, who'd made the video and about the evidence in it, the storage unit, invoices, opium, a cache of oxygen tanks, the bank's ties to names of Pakistanis on the government watch list, the accountant's office, the flash drive and how all of those facts are beginning to connect. The frustrating question is, though, how does Sarita's trafficked situation play into this? Is she a lone case of a kidnap victim who has no connection with the other crimes, or is human-trafficking a much bigger piece of this criminal operation?

The one certainty that's come out of this conference call is that the information about the recent explosion on base, along with the oxygen tanks and a phony, free-moving, reinforced steel truck has the major general's undivided attention. "At the moment there's no proof," he tells them, "but it's not out of the realm of possibilities for the armored truck to become a weapon of mass destruction, a jumbo, homemade, fuel-air explosive. A bomb that can create overpressures equal to an atom bomb and even though there are other conjectures to consider here, just a hint of the possibility of a thermobaric bomb makes this a matter of national security which must be dealt with immediately."

The council has also determined that the three women, Julie Bishop, Linda Stevens and Sarita Stevens, cannot disappear into protective custody. They are the keys to uncovering timely, accurate intelligence because of their close relationships to the suspects. There is no choice other than to use the women to help gather intelligence of when, where and what a counterfeited, undetected armored truck is being used for.

At 6 a.m. Tuesday morning.

Ira looks out the kitchen window of the rectory while on the phone with Agent Herroso. He has assigned him the duty of getting close to Sarita without alerting Lee Stevens, which will be a tough assignment, because traffickers keep a tight rein on their victims.

Carlos' assignment is to stay with Linda and guide her through what she should say to Sarita and Lee during staged phone calls to them. It is also his job to inform Linda that the little girl she believes she adopted had been trafficked into the country by a group of gangsters which includes her husband.

At 7:00 a.m., Ira leaves Linda in Carlos' care. He and Julie, dressed in military fatigues, leave for the Customs and Border Patrol Station in Imperial Beach where they keep patrol horses corralled. He had a long conversation with Julie after his vision yesterday and learned that she's not only an accomplished rider, but that her grandparents owned a ranch adjacent to the foothills of Otay Mountain, and when she was young she spent her summer vacations with them. She'd ride for hours on horseback, getting to know every inch of the terrain and trails, both on and surrounding her grandparents' 200 acre ranch.

He listened closely to her words, letting her reminisce about a favorite hidden trail off the south side of the ranch where she'd ride alongside a babbling, crystal-clear stream. When Father Lelo heard her tell Ira how much she'd loved it, because it was so secluded, and shaded that moist lichen hung from the branches of the trees, he remembered his vision in Dewey's office. She continued, telling them that nobody else that she knew of, knew about it and at the end of the trail was a fire tower, which reminded Ira of the vision he'd had of Rocko in the hospital and the fire tower reflecting in the dog's eyes.

She continued talking about the fire tower, saying she'd climb it and from the top she could see the roof of a shabby, old, abandoned building surrounded by trees. She used to pretend it was where the bad guys would hide out. Ira asked if she could remember how to get there and she said that she believed she could still find the way.

By 7:30 a.m., Ira and Julie pull into the Border Patrol's parking lot at Imperial Beach and Ira puts the truck in park. He turns to Julie. Her skin is pallid, she's exhausted. Asking this from her is asking a lot, but even though she hadn't slept last night she insists on riding to find the trail leading to the tower, hoping it will occupy her mind enough to ease some of her pain.

"I'll be right back." Ira gets out and walks to the horse corral. He bridles, then leads three rescued mustangs out of the gate. One white stallion with pink-rimmed eyes and two chestnut colored mares, one of them with a black mane and black socks. After he ties them to a hitching post, he goes back to the truck and grabs his leather pouch, then invites Julie to follow him inside the station.

The first thing that catches Julie's attention when she walks through the door is a muscular German Shepard with a silver sable coat with his ears perked high. His name is Gustafson, Gus for short. He's a search dog, cross-trained in Air Scent and Human Remains Detection and is rumored to be the best dog on the force, so reliable in archeological finds, in fact, that he's dubbed Gus the Rock. His most notable claim to fame was a hip bone from a child who went missing thirty years ago.

Ira stoops in front of Gus to let him smell his hand and the stick. Even though Gus is not a ground-tracking dog, Ira wants him to smell whatever scent cells remain on the wood.

Gus's handler, Sergeant Kate Nelson is standing next to him. She's a dark-haired, brown-eyed, Border Patrol Agent dressed in typical BP fatigues, green cargo trousers, work shirt and a bullet-proof vest with a pistol in her side holster She is an expert in canine search and rescue. Her hair is pulled back tight in a ponytail and she's wearing a black headband. Ira has known Kate since he joined the BP.

At 7:45 a.m., the horses have been loaded onto a trailer and they're heading to Otay valley.

By 8:30 a.m., they're riding on horseback through some of the most remote range and pasture land in North America, stopping on occasion to check out the spectacular views of the canyons a short distance from the Mexican border. As they approach the far south corner of the ranch they see a gigantic oak tree, a distinct marker for where the trailhead begins. Its trunk is massive and split at the bottom. There is a hole big enough for Julie to remember sitting in when she was young.

As they ride closer they can see the overgrown inlet of the trail leading into a dense, wooded area. Although the trail is thick and wild, there is a grouping of stones alongside the entrance arranged in a undisturbed labyrinth pattern; one for each time she used the trail.

Julie dismounts her horse, and stoops next to the stones. The remnants left from her childhood bring back a flood of memories of a simpler time. She traces her finger along the rubble shrine of her youth, thinking about the time she'd brought Greg here when they were first dating, a time of youth, innocence and invincibility. Hot tears sting her eyes. She takes a deep breath and fights back the urge to scream, but can't hold back the tears.

Ira dismounts and stands next to her. Kate also dismounts. Gus senses her grief and lowers his shoulders. They give Julie their mournful support in respectful silence.

After a few minutes, Julie wipes her eyes, then looks up and nods at Ira. She's ready to move on and he helps her mount the stallion.

She leads them up the craggy slopes of the trail through the dense overspread of the woodlands. After they've been riding for several miles they come upon the crystal clear stream that she'd talked about. They stop and let the animals drink the cool water as it bubbles through the rocks while they drink from their canteens. Once they're rested and refreshed they begin to follow the trail along the stream. It winds to and fro and they slowly make their way up the foothills ascending Otay Mountain.

At noon they stop and dismount letting the horses drink again and giving them their oat bags. As they sit in quiet tranquility, they listen to the water trickle through the rocks and the birds chirping high in the trees. They eat their lunch of smoked turkey sandwiches, roasted almonds, and oatmeal cookies in the cool shade of a sturdy tree. Gus enjoys his all-natural high-protein chow and a piece of natural beef jerky. When they finished eating, they mount again and continue following the trail. An hour and a half later when they stop once again to let the horses drink, Ira dismounts and stands in deep thought, staring into the clear, running water.

Startled, then anxious, Gus lifts his nose high in the air and a hawk's cry pierces the treetops. Gus smells the cat before he can see it and he lets out a bark. Ira turns in Gus' direction and a cougar leaps from behind a thicket and pounces, scraping his claws across the rocks, then digs them deep into a tall pine, shredding the bark as she climbs.

The cat startled everyone, the horses buck their heads and Gus lets out another bark, then sits down and looks up at Kate. "Easy boy," she says, with her pistol drawn and her heart pounding in her throat.

The cat stops on a branch for a moment, looking down at them and lets out a loud snarl. This time, Julie and Kate's horses rear up, and Ira's horse takes off. Ira pulls his pistol. The cat claws her way to the top of the tree where she disappears into the thick branches. Ira watches, helpless as his horse runs away. He turns to the two women, furrowing his brow, letting out an exasperated growl of his own. Julie dismounts and begins to unbuckle her saddle. "We can ride together. I'm pretty certain that the tower is less than a mile from where that cat came from."

Ira slides his pistol back into its holster, while Kate covers them with her pistol. He walks to Julie's horse and lifts the saddle off for her, setting it on the ground. She hands him the reins and he mounts the horse's bare back, then he takes Julie's hand and pulls her up behind him. He gently guides the horse with the reins in the direction that the cat came from while Kate follows behind, pistol ready.

After riding a few hundred yards they see light blinking and shimmering through the trees. Then after a few hundred more, they emerge from the wooded trail onto a narrow dirt road.

All three look up at the metal rungs of a ladder scaling the side of an old fire tower.

Ira halts the stallion, whispering. "And so it is." He sits for a moment, recalling the glimmering in his visions, a sense of déjà vu creeps through him, he nudges the horse forward. They approach the tower on the narrow dirt road and stop in front of it as Gus lifts his nose high in the air and begins wagging his tail. He's sending Kate a signal, indicating that his trained nose, forty thousand times more sensitive than a human's, is picking up cell scents. Kate looks at Ira, then dismounts her horse. She holds her hand out to her side and gives Gus a command. "Find boy, find."

The powerful Shepard takes off with his nose to the ground like iron takes to a magnet. He darts back and forth, then around in circles, then back and forth again, his tail wagging. He lifts his head and barks, then trots along the dirt road, nose back to the ground.

He's moving toward a grove of trees twenty yards away, when Kate once again gives him the command. "Find, boy."

Ira dismounts, helps Julie down and they tie their horses to the tower. They follow Gus on foot into a grove of trees. Once on the other side of the grove, they watch Gus do his stuff.

Sniffing round and round, his tail wagging hard, Gus finds a spot where he begins to paw at the ground, he stops to bark and then paws at the spot again. Then he stops and looks at Kate, indicating a find.

Kate coaxes him some more. "That-a-boy, work it, Gus. Find boy, good boy, find." Kate waits for the confirmed sign. Gus circles a ten-foot radius and the circles get smaller and smaller until he paws at the ground once again, sits on his hindquarters, looks up at Kate, barks and lies down in the same spot. Kate turns to Ira. "It's a hit. That's his confirmed signal and position."

Ira nods, then gazes up at the tree branches hanging above the spot. He is looking up at the branches from a tree included in a scant stand of Tecate Cypress. Gus is sitting on the find just beneath them, his tail wagging beneath him as he waits for his reward.

Kate takes her backpack off, reaches in for a piece of jerky for Gus and then pulls out an entrenching tool. She unfolds the collapsible shovel and holds it out for Ira to take.

He begins to dig in the dirt with gentle sweeps and after he's moved a few shovels full, the moment he's been waiting for all of his life emerges from the earth. A piece of bone falls from the shovel to the ground. They stare at its unmistakable form: a piece of rib bone, three inches long, splintered in half. Ira swallows hard, fighting the urge to howl like a wounded wolf, as brine pools in his eyes and spills down his cheeks. He quickly wipes the tears away, getting hold of his emotions as he stares down at his mother's rib bone. There'll be time for the grief to overcome him later. For now, he will continue with the task at hand.

He stoops and picks up the bone with his bare hands. *He's whirled into another place and time. He covers his head, screaming, as a whip cracks and rips through his skin. The butts of rifles slam into his body; the blows are horrendous and violent. A sharp hook, a meat hook, tears into his chest and then at once, like he's being hit by a huge wave he falls forward on the ground, and snaps out of the vision.*

He looks up at Julie and Kate standing over him and with the eyes of an assassin he clenches his jaw and veins protrude from his neck. He says to them. "So help me God I'm going to spend the rest of my life searching for the people responsible for my mother's death and even if I can't find them, for her sake, I'll spend the rest of my life fighting human traffickers and destroying them." He pulls a leather pouch from his pocket, stares at the rib bone in his hand, then glances up at the Tecate Cypress trees. Their presence assures him that this is the place where his mother died and that this bone belongs to her. He puts her bone into the leather pouch.

In that instant, once again Gus' nose is in the air, alerting Kate of something more. He barks, then darts to a spot meters away where dried weeds and thick brush have overcome an old concrete slab. It's a place where a building once stood.

Ira puts the pouch in the pocket of his cargo pants and they walk to where Gus is. Julie looks down at the concrete foundation. "This is what's left of that building I'd see from the top of the tower." They watch as Gus paws at the concrete. Kate looks at Ira. "We need to bring a search team up here, there's more to be found."

Then all at once, the three of them turn in the same direction as the humming sound of truck engines emerge from down the hill. The vehicles are distant, but they're heading up in their direction. They remain still while listening, until the motion stops and the engines idle shy of them by a couple hundred yards.

Ira draws his pistol and indicates to Kate to keep control of Gus, he signals he's going to have a look down the hill. Having vowed to protect Julie he motions for her to follow him.

He leads her down the slope, boots sliding on the loose gravely rocks. He holds her arm, helping her through the bramble and thick brush as prickly thistles catch their sleeves and pant legs. They stay low, using the scrub and chaparral for cover as they descend closer to the sound of the idling trucks.

As they near, they crawl behind a huge boulder and peek around it, Ira's head above Julie's. They see a building made of corrugated metal, painted in desert camouflage and surrounded by a chain-link fence topped with barbed wire. There is a huge generator at the back of the building and the two trucks are idling alongside. One of them is an armored vehicle that Julie recognizes right away. It's from the security company that Greg's bank uses. She had seen it on many occasions while visiting Greg for varies reasons at the bank, it's hard to overlook a security truck. Her eyes moisten and she narrows them as she remembers Greg, while focusing on the insignia of Guardit Security, wondering, *what the hell is their truck doing way up here?*

They study the scene as they crouch behind the rock. Ira's dark, intense eyes shift from one vehicle to the other, watching as the driver of the pickup gets out, slings his rifle onto his shoulder and moves to a huge makeshift door in the side of the foothills; a thatching made from tangled brush and prickly rubus stems. He grabs and pulls, dragging it away from the rocky gorge, exposing a cave in the bluff. Then the driver of the armored vehicle drives the truck inside.

When they pull the thatching back into place not a trace of the armored vehicle can be seen.

Ira unbuttons one of his pants pockets and pulls a GPS out, checks the coordinates of their location, he taps Julie's shoulder and takes her hand, guiding her back up the hill.

As they untie their horses, Ira tells Kate what they saw, she shakes her head in disbelief. He mounts the stallion and then pulls Julie up behind him.

The ride back is hot; even the shelter of the tall trees cannot cool the stifling midafternoon air and Julie is spent. She withers and she eases herself against Ira's back, lays her head on the back of his shoulder and closes her eyes.

A warmth flows through Ira and he turns to her. "Rest," he whispers, catching a whiff of her sweet-scented hair. He pulls her arms tighter around him. "You're safe now."

The trip is quiet; their minds occupied within their private thoughts. The slow gentle rocking of the stallion's gait relaxes Julie enough for her to fall into a dream.

*Ira takes her hands and pulls her closer, his breath on her face. She knows she should resist, this isn't right, it's too soon, but she's tortured by loneliness. She's paralyzed, and though she tries, she can't move. His eyes, like a dark, starlit, summer night draw her in, warm and inviting. He brushes his lips on her forehead and then slowly moves downward, first kissing her lips, then her chin, and down her throat past her–*. She wakes with a start, and Ira notices her body jerk.

"It's okay," he reassures her, "you're safe, Julie."

Blood surges to her cheeks and she flushes with embarrassment and guilt. She's glad he can't see her face. Ira is none the wiser.

As they ride, Ira begins thinking. He is certain that by now Carlos has told Linda what the Feds know about Lee and Ted Silar and nobody on this planet would want to be in Linda's shoes at present, Prada or not. Julie, who hasn't even had a chance to mourn *her* loss yet, is in for another jaw-dropping wallop when she hears what Sarita told INTERPOL about being sold and held against her will.

He knows he has to tell Julie before they get back, but he decides he'll tell her after they've dropped Kate and the animals off. Right now she needs to rest.

# CHAPTER TWENTY-ONE

## Beyond the Fringe of Human

Carlos had gained some respect from Linda when they'd first met in her hotel room and given the shocking conversation they're about to have, it'll come in handy. His college degree includes a heavy minor in psychology and it's the reason Ira chose *him* to lay bare the onslaught of revelations about to collapse Linda's world.

It was two days ago on Sunday that Carlos first brought Linda to the rectory and they've spent long hours talking. Not just about Lee's accounting habits and Sarita's lies about college, but also about their family dynamics.

He'd become suspicious of the Stevens' when he'd learned that Sarita didn't have an original birth certificate, but then after Linda told him that Sarita had lied about being in college and that the lies were down to the last detail, like her class schedule and professors names, that things began to click in Carlos' mind. There was no reason for Sarita to lie, it made no sense and as he asked more questions it became clear to Carlos that Lee Stevens had been the lead caregiver in Sarita's upbringing. He's got a hunch that Lee is the mastermind of the college scam, he is the one with motive, motive to keep

Sarita under his control, to keep her working for him. So Carlos asked Herroso to dig into Lee Stevens' past, starting with grammar school. He knows from experience that where you find lies, you'll find secrets.

The rectory has become an undercover command post, complete with laptops and printers and Carlos has just received an e-mail back from Herroso regarding Lee Stevens' past.

He pushes the last bite of his croissant into his mouth and brushes the crumbs from his army-green t-shirt. He sends the e-mail to the printer and finishes chewing while the document prints. Once finished, he stands, sipping his coffee, reading the information. He's disgusted, but not surprised as he reads the words that confirm what he'd suspected all along about Lee Stevens. He is the mastermind behind Sarita's lies and much more. The e-mail reads.

Lee Stevens had exhibited social problems as far back as fifth grade. Florence Nyberg, a fifth grade guidance counselor, made journal entries about a young Lee Stevens. *After counseling Lee Stevens, I believe the boy exhibits a conduct disorder which I considered severe enough to suggest to the parents that the boy undergo behavioral therapy; he lacks emotion, ignores rules, bullies, and lies on a consistent basis.*

That suggestion was not followed.

Then, in high school, a psychologist concluded that Lee Stevens displayed emotional vacancy. He gave examples, one of which referenced a biology experiment involving a mouse.

The psychologist wrote that Lee Stevens went to great lengths to fabricate a tiny screen cage in which to place his mouse's nourishment. The arrangement required that the mouse run circles around the cage day and night trying to get at the food. It couldn't chew through the screen because Stevens had sedated the mouse with ether and filed its teeth down to nubs. Within a few days his mouse died of starvation, dehydration and exhaustion, most likely in a lot of pain. Some of his classmates commented that he seemed to get a kick out of knowing the mouse was suffering.

By the time he was a freshman in college Stevens' personality flaws began to affect the humans around him. When he took his first job at a local business supply chain store he began to steal credit card numbers and sell them to neighborhood thugs. He didn't need the money; his parents were well off. He did it for thrills, for the psychological pain it caused the card owners and the challenge of not getting caught. When a female employee became suspicious of him and confronted him, he planted some credit card numbers in her locker and then waited for her after work one night. He conned her into talking things over and after she'd gotten into his car, he drove her to an abandon parking lot and raped her. When she went to the police and reported the rape, he pinned the thefts on her. He told the cops that she made up the whole rape story because they got into a lover's quarrel after having consensual sex. He had threatened to expose that she'd been stealing. He told them to search her locker if they didn't believe him. They went back, searched the locker and finding the credit card numbers, arrested her an hour later. She was kicked out of college and sentenced to two years in a woman's correctional facility. Lee was the key witness against her.

He let his father, an attorney, who handled his case, drag that innocent nineteen year old girl through the mud without so much as a flinch of remorse. The college dean suspected the girl was innocent and requested that Lee Stevens be evaluated by a psychologist. He was, but the psychologist was chosen by his father. While no proof was ever discovered exposing his crime, enough questions were raised by the college dean's request to free the girl.

Carlos is certain that Linda has no idea about Lee's hidden life. People who have personality disorders like Lee's are persuasive masters of deception. So Carlos has his work cut out for him where Linda is concerned. Breaking the news to her about her husband's deviant side is not going to be an easy task. She is a hard-driven, successful and respected business woman with a good-sized ego and a need for perfection. It's an understatement to say that she'll not easily accept that she's been Lee's unsuspecting dupe for her entire marriage. Lee preyed upon her, using the very qualities in Linda that made her successful to advance his sinister double life. It's going to be difficult to get her ego to accept the truth and the truth is, she has been fooled, scammed and double-crossed in the worst possible way by the person she most trusted.

It is human nature to want to resist unbearable reality when everything seems good on the surface, and on the surface, *Linda's* life couldn't have been better, but there are millions of psychopaths in the country. That fact alone is hard to believe, let alone finding out that you are married to psychopath. It is also typical human nature to believe that all humans are basically good and decent, that all people feel empathy and guilt on some level and it is assumed that being human means having a conscience. It's because of those thought patterns that psychopaths like Lee Stevens are able to hide themselves among us. But what you see is not always what you get when it comes to human beings and Carlos knows that the statistics concerning psychopaths are astonishing.

It is estimated that one in every twenty to twenty-five people have psychopathic personalities. Most are not hardened criminals, murderers, or for that matter, even strangers. They come from all social standings, from boardrooms, operating rooms, class rooms and yes, even situation rooms, living among us as bosses, co-workers, teachers, politicians, neighbors, friends, siblings, even parents, who have a dangerous defect in the paralimbic system of their brains. They are born without a conscience, so their entire life is dedicated to self-gratification. They've learned to mimic those of us who do have a conscience in order to live among us, but they'll obtain their self-gratification at any cost to whoever gets in their way.

During a long conversation with Ira last night after the teleconference, Ira told Carlos that Sarita Stevens was the one who informed INTERPOL about Lee Stevens' criminal activities and that she'd given them some explosive information.

She told Interpol that Lee Stevens has connections to criminals from Pakistan and that human-trafficking may be part of the whole criminal enterprise. She also said that Greg Bishop was set up by the Castello gang and board members of the bank where he worked. If that wasn't jaw dropping enough, she'd also told them that she'd been sold to a judge in the United States when she was eight years old, providing sex for him, then been sold to Lee Stevens. She has been in sexual servitude to Lee Stevens since she was thirteen.

"Damn." Carlos has seen a lot in his line of work, but Sarita's story blew him away.

He'd been awake for most of the night digesting what Ira told him about Sarita and planning how he would reveal the information to Linda. He decided to approach it one step at a time, bit by bit, but there's no question that because of the speed that this investigation was moving, it had to be done this morning

Linda's normal lifestyle has been cramped by a lumpy twin mattress and a tiny washroom facility at the rectory, but she's doing her best to adjust and make do. She takes one last glance at her reflection in the mirror of the medicine cabinet. Then she walks to the kitchen freshly showered, dressed in a pair of sun-bleached jeans, black pumps, a black sleeveless blouse with ruffles down the front and a long, knotted strand of pearls around her neck.

She is worn down and sleep-deprived from her own circumstances, not to mention her sympathy for Julie because of Greg's death and you can hear it in her voice. "Good morning." she mumbles, as she passes Carlos on her way to the kitchen counter where she pours herself a cup of coffee. Then she sits down in a chair across the table from him. She boots her laptop up and tries to engross herself in her work.

For the next twenty minutes she stares at her computer screen, reading e-mails with her coffee cup pressed against her lips.

She looks up, bewildered, when Carlos strikes up a conversation telling her about his college education and his minor in psychology. After a moment she stands up without replying, walks to the coffee pot and pours another cup. While she's pouring, she's thinking, *With everything I have on my mind, how rude would it be if I just told him out right that I'm not interested in his idle chit-chat?*

She turns back around to tell him how she feels, but before she can get the words out of her mouth Carlos speaks first. "Linda, I have something important I need to talk to you about."

She sets the pot down with a lackluster sigh, and walks to her chair, thinking, *There can't be anything left to tell him about Lee and Sarita.* She peers into his dark brown eyes for a moment and reads the seriousness in them. Knowing this means he needs her undivided attention, she sets her cup on the table and logs off her computer.

Carlos prefaces the conversation by describing the duties of the USBP. "Linda, my role as a United States Border Patrol Officer, put in the simplest of terms, is to deter and apprehend illegal entries into this country, including terrorists and their weapons, drug smugglers and other contraband and people who traffic in humans. I'm sure you understand this, right?"

Linda nods. "Does this have something to do with Greg's death?"

"Yes, we believe so." He hesitates for a moment, then in an unpretentious tone, "Linda," he says, "how much do you know about human trafficking?"

She raises her eyebrows, caught off guard by the question. "Human trafficking?" she repeats, wondering what human trafficking has to do with any of this. "Well, I have to confess it's not something I think about every day. It's not like it's something that comes up in conversations in *my* line of work, but of course I know of it. What does this have to do with Greg?"

Carlos leans forward, ignoring her question. "What I mean is, do you have an image in your mind of how it happens and who the victims are?"

"Yes, it's horrific. It happens in poor countries. Human traffickers trick people into thinking they'll lead them to a better life, then force them into slave labor or prostitution. It's appalling when you think about the reality of it."

Carlos nods. "Yes, it is, and it's technically defined as a process, not as a single act. It's the abuse of power over the vulnerability of a human being. Coercing, or forcing anyone into doing something they don't want to do with the use of violence or threats, for one's own profit or self-gratification is considered human-trafficking. In other words, you don't have to move victims around from city, state, or country to be trafficking a human being."

Linda tosses her hair to the side while warily fingering the knot on her strand of pearls. "And why are we talking about this?"

Carlos looks down at his coffee cup for a long moment before he speaks again. "We already talked about this yesterday, but when I asked if you knew why Sarita chose to work at your husband's orthodontics profession rather than in the fashion world with you, your answer was vague, saying just that you wished she'd chosen to follow in your footsteps instead. I'm going to rephrase the question. Did Sarita have a choice of whose footsteps she followed?"

"I can't believe you just asked that!" She eyes him, annoyed. "Of course she had a choice. I raised my daughter to be an independent woman. Just what are you insinuating anyway?"

Good, Carlos thinks, she's got an idea of what I'm leading up to here. "Doesn't it seem at all odd to you that she'd choose to be a dental assistant instead of a fashion designer like you?"

Linda narrows her eyes, vexed by the question.

Carlos doesn't want to anger her, he just wants to plant a seed. He backs his intensity down a notch, and begins to approach the matter from a different angle. "Linda, from what you told me about your career, you travel a lot and so Sarita had to spend a lot of time with your husband while she was growing up, right?"

"Yes," she says with some resentment, "but what's the relativity here? Lots of fathers take an active role in rearing their children. Does the Border Patrol consider that a crime?"

Carlos shifts his eyes away for a moment and lets out his breath, then he turns back to her. "It's relative in this case and we need to discuss it."

Linda takes a sip of coffee then, peering at Carlos above her cup, she says, "He may not be a perfect man, Carlos, but he's a good father. He made sure she had everything she needed growing up. He was there for her when I couldn't be. He drove her everywhere she needed to go, recitals, music lessons, doctor's appointments, you name it. I couldn't do that. I had to travel and if it were the other way around no one would even bat an eye. She's loyal to him, I understand that and I don't harbor ill feelings about it, nor has she ever shown any ill feelings about my career and my traveling."

Carlos, understanding how on the surface it all seems logical, nods, but continues to push. "Have you known Sarita to lie about anything as she grew up? I mean, did you ever catch her in any lies other than this college thing?"

Linda stiffens as his words pierce her.

He reads her reaction. He is contrite, but knows he has to press her. "I'm sorry to bring up the lying again, but we need to get to the bottom of this. Sarita has no motive, no reason to lie about college, so there must be someone else behind it and if so, then she's in danger, too."

Linda swallows hard, clasping her fingers tight around the knot in her pearls. This hits home and she blinks away moisture from her eyes. Her motherly instincts have kicked in and she stares at him for a long moment, her chest now rising and falling with unease. Then she whispers. "Yes, perhaps you're right." She thinks for a moment longer, then she says to him, "I've never noticed any lying. How could I possibly know if someone I trust is lying unless I'm trying to catch them in a lie and why would I try to do that to someone I trust?" She shifts her glance to the window and then looks back into her coffee cup, avoiding eye contact with Carlos. "Though there are two things that I've noticed for sure, she is always somewhat detached, which I feel is explainable. It stems from her past, the tragic loss of her parents in a car accident at a tender young age, before we took her in. The other thing that I've found myself pondering is her lack of motivation, but I also attribute that to the shock and trauma of the accident." Linda looks up from her cup. "This is uncomfortable, talking about something so private, but we did provide her with weekly counseling and after a few months the psychiatrist said she was doing fine and that she didn't have to come back."

"How did you find the psychiatrist? Was he a referral?"

Linda stares at him, then shifts her eyes away.

He can tell that she's thinking deep about her answer. Lee has been in control of Sarita's entire upbringing and she is presently feeling the sting of it. She shifts back to him and answers in a thwarted tone. "Lee knew him."

Carlos remains non-judgmental. "And naturally you trusted your husband's choice. You were busy, grateful that he knew someone and in fact Lee had time to make all the decisions when it came to Sarita, right?"

Linda leans back in her chair, not liking where this conversation is going. She rubs her temples. She leans forward again, looking him in the eyes, answering in a rigid tone. "Agent Carlos, you seem to have something specific on your mind about my husband's blameworthiness. Can we just cut to the quick here?"

The subject of Lee's control over Sarita is what Carlos has been driving at and although he would like to cut to the quick he knows he can't just blurt out that her husband is under suspicion of having ties to the Castello gang's, human-trafficking activities and that Lee has been using Sarita as his sex slave for seven years. He's got to continue to handle this with kid gloves to get through to Linda that nothing she's about to learn is her fault and that she's been targeted by a special type of psychopath, a malignant narcissist, who's carefully contrived a façade called a family life and built it around *her* to disguise his insatiable need for sadistic control. Carlos is almost ready to show her the e-mail from Herroso, but first he has one more question. "Can you think of anything that Lee has ever done in the past that you know of that would have made you question his integrity?"

"No."

Carlos lifts a piece of paper off the table. "I have an e-mail here that I want you to read. It's regarding your husband's adolescent years, right up through college." He hands her the sheet of paper.

She's reluctant at first staring hard at Carlos, but then takes the paper and begins to read. As her eyes move back and forth across the page her expression changes from reluctance to absorption, then to shock. She looks up and snaps. "Where on earth did you get this rubbish from?"

Carlos stares into her eyes. "The FBI obtained it for me." Then to reinforce its validity, he adds, "There's corroborated documentation to back it up."

If Linda weren't already sitting down her knees would have buckled beneath her. A huge fist has just gripped her chest, squeezing the air from her lungs. She lifts her hand to her mouth and sits for a moment, deep in thought. She had no idea about any of this. Lee was a gentleman when they'd met, charming and confident, his father a reputable attorney, his mother quiet and reserved. They'd been engaged for a year before they married and Lee is a respected member of the community serving on boards like Point Loma High School and The United Club. She looks at Carlos, her eyes full of doubt. "This has to be a mistake. How could I have not known about any of this?"

"It's not your fault. People with malignant personality disorders like Lee are masters at fooling people and hiding their lack of emotion. Often they rise to the top of their fields. And they do that by manipulating networks of people to help them get to positions of authority."

Linda looks up from the paper and stares at Carlos for a moment. "Are you saying my husband is a clinical psychopath?"

Carlos locks eyes with her. He nods, voicing an adamant. "Yes."

She shifts her gaze, staring at the floor as she's swept back in time to the restroom at Johnny Rockets on Camp Pendleton. Back then she'd dammed all thoughts about what Lee was capable of, concentrating on Sarita's lie instead, but now, the gates are leaking like a sieve and the dam is about to give way.

There's always a delay in accepting the truth, whether good or bad, but at some point the realization begins to set in.

She sits frozen, staring for a long moment, letting denial run its course first, even though she's holding the proof in her hands. "It's impossible," she says without blinking, "How could I have been so blind and for so long. It's just *not* possible and Sarita." She stops in mid-sentence and shifts her attention back to Carlos. The thought of Sarita snaps her out of denial like the crack of a whip. "She's a good girl! She's never caused any trouble!" She stands up, making her way across the kitchen to the window. She stares out at the long reaching branches of the chestnut tree, thinking about her daughter's lies. Then she thinks about Lee, *the late nights, the drinking, the gambling,* and she mumbles as if talking to herself. "There's no explanation for Sarita's lies, except that he put her up to it." She whirls around, her green eyes ablaze. "Why?" She snaps at Carlos. "Why did he put her up to it?"

Carlos knows why, but he's not looking forward to telling Linda the rest of Lee's sordid secrets.

Linda charges forward not taking her eyes off of him, then stops and hangs over him like a dark thundercloud about to explode in a torrent of rain, her wrath apparent. After reading the e-mail the thought of leaving the bulk of her daughter's upbringing to Lee sends chills down her spine. She stares down at Carlos and in a haunting tone she says. "I'm not a person easily deceived, Carlos. I have a successful company that I run like a well-oiled machine. I have hundreds of people who can testify to the fact that it's very difficult to pull the wool over my eyes." She narrows her intense stare. "Tell me straight up, Carlos. What other skeletons has Lee been hiding, because judging by the look in your eyes, his closet is brimming with decay."

"The first thing that you need to remember, is that none of this is your fault."

Linda jabs her finger into her own chest. "*My* fault?" She shouts. "What isn't *my* fault?"

"Please sit down. The remainder of what I have to tell you about Lee is going to be an even greater shock."

Linda's heart begins to pump in her chest as she stands staring down at Carlos. Then a dreadful feeling spreads through her, a choking feeling as if she has ingested strychnine. She tries to swallow, but her mouth and throat are dry and she sits down in slow motion, not taking her eyes off Carlos. Her eyes are like a fire storm while her mind puts two and two together. She braces herself.

"Linda, this isn't easy for me to have to tell you this, but straight up, your husband is a pedophile and he has been using Sarita as a sex slave ever since he bought her and brought her into your house. He is vacant of morals, he's psychotic and is capable of any heinous act."

Linda sits frozen, staring at Carlos for a long time. Then she presses hard on her chest, struggling to breathe and truly comprehend the revelation. "Oh my God!" she utters, breathless, as the blood drains from her face, and she doubles over, gasping.

Carlos stands and rushes to her side, sympathetically he rests his hand on her back. "Slow down, try to breathe slow, breathe slow." He stands at her side, coaxing her until she's able to catch her breath.

She looks up at him after a few minutes, still light-headed. His eyes tell the story. Then grasping the table-top as if she's just been hit with a club, she whispers. "Is this first-hand knowledge?"

Carlos swallows. "Yes. From Sarita."

She holds on as rage roils to the surface and fury takes hold, her green eyes smolder as she curls her lip. She turns away from his gaze as the agony she feels for Sarita fills her body and stings her eyes. She blinks as hot tears stream down her cheeks in shame. "That son of a bitch!" Her voice icy. "I'm going to kill that *son of a bitch*!" She emphasizes in a hiss. "How could I have been so blind?" She stands up and begins to pace, guilt gushing through her, she rants in pure anguish. "I hate him! That bastard, I hate him. I'll kill that son of a bitch, I swear to God I'll kill him." She stops and her eyes drill into Carlos'. "I swear, Carlos, I'm going to kill that fucking bastard." She doubles over, sobbing.

Carlos takes hold of her shoulders and walks her back to her chair. She rails on about Lee. "I hate him, I hate that filth of a man. How could he do this? I've never been so mortified in all my life." She pushes Carlos's arm away and sits down with her face buried in her hands. "Oh my God, poor Sarita, I'm so ashamed; this is unforgivable. I'm so ashamed, I can't even look at *you,* how can I ever look at her? How will she ever be able to forgive me?"

Carlos pulls up a chair in front of her. He sits down and peels her hands away from her face. "Linda, this isn't your fault. This is Lee's doing; he's the guilty one."

Streams of tears laced with black mascara roll down Linda's cheeks.

Carlos retrieves a box of tissues from the living room and pulls some out, handing them to her, then he sets the box on the table in front of her. He sits back down, "Linda, people like Lee live beyond the fringe of humanity. They learn at a very early age how to carve out a life founded on and constructed from lies because they haven't any emotions of their own. And then they use that life to deceive and manipulate others in order to appease their insatiable sense of entitlement."

Linda looks at Carlos through swollen tear-filled eyes while reaching for tissues.

Carlos drags the metal garbage can closer to her chair. "When a person is a victim of someone who exhibits antisocial personality disorder, they always blame themselves, but that's the reason these pariahs keep getting away with it. The best way to bring about justice is to work with Ira and me and the rest of the team to lure these ruthless scumbags to a cliff and drive them off."

She looks up from the soggy, mascara-stained tissue that's in her hand, her eyes red and burning. She furrows both eyebrows and her lips quiver when she says her name. "Is, S-Sa-Sarita helping you?" She tries to catch her breath.

Carlos nods, staring her in the eyes. "She's come forward with strong evidence for the authorities and she's agreed to continue to cooperate behind your husband's back."

Linda brings the tattered tissue to her nose, she blows and wipes it, then drops it in the garbage. She grabs another tissue and holds it to her eyes for a long moment. Taking a huge breath, she shudders as she exhales. "She's a brave girl. I have to be brave for her."

Carlos nods. "You can talk to Sarita as soon as we hear from Agent Herroso. He's the FBI officer in charge of contact with Sarita."

"Oh, my stars," she says in a small voice, "I-I don't even know what to say to her, or where to start."

"I'm sure, as with any other child, she loves her mother. Reassure her of *your* love for her and make sure she knows none of this is her fault, either."

Later that afternoon as the sun sets, not knowing where the time has gone, Linda is still sitting at the kitchen table with Carlos when they hear a vehicle pull up. They wait with eyes locked in silence.

Ira has told Julie everything he knows regarding Sarita and what his men have been able to establish about the slavery ring while driving her to the rectory.

When they arrive the first one through the kitchen door is Julie and the first thing she sees is the box of tissues on the table. She looks at Linda and she knows that Linda has joined her in sorrow. As Julie makes her way to Linda's side, Carlos stands, moving his chair out of the way, allowing the two to embrace while he and Ira look on.

# CHAPTER TWENTY-TWO

## Band of Silk

After Sarita's Hot Tip call that went to INTERPOL which prompted the appointing of a leadership council and a full-out investigation, Linda had to feign coming back from her sick mother's side in San Francisco to play the role of a grieving friend and attend Greg's funeral with Sarita and Lee. Even though her first instinct was to castrate him, then strangle the life out of him, she had to pretend total ignorance of Lee's double life and because of his extreme self-absorption and narcissism she was able pull it off.

Lee insisted on picking Linda up from the airport to drive her to Greg's funeral and had given Sarita orders to meet them there. Not because he gave a damn, but because he has to make it appear to others as though he does and as usual he has to keep his eye on Sarita.

At his pompous best, he leads Linda into the funeral home like an Academy Award winning actor, dressed in a black, double-breasted Armani, white shirt, and red tie, removing his dark Oakley glasses as if he were stepping onto the red carpet.

Linda follows him in, somber, wearing a black couture suit, a calf-length skirt clinging to her hips and a silk, monochromatic scarf jutting from the top of a short, cropped jacket. Her hands are covered with black lace. Her grief-stricken face, hidden by an angled black veil hair-piece, is not for Greg. Her grief and tears are for Sarita.

She spots Sarita standing by the registry, wearing black from head to toe, a vintage '70s Chanel pantsuit, and dagger calf-length boots. In the moment that their eyes meet for the first time since Sarita's revelations about Lee, it is as though two lightning bolts collide and a fiery singe spreads through the funeral home's foyer, charring the walls. For a long moment they stare at each other, Sarita lowers her head in shame.

Linda tries to reach out to her, but Lee steps in between them, giving Sarita an authoritative hug. Linda stops in her tracks, standing there disgusted, as hate sweeps through her body and her eyes bore holes into the back of Lee's skull. She watches Sarita wither as Lee forces his hug on her and she feels herself shrivel, appalled that she'd allowed this to happen to Sarita.

As soon as Sarita pulls away from Lee, Linda hugs her tight, relaying how much she loves her with her arms and how miserable she is for allowing this to happen. They hug, holding each other tight for a long time. Then Linda pulls away and sends Sarita a silent message of sympathy through narrowed green orbs, shrouded by a black veil.

She takes Sarita's hand and they settle on chairs close to Greg's empty coffin, sitting hand-in-hand, while Lee establishes himself next to them trying to emulate a patriarch of a grief-stricken family. He's thinking that their grief is for Julie.

Julie stands between her parents a few feet away in a black Versace dress and a triple strand of pearls braided around her neck.

Her mother, a few inches shorter, but bearing a close resemblance to Julie, stands polished and refined in a dark navy pantsuit holding a dainty white handkerchief in her fist and her father dressed in his formal dress blues has his arm wrapped around Julie's waist for support as she sobs in front of Greg's picture displayed next to his hand-polished casket. Her body is shuddering, her hand is clutching a mass of worn-out Kleenex pressed to her nose and her head's resting on his shoulder. She remains standing between her two pillars of strength the entire time, shaking hands with an endless stream of people who are there to pay their respects.

Father Lelo is there, he's been asked by Julie's dad, Colonel Price, to say a few words at the service. Ted Silar came with Dorothy Cache, and they're seated one row behind Lee, Linda and Sarita, along with other co-workers from the bank.

Ira, with his hair cut short, is occupying a place in the back of the room where he chose to perch early on and where he will remain for the entire service, inconspicuous among a handful of Marines. He watches Julie helplessly, wishing he could comfort her in her distress. He also keeps his eyes nonchalantly on everyone who arrives.

When he saw Sarita walk into the parlor, her striking beauty, dark and flawless, floored him. He knew right away from the description he'd been given that she was the one who was the slave girl. He had a hard time looking away, not only because of his empathy for her, but there was something more. He monitored her with considerable curiosity, having a hard time peeling his eyes away. Then Silar walked in and he saw Sarita's body tense up. When Silar walked past her, he watched her sink in her chair as the honcho banker gave her a stiff, authoritarian glance. Ira scribbles a note on a piece of paper, *dig further into trafficked girl's past*.

Silar has never seen Ira, doesn't even know who he is, but still, even though Ira felt he had to attend the funeral, there was a small element of danger in him being there.

Sarita and Linda excuse themselves and take a few minutes to be alone together in the restroom. They pack a lot of love into a few minutes. Linda whispers that she "knows," and strokes Sarita's silky black hair, repeating again and again how sorry she is for being so blind.

Sarita pulls away and with an expression of maturity that no one should have at her age, looks deep into Linda's eyes while narrowing her own, refuting Linda sharply. "None of this is *your* fault; it's *his* doing, not yours! He's deceived everyone in his path."

In that moment they wanted to run out of there, to leave town together, to be able to talk, to get help, to heal, but as hard as it was to stay silent, they both knew that they had a job to finish and united they would make Lee pay.

They vowed that after he was arrested, they would take a long trip to a secluded island somewhere where they could rest and bond. They knew that being responsible for putting Lee behind bars for the rest of his life would be the sutures that would begin the process of healing their wounds.

Linda takes a phone out from her purse and gives it to Sarita, who slides it into her boot. This phone will be the line of communication from Sarita to Ira and his team. It's the line that will choke the life out of a modern-day slavery ring.

After the funeral, Linda tells Lee she needs to return to her mother's side in San Francisco before leaving for a fashion show in Milan and that she'll be gone for a few weeks, but in fact she'll go back to the rectory, which is now the command post and help with the investigation. She'll communicate with Lee when she has to, but she'll be able to talk to Sarita daily on the phone that she'd given her.

Sarita's fate sent her to the inner recesses of one of the worst types of human cruelty imaginable, sex slavery and because she's a victim she's passionate about doing something about it. She will remain in the same daily grind, shackled by Lee's manacles for a while longer, but with nothing to lose and everything to gain, she'd affirmed to Linda that the end would justify the means and it would be bearable by her if she could be the cause of Lee's ultimate demise. Linda knows Sarita's intentions are good, but worries in the back of her mind. Questioning whether when the time actually comes, will Sarita have the strength to cut loose the cords that bind her and go beyond the contention of her safety to betray her captor? She prays silently that she can.

Julie sits alone in a chair by Greg's coffin at the end of the service limp. Drained and bone-weary, she stares down at a soggy, crumpled wad of Kleenex in her hands. Her parents are standing in the foyer saying goodbye to the last of the visitors. Father Lelo is the last one out the door. They have invited him to a small lunch gathering of family and close friends at their house and even though it made them cringe they've been instructed to invite

Greg's boss, Ted Silar and Dorothy Cache also. They were invited in order to keep things looking as normal as possible and as the saying goes, "keep the enemy close."

Father Lelo keeps an eye on Silar while at the luncheon, noting that his masquerade of sorrow could win him an Oscar and he realizes that Julie's getting an eyeful, too. More than once he's caught her peering in Silar's direction, her once bright blue eyes now narrow and cold. Dorothy's grief is genuine, though and she and Julie spend most of the luncheon consoling one another.

Julie's been asked by Ira and his team to use her relationship with Dorothy to try to glean whatever inside information she can about the bank and its oddball branch in Junction City, adding that Julie must do it cautiously.

Three long weeks after Greg's funeral, Ira and the other undercover agents are still working non-stop round the clock on the case. Ira hasn't seen Julie since the service; she's been staying at her parent's house on Camp Pendleton where she's safe and where her parents are helping her take care of her affairs. The thugs responsible for the explosion on base won't dare step a foot anywhere near the Marines, which is good for Julie. She needs to rest and heal and Ira felt he should give her some space while she's mourning, but these last three weeks seem more like three months to him. He needs her to start nosing around in the bank's business and he's anxious for her to get started, but more than that, he'd like to see her again. During the day he's immersed in his work, but at night when he's alone after a long hard day he thinks only of her.

He stares up at the ceiling in the dark, with his hands clasped behind his head, waiting for sleep and wondering if a woman like Julie could ever want to be with a man like him. *Bishop and I are so different,* he thinks. *Bishop was suave and polished, had money, could buy her the moon. Would she ever settle for a man with less?* As soon as he thinks it, a voice in his head says loud and clear. *No way, dude, forget it!*

He rolls onto his side releasing a deep breath. He can't help himself, he just can't stop thinking of her. He has memorized every detail of that horseback ride with her on Otay and the legends engraved in stone, sojourning on a shelf in his mind. Hidden deep inside him is an aching, a longing to see her and his spirit calls to her at the threshold of his dreams. The scent of her hair embodies his nostrils as he breathes in. The softness of her skin, and the warmth of her body next to his emanates to his bed and he sees her face in his heart. He knows he stands no chance, but she relaxes him, puts his mind at ease, quells his nerves and he drifts to sleep thinking of her.

It is a clear September night and the windows in Julie's bedroom at her parents' house face the mountain. As she lies staring out at a cluster of stars, she thinks back to when she and Greg were in the hot tub together. The stars were plentiful that night, too, and that was the last time she'd made love with him. She covers her mouth as grief overcomes her and tears spill from her eyes as she thinks about the two of them together.

She wipes the warm, wet streams from her cheeks and rolls onto her side. She's so lonely, she feels as though her chest has been carved hollow and that she might perish herself. She thinks. *How can I go on like this? It's impossible to shoulder this pain alone, and yet, the one who would have helped me through this pain is the one who caused it.* And for the first time since Greg's death, Julie feels anger toward him. *How dare he allow Silar to lure him into that sinister world? Where was his regard for my safety and our future? He's ripped my entire life to shreds and left me empty and yet there are so many questions left unanswered.*

She curls her knees to her chest and absently reaches out to the vacant spot next to her, seizing a fistful of empty sheets. Realizing she'll never get the answers from him, that she'll never even hear his voice again, her loneliness smothers her like a wet blanket smothers a fire. Unable to escape the mantle, she cries deep into the night, empty sheets crushed tight in her fist.

On Monday morning as Sarita stands in front of the mirror tying her hair in a pink scarf before leaving for work, she reflects on the intelligence she had just given Ira over the phone about a call she'd overheard last night, where Lee had mentioned the word Junction twice.

She stares at her reflection in the mirror as Ira's voice lingers in her mind. There's something about him that she can't easily dismiss and she contemplates her feeling for him for a moment longer, perplexed as to why her thoughts of him persist. Then she thinks about Julie. Ira has just told her he's going to try to arrange a meeting with her today to see if she's ready to meet with Dorothy over lunch to try to get some details about the Junction City branch that only a secretary would know, like how often Greg went down there and on what days. Ira assured Sarita that he's been moving things along as fast as he can.

She lets out a heavy sigh, brushes her bangs to the side, and takes one last look at her reflection.

She gathers her purse and keys, then leaves to spend the day at the office with Lee. The one and only thing that keeps her from fleeing this abhorrent circumstance is her knowing that she's leading Lee to his own slaughter and that then she'll be free to pursue her dreams.

After Ira finishes his conservation with Sarita, he calls Father Lelo and asks him to give Julie a call to see if she's up to meeting with him somewhere later today. Julie agrees and just two hours later, Father Lelo's ringing the bell at Julie's parents' house.

As he waits for Julie to come to the door, Father Lelo thinks about what Ira had revealed to him this morning about the armored truck company. After the FBI questioned company executives long and hard, they verified that the company was not involved, but that the truck is in fact an exact replica of a *Guardit* armored vehicle. A clever scheme, Father Lelo thinks, enormously alarming, since an armored truck is never pulled over and searched on a busy highway. Therefore, it's able to transport anything without suspicion. Being a Marine, Father Lelo can't help but stew over how dangerous this is to homeland security.

When Julie answers the door she's dressed casually in a pair of stone-washed jeans and a cream-colored tank, layered with a faded celadon hoodie. Her blond hair is spilling freely over her shoulders. She tells her mother she'll be back in a couple hours and then leaves with Father Lelo to meet Ira.

Father Lelo drives her to the San Luis Rey Mission church where she and Ira can talk in a private room at the Sierra Center. Julie's been cooped up for the last three weeks and to her it feels good to get out into the world again.

Father Lelo walks her down the hall to the door of a small conference room.

Ira is waiting inside anticipating their meeting, dressed to blend in like a tourist, wearing a pair of jeans and an Anaheim T-shirt with a camera case hanging round his neck. He stands when Julie steps into the room and the faint scent of her perfume drifts into his nostrils electrifying his senses. As their eyes meet, his pulse quickens and his heart's pumping so hard that blood rushes to his head and its making his ears ring. His breath catches in his throat.

She freezes, locked in his stare. Then her thick lashes flutter as she takes him in, once again struck by his incredible symmetry. *His hair is cut short now,* she thinks, but he's even more attractive than she remembers. A tinge of contrition surfaces when Greg pops into her head, and she feels guilt about the painting of Ira on the rearing stallion in the closet of her studio. And suddenly like déjà vu, she remembers the kiss in the dream she had while riding bareback on the horse with him on Otay. Her cheeks feel flush and for a quick second she looks away, trying to hide the conundrum of emotions brought on by the memory of the tender, passionate touch of his lips. Flustered, she offers her moistend palm in a handshake, trying to act as casual as she can. "Hello, it's nice to see you again." She says in a demure tone.

He tries not to swallow *too* hard, and answers, "I wish it was under better circumstances, but." He struggles for the right words and the moment he touches her hand voltage surges through his body and his thoughts spin out of control. He scrambles for what to say next, but all he can come up with is. "Please have a seat."

She smiles letting go of his hand and he helps her push her chair in. Her blue eyes follow him back to the other side of the table, unable to ignore his toned, muscular backside even through his denim. She's been so secluded and caught up in her sorrow that she hasn't given the rest of the world much thought. She had lost track of time, but now that she sees Ira again, her senses have been awakened and she's eager to hear what he's learned in the investigation so far.

Ira can see by her lack of color that she has been worn down by her husband's death, but she's still beautiful and she bears an inner strength that can't be bridled; he admires her for *that* even more. As he sits down across the table from her, he has to remind himself to both breathe normally and to focus on his job.

He talks to her about Sarita and some of the latest intelligence that she's been able to collect for them. He also tells her that they know that the enemy's been inside her house, because when they went to retrieve the secret phone and gun that she'd told Father Lelo about, they were gone.

Julie is hanging on his every word, engrossed in the events that eventually led to Greg's death. At times her jaw drops open and long moments pass before she takes a breath, alarmed by the cunning and the repulsiveness of the crimes and the magnitude of the other criminals involved with Silar and Lee Stevens.

Ira tells her that Sarita's spying has linked a Mexican crime gang and a band of Pakistani criminals living in the U.S., to Ted Silar and Lee Stevens' business activities and associates, concluding that Lee Stevens' abundant inventory flow of composite oxygen and his plentiful orders for narcotic suppositories are being used on human-trafficking victims and that the armored vehicle they saw on Otay is a fake, most likely being used to transport sex slaves. The oxygen they believe is playing a part in keeping the victims alive, which means they must be transporting them from a significant distance. They've also concluded that the victims are most likely children and the narcotic suppositories are being used as an inexpensive form of sedation, suppressing the children's motion and breathing. Also, the suppositories could be used for other sinister purposes that he can't bring himself to consider.

Julie stiffens her spine. She is horror-struck by the sex-trafficking of children and the word Mexican crime gang is enough to scare the daylights out of her, but the words "Pakistani criminals in the U.S." makes her soul shiver. To say that she's frightened is an understatement and she sits still for a moment, not able to make a sound. Her mind wants her to go back to her parent's home, to hide, to be safe, take refuge from a world filled with greed, torture, slavery, bombings, jihad and senseless slaughter, but she can't turn away. Across from her sits a true hero, a man righteous enough to stand and fight the enemy and she wants to help him fight the evil.

When Ira finished talking, Julie glances up from the table, pain evident in her eyes. "These monsters have to be stopped, whatever it takes and without question. I'll try to arrange a lunch with Dorothy this week."

Ira's gratefulness can be heard in his sigh of relief, but still, his eyes are full of apprehension for her. He is not thrilled with putting her in the dangerous position of spying.

He takes a phone out from the camera case and looks her in the eyes.

"This is a special phone, Julie, the only person who will ever call you on this phone is me and it's important that you follow these instructions to the letter. There's just one number programmed into this phone and it's mine, so if it rings and my name doesn't come up on the caller ID, don't answer it under any circumstance and never use it to call anyone except me." He slides the phone across the table to her.

Julie nods – her stomach full of butterflies she asks with fear in her voice. "Ira, are we going to be okay? I mean everyone, Linda, Sarita, my parents, Father Lelo, everyone? Are we all going to make it through this?"

He knows she's frightened. She knows firsthand what these monsters are capable of, from the spooks tailing her and Linda, to what they've done to her husband, not to mention the deadly snakes planted in her backyard and he wants nothing more than to comfort her, to promise her that everyone will be okay, but he can't. All he can do is look at her from across the table and tell her, "We're going to do everything in our power to protect all of you."

He wouldn't blame her if she wanted to hide from this nightmare, to go back to her parents and sequester herself where she's safe. Part of him wishes she would, but she's their best chance at obtaining key information about Junction City and they need her to help them stop these bastards.

After his meeting with Julie, Ira went to the firing range for practice. No matter how hard he tried, he couldn't stop thinking about *her* and all the *what ifs* that could happen with her spying on the bank. What if the Bureau pushes too hard? They've already had an indirect hand, *through me,* in getting her to use Dorothy for info. His reaction when they first hinted about using her was, *no way Jack*, but they were persistent and they weren't using kid gloves. What if they push her to get close to Silar? What if Silar starts to suspect her and what if the thugs put a contract on her life, like they did her husband?

When Ira retrieves his target score, it's 348/360. "Yuck." He wrinkles his nose. "Terrible." And it is, for him.

He shoves his ear gear and glasses into a duffle bag and leaves for the office.

Agent Herroso is sitting in front of Ira's unkempt desk waiting for him when he walks in. Ira throws his hat on the empty chair next to him, he takes his seat on the other side of the desk.

"What's up, Hero?"

"Ira, how's it going? Just got some inside intelligence from a mole that's been underground embedded in the Castello gang for the past two years. This is so top secret I had to come to you in person, in private, at a place we can trust that isn't bugged. You know how sensitive these matters can be."

Ira scoffs sarcastically. "Is a Russell's Viper poisonous?"

"Right. Anyway, the mole's been hauling stolen electronics and fake designer stuff for Castello for the past two years, jeans, purses, watches, things of that sort. Nothing big time yet, but he's reported that he's had a conversation with Castello himself and Castello's ready to bump him up a notch, told him he likes his trustworthiness and that he's going to be reassigned to an important job as a switch driver at the U.S. Calexico border, driving a semi. HQ told me that I should pass the info to you, given the timing of it, it may have something to do with this trafficking case."

"Good, thanks." Ira makes a note. "It's an interesting detail that could turn out to make a difference for the advanced planning of this operation. I'll start researching the U.S. Maquiladora companies across the border and the trucking companies that haul their goods."

Herroso stands up. "You may want to make a list of the American banks down there, too."

Ira nods. "Already have."

"Well that's it, then, that's all I was sent here for. I got other things to do, so I'm outta here."

Ira stops him. "Hero?"

"Yeah, man."

"Have you ever gotten to the point in your life where thinking about someone has become an obsession?"

"You mean like a woman?"

"Yeah, like a woman."

"Yeah, dude, of course."

"What'd you do about it?"

"You mean to stop it?"

"Yeah."

"I married her, dude." He walks out the door, leaving Ira staring at an empty door frame.

"Great," he mumbles, "like that'll ever happen."

At the end of the day, Ira unzips his briefcase and stuffs another file inside. "Work I can bring home with me," he says to his desk as he rummages around for more files. He checks his watch, five thirty already, better wrap it up, he's thinking. Father Lelo's coming over tonight for Rosa's famous chicken dinner and she said to be home by six-thirty sharp. As he's about to walk out the door his phone rings. When he checks to see who it is, his heart rate bumps up significantly, but he answers in a stiff tone. "Julie! Are you okay?"

"Yes," she says, sounding perturbed, "physically, I'm fine, but mentally I'm spooked. Ted Silar just called me, and asked me to have dinner with him tonight."

Ira felt as if his blood had stopped circulating. He's stunned silent.

"He said that he's been thinking about Greg and he misses him and that he knows I must be feeling a million times worse than he does. Then he asked if I'm up for going out for a bite. He said it would be healing for the both of us. Ira, I was so caught off guard, I didn't know what to say, so I said that I would and we're meeting at the Barbican Lounge, on South Coast Highway at seven tonight in Oceanside. . . . Hello? Hello? . . . Ira? Are you there?"

"Yes, yes, I'm here. Just a bit surprised, that's all."

"So am I, I certainly don't want to have dinner with him. I hate the man, he really scares me, but I'm afraid he might get suspicious if I don't. Can you help me? I've never had to do anything like this before. Can you coach me on how to act and what to say?"

Ira knows it's too late to meet with her somewhere, he'll have to do it over the phone. So he spends the next forty-five minutes mentoring her, trying to build her courage, telling her that she needs to do more listening than talking and when she does talk, he tells her, talk about Greg. Play on Silar's sympathy and don't stay out with him too long.

"Don't worry, I couldn't be swayed with a firing squad to stay any longer than I have to."

After he hangs up the phone he calls Herroso and tells him he needs him to go to the Barbican Lounge in Oceanside and keep his eye out for an attractive blonde with an older man.

"Are you kidding, Ira? That's three quarters of the population of California."

"Hero, I'm not joking, this is important. It's Ted Silar from the bank and the late Greg Bishop's wife. It's our responsibility to make sure she's safe."

"Okay, I can do that, I got a glimpse of her at Jomoka's Bean Shack when she dropped the Stevens woman off. I'll handle it."

"Thanks and Hero, when they leave make sure she gets home safe and –" he hesitates.

"And what?"

Ira was going to say call to let me know when she's home safe. "Nothing," he says, hiding his feelings. "It's not important."

Carlos has his hands full at the rectory. He steps outside the door yelling over his shoulder, "Linda! Just what in the hell is that?"

Linda comes out behind him and with a pleased smile says, "It's a truck from my fleet."

"I know it's a truck. What's it doing here?"

"Delivering my mattress." She steps past him and walks toward the truck.

"Your what?"

"My mattress."

"Your mattress!" He throws his hands in the air. "Linda, you can't."

She turns around interrupting him. "*I can't* work when I can't sleep, and I can't sleep on that lumpy mattress any longer."

"You can't just place an order for convenience and have it delivered to a secret command post!"

"Don't get angry with me, Carlos. I ordered one for you, too."

Carlos catches up with her at the back of the truck. "Linda!" He says, his voice elevated. You've put us in danger, don't you understand that people like Lee and his cohorts hire criminals to kill people like us? Who's this guy here?" He points to the driver who has just come around the corner. "He could be a hired assassin."

"Relax, Carlos. This is Javier, he is from Honduras. He's in the USA on a work visa, and it's about to expire. He knows that if something were to happen to me he'll have to go back to the inhumane working conditions of the banana plantations. Needless to say, Javier is very loyal to me. He understands English, so when I told him that nobody is to know about this, nobody will know. He's one of my personal assistants. You see Carlos, you're not the only one who works in a dangerous occupation. The fashion world is a cut-throat business, so I make sure I have loyal people around me. I have resources of my own for keeping secrets.

Javier reaches for the handle and pulls open the door of the truck. Carlos looks inside and lets out a huge guff of air. "I can't *believe* you did this, Linda."

"What? Is a twin not big enough?" She says in an innocent tone.

"Linda you *know* damn well what I mean, this is unheard of. I'll be a laughing stock with the guys, and mince-meat with HQ."

"Hah," she shrugs, making light of it, "If you don't want them to know, don't tell them. Now if you don't mind we need to step aside please, so that Javier can carry these inside."

Lee pours himself a scotch, then sits down at his desk. "Why hasn't Linda called, she used to call regularly when she went away."

"You know *her*," Sarita answers. "She's probably hanging around with the top designers in the business at Gucci's lounge, in Milan, sipping champagne over a fashion spread right now."

Lee sneers. "Or maybe she's standing on the balls of The Bull of Truin." He retorts sarcastically. He sets his glass of scotch down. "Anyway, she should check in more often, I don't need her sneaking home in the middle of the night unexpectedly to surprise me and me not being there."

"If it'll make you feel better, I can call her tomorrow and ask her for sure when she'll be home. She would tell me if she planned on surprising you."

"You do that. Then tell her to call me. I want to talk to her."

Sarita walks to the door of his office. "I have a few things I have to do at the front desk before I leave." Lee waves her off and resumes reading his e-mails. When his phone rings, Sarita stops in her tracks and backs up and, leaning her body next to the wall by his door, she waits to see if she can hear his conversation. He doesn't lower his voice so she hears him quite well.

"It's good, Ted. Castello will be there when the shipment arrives, but who is this Abdullah Najibullabullal? Fuck, I can't even pronounce it. Who is he?" Lee asks, perturbed. "How come I've never heard of him? . . . No, Castello never mentioned him to me; who could forget a fucking name like that? Who is he?"

Sarita is thinking she's got to get to a pen to write that name down. It sounds like he's someone important to Silar and she's sure Ira will want to know about him. She moves to the front desk as quiet as possible, spells the name the best she can on a sticky note and slips it into her shoe. Just as she's about to sneak back again, she hears Lee stand up and then sees him close his door. This time, with palms sweaty and heart thumping, she nestles her ear tight against it, so she can hear his words clearly. It's necessary for her to be accurate with the information she is gathering for Ira, but right now she can't believe what she's hearing, will anybody believe it?

Lee's fired up. "I knew Castello was an eccentric, sadistic SOB." He chuckles. "But a harem of ten virgins from Afghanistan in burqas? The real deal? None over twelve years old? Fuck, he's demented. They'll be catering to his every whim . . . yeah, you're not just a kidding it's a fantasy come true. The only difference between the female sex slavery over there and ours over here, is that over there it's legal and called marriage." He says laughing. "So, what kind of a production's going on up on Otay now? You've taken it to the next level then, a regular Hollywood movie set? Don't forget my cut; that porn is gonna make a mint . . . Six months already? Damn time's flying. Don't worry, I got the matter settled with the OB doc; he was stalling, wanted more money, but he's willing to do it now. He'll be there when it's time for the bitch to deliver. Yeah, I gotta get going, too. I got work to finish up here. So who's your date with? Shut the fuck up, Bishop's wife? You're kidding! You trying to wiggle into those panties now?" He grins. "Good luck, Ted, talk to ya later."

Sarita's hand is covering her mouth, she is sick to her stomach and she flees to the restroom down the hall.

Lee comes out of his office, and walks to the front desk looking for her. "Where'd you go?" he yells.

"I'm in here," she answers from the restroom in the most normal tone she can muster, huddled as far away from the door as possible with her arms folded tightly across her roiling stomach. "I think the salad I had for lunch had some bad chicken in it. I'm really sick." Sarita, sickened by what she has heard is trying not to crumple to her knees.

"I've got poker tonight. You lock up, then get home and stay there. I'll be calling the land line to check on you as usual and I'll be over to your place when I'm done. And Sarita, think of a new game for tonight, maybe you can be a harem girl or something. Ha!"

She hears the office door close just in time to drown out the sound of her heaving. With hot tears and mascara streaming down her face, Sarita hangs over the toilet, gagging and retching from the thought of what these monsters are doing and the hell she's living in.

Ira paced back and forth in his room till late in the night, then tossed and turned before he fell asleep thinking about Julie and what Ted Silar is up to and when sleep finally came he fell into a dream.

*A middle-eastern man is kneeling in front of him, his hands are bound, and a gag has been forced into his mouth. His fiery eyes smoldering with hate. Then out from a cloud comes a whirling wheel of golden light, and it lingers above his head. Raina appears out of the spiraling light. She holds a thick, coiled snake above his head; a bold chain pattern runs the course of its back. It appears to Ira to be one of the snakes that bit him, and it sends shivers through his spine. This time, though, the snake is docile. Then the bound man spits the gag out of his mouth and begins to hiss; his tongue is split at the tip like the licks of a flame, and it darts in and out of his mouth. Then his teeth turn to fangs. Ira looks above his head and watches as the coiled snake straightens and becomes rigid. It evolves into a stick, dripping with blood.*

He is startled awake, his palms are sweating and a thick knot has formed in his stomach. The dream is profound. He knows that the man in it is responsible for his mother's death. He ponders the dream's meaning long into the early morning hours and determines from his contemplation that the world's demise when it comes, will come, not from a reptile in a garden, or a woman with an apple, but from real men with deadpan eyes who have no conscience, no soul.

At breakfast, Rosa pours Ira a cup of coffee and sits down across from him with a cup of tea. "I haven't heard you pace in circles like you did last night since you were fourteen. Is there something you want to talk about?"

"You could hear me?"

"Yes, but I had already noticed that something was eating you at supper last night, instead of you eating your supper. What is it, son? What's wrong?"

Ira doesn't want to spill his guts about Julie, but he tells Rosa that the pressure of this undercover operation is getting intense and then he describes the dream he had in detail. Rosa listens without interrupting or questioning.

When he has finished talking she nods her head as if she had been there. "I have seen this man in my dreams, also. I am certain that you will soon come to know who he is."

"How do you know that?"

"Because in my dream, there was a sister who told me that you would."

Ira stood listening, perplexed for a moment. Then he turns and sets his cup in the sink. "I'll be home late tonight, go ahead and eat without me."

After he leaves, Rosa sits and thinks about her dream, her hands wrapped around her cup.

Ira calls Herroso on his way to the office. He knows he should wait for Herroso to call him, but he's on pins and needles about Silar and Julie and it gets the better of him. "What's going on, man?"

"Ira, what's up? You calling 'bout Silar and the Bishop woman?"

"Yeah, what happened?"

"Nothing much. They ordered food, which *she* just pushed around on her plate. He ordered a bottle of wine and poured her a glass, which she didn't touch and they talked very little. It looked to me like she wanted to bolt from the minute she got there until they left. He walked her to her car and opened the door for her, then he put his hand on her back and it looked like he was trying to get her to linger, but she got in fast and left right away."

Ira's eyes narrow as he listens. "That son of a bitch," he whispers under his breath.

"What was that, Ira? You're fading in and out, I didn't hear what you said."

"I said, 'So that's it?'"

"Yeah, that's it. I followed her home and she got there a little after eight."

"Thanks for the report, Hero. Catch you later."

"Later, Ira."

Ira drops his phone in his shirt pocket.

What a low-life scumbag. What kind of a dirtball tries to take advantage of a newly widowed woman? A bloodsucking louse, that's who. A parasite of the worst kind, one with suspicions and something tells Ira he's not the type who is going to forget about the wife of the employee he was responsible for killing, ever.

The warm lavish water cascades down on her face, and she lathers herself like she's just stepped out of a cesspool. Just the thought of sitting across the table from

Silar last night makes her feel dirty and even though she'd showered after she'd gotten home, she still feels dirty. She knows when a man is sexually tempted and even though it was subtle, he was dropping hints.

"Yuck," she says out loud as she scrubs harder.

I can't wait to talk to Ira about this, he'll make me feel better, I know he will.

When she steps out of the shower she can hear the phone ringing in her purse on the chair by the bed. That's him now, she thinks and she hurries to dry herself off, then dashes across the bedroom to get to the phone before it stops ringing. Her heart sinks when she remembers Ira gave her a special phone and that's not the phone that's ringing. It's the attorney who's handling Greg's estate. She lets the call roll into voice mail. She finishes dressing with a lack of enthusiasm. Her mom has made plans to try to lift her spirits and she sighs a heavy sigh just thinking about it.

Ira spent the entire ride to the office with his ear glued to the phone. Now he's sitting at his desk massaging the bridge of his nose. He'd talked to Sarita after calling Herroso, and she reported what she'd heard Lee saying to Ted yesterday, giving him a new name to check into. Within seconds he was on the phone with Lucius asking him to dig up everything he could, if anything, on a man named Ab dul a, Na gi bull a, as Sarita spelled it to him.

Then he called Father Lelo and told him the chilling new info that Sarita gave him about the Afghan virgins, a pregnancy, an OB doctor and porn productions that she'd overheard Lee talking about on the phone. His mind began hatching ideas while he was still on the phone with Sarita, on the how and when. The where, she'd told him, was on Otay Mountain. Father Lelo was appalled, almost moved to tears. He insisted on being a part of the team that made the rescue and he began discussing with Ira how to infiltrate the compound with minimal danger to the children.

From the details Sarita had given Ira, it seemed rational to assume that there is a porn studio inside that compound on Otay involving Afghan children and as implausible as it may sound to the world, instead of forcing the sex slaves to have abortions, they're going to start delivering their babies into slavery and the porn business from the moment of birth. They are creating a sub-genre of humans. It is deplorable, despicable and repulsive, hard to even think about, but these monsters are making it happen here in the United States and they've got to be stopped.

Just as Ira thinks things can't get much worse, his phone rings. It is Lucius calling him back. "Ira, got some info for you."

"Damn Lu, that was fast."

"Yeah, well, it turned out to be a grand-slam, buddy. I'm confident the name you gave me is actually spelled Abdullah Najibullah. He's in the database. He's a refugee who fled Afghanistan during the Soviet occupation in 1980. Najibullah, is also known as Daboia. He made a name for himself as a young man spying for the premier Intelligence service of the Islamic Republic of Pakistan, after fleeing a Soviet bombing raid of his village, my sources said. Besides channeling money to the mujahideen for the Islamic Republic, he played a key role in the capture of a large cache of Soviet weapons in transit in

1982. Apparently he was able to do this through his connections to Afghanistan's local transit mafia. The weapons subsequently landed in the hands of guerilla militants; the mujahideen groups fighting the Soviet Army at the time, and in exchange for his intelligence he was given safe passage on a London bound British Airways plane.

It is believed he slipped into the U.S. under the radar, due to a misspelling of his name on a background check early in 1983. And now, here's a bit that you're going to find really interesting. Because he had eluded capture many times while crossing the border from Pakistan to Afghanistan on spying missions, playing both sides, his spy nickname became Daboia. I looked up the word Daboia and found it's from a Hindi word meaning "that which lies hidden," and guess what? It's also the nickname given to the Pakistani Russell's Viper for its disposition, its elusiveness and its ruthlessness." Daboia hadn't surfaced anywhere in a good way, or, for that matter, in a bad way up until now.

Ira's floored. "*Holy* shit! Russell's Viper! Son of a bitch, Lu, my brain is spinning. Great job!" Ira sits back, letting it sink in for a moment. "I got a lot to sort through here and I need to start working on a plan to stop this raw sewage from hitting the fan. Give me a call if you learn anything more about Daboia. Oh yeah, before I forget, did you find anything else out about Stevens' daughter, Sarita?"

"Will do on Daboia, and no, nothing on the girl yet, I'm still digging into her background. Later, Ira."

Ira sits in repose for a moment, thinking. He is beginning to realize that this is the man from his dream. The man that the woman in Rosa's dream said he would come to know soon, the man responsible for his mother's death. According to the intelligence given to Lucius about Daboia and the Afghanistan Transit Mafia, it's not so far-fetched to think he could be involved in human trafficking and his tentacles are straight from the mid-east, where the slavery of women is pretty much legal; where you pay a dowry for a woman or child once and then you own her. Here, he's going to make a community of sub-humans, sex slaves used to make an enormous amount of residual income. Income for what though? Terrorism? If so, then the male children born could become suicide bombers or be groomed for the mujahideen; thus bringing a national security aspect to the Daboia's evil plan. He went over the whole thing in his mind. "Son of a bitch," he whispered, "If that's what's going on, than this country has a mid-eastern terrorist group working to take us down from within.

Taking some time, he gives serious thought to the situation and considers who would make the best team to send in, to take these bastards down with minimal risk to the children. He thinks long and hard.

Julie's sitting at the kitchen table holding Miss Jingles on her lap. Her father and mother have been taking care of Julie's household matters, picking up the mail, watering plants, etc.. Her mother is insisting on going to Balboa Park for some light shopping and lunch today, just to get Julie out of the house and back into some sort of normalcy, but Julie doesn't feel up to it; she never feels up to it anymore. She sits at the table, petting Miss Jingles while looking at her mom across the kitchen standing at the sink with her hands in the dishwater. She knows what her mom is thinking right this minute. *Poor Julie, with her elbow on the table and her hand holding her chin up, her kitty in her lap, it's all she has left of her and Greg; she must be pining for him.*

*But I'm not,* Julie wishes she could scream out loud. I'm brooding because Ira hasn't called me yet and I've been waiting for him to call all morning. What would her mother do if she came right out and said, "He makes me feel better, Mom; there's just something about him that makes me feel alive?" She'd disapprove, that's what she would do. Julie feels bad for Greg, bad for what happened to him. She is sure Greg was forced into his criminal activities with death threats, but her question is that if he called the FBI in the end, why didn't he call them in the beginning? Every time she thinks about it the anger surfaces and it feels as though a black cloud is hovering above her head.

"Dear, you look so rundown and pale. A little sunshine and some nutrition will be good for you," her mother tells her while rubbing some lotion on her hands.

*Fine, let's get it over with,* Julie thinks, as she sets Miss Jingles by her food dish, she picks up her purse. Her mom follows her out the door.

The breeze rustles the canopy of a quaint café in Balboa Park and Julie checks her watch over the remains of their lunch. She'd been certain that Ira would have called by *now,* wanting to know if she'd got home safe and what she and Ted Silar had talked about. *This is annoying, why hasn't he called*?

Just as she's thinking about that situation, Ted walks up from behind. Her mother looks up at him, recognizing him from the funeral and trying to act amicable, she clears her throat with a forced smile.

Julie, sensing her discomfort, turns around and looks up. "Ted!" she says as her brain collides with an asteroid, then she stammers. "What are you doing here?"

"Julie, it's a pleasure to see you again so soon." He's dressed in a light gray suit and pouring on the charm. "I frequent this little bistro for lunch quite often. It's one of my favorites. What a pleasant surprise to find that you like it, too."

Julie's skin is about to crawl off her body. "Oh, I never come here; the food is much too rich for me."

Ted laughs. "No wonder you stay as healthy looking as you do."

Julie didn't like the way he looked at her.

"Mind if I join you?" Ted asked.

"Well, actually we were just about to leave." Julie picks the check up off the table.

"Let me get that for you and I won't take no for an answer," he tells her with a smile as he takes the check from her hand. "Perhaps we can have dinner again sometime?"

She forces a smile. "I'm not feeling well these days, Ted and I need to get going," she says, trying to avoid angering him with a flat-out rejection. "Thank you for lunch and have a nice day."

He watches her and her mother weave through the tables as they walk away. She's way to cool to me, he's thinking. I was her dead husband's boss, it would be normal for her to respect me, even feel a sense of closeness to me. I've known Greg since he was in high school. There's something not quite right about the way that grieving widow treats me.

By the time she gets back to her parents' house, Julie has a splitting headache. She's irked by Silar's advances toward her and even more frustrated that Ira still hasn't called so she can tell him about it. She tells her mother her head is pounding and that she's going to her room to lie down for a while.

She takes the phone Ira gave her and sets it on the nightstand, staring at it for a moment. What would he think if I called *him*? But what would I say to him. Why haven't you called me? No, I simply tell him about Silar showing up at the restaurant today. He would want to know. She calls Ira's number, it rolls into voicemail, She hangs up frustrated.

When she awakens, the sun is low and dusk is fading the shadows and for a moment her mind is cloudy. Then she remembers where she is and she thinks about the phone. She sits up and reaches for it, checking to see if he called. She shrinks back down and stares up at the scant shadow of the light fixture on the ceiling. No call from him. It irritates her, and she hates felling like this.

All cell phones are turned off and the meeting is a closed-door gathering where nothing that's said will leave the room.

"The point is, it's an unprecedented crime and it needs to be handled with an unprecedented approach."

Ira's voice is strong. "Their ability to detonate a bomb on a military base and move a counterfeit armored truck around without detection speaks volumes about their capability. I wouldn't suggest this if I didn't think it was absolutely critical that we surprise them with something so unexpected, we catch them red-handed. It's necessary, so we make sure they die in a prison cell somewhere and not disappear underground."

Major General Weston is touchy about the explosion on base and he peppers back. "I don't need to be reminded of the threat that this enemy is, young man." He stares Ira down for a moment. "I've seen plenty of evil in wartime, but this is the most heinous crime I've ever heard of. If al-Qaeda were to get its hands on child porn made with Muslim children in the United States and release it on the Internet for the world to see, I don't think I need to describe the magnitude of the shit storm that would hit the globe. It is not just a matter of human trafficking, it's also a matter of national security that must be dealt with swiftly and silently."

Father Lelo's been quiet all day, a spectator until now. "Excuse me, I know I should remain a bystander in this, but everyone's been here hashing this out all day and since I'm the one who brought us all together and with all due respect to General Weston, I'd like to put in my nickel's worth. There's only one shot here and if we fail they'll slip underground and surface somewhere else, likely even stronger. It sounds like Daboia and Castello will be at the compound when that shipment of children is delivered. I think Ira's idea about using burqas could work. I think the best team for the job in this case would be female Marines. We need people who are small enough in stature as to emulate children beneath burqas, but tough as nails and trained for battle. I think an all-female Special Operations team would be most beneficial for this type of engagement. It gives us the best chance of getting inside that compound and taking their two top men out with less risk to the lives of the children inside. And the silk that Ira was talking about has been on the Office of Naval Research's list for decades. As you know, it's already been replicated and can make a traditional flak jacket, or in this case, a flack body suit, that's virtually weightless which could be worn under the burqas. I'm not a man who readily accepts that violence is the answer, but I'm smart enough to understand that sometimes war is a moral necessity to fend off evildoers who have nothing to offer but oppression. This plan would save and protect the lives of innocent children while assuring as few casualties as possible for our troops."

Major General Weston's patience has been tried numerous times throughout this meeting, but he agrees that the interior of the compound needs to be breached and the children inside need to be protected before apprehending the enemy. "I'm not jumping up and down about this idea, but the thought of children being killed when they're the reason this mission is going to be executed in the first place is not anything I want on my shoulders. I agree the best chance we have is to secure the building from the inside first, but a female Special Ops team has never been used before. I would insist on a back-up team of men around the perimeter of the building and a sniper team somewhere in the foothills. But first I have to sell it to the Pentagon. My first inclination is that they'll never approve it. However, I'll try to make the argument with the Secretary of Defense, using his own statement that the armed services will continue to review additional job positions that may be opened for women, and I quote, 'Ensuring the mission is met with the best qualified, and most capable, regardless of gender.' Even though the words have been said, 'best qualified and most capable' are relative terms. So the odds in favor of this idea are not good. Now, if that's all, gentlemen, my time is valuable, and I've given you plenty of it. Colonel Kendall, I'll get back to you, when I know the answer."

"We're obliged, General Weston."

When Ira walks out of the meeting room, he turns his phone on and checks his watch. It's going on 7:30 p.m.. The whole day is shot and he hasn't had a chance to talk to Julie yet. He looks at his phone and is surprised she tried to call. He calls her number.

When Julie sees it is Ira calling, a warm sensation flows to her cheeks, but she answers the phone in a flat tone; trying to hide her eagerness. "Hello?"

"Julie, it's me. Is now a good time?"

*Is now a good time? Last night or even this morning would have been a good time.* "Yes, it's fine," she says, her voice composed.

Even though it's good to hear her voice and he's glad she's safe, it sounds to Ira as though Julie doesn't want to be bothered, almost unfriendly, as if she wants to get this over with quickly. He decides to not annoy her further, and keeps the conversation on a dutiful note so avoiding cordiality he cuts through the chase. "What did Silar talk to you about?"

Julie's eyebrows knit together. Why all of a sudden so aloof? She thinks, hating the unsettled feeling in her stomach. She responds with a reserved tone of her own. "He spoke about Greg most of the time."

"Did he mention anything that would be relevant to this operation?"

"No, he kept saying things like he misses Greg and he can imagine how lonely I must be. He did ask me if I've gone through Greg's things yet. He said sometimes it helps the grieving process."

"He's trolling, fishing to see if Greg left any trace of evidence behind. He's up to his eyeballs in the cause of Greg's death and he's using you to find out if there's any proof of it lying around. Did he ask you to go out with him again?"

I didn't go *out* with him, I *met* him there, she is thinking, a tad rankled. "*No,*" she emphasizes. "But he did ask me today."

"Today!" Ira's voice is raised. "You met him today too?"

"*No,* I went to Balboa Park with my mom for lunch and he showed up there."

"You mean out of the blue, he showed up out of the blue?"

"Yes, and to be honest, I don't like the way he looks at me, like I'm a conquest or something."

"He may be tracking your movements."

"Oh, my god, Ira, that scares me."

She is vulnerable, Ira thinks. What Silar did to Greg is merciful compared to what he'll do to her if he finds out she's working with law enforcement. Silar is a dangerous man and a womanizer and he'll keep hounding Julie until he gets what he wants. So Ira's going to have to keep her out of Silar's physical presence, yet if she comes off too cold and makes herself unavailable, it will throw up a red flag. There's only one thing he can do. He must remove Julie from the equation, perhaps send her on a vacation to heal from the loss of her husband, or at least he must make Silar thinks she is going away.

"Julie, if you could go anywhere in the world, where would you go?"

Julie narrows her eyes. "Greg asked me the same thing. He said he'd like to take me somewhere and spend a mint on me. He asked me how I felt about that and where I would want to go."

"What did you tell him?"

"London, I'd like to travel around England."

"Well, that's where I'm going to send your phone, but you'll go to the rectory."

"You think that's how he's tracking me?"

"That's my guess."

"But won't he get suspicious if the phone just sits at the airport?"

Ira has to smile at her innocence. "I'm sure we can find someone across the pond who'll be willing to take it sight-seeing for you."

There is not a cloud in the sky this morning as Carlos bounces along the dirt road going to the rectory. He's just hung up from talking with Ira when he hits the roughest part and the washboard vibrates the targets and ammunition he just bought to the edge of the seat. He pushes them back to keep them from tumbling onto the floor.

When he walks into the kitchen his arms are full. He sets everything down on the counter. Linda acknowledges his presence with a slight shift of her eyes, then continues to pound out an e-mail. After she's finished she looks up at him and says, "I'm not going to be able to stall much longer without going home. Lee's bouncing off the walls. I had to call him this morning because he was complaining to Sarita that I'm not calling him enough. Poor Sarita! God, I can't stand the thought of her living like that any longer. When is this nightmare going to end?"

"Not soon enough for anyone," he empathizes. "Hopefully, a couple more weeks is all. As a coincidence, I was just talking to Ira on the way here. He told me that Ted Silar is on Julie Bishop's tail. He is sure Silar's tracking her. So Ira wants to pretend he has sent her to London and what we want to know from you is how well do you know London?"

Linda watches Carlos as he loads rounds into a Colt .45. "Quite well. London's become a fashion mecca. Why do you want to know?"

He snaps the chamber shut. "I was hoping you would say that, because you are going to pretend to accompany Julie there." He lays the gun down on the counter and picks up a target, holding it to his chest. "You're going to learn to shoot a gun, just in case you have to protect me from anyone who may have followed your mattresses out here."

She leans back, folding her arms across her chest, staring at the black silhouette of a human torso on Carlos' chest. Lee enters her mind, and mischief surfaces in her expression. "Well, of course, I'll have to find something suitable to wear to the firing squad, I mean range."

Carlos smiles. "The *range,*" he emphasizes "is in the backyard."

"The phones are switched, the calls are forwarded and the phones have been packed into a box which should be boarding San Diego's Southwest, flight 8010 about now. I've just dropped Julie off at the rectory," Father Lelo is telling Ira.

"Good. She told Silar three days ago that she was leaving. It seemed to pacify him when she said that it was Greg's wish to lavish her with a trip and that she was going to honor his wishes, but he sounded dejected when she told him *Linda* was going to escort her. And Lee Stevens put on an Academy Award performance pretending that he was peeved that Linda was meeting her in London."

Father Lelo steers his truck to the Camp Pendleton exit. "It's hard to believe that people like that exist."

Ira changes the subject. "Any speculation when Major General Weston will get back to us?"

"They know they don't have time to waste, so I hope within the next twenty-four hours. I'm on my way to visit some Marines at sickbay right now and afterward I thought I'd try to call him."

"Let me know when you've gotten word from him. I'm going to teach Julie how to shoot a gun today, so I'm driving to the rectory now."

"She told me you were going to give her instructions and yes, you'll be the first to know what General Weston tells me."

When Ira drives into the driveway of the rectory, Carlos and Linda are alongside the building wearing army-green utility clothes and protective head gear. Carlos is standing behind Linda teaching her how to shoot a pistol at a target. Julie is leaning against a tree several yards away, watching.

Julie is wearing a pair of skinny jeans, brown boots, and a white tank top, looking casual with her hands in her pockets and her hair pulled back in one long braid, yet Ira can't help but notice there's refinement in every detail about her.

Through the corner of her eye, Julie catches a glimpse of the silver Toyota Tundra pickup truck rolling into the driveway. She turns, and through the dust kicked up by his tires, she sees Ira through the window when the truck comes to a halt.

Ira's pulse quickens and he wonders if she's as nervous as he is. This is the first time they'll be close to one another since being in the private room at the Seirra Center, and this time there won't be a table inbetween them. *Cool the engines,* he tell himself *and stop gawking like an idiot.* Tiny beads of perspiration form on his brow. He takes a good deep breath and gains control.

She can see him leaning over in the truck, now gathering things in his arms. She is almost breathless with anticipation, her heart rate quickens. *Jeez Julie, pull it together,* she thinks as she takes a long, cleansing breath.

Ira gets out of the truck and slings a canvas bag onto his shoulder, he stacks his arms with safety glasses, ear protectors and cardboard targets, all riding on top of a six-pack of cold, bottled iced tea. He's wearing a black sleeveless T-shirt, and dark-tan cargo pants.

"It's getting warm out." He raises his voice above the gun fire and in between shots he shouts, "I thought you guys might like something to drink, I brought iced tea, it has lemon in it." *Ok enough, stop the mindless babble,* he thinks.

Linda and Carlos both turn around and Carlos acknowledges him with a wave, then they finish shooting their rounds.

Julie walks toward him, reaching out to lend a hand, as he edges toward an old wooden bench. "Let me help you with some of that," she says, in an elevated tone.

One of the ear protectors gets tangled up with one of the bottles and when she tries to take the six-pack from him, the ear protector falls to the ground. "Oops, sorry."

They both bend down to retrieve it at the same time. The neckline of Julie's tank top falls away from her skin, exposing a moderate amount of tanned cleavage. The view catches Ira's attention and for a moment you couldn't pry his eyes away with a wrecking bar.

She notices and feels him staring, which sends subtle shivers through the course of her torso down through her thighs. Then she feels her cheeks turning rosy.

When he shifts his eyes back to hers, he realizes she's watching and for a moment they're trapped in a captivated stare.

Ira is the first to break away when he hears Carlos call out, "I'll take one of those teas now," and he sets his arm load of stuff down on the bench.

Carlos and Linda walk over to Julie and Ira.

"Linda's a quick learner," Carlos tells Ira as he slides his safety glasses up on his head. Then he takes a bottle of tea, opens it and after a few swallows, adds, "We've been at it for a couple hours now. I think it's time for a break." Ira nods.

Linda turns to Julie. "It's not as bad as I thought it would be. It's somewhat taxing on the arms, but it's challenging and I like a good challenge."

"Well," Julie says, unsettled by the thought of shooting a gun, "I'm thinking I'm about to make a complete fool of myself. I know nothing about guns."

Carlos pats Ira on the back. "Don't worry, this guy here knows a thing or two about shooting. You're in good hands, you'll be comfortable before you know it. The target's all yours."

Ira takes a Colt .45 out of his canvas range bag and straps the holster to his hips. Then he picks up one of the targets and turns to Julie. "Okay, shall we get started?"

Linda smiles at Julie. "You'll do just fine." She and Carlos walk into the rectory.

Ira runs through a physical description of the pistol with Julie explaining to her how it works after which they put on their protective gear. "Okay, Julie," Ira says loudly so she can hear him over the ear plugs, "you stand right here." He takes her shoulders and guides her to a spot, then points to the ground. "Put the tips of your toes there, at the line."

He stands behind her with his chest pressed tight against her back and brings his arms up around both sides of her shoulders, enfolding her between his biceps. He places the gun in her hands and with his hands on top of hers, he guides her finger to the trigger and then rests his finger on top of hers.

Julie's mind is blur. She can smell the lingering clean scent of the soap on his skin and she knows she should be concentrating on the target, but her thoughts are on his thick shoulders and his iron-hard arms around her. *I like this,* she's thinking. "I've never done this before," she says.

"I know," he says, his finger continuing to rest on hers, while he thinks, *neither have I.* "Now look at the bead on the end of the barrel and place it where you want the round to hit." He lets go of her hands. "Okay, when you're ready, squeeze the trigger gently."

Julie squeezes the trigger and closes her eyes at the same time. She misses the target completely. "Where'd it go?" She says, opening her eyes.

"Way high; try again."

She squeezes again, and just grazes the lower right corner of the cardboard. "That's not where I was aiming," she says, perturbed, and after a few more misses, she gets disgusted. "I'll never be good at this."

Ira is patient. He smiles. "You're closing your eyes in anticipation of the shot. Let's try it again, this time keep your eyes open and put your cheek up against my cheek." He leans over her shoulder and moves his face close.

In that same exact moment she turns toward him and her lips graze his cheek. She pulls back in surprise, her eye-lashes fluttering. She says, "I have to do better," nervously, trying to deflect his attention from what just happened.

Her warm breath sends a shiver down his spine and he smiles at her. "You will."

He turns toward the target again.

She stares at his profile for a moment, not able to ignore the sheer confidence displayed in his expression. *He must be really good at this,* she thinks. Then she lays her cheek next to his and aims the pistol at the target.

"Okay, now relax," he says, "keep your eyes open, let all your breath out, now squeeze the trigger." She does what he tells her, and the bullet smashes through the black silhouette's abdomen. She turns to Ira, her blue eyes twinkling. "I could do this all day," she laughs.

"So could I," he says in a low whisper.

It has been two weeks since the Department of Defense gave the go ahead to assemble a female commando Special Ops team to raid the child porn compound on Otay. Major General Weston has chosen Captain Karin Channary to lead the team. She will also be wired for monitoring in real time.

Father Lelo has volunteered to fly a chopper to carry Ira, two snipers, and four backup Marines to the foothills when the time comes. Father Lelo and Ira will be able to watch the raid live from a field command post set up on Otay. The operation has been dubbed Operation Golden Orb, not just because of the spinning gold orb that recurs in Ira's visions, but also because of the Golden Orb Weaver spider found in Madagascar. The spider's drag-line silk is as strong as steel and lighter then Kevlar and the Navy's scientists have spent many years researching and developing a textile imitating the silk which could be used for body armor. The mission for the female Marines is to covertly overtake the cargo of children and switch places with them at the bank in Junction City, where the transfer of the children from a truck to the phony armored vehicle will take place. The female Marines will be wearing traditional burqas, over two-piece body suits made with the imitation spider silk. They will each be armed with a high-powered taser and a semi-automatic Baby Browning pistol, strapped to the inside of their thighs.

Sarita had called Ira three days ago and told him that the plans for the delivery of the Afghan children to the compound on Otay was close to being executed. She thought it would be happening within the next few days.

It is a clear late afternoon in October and the sun is making its descent. Ira is dressed in camouflage gear and is standing in the rectory talking with Herroso, Father Lelo and the six Marines assigned to operation Golden Orb.

As the sun edges closer to the desert floor, a call comes into Linda's phone.

She's sitting in the living room with Julie. Ira shifts his dark eyes toward her. His guess is dead on. Linda motions that it's Sarita. Herroso hustles to the communication equipment on the kitchen table.

Linda touches the screen on her phone and answers it after the chatter in the Rectory has turned to silence. "Hello?"

"Mom," Sarita says in a hushed voice, then she articulates each code through the phone clear and quick. "Raina, Bank, 18, 94, Sam, X, Mat, 8, Cal, Oco, 98, 8." Then she hangs up.

Linda looks at Herroso, who nods, signaling he's heard the coded message through the phone tap as he's writing it down. He tears the note off the pad and hands it to Ira.

Ira reads it, he checks his watch. "They're mobile," he says. "It's starting, they'll be in Junction City at 1800 hours via Route 94." He walks to the map on the table, and taps his finger on one of the red push pins. "They're in a Samax rig, Hazmat placard 8." Then he trails his finger along the map. "Coming in through the port at

Calexico to Ocotillo, on Highway 98 and then Highway 8." Ira pulls his phone out of his pocket and pushes a speed dial number, for General Weston. Once he has the go-ahead from the Marine Corps, he shouts the code word, "Raina! It's time, boys. Let's move!"

Everyone has a job to do and as with any military assignment they make it happen, quickly!

Herroso picks up the phone and calls the number for the San Diego Airport. General Weston has made an arrangement with Southwest Airlines to delay a Boeing 737's flight to Mexico until Herroso's call. Then it will fly over the compound site on Otay Mountain with precision timing to drown out the sound of Father Lelo's chopper when it lands in the foothills. Herroso tells Southwest to stand by.

The six Marines that General Weston wanted stationed outside the compound have been waiting at the rectory. They zip up their flak jackets, double-check their rifles and clips and grab their gear.

Two of the Marines are scout snipers. Corporal Donavon Franks is a med school dropout who explained he prefers the elite School of Infantry at Pendleton to the School of Medicine at Berkeley, and his nickname is One Shot Doc. His partner, Al McKnight, is also a deadly shot, but tonight he'll be the spotter. He and Franks will lug their equipment up into the tower that Julie played in as a child, about 300 meters from the compound. The other four Marines will secure the compound's perimeter.

Ira reaches for a duffle bag with his gear in it and slings it across his shoulder. Then he grabs his M4. He stops for a moment and turns to Julie, who is standing across the room. Their eyes lock unwaveringly in frozen silence. They have become close in these last three weeks and she's worried about his safety.

Julie tugs at her maroon cardigan, pulling it tight around her body, still fixed on his eyes, then she folds her arms across her chest. She knows what it's like to say goodbye to someone, never to see them again. She swallows, choking back her tears. "Be careful," she says in a soft-voice, forcing herself to believe that she will see him alive again.

Ira's eyes are dark and intense. "You know what to do," he says, not a question.

Julie reaches into her sweater pocket and pulls out her phone. She holds it up.

Linda shifts her eyes toward him and they both look at Ira with affirmation.

He hesitates, his eyes lingering on Julie for a moment longer. He wishes he could say something to her, hug her, or kiss her goodbye, but he can't, not in front of his comrades and not in front of Father Lelo. What would they all think? He gives her a nod, turns and looks at Father Lelo.

Julie bites down on her lip and a tear slips from her eye.

Father Lelo, dressed in a gray-green flight suit, stuffs his rosary into his top pocket. He grabs his rucksack, tosses it onto his back, then with the sign of the cross, he gives everyone in the room a blessing for a safe return, including in the blessing, a prayer for the safety and rescue of the enslaved children on Otay. When Father is finished, they all follow Ira out the door.

He crosses the gravel driveway with long strides and climbs into the cockpit of the chopper while checking his watch. According to the U.S. Navy observatory, the sun is calculated to set at around 6:50 p.m., about fifty-two minutes from now and they'll want to be in the sandbox and situated before dark to count the number of adversaries, and to wait for the arrival of the armored truck.

Within minutes, six young, tough-as-steel Marines, faces streaked with camouflage paint, helmets buckled at the chin, adrenalin pumping hard beneath their vests, are on the sideboards of the idling chopper. Their leather gloves grip the Iron bird. The turbulence from the rotors sends a plume of swirling sand into the air, and a heavy pounding in their ears. A thin layer of dust begins to settle on their goggles.

As the chopper levitates, then hovers, Julie, Linda, and Herroso stand in the doorway of the rectory, watching Father Lelo, curled into the cockpit with his knees to his chest and a bulky headset fixed to his ears. He tilts the chopper to one side and swings her tail rotors around. Father Lelo grips the lever and pushes it forward. Ira is watching from the passenger seat. The bird takes off in a shot like a huge black hummingbird against the dimming orange of the setting sun, heading toward Otay Mountain.

On this evening, as people all over America dine, watch TV, gamble, worship, ride the subway, shop, jog, read a book; in other words, while American's are busy being free, a mission is quietly being launched by the heroes of this free land to snuff out a reign of terror, to stop slavery from spreading and to save, at least some oppressed and helpless human beings from a life of subjugation.

Operation Golden Orb is launched at 4:54 p.m.

Linda and Julie turn and walk back into the rectory.

Linda calls Lee's number. Julie calls Ted Silar.

Jorge Sanchez grinds the gears of his Samax Tanker, slowing it to a crawl in the squash of traffic, inching their way toward the USA's port of entry in Calexico, California.

Jorge has all his paperwork in order, but crossing the U.S. border hauling hazardous waste is still a nerve-wracking event. Even though he's crossed the border here many times before, there is always the chance that your load has not yet been cleared for a go-ahead, causing a serious delay and usually a migraine headache.

As Jorge sends pressure through the lines and the brakes bring the tanker to a halt, an armed CBP officer emerges from the booth and walks toward the front end of the truck, checking his decal. The officer seems to recognize the truck and it looks like this is going to be quick and painless. He walks around to the driver's side and Jorge rolls his window down.

Hot, heavy exhaust fumes assault his face and wend their way into the truck's cab as the officer looks up and gives him a slight nod. "Afternoon. Driver's license and paperwork," he says, unsmiling.

Jorge has a trucker's passport, a FAST card, in his wallet. He digs in his back pocket and pulls it out. Then he reaches for the required Hazmat shipping papers, along with the thick manifest of paperwork required to cross.

The officer attaches the cards along with the paperwork to a clipboard and walks back to the booth while flipping through the documents.

As Jorge waits for the officer, he watches as a drug-sniffing German Shepherd scurries around the red cab of an 18-wheeler that's been pulled into the secondary lanes. Moments later, two officers seize the driver, handcuff and pat him down. Jorge taps his fingers on the steering wheel while he watches, wondering if the drugs were planted on that poor guy's rig by a cartel, or if the driver is the actual offender. Then he wonders whether the U.S. will ever get serious about curtailing the profuse flow of contraband gushing into it. That, he thinks, would take a significant increase in military resources.

Jorge has no idea to what extent the evil that smuggling has reached. Innocent himself of all criminal doing, his rig has been bought off by Daboia's cartel and is being used as transport. He is totally unaware of the fact that a load of living, breathing female children, bound, gagged and drugged have been smuggled into the dark underbelly of his truck through a modified, but concealed hatch door. They are treated like animals being sent to slaughter, unable to even breathe except for the oxygen tubes shoved into their noses. They are facing a future that is literally worse than death.

The CBP officer emerges from the booth, walking toward his truck. Jorge rolls his window down, assuming that's he's been cleared, yet with a twinge of angst knowing there's never a guarantee.

When the officer appears at his window, he doesn't hand Jorge his paperwork right away. Instead, his eyes wolf-like and suspicious, stare into Jorge's eyes. "Where's this load heading?"

"Samax in San Diego, sir."

"What route?"

"Ninety-eight to Eight."

The officer hesitates and then he nods, handing the paperwork to Jorge. "You're one of the few maquiladoras that dispose of that shit properly," he says under his breath, while stepping back and waving his hand. "Proceed through."

Jorge revs his diesel engine and shifts into gear. He rolls the truck through the gates of the border into a north-side parking lot.

From there a U.S. driver will take the load. Jorge hops down out of the truck, leaving it idle. The new driver nods at Jorge, and signs for the load.

As Jorge walks back across the border to a car that his company has waiting for him, the new driver rolls away in the Samax Tanker. The driver is Agent Mike Crosby, the agent who'd been placed by the FBI as a mole inside the Castello organization two years ago. For Crosby, getting the assignment to drive this particular truck was a stroke of luck for the FBI, even though they were ready if they needed a plan "B." Sometimes they say in the Bureau, "It's better to be lucky than smart."

Ira's buddy Carlos has been assigned as a lookout and is parked on the U.S. side of the border in a white Nissan Altima. He's been watching the flow of trucks crossing the border for an hour now, but has been paying particular attention to the trucks with Hazmat class 8 placard, and he's been zeroed in on Jorge since he pulled up to the inspection station a few minutes ago. Carlos calls Ira and reports the driver switch to him.

Ira, having the hideous knowledge that inside the pitch-black belly of that hazardous tanker are young girls bound and doped up, relying on oxygen masks for life, is worked up and edgy. The next fifteen minutes will seem like an eternity.

Crosby, the mole, is driving the tanker to Junction City where he'll stop to refuel behind Camp Corners' convenience station. He calls his contact with the

Castello gang, to let him know that he's on time and will be at the bank as planned. Back at the rectory, Herroso is listening in on the call through the phone tap.

Crosby will pull up to the diesel pump in the poorly lit parking lot behind the bank at Camp Corners to refuel. The plan is that four of Daboia's men are expected to be waiting inside the bank to transfer the human cargo from the tanker into the armored truck. The last leg of the journey is the long, remote, inky stretch of Highway 8, bestrewed with tactical check points known for delaying vehicles for up to forty-eight hours. That would be much too long to keep the human cargo alive inside the tanker, which is the reason for the phony armored truck.

At the same time, Ira, still in the chopper with Father Lelo on his way to Otay, is juggling phone calls above the noise of the blades. Swimming in messages from Carlos, Herroso and Crosby, along with updating Captain Karin Channary on the radio, Ira's got his eyes, hands and ears full.

Channary and her commandos have moved into position inside the bank. The ten physically fit female Marines had been dropped in the desert two meters behind the bank, wearing black bodysuits made of light-weight armor, carrying blue burqas in backpacks, and other gear on their backs. They crept in low, through the long treck of the harsh desert terrain without a sound, moving into position using shadows and scrub brush for cover. Gradually and in turn, they entered the bank through a window in the back, slipped the burqas on, and entrenched themselves in the main lobby. They waited for Daboia's men and ambushed them unexpectedly as they entered the side door of the bank. Totally surprised, each thug's eyes went wide in amazement as they were seized by the burqa wearing women. They have been immobilized, bound and gagged at gunpoint, except for one. The women are forcing him to take Daboia's calls, to assure Daboia that everything is going according to plan.

After receiving information from Carlos that the hazardous tanker had just left Calexico, Ira gives a go-ahead on the radio to a chartered bus to also leave Calexico. The words Jamal Desert Casino written in bold, red letters above the front window is a ruse. The chartered bus will also pull up to Camp Corners. The bus has two purposes. First, it will be used to shield the view of possible lookouts from Daboia's crew and second, it will be a mobile hospital carrying medical supplies and EMTs for the children, along with a holding cage for Daboia's men.

The tanker truck carrying the child victims will drive to the back of Camp Corners next to the fuel pump.

Soon after the tanker comes to a halt and begins refueling, two of Ted Silar's men will drive up to the bank in the phony armored truck and back it in alongside as if it's picking up cash.

Moments later the chartered bus will arrive. The driver will slow the bus to a crawl in front of Camp Corners to obstruct the view of the rescue of the children, and the female Marines hustling into the back of the phony armored truck.

The non-driver "guard" of the phony armored truck will be replaced by an undercover Border Patrol agent who will force the driver at gun point to continue communicating to Daboia as if nothing were wrong.

A light, westerly breeze rustles through the branches of the chaparral beneath the faint, waning moon of Otay Mountain, while a Boeing 737 leaves a deafening trail low above her foothills. Father Lelo sets the chopper down in a clearing on the slope 1600 meters behind the fire tower at the same time.

The six Marines, two snipers, and four recons, have their boots on the ground with a heap of gear and ammo on their backs before the chopper touches down. In an instant, they branch out into the night skulking through the rocky silted loam of Otay's wilderness. Four of them take off fast down the slope toward the perimeter of the compound. They slide over the top of the fence in seconds, landing with bent knees low to the ground, then crawl on their bellies to their positions, using the dense scrub for cover.

The two snipers crouch low moving up hill, prowling noiselessly through the swaying shadows of the almost impenetrable thicket of scrub oak. They scale the fire-tower like two panthers in the night with ears pinned back, alert and aggressive. When they reach the top, they secure a position that overlooks the foothills and vigorously unpack their gear. They discuss range, wind, drift, and trajectory in a low chatter from their position high above the compound.

Ira and Father Lelo edge their way into position at the old cement foundation where Raina was held captive twenty-five years ago and where they've set up their field command post. They both know that this could be the longest night of their lives.

Minutes ago at Camp Corners, the women Marines packed themselves into the armored truck and are now on their way to Otay. All the Commandos are petite, just barely able to meet the requirements to join the Marine Corp. They hope now to pass themselves off as children. They are riding in darkness, in silence, disguised in blue burqas with only the whites of their eyes visible through the small mesh screen of its veil. They ride shoulder to shoulder, hands folded in their laps, their hearts pounding hard against their chest.

Their thoughts are on the uncertainties that lie ahead. Will they be able to trick a man who is an elusive mastermind and take him and his men by surprise? Or will they be the ones surprised when the back door of the truck opens and they're slaughtered by a ferocious spray of automatic machine-gun fire, shot while crammed tightly in the back of the armored truck?

Their brave hopes are in Ira's plan. If it works, they'll be taken inside the compound for inspection, where the possibility of the element of surprise would give them a 50/50 chance.

From their crow's nest in the fire tower, McKnight stands in the cool night air beneath a blanket of stars, scanning the area with night-vision gear, mapping out the area of engagement and recording target reference points. A light fog begins to drift in. McKnight's body stiffens as he sees movement at the compound.

Six men dressed in militia-like uniforms, pant legs tucked into boots and AK-47s slung on their shoulders, emerge from the door of the corrugated metal building. One of them is talking into a radio and within moments a black, brutish-looking Chrysler 300 sedan, with just its fog lights on, pulls into view from beneath the canopy of the trees. The sedan rolls to about thirty feet from the door of the building, then stops in the shadows of the trees.

McKnight whispers into his radio, telling Ira what's happening below. McKnight thinks it's possible that Daboia and Castello have just arrived. The driver and front passenger get out of the car first, drawing their pistols. Then the two honchos emerge from the backseat. For a moment McKnight can see their faces lit up by the dome light. One of them is of mid-eastern decent and wearing a dark suit, and the other is a short, thick-shouldered, barreled-shaped man carrying a black duffle bag. McKnight consulting a picture confirms that the man carrying the duffle bag is Jimmy Castello. He watches, scrutinizing their movements until they disappear inside the building. Two of the armed men stand guard outside the door, while the other four begin to patrol the outside of the building.

With just the crescent of a pale moon to light the ground, McKnight constantly monitors the current weather conditions and has added the moisture of the fog into his estimates. He also adds the Chrysler 300 to his list of target references points.

Franks, the other sniper, is busy threading a suppressor onto the barrel of his rifle when McKnight spots flickering lights bouncing up the mountain road. He signals to Franks and again radios the information to Ira. Franks whirls around, laying the barrel of his rifle on the tower railing. He puts the crosshairs of the scope on the lights. He watches as the dim headlamps sway and bounce while the vehicle moves through the thicket.

A few seconds later, the phony armored truck emerges from the trees. It rolls toward the door of the metal building. The guards at the door yank their rifles off their shoulders and aim at the truck. In a world where trust is nonexistent, they keep the guns pointed at the windows as the truck comes to a stop alongside them.

Franks watches through the crosshairs of his scope as the gunmen exchange words, their fingers still on the triggers.

The driver of the armored truck is a man of average height, with boxy shoulders, sandy hair and a pockmarked, oval-shaped face. He's been around the block a few times and he knows that if he blows the whistle on his passenger, the undercover Border Patrol Agent, he'll be shot right along with him. So for the sake of self-preservation he keeps his hands on the steering wheel, staring straight ahead and says the code words, "Baby Camel" in a flat, dry tone.

One of the gunmen keeps his aim while the other opens the door of the building. A spear of light is cast along the ground, illuminating him as he stands shouting to the men inside. Then he closes the door and walks to the back of the truck.

The driver remains in his seat, but shifts his eyes to the side mirror. The gunman motions with his rifle for him to unlock the back door. He pushes the button on the dash and the electronic lock buzzes, then clicks and the guard pulls the handle of the heavy door.

As the door swings open, faint moonlight hits the tiny camera sewn into the corner of the mesh screen of Captain Channary's veil, and in an instant Ira and Father Lelo can see the world through a "victim's" eyes.

Yesterday at this time, Channary was safe within the fortress of her military base, preparing for this mission, but in reality nothing can prepare you for a moment like this one. Her heart is racing, pounding high in her throat, and behind the tightly woven lattice of the veil her dark eyes dart back and forth as she surveys her surroundings. The thick silk is stifling, making it difficult to breathe, but she keeps her composure and remains still. It is dark and all she can see behind the gunman's AK47 are trees and thick brush. Seconds later, her eyes meet the gunman's glare through the tiny thick squares of netting. Pangs of panic rush her senses.

It's not hard to show fear as he waves his rifle, motioning for them to get out.

The gunmen stand at each side of the back of the truck, using their rifles to impel the women out, shouting and prodding them with the barrels of their guns.

It's chaotic and terrifying and Channary can't help but think if a trained, well-armed Marine feels this much fear, what must the fear be like for a child or an unarmed adult? She wobbles and hops down from the tailgate of the truck, bent over, pretending to be a weak child. One by one the women Marines follow her, hidden beneath their oppressive burqas. With their shoulders slumped forward and their heads lowered, they appear small enough to pass for children. The gunmen, for the time being seem to have been fooled and they force the women into a single line.

Captain Channary touches the handle of her pistol with a sweaty palm, relieved to have made it out of the truck and then she touches the powerful lipstick-sized taser for courage, knowing that the weapons and the armored body suit beneath her burqa are all she has to get her out of this alive.

Once they're lined up, the guards push them toward the building with their rifles, driving them forward with the hard, steel barrels.

Ten petite women Marines dressed in blue shuttlecock burqas, march like penguins toward the icy, sinister depths of Daboia's world. They stagger forward to whatever fate awaits them, they disappear inside with their arms held close to their sides near their weapons.

Captain Channary is the first to cross the threshold and immediately a blazing light stabs her eyes. She blinks and squints, struggling to keep them open, trying hard not to panic, not to brandish her weapon prematurely. Then after a few seconds her pupils adjust and she looks around, scanning her surroundings, making sure Ira and Father Lelo get a full view of the inside of the building from the images transmitted by her tiny camera to their monitor at the command post.

Ira and Father Lelo are glued to the screen as she scans the inside of the gray, windowless, metal building. It's partitioned off in different sections. On one side, toward the middle of the building is a row of metal tables, three of them, each with six folding chairs. The area appears to be a makeshift cafeteria. Along the right side stands a plain wooden counter where a camp stove sits, along with a giant plastic container holding water. Next to it stands an old refrigerator. Along the left side, partitioned off, is what appears to be a movie set. Both Father and Ira watch the screen with growing disgust as Channary's camera lingers on the simulated bedroom lined with camera dollies and spotlights. Chains and hand-cuffs are attached to the headboard and a rack with small-sized clothing on hangers is off to the side. On the floor next to the bed is a metal trunk.

Ira stares at the hand-cuffs, deeply disturbed. His thoughts take him back to long ago. When his mother was alive, his guts twist thinking of what she must have endured at the sinister hands of Daboia. He's sickened by what these children and all trafficked victims suffer. They live in a prison of unimaginable brutality, of fear and sexual torture and most of them *are* children. He thinks about Sarita, the girl held as a sex slave by Dr. Stevens and wonders why he is especially sensitive to her plight. Then a mélange of thoughts drift through his mind, he thinks about Pela and about Ruby and Lolita and the kindness they had shown him. Then he thinks about the perpetrators of human trafficking and how evil these monsters are, how they took all he loved away from him. Perhaps Sarita reminds him of Pela, perhaps if he can save Sarita and these children, it will put a balm on the deep wound of Pela's death, the vivid bloody scene of which is etched in his mind and still haunts his soul. His eyes glaze over with moisture; he quickly blinks the dampness away.

Channary scans the back of the building. It was a staggering scene, almost too much to absorb. Her mouth goes dry and chills run the course of her spine. In the darkness at the back of the building stand large cages, kennels with metal bunk-beds, with children lying in them.

Father Lelo and Ira stare at the mind-numbing scene. Ira is furious, his dark eyes narrow to the size of mere slits. Father Lelo's neck muscles tighten. He grits his teeth while rage grips his expression.

Then Channary turns toward Daboia standing in his well-cut, expensive black suit.

From the field post, Ira sees his mother's murderer for the first time and his hands tighten into fists.

Channary stares at Daboia for a long moment and Ira glares at the monitor. Daboia's expression is ominous, suspended in blackness, cold and motionless as the ocean's depths. Ira watches the soulless man as he points to a wall and directs the children to line up against the wall.

Channary turns to Castello, short and stubby, with puffy jowls and blotchy skin. His eyes are wide and wild, full of anticipation like a rabid predator stalking its prey. He salivates, practically drooling as he watches the procession of burqas parade into the room. The metal door of the compound is slammed shut.

Daboia, thinking the Marines are Afghan children, shouts a command in Pashto, and the gunmen once again start prodding with their guns, shoving the children toward the wall.

Once they're lined up, Daboia shouts to them again in Pashto, telling them that they have no choice but to obey his every command or they will be punished. Then he claps his hands and a girl, a young teen, is pulled from behind a screen by one of the gunman. Her face is mutilated and scarred from drops of acid, her arms and legs scored from the end of a whip. This, he tells them, is what happens when females disobey. Then he shouts at them again, telling them to put their backs against the wall, and the guards shove them backward with the barrels of their guns.

Captain Channary was prepared by the military, taught Pashto, and the others had been instructed to watch and follow her lead, though none of the female Marines need to understand Pashto to know what's going on. Veritable evil needs no translation; it has a universal language of its own.

Daboia turns to Castello and demands that the duffle bag, stuffed with money, be opened and counted before he'll allow Castello to inspect the merchandise. Castello motions to his guard, who takes the bag to Daboia. The tension in the building could set off a landslide.

Once Daboia is satisfied that the money is good, he turns to the children and orders them to remove their burqas. Channary is about to shout the order to make their move when shots are fired just outside the compound door.

Everyone freezes, except for eyeballs darting back and forth, nobody moves a muscle. The shot wasn't planned. Channary knows something's gone wrong.

Outside, alongside the armored truck, the undercover Border Patrol agent is lying face down in a pool of blood, shot execution-style in the back of the head by the driver of the armored truck, who is now heading toward the door of the compound to warn Daboia of the surprise attack.

Up in the tower, sniper Franks has his crosshairs on the center of his back. He squeezes the trigger just as the man is reaching for the door handle. In a split second the .50 caliber bullet smashes through his spine, blowing his rib cage apart, and virtually cutting him in half, spewing bloody shreds of flesh all over the door. His midsection is blown out of him and he's dead before he hits the ground.

McKnight radios to Ira that the undercover BP officer is down and so is the man who shot him. Father Lelo lets out a huge breath from his lungs, and drops his head in silent prayer.

Ira's furious. "Son of *bitch*," he says standing up, too irate to remain sitting. "We lost a man because of that scum."

Then short bursts of machine gun fire ring out into the foothills. Daboia's men guarding the outside of the compound realize what happened and they're running for cover, shooting at the tower.

Both Father Lelo and Ira hit the ground, staying low and covering their heads, as bullets bounce and ricochet off the rocks of the hillside. The four backup Marines hidden around the perimeter of the compound had positioned themselves in preparation for this and in minutes are able to locate and kill the gunmen one by one.

At the same time inside the compound, Channary has no choice but to deliver the code word. "Raina!" she shouts. In an instant, the women tear off their burqas and point their tasers, leaving their guns tucked into the holsters strapped to their thighs. They have orders to bring the criminals in alive for interrogation, if possible. "It's over, you sub-human sons a bitches," she snarls.

They lunge at their targets, volts of electricity flying through the air. Daboia and Castello are startled frozen for a moment, the look on Daboia's face is one of sheer surprise, but in a split-second his expression contorts to pure hatred. Channary sets her sights on him.

She sends the taser's maximum charge through the air and the barbs hit Daboia square in the chest. Every muscle in his body constricts, his eyeballs roll up, he quivers, then collapses to the floor, his bladder empties, his bowels loosen and ooze through his tailored suit. He lies shaking in his own excrement as drool begins to trickle from the corners of his mouth. Captain Channary reaches down and seizes the .45 hidden in the inside pocket of his suit coat. She rolls him onto his stomach and then cuffs him.

At the same time, Sergeant Amber Jamison tasers Castello. He's lying on his back, his body shuddering and with vomit flowing from his mouth.

One of the gunmen doesn't go down from the taser, he's weak and shaking, but still on his knees. He aims his gun at Channary. Amber rushes him, shoves the prongs of her laser into his groin and knocks the gun from his hands just as it goes off. He squeals in pain, wets himself and collapses to the floor.

Daboia's personal guard has managed to sidle away from the chaos, concentrating on the bag of money. He grabs the black bag, pulls a handgun from his jacket pocket and seizes Channary from behind, pressing the barrel of his .45 to her head. He pulls her to the door, shouting, "I'll blow her fucking head off! Don't follow! I swear I'll fucking shoot the bitch!" Then he bursts through the door, using her as a human shield. He drags her through the blood and guts of the man who shot the BP officer and then over the dead BP officer who's lying face down. He pulls her toward the armored vehicle, then jerks her behind it slamming her body into the tailgate. He rummages inside with one hand and yanks out an oxygen mask, using the thick tubing to bind Channary's hands. He plans to get to Daboia's car using her as a shield and escape with the money.

Ira and Father Lelo lost their visual after Channary threw off her veil and in the scuffle, the camera attached to her body armor malfunctioned. Now all they can do is wait, frowning, worried, with tight lips for updates from Franks and McKnight.

Because of the position the armored truck and black sedan are in, none of the ground Marines have a shot at the gunman, but Franks is watching through his cross-hairs. "Damn," he says; he, too, has lost visual.

McKnight is standing directly behind Franks. He's watching through night vision binoculars waiting for another sighting. He had already logged the black Chrysler as a target reference point. Now he stands in silence, concentrating, making mental calculations, narrowing the TRP to the driver's-side door.

Suddenly, Captain Channary is in sight again. Her hands are tied behind her back and the gunman has a gorilla grip on the collar of her body suit, twisting it, choking off her windpipe. He's shoving her forward with a gun jabbed into the back of her head. He's wild-eyed, unpredictable, a crazy man with a hair-trigger and he's thrusting her back and forth, dodging this way and that while crouching behind her, making himself an impossible target. He advances toward the car. Then he stops, looks up in the direction of the tower and while cowering behind her, he pushes the barrel of the pistol into the side of her cheek as a warning.

Channary feels the hard metal smash into her skin beneath her cheekbone. She cries out after biting her tongue, and blood squirts from her mouth.

McKnight and Franks both know there is no chance he will let her go. Even if he manages to escape he will kill her.

The choke hold he has on Channary has her blood pumping and pounding in her temples. Her tongue is throbbing from the gouge bitten into it, her brain is lacking oxygen and she feels as though her head is going to explode, but she puts up a resistance, shuffling, trying to buy the snipers some time. It's her only chance to survive.

As the gunman approaches the car, he slams her into the driver's door and pins her there, keeping his head and body behind hers. He slides the bag of money off his shoulder, opens the door, and shoves it inside. McKnight knows that Franks literally has one shot at this.

He gives him the data, his voice deep, his throat dry, pure adrenalin replacing the blood in his veins. "Hold center, three mils, two o'clock."

Franks positions his rifle to two o'clock and peering down the tube of the scope he dials in the crosshairs. His forehead is glistening with sweat. He tightens the grip on his gun and focuses on the area he wants his bullet to hit. Then he steadies his breathing. "Ready," he says, and waits for his cue.

After hesitating for a few moments, the gunman pushes Channary's head down and shoves her into the sedan. For one half second the gunman's head is exposed.

"Send it," McKnight tells Franks.

Franks squeezes the trigger, and in a micro second the bullet hits, then exits the back of the gunman's skull. Fragments of bone and brain matter along with blood spray through the air. He collapses headless to the ground like a flimsy nightgown. Franks lowers his scope. "Nighty night, lights out," he says, as the smell of gun powder drifts through the night air.

McKnight radios to Ira. "Hostage situation secured. Gunman is down, I repeat, gunman *is* down."

Captain Channary hesitates for a moment, looking up through the window in the direction of the tower, then she climbs out of the car, coughing and choking, spitting out blood. Staggering, half crawling with her hands tied behind her back, she stumbles toward the building.

Ira grabs his rifle and Father Lelo his rucksack. They both make a dash for the compound, sliding down the loose gravel and forcing their way through the thick brush. Once inside the building they find that the Marines have it secured. The building is filled with an overwhelming, reeking stench and there are men bound and gagged lying in fetal positions everywhere.

Ira and Father Lelo survey the scene. Daboia and Castello are both on their knees with their hands behind their backs. Ira's jaw is clenched tight and he stares at Daboia. Then through clenched teeth, he tells one of the Marines, "Take the cuffs off him."

Father Lelo sets his rucksack on the floor and unzips it. He reaches inside and pulls out a towel. He throws it at Daboia and it lands on the floor in front of him. Ira steps closer to Daboia. He can hardly keep from losing his cool, from hurling profanity, from smashing his fists into Daboia's smug expression, from grinding the heal of his boot into his throat, but he's not about to throw his career away for a scumbag like this.

Instead, he picks up the towel and a burqa discarded by one of the female marines, walks over to Daboia, and sticks his finger in his face. "You stinking piece of trash, you make me gag! SDPD is on their way up here, you get to ride to your new home with some of San Diego's finest, but you're going to wipe some of your stinking filth off yourself and put this Burqa on before I allow you anywhere near one of their transport vehicles.

One of the female Marines unlocks his cuffs. "Clean this filth off yourself. Now!" she shouts in Daboia's ear.

He begins cursing and calling her names, swearing he won't tolerate the insult of being forced to wear a woman's garment.

Ira takes out his pocketknife, rips the towel in half, and stuffs one end into Daboia's mouth, then he aims the barrel of his rifle between his eyes and with a lethal glare, says, "Do as you're told, you slimy son of a bitch or I'll make you wish you were dead."

Daboia struggles and tries to spit out the rag, but Ira pulls a taser out of his pocket and aims it at Daboia's crotch. "Leave the rag in and do what you're told." Then he leans down and with emphasis, says, "This is personal for me. I'm not going to warn you again. Do as the woman tells you to do!" He sticks the taser in his crotch and gives him a quick jolt. Daboia squeals.

Some of the female Marines have gone to the back of the building where the young children are locked inside the kennels, bringing blankets from Father's rucksack. Others are sorting through filing cabinets, boxes, photo mailers, and computers. They gather enough evidence to lock Daboia and Castello away for life.

Back at the rectory, Linda had left a message for Lee and he's just returned her call. She's about to send a speeding locomotive straight at him. "Lee," she asks, "where are you?"

He's standing in Sarita's living room. "I just left the office, I had some work to finish up, but I'm on my way home now. Why?"

This is Sarita's moment to prepare for Lee's demise. She leaves the room and goes to her bathroom, closing and locking the door.

She quietly opens the closet. Hidden beneath a stack of towels way in the back is a wire- tap. She digs it out, turns it on, and with shaky hands she fastens it to the inside of her bra. The anticipation of this moment has frayed her nerves, leaving her rundown, broken and unsure, wondering if she'll make it through this. She tilts her head back and closes her eyes, tears seep from the corners of them. She's nauseated, almost at the threshold of vomiting. It's almost over, she thinks, calming herself. She takes a few huge breaths, trying to quell the queasiness in the pit of her stomach. She squeezes her eyes shut to force back her tears and telling herself again that it is almost over thinks, *hold on, hold on, hold on.*

She is the key to her abuser's demise. He has had absolute control over her for many years and she wonders if she has what it takes to bring Lee down. Will she be able to play him for a fool, face to face? Will he fall for Linda's phone call? Or will he smell Sarita's betrayal and fear and become suspicious. She's uncertain, and beyond frightened, but she has to try.

When she emerges from the bathroom, she glances through the bedroom door to check to see where Lee is. He is across the living room staring down at his phone with a sour facial expression. Sarita steadies herself and walks into the living room pretending to know nothing about the phone call, but she's shaking inside and on the verge of a breakdown. She eyes him with an innocent expression. "So, how's the trip in England going?" she asks in a soft voice.

He remains in deep thought, contemplating his next move, he wasn't expecting this bombshell, and he's visibly shaken. He swivels his head around and glares at her. "Linda said that Julie's dug up some information in Greg's banking files about Silar arranging a fake adoption for you and that she's taking the first flight home so she can get back here by tomorrow to start digging into the courthouse records." Then in an accusing manner he says. "She's not happy with you or your relatives for causing this trouble, Sarita. The best thing to do is to get you back across the border tonight." He knows that the U.S. authorities would have to jump through hoops to get consent from the Mexican authorities to pursue him across the border and he'll be long gone. "We need our passports and some significant cash. We'll have to stop at the office to get it from the safe." He looks her up and down, glaring like he could squash her for causing him this aggravation. "Well, move, damn it! Pack a bag!"

As she's packing, she's relieved that he's fallen for the ruse and is doing exactly what she'd predicted he'd do. Or at least it seems like it.

Lee goes out to the garage and opens the glove compartment of his car. He checks to make sure there are rounds in the magazine of his 9mm Ruger.

Julie is on the phone with Ted Silar, who's still at the bank in his office. She's disguising her utter disgust for him and in an innocent tone is telling him that she's found some disturbing information in Greg's belongings and that one of the things she found was a note Greg wrote. The note was not really written by Greg. It's part of the set up.

"I'm positive he wrote it," she says with sadness and distress in her voice. "It's written in his unmistakable, meticulous penmanship. I'll read it to you. *If you've found this note then I'm dead and I believe someone at the bank is responsible. I want you to go to Lee Stevens' office, because there's proof about why I was murdered hidden in the safe in his private bathroom.* Then, trying to sound concerned, she tells him, "I'm afraid you might be in danger, Ted, and the police will most likely come to the bank and question everyone after I turn this note over to them."

Frowning and tense, Ted stands up from his chair, but keeps his cool. He thanks her in a polite, soft-spoken voice and hangs up. He's not surprised she's back from England. Her phone arrived back home this morning, but he is surprised that she's found a note in Greg's belongings. His men were sure they had removed everything incriminating from the Bishop's house. He stares down at his desk, fixed on his glass of scotch, processing the seriousness of the matter. There are a lot of dangerous people involved in this trafficking operation and his mind reels backward to the moment he first met and shook hands with Daboia. As he recalls, the man had the warmth and charm of a wet blanket on a winter night.

Castello had introduced them to each other. Daboia, needed a "good banker" because he had lots of money that needed special attention and he'd pay a premium price to have Ted and his bank take care of it for him. Ted didn't give a rat's ass how Daboia was earning it, he assumed he was in the drug trafficking business like Castello and according to Ted's way of thinking, selling heroin was an honorable felony compared to this human-trafficking shit. "Fuck," he says out loud. Then, thinking. *That fucking half-breed Arab bastard knew what he was doing all along. He used Castello to find someone like me; a banker willing to launder his money. The fucking jerk-off snared me into his human-trafficking business. That's why that phony armored truck was available so fast; it wasn't just an idea, it was already in the process of being built. Then I find out from one of Castello's newbies, by the slip of the tongue, that it was funded by al-Qaeda. That son of a bitch, Castello!*

*He gets me into this up to my eyeballs and now I find out that the idiots who work for me missed some evidence at Bishop's house. Could things get any fucking worse? I have to get hold of whatever's in Lee's safe, or I'll be joining Bishop.*

"Goddamn fools," he whispers under his breath. "They're going to be the cause of me getting my head chopped off *and* thrown in the Bay to sleep with the fishes."

He doesn't bother calling Lee, because now he thinks that Lee keeps evidence in his safe that can be used as blackmail and that Lee and the board will use it to send him up the creek. He has to get his hands on that information. First he tries calling Castello to see if he knows anything, but doesn't get an answer. Then he scrounges through his desk looking for the phone number of an old high school chum by the name of Garrett Newton, an ex-con that in his heyday could crack the main vault at the U.S. Treasury building.

Newton, having forfeited his penthouse view of the bay after a twenty-year stint in San Quentin, is reluctant at first, but Silar tells him it's just a small job, nothing to it and he'll make it worth his while.

Later that evening Newton meets Silar in the deserted parking lot behind the orthodontics building. The night air is damp and heavy, and a low-lying fog obscures the ground. He parks his car beneath the shadows of the huge oak trees. Then he digs a pair of snug-fitting, black leather gloves out of his tool bag and tugs the protective coverings over his hands. Closing his car door without a sound, he carries his black, cylinder-shaped canvas bag of tools toward the building. Silar, wearing a long black topcoat with the collar turned up, is standing under an oak tree in front of Newton's car with his hands in his pockets. Inside his right pocket is a .357 Sig Sauer. He follows Newton along the edge of the parking lot, using the shadows for cover, to the building's south-side windows. Then he stands watching as Newton scores a huge circle with a glass cutter in one of the lower-level windows.

Once inside the office building, they hear voices and Silar realizes that Lee is there with Sarita. "Fuck," he whispers, his face twisting into a scowl, "we'll have to come back later." but when they turn around to leave, they're surprised by the barrels of two .45 caliber Glocks.

Before Silar and Newton got there, Nobel and Lastad wired the place with cameras and bugs and waited for the sting to unfold. Now, without wasting any time they slap the cuffs on the pair, frisk them and confiscate their weapons without incident. They gesture for them to stay quiet and then pressing their guns into their backs they nudge them down the hall to the waiting area of the front office.

Silar and Newton walk into the waiting room with their hands cuffed behind their backs, followed by the two detectives. Lee turns around when he hears someone walking up behind him. The blood drains from his face when he recognizes Ted. He's ghostly white and he stands with his mouth hanging open, staring at him. Then, like a scared rat, he turns and scurries for the door, but before he can turn the knob the door swings open.

Lee reverses his motion in an instant and throws his hands in the air. He's now staring down the barrel of Herroso's M4 riot shotgun. The arrest might have turned into a hostage situation and Herroso came prepared.

"FBI! Put your hands on top of your head!"

Linda is behind Herroso, dressed in an olive-brown T-shirt, khaki cargo pants, and a nylon belt, with her green eyes blazing. As instructed, she remains at a safe distance outside the door. It was dangerous for her to be there, but nothing could keep her away. Her daughter was on the edge of a breakdown and after pleading her case unremittingly, she was given clearance for the sake of Sarita's emotional well-being. After all, they would need Sarita to testify against Lee and there was a weighty chance, as with all Stockholm syndrome victims, that she could change her mind at any moment and empathize with her abuser.

Within a half second Herroso's behind Lee, yanking his arms around his back. "You're under arrest, asshole," he says as he slams a pair of cuffs on him then pats him down.

Lee of course feigns innocence. "For what?"

Herroso points his finger at him, and then at Ted. "For trafficking in humans, both of you."

"Human trafficking? You're fucking crazy! What the fuck are you talking about?" Lee snaps.

Ted remains silent, he knows it's best to keep his mouth shut and he hangs his head down, staring at the floor. Newton stares at Ted, furious.

Lee turns to Sarita.

She grabs her chest. She is so scared she can hardly breathe; she feels trapped by his penetrating stare.

Linda watches from the doorway. A wave of dread rushes through her. "Don't cave now, baby," she whispers.

Sarita grabs the top of her white silk blouse. She reaches down inside and rips the wiretap out of her bra and rushes to Linda's side. Linda grabs her and with a huge sigh of relief she wraps her arms tight around her. Sarita buries her head in Linda's shoulder.

Linda glares at Lee.

He glowers at Sarita, his eyes like flame-throwers. "You worthless bitch, you backstabbing whore! You seduced me and now you pretend that I was the one that initiated this affair." He shifts his beady eyes to Linda. "You believe this conniving little Mexican half-breed? She's nothing but a tramp, a slut, she's been that way since we took her in."

Sarita should have been hurt by his words, but she's beyond hurt, she's numb and she doesn't look at him.

Linda loses her cool. She lets go of Sarita, and rushes across the room before Herroso can stop her. She backhands Lee's face so hard it leaves a welt on his cheek.

The sting makes his eyes water and he sneers. "Look at you, dressed like a common street bitch." He nods his head in Sarita's direction. "Look what she's done to you, Linda. She has pulled you into the gutter with her."

"Shut up!" Linda points her finger practically jamming it in his eye, making him flinch. "You are an evil man. I know what you've been doing and the authorities can prove it. She hisses between clenched teeth. "You disgust me."

Herroso steps forward, yanking Lee's arms up, making him grimace in pain. "Hey, hey, hey." He looks at Linda. "There's no reason to insult us real men, by calling *him* a man.

Linda's eyes are smoldering, practically burning holes through Lee's skull and Lee glares back. "I'll never do any time, Linda. My father will never let that happen. So watch out tomorrow when my bail's made. I'll be home waiting for you to put my supper on the table."

Linda lifts her chin with scorn. "Apparently you don't know what wearing a federally approved wire-tap means to a criminal case. It means your bail's going to be denied and that you're going to spend the rest of your life surrounded by cement blocks and steel bars."

She turns her back on him and walks over to Sarita. She wraps her arms around her, hugging her close, whispering, "You're safe now, safe with me, it's all over, baby girl, he'll never hurt you again." As she says it, tears pool in her eyes, she turns her attention to Herroso. "Please get him out of our sight."

Herroso shoves Lee toward the door. "Move it, dirt ball. Today's garbage day and it's time to throw out the trash."

Sarita turns her back on Lee as Herroso forces him out the door. Noble and Lastad follow with Silar and Newton.

Linda reaches down and lifts Sarita's chin up. For a few moments they lock eyes. Tears stream down Linda's cheeks. "I'm so proud of you," she whispers. "You're so brave and I promise I will spend the rest of my life making this up to you."

Sarita closes her eyes and puts her head back down on Linda's shoulder, exhausted. She releases a long breath, feeling as though she hasn't slept in years.

They turn and walk out of the office, heading to a beach house on Windansea Beach in La Jolla where she has made arrangements to stay for a few weeks until she gets everything settled at *Lines of L' Attitude*. Then they will fly off to Atiu, a remote island in the Cook Island cluster in the South Pacific. Linda couldn't bear the thought of taking Sarita home, or to Sarita's condo.

Ira and Father Lelo have boarded the chopper and are now en route back to the rectory, both men reliving the last few hours quietly in their private thoughts as they ride. As Ira stares down through the side window at the tree-tops passing beneath him, his thoughts turn to his mother, to the circumstance and the aftereffect of her death that led him to this ordeal. He wonders what life would have been like if she and his grandfather, Samuel, had lived. Would his mother have married? Would he have siblings, nieces, nephews? Would they have gone on family outings together, to baseball games, to the lake for picnics? There's so much that he missed out on in life because of the horrible crime against his mother. He will never forget. Not a day goes by that he doesn't think about her and the brutal way she died and as of late he's been thinking about how his only blood relative, his grandmother, is getting up in age, and it saddens him to think about life without her. He looks away from the tree tops, out the front window into the dark night sky, lit by the pale moon and a sparse spattering of stars. He is thinking. *Human trafficking took away the family and life I should be living right now. Some people might have spent their lives trying to forget the pain and sorrow, but I'll never stop fighting for the victims of this selfish, greedy, and foul crime.*

# Epilogue

## One Month Later

The rain started with a downpour accumulating a half inch in an hour, then slowed to a drizzle that has stayed for the last couple days. November has been a soggy month and with December drawing near, typically the wettest month in Southern California, it looks like it may be an above average year for precipitation.

At least it's just a light steady shower, not coming down in sheets, Ira's thinking, as he holds Rosa's umbrella for her. The dark sky and dreary weather match the mood and garb of the small gathering of people, four to be exact, at the old cemetery on the reservation.

As Rosa places the urn containing the fragment of Raina's rib bone wrapped in the blood stained handkerchief down into the grave, Father Lelo begins to recite the first rite of The Burial of the Dead, then finishes with the Lord's Prayer. He wasn't able to attend the traditional funeral held for his good friends Samuel and Raina years ago, so he has taken this opportunity to perform a Christian burial for them now. Rosa didn't mind at all, she actually welcomed the ceremony. During her years in exile, she often recalled with affection the days when she would go to church with her family to hear Father Lelo's homily; it was what got her through the day.

Rosa kneels at the side of the grave while staring down at the urn, reminiscing. Remembering vividly the moment when a young priest named Lelonis Kendall, dressed in black from head to toe with the white of his clerical collar showing, lifted the newly baptized infant, Ira, high above his head and presented him to the members of an aloof congregation. As Raina watched, her expression of pure love transcended the traces of scorn in the pretentious smiles on some of the faces in the pews. Father Lelo had noticed the harsh undertones within the parish that day, and he began to admire Raina, an unwed mother, even more for her courage. Beginning that day he practically became a permanent fixture in the Notah household, a loyal, adopted member of the family.

When Father Lelo finishes his prayer he makes the sign of the cross, and Rosa begins to shake her gourd rattle while chanting a prayer of her own. Laying the last of Raina's remains to rest will free her spirit from the earth, in accordance with the Kumeyaay tradition.

Ira passes Rosa's umbrella to Sarita, who is standing by his side and he picks up a shovel. He begins to cover the urn with dirt and tears fill his eyes as the last trace of the vessel disappears. He bows his head and swipes the tears away, fighting back the sorrow of letting her go. Having a piece of her bone with him gave him comfort and seemed somehow to make him feel closer to her, but he knows he must let go. Sarita notices his quiet grief and she sets her hand on his shoulder in a comforting manner. She had never met Raina, of course, she'd died before Sarita was born, but in the past month she'd learned a lot about her. Her circumstance was similar, held in slavery by cruel men and that made Sarita feel connected to her.

Ira and Sarita's lives had been shaped by tragedy and oddly enough in a strange twist of fate, tragedy is what brought them together.

After Agent Lastad had finished digging into Sarita's past, he'd called Ira and told him who her parents were. Ira sat in silence with his phone glued to his ear. The names Domingo and Anita Salazara rang through his head like a blaring siren. He knew of the couple, he had seen them once. It seemed like a lifetime ago, but he remembered them from down in Mexico at Hallia's place when he was nine years old. Anita was Hallia's oldest child and Domingo was her husband. The couple had stopped by the rancheria one day, and nobody knew it at the time, but Anita was one month pregnant with Sarita. Domingo was the man who had raped Raina. He is both Sarita and Ira's biological father. They are half brother and sister. Words could not describe the complicated emotions that passed through Ira in that moment of revelation. Shocked, would be the only word that could come close. To learn he had a sister was difficult enough to absorb at age thirty, but to realize that both his mother and sister were victims of human trafficking left him speechless. The following day when he'd approached Sarita with the news, she was equally shocked and they spent the rest of the day trading memories and information about their families.

Linda postponed her and Sarita's trip to Atiu, to let Ira and Sarita spend time together, knowing that it would be beneficial to both and therapeutic for Sarita. She also wanted to grant Rosa's request that Sarita be at the burial. After all, Sarita was Ira's sister and Rosa began treating her like a granddaughter immediately. Linda couldn't have been happier for Sarita. She knew her pain and wounds were deep and she was going to need lots of love and family to help her heal from the trauma.

After they left the cemetery, Ira dropped Rosa and Father Lelo at home and took Sarita to the beach house in La Jolla. He then headed over to Julie's house, hoping that she would be finished meeting with her estate attorney; an appointment that came up at the last minute and could not be rescheduled. After the sting operation and the arrest of Ted Silar, regulators from the Office of the Comptroller of Currency slapped the bank with a cease-and-desist order. All of Julie and Greg's assets were being held by the bank which was making Julie's life hell. If not for the extreme importance of the matter, she would have been with Ira at the cemetery. Instead, she gave him a key to her house, and asked him to wait there for her if she didn't get home before he got there.

As he turns into her driveway, he sees her emerging from the front door of the house, still dressed for her meeting, wearing a dark blue suit, with a cream-colored satin blouse and black boots. She waves at him and smiles. She'd just gotten home and saw him pull into the driveway. She met him half-way down the walk. She wrapped her arms around him, hugging him close. He closed his eyes, immersed in the feeling of her body next to his.

He holds Julie tight, embracing her as if he'll never let go. She senses his need to surrender himself, to give in to warmth, trust and love and to forget his secret fears and those memories of rejection and abandonment. Even though his body is rock hard against hers, it feels as though he has collapsed, as though he has melted into her.

She pulls her face away from his shoulder and looks deep into his eyes. He kisses her lips, gently at first and then with a yearning that he's never felt before with any other woman. They stay locked in their passion for a long time, not caring who might be watching. Then she pulls away and leads him inside her house where she will satisfy his hunger and thirst and soothe his aches. She will care for him in the manner in which he deserves to be cared for. She will never betray him or abandon him. Whether her life is very long or closes tomorrow she will love Ira until the end.

# Meet Barbara Bolton

Barbara was born and raised in a small town in north western Wisconsin. At the age of sixteen she moved to an even smaller town in the U.P. of Michigan.

Bolton married one of her best friends, Ken Lillie, at the age of twenty-two, when he was fresh out of the Marine Corps boot camp. Although no longer married to Ken, they have a daughter, Amber Lillie and remain friends. It was Ken Lillie, who was the channel for the inspiration for this book.

It was while they were stationed at Camp Pendleton and living in Oceanside, that she and Ken along with another couple were driving along a highway when she noticed a white piece of cloth hanging from the tall grass at the beginning of a path on the side of the road, and the scene repeated every so often as they drove along the highway.

She asked, out of curiosity what the white flags were for and she and her girlfriend winkled their noses at the answer. She was told, the paths lead to the where the migrant workers and military personnel brought their whores. That was in 1983, and it was believed back then, that the women selling themselves were prostitutes. In reality they were not just women, but also young children, and they were not selling themselves, they were enslaved against their will.

It wasn't until roughly twenty years later that people stopped looking the other way and began to realize this was an underground world of sex slavery in the produce fields of southern California.

Bolton said that she saw a video on the news called the Fields of Shame in 2003 and realized that she had lived among it, practically in her back yard, and without meaning to she also turned away in disgust. Many times throughout the years following that broadcast, she'd thought about and wondered how many women and children had been tortured, beaten, and died as victims of this brutal crime since 1983.

In 2008 when Bolton's home business slowed down in the financial crisis, she decided to start writing a novel about human-trafficking in her spare time. She hopes it will help the people who work hard at trying to stop this growing problem, by bringing more awareness to it.

Bolton still lives in Wisconsin, with her remaining cat, and is an avid gardener.

# Acknowledgments

It is with deep gratitude that I wish to thank and acknowledge the Holy Spirit and a host of individuals who helped me, had patience with me, and stood by my side through the long and tedious process of writing this novel. First I would like to thank my family; mom, dad, brother and sisters, and friends for their understanding when I would decline lunch, dinner or picnic invitations, because I wanted to meet a deadline I'd given myself. Thanks to Pattie Kay, and my beautiful daughter Amber for dragging me out of my hermit life to a new restaurant every so often, or for a walk, just to get me out of the house. Thanks to my college professor Ken Bowman for his inspiration to write, and also to my professor Patrick O'Neil for his encouragement and prodding to finish my novel. Without these two extraordinary teachers I would have never started this project. Thanks to Carlos Hernandez for translating my Spanish, and Carlos, I really appreciate that you didn't laugh at me.

Thanks to Miami-Dade Fire Rescue, for their expert knowledge on snake bites, specifically the Russell's Viper. Thanks to Dr. Michael Kryda, for taking time to talk with me about his medical knowledge and hospital protocol. Thanks to Ken Lillie, for his Marine Corps knowledge and my brother Randy Bolton for teaching me about guns. Thanks to Father Landerville, for being a good, down to earth priest I could talk to and get to know. A special thanks to Betty Pound, my spiritual healer at the *Inner Well* for her clarity and guidance. Thanks to Dorrie O'Brien, my content editor and mentor, for helping to make my book deeper and richer. Again, a deep heartfelt appreciation to Ken Bowman for editing my final draft. Thanks to Gail Cross at Desert Isle Designs for a beautiful cover. Thanks again to my friend Pattie Kay, my first critic who read my rough and raw manuscript before it was edited, and miraculously saw a bit of potential in it, and also for helping me with the monumental task of proofing the final draft. And last but not least, thanks to my love, my soul-mate, my best friend, without whom this project would not have come to fuition. Everything around you flourishes my darling, including me, I love you.

# Authors note:

While standing in the bookstore of the Adrian Dominican Sisters Mother House in Adrian, Michigan many years ago, a refrigerator magnet on display caught my eye. It was a simple black square with white lettering. It said.

> what would you attempt to do if
> you knew you could not fail?
>
> (unknown)

The answer that entered my mind immediately was. *Write a novel.* The magnet still hangs on my refrigerator to this day, and a matching coffee mug graces my kitchen cupboard. I used the mug most mornings as I wrote this book.

I ponder the Adrian trip often, and I can't help but believe that my visit to the Mother House was the spring board which catapulted me to begin writing this novel. God truly works in mysterious ways. Peace to you Sisters.

Adrian Dominican Sisters mission and vision
**Seek Truth - Make Peace - Reverence Life**

28461288R00369

Made in the USA
Middletown, DE
15 January 2016